TIME SE

by N E Shawsone

Any similarity to anyone living, or passed, within this fictious story,

is purely coincidental.

Chapter 1

Belfast, like every capital city in the world, is the same during the morning rush hour. A homage to a volcanic eruption. Commuters race from suburbs, outskirts, and boroughs toward the city's arterial routes. Coagulating and slowing, the mass merges into one, the closer they inch toward their destination. However, on the Upper Newtownards Road, one of the major corridors into the city, there was chaos. Ongoing roadworks had reduced the traffic to a single lane. Horns beeped continually. Muffled screams of anger and frustration as vehicles jockeyed to join the single lane. For one particular person, this was a bad scenario.

The hotel room on the outskirts of East Belfast showed no signs of life, lined curtains suppressing any glimpse of daylight. A standard quilt dumped on top of a bed, displayed indeterminate shapes. The room littered with discarded clothes. Ash trays piled high with cigarette butts and the occasional marijuana roach. On a dressing table, a myriad of wine, miniature vodka, brandy and water bottles lay scattered. A grunt from the darkness under the quilt was a cue for a hand to creep free. It scrambled and scuttled crab like amongst the debris of loose change and keys until it reached its prey, a back lighted wristwatch.

'Shit! Bollocks! Oh no, no, no! Look at the time!' squealed John Patterson ripping the quilt away.

His bed mate, Orla, struggled to open her eyes. When she focused, she stared at his back on the edge of the bed as he poured himself into clothes in a practiced manner.

'I can't afford to be late today. I need this!'

A dreamy grin descended on Orla's face, disguising her lurid thoughts. She reached across to stroke his back.

'Why don't you phone in sick and spend another few hours with me?'

'What part of I-can't-afford-to-be-late do you not understand?' Patterson snapped without turning.

The sharpness of his reply would offend anyone who didn't know him, but she did, smirking at his sarcastic attempts to control panic. He quickly pulled on a shirt and hoisted his trousers. There was a dull thud as a heavy object fell to the floor and bounced off his foot.

'Shit!' Patterson shrieked, kicking out at the offending object.

He fell back onto the bed and grabbed his injured foot. Orla turned on the bedside light and crept toward him. 'Here. Let mummy take a look.' she purred in a teasing tone. 'Do you want me to kiss it better?' Her hand slid along his thigh toward the groin.

'No, I don't.' he finalized, gripping her hand playfully as he sat up beside her. A huge part of him would have loved to have slipped back into bed and felt her nakedness against his, but the thought of missing a lucrative pay day overtook any conceptions that arose. He was in enough trouble as it was. He took Orla's face in his hands and glared into the bottomless pools of her eyes. She was stunning. He often questioned what she saw in him, yet remained blessed with his luck. Patterson leaned forward and carefully planted his lips onto hers, a reaction that animated them both. Tongues darted in and out of alien mouths before Patterson reluctantly backed off, rising to leave.

'I will see *you* soon, my dear.'

Orla smiled, glowing deep inside. 'John?'

He turned back to her.

'I lo…'

'Shhh!' Patterson hissed. 'Don't say that. You can *never* say that. Remember? We agreed!'

Orla accepted the inevitable retort and lay back on the bed, appearing more inviting. The quilt had slid down revealing perfect breasts, her sultry glare locked on him. She had an inner strength when they were together. Strength she never wanted to lose. She also had plans for their future, but would have to wait for a more appropriate occasion to share them. Patterson bundled his remaining belongings into his pockets as he headed for the door, but before leaving, he collected the offending item that had almost crushed his toes. He checked the safety catch and slipped his 9mm Walther pistol into a belt holster on his trousers.

'Call you later.' was the last thing Orla heard before drifting back into a beautiful slumber where she dreamt that Patterson was back beside her.

~

Sparks spewed into the night sky as another plank of wood was tossed onto the bonfire. It was the night before the celebration of Protestant William of Orange's victory over the Catholic King James, at the Battle of the Boyne in 1690. It was the same every eleventh night of July throughout Northern Ireland. Belfast traditionally had the largest bonfires, each Protestant enclave vying to outshine their contemporaries. The celebrations symbolised Protestantism more than historical events, a celebration that seemed more important than ever. Sectarian violence had spread with the speed of a plague, each tribe growing more ignorant and suspicious of the other. The west of the city was a swarm of settlements randomly located, heightening the wariness of attack. Catholic and Protestant families were forced out of respective areas. Years of friendship between working class neighbours went up in smoke quicker than their previous homes being incinerated. Garrisons were formed, as each side feared the other was drawing up battle plans for a final solution. The old Marxist, Official Irish Republican Army, had spawned a devil child in the Provisional IRA; a ruthless paramilitary mob intent on defending their areas, whilst inflicting casualties on their sworn enemies as well as the British Government. The parallel fear felt by Catholics was the reason the Protestant communities allied together to form their own army. The Ulster Defence Association. Thirty-five-year-old, six-foot-tall, shipyard welder, Jackie Smallwood was one of the founder UDA members and looked upon by many as the natural leader. He wandered along the staunchly protestant Shankill Road, heading for Tennent Street, an urban artery connecting to Crumlin Road, the site of the Belfast

Crown Court and Victorian jail. It was the gateway to many Catholic strongholds. For that geographic reason, he had decided to show solidarity with the vulnerable, establishing his headquarters, and war office, above Tennent Street Protestant Boys Flute Band Hall. He felt secure. This was his area and no one or thing would ever change that. The abject feeling of security was borne from the size of his 'army'. Promoting the notion of self-defence in the Harland and Wolfe, mainly Protestant, shipyard, he had been overwhelmed by the response of his 25000 colleagues. It was if they had been waiting for someone like him to create their voice. These were solid, working-class men who would fight tooth and nail to protect their families, areas and heritage. They had access to materials and expertise within their workplace, to manufacture a deadly arsenal of zip guns and pipe bombs. Battalions had been established throughout the city with companies in the heartlands throughout the province. They were, in every sense of the word, loyalists. Although somewhat confused loyalists. Their British government appeared to be acceding evermore concessions to the Republicans. The loyalists, totally devoted to their monarch, were convinced they were being betrayed. It appeared to be only a matter of time before they would be abandoned to the clutches of the South. Smallwood had convinced the masses it could not happen if they had unity of thought and action. The UDA, the epitome of this ethos. Smallwood smiled, pondering the oxymoron of creating a Protestant Republic. Uncomfortable with the role of leader, he had created a united council with shared responsibilities.

Smallwood was a moderate drinker with an impressive physique, honed from twelve-hour shifts as a welder, like his father before him. He had inherited his father's organisational skills, the ability to listen and earn respect from others. Following in the family tradition, he became the union shop steward. He had also inherited his father's violent temper, struggling for years before succeeding to control it. Above all, he had hated his father with a passion. His mood took a downturn on recollecting the squeals of his mother as he sat at the top of the stairs in their tiny terrace house as a child. Both crying at her plight and angry at his father. Sounds of thuds, slaps, breaking of glass and demonic roaring. The worst sound was the pleading voice of his defenseless mother, while his father vented his rage. Sounds that would haunt him for a lifetime. He had once gone to his mother's rescue and was rewarded with a ferocious jaw cracking punch, the pain of which helped numb his body, distracting attention from the kicks that fractured three of his ribs. Throughout the ordeal, Smallwood never once cried, nor lost eye contact with his father. What was ingrained in him that day was the feeling that it was right to defend honour.

'Maybe I have the old bastard to thank after all,' he mused. For months after the event, his mother never verbally thanked him, mostly through fear. She gesticulated her thanks. Her most endearing habit was calling him 'my wee man'.

She held him closer, more often, drawing strength from his nearness. He was more than happy to reciprocate. However, the abuse continued, escalating in ferocity and regularity.

Fate seemed to be the only relevant body prepared to help protect them. Attending work on a winter's afternoon, his father had a liquid breakfast of vodka. The frosty conditions made the bare metal scaffolding in the enormous dry dock a perilous place for the sober. It was to prove a death trap for the inebriated. The youthful Smallwood was confused, holding his mother as she wailed at the news of her husband's death. He prayed he had suffered. He couldn't understand how she had any feelings for this monster, and the harm he bestowed on her. On them both. Obscure marital loyalty was above his young perception. He reluctantly attended the funeral, displaying no emotion.

Chapter 2

Patterson hurried from the lift to the hotel car park, racing toward his silver BMW. Unknown to any onlookers, he surveyed the scene with a trained eye on approach. Fumbling his keys and deliberately dropping them beside the driver's side of the car. Instead of leaning down to retrieve them, he knelt in a practiced fashion, hands on the keys, expertly checking under the car for any signs of tampering. Loose wires or a taped package were Patterson's worst nightmare. Satisfied, he opened the car door and slid into the expensive leather seat. This was the car of a single man and he knew it. His colleagues were too tied up with families and domesticity, to be able to experience the delights of such a machine. He also wondered how much longer he could afford it.

Praying that the city bound traffic along the Upper Newtownards Road would be minimal at 6:45am, he reached the exit to find there wasn't as much as a space to squeeze into. 'Aw shite, I forgot about those bloody road works!' He slapped his hands on the steering wheel and considered trying to cross the road to tackle the congested traffic. It was an insane idea, like so many ideas in his life, he gave no thought to forward planning and possible consequence. He couldn't join the queue heading in the right direction never mind cross it Pushing a button on his stereo radio, he heard the chorus of Kiss's 'Crazy, crazy nights.' It was a welcome distraction, that returned his thoughts to the previous 10 hours, a devilish smile creeping across his face. He'd met Orla almost a year ago in The Wellington Park Hotel, in the university area of Belfast. Both were there with friends.

He noticed her immediately, her beauty radiating amid her crowd. He was mesmerised, hoping she had noticed his obvious interest. Patterson was delighted when he approached the bar to order drinks, she had been assigned the same role. He cringed with embarrassment, recalling the first ever words he offered…

'Do you come here often?' Patterson felt gormless at the finishing syllable. A satisfied smile broke out on his face remembering how Orla failed to suppress her feelings, almost choking with laughter. She touched his arm to register intrigue. Their early rendezvous were tentative; unlike their immediate physical attraction. They shared the bare essentials of each other's backgrounds. Orla, a Catholic from the West of the city and Patterson, a Protestant from the East. Unwritten rules were established. They would never travel to each other's areas on Patterson's insistence. In his case, and at this stage of the 'Troubles', it could prove fatal. Their early meetings were in neutral, safe places. Bangor, Holywood, Lisburn. Meeting for drinks soon elevated to car back seat liaisons that developed into all night hotel room sessions, the love making ferocious from the start. Both felt the crevice of a gap when they departed, wondering if it could ever be filled. He ascertained she was married; instinctively aware she was unhappy. Orla tried to avoid any mention of her spouse. Occasionally when she accidentally slipped, it was with dread. Without offering opinion, Patterson read between the lines, wondering what sort of coward it took to terrorise a woman. They grew closer, continuing to share the minimum amount of personal information and Patterson avoiding any reference to his job.

She knew, as every civilian of this era knew, he was some sort of security forces, though shied away from challenging him, as the mention of his vocation could spell the end of a beautiful relationship. Her reaction to his self-imposed notoriety was always as surprising as it was welcome. She would hug and make love to him with so much passion as if she was thanking him for the supreme sacrifice he was making. Even though she had no idea of his surname nor address, she felt safe. The Downtown Radio announcer dragged him from his warm thoughts. *'It's almost 6:45 and if you're heading into Belfast, be sure to avoid the Knock junction of the Upper Newtownards Road...'* 'I know for Christ's sake!' he snarled at the invisible voice. He was annoyed at the announcer. Annoyed at the traffic. But it did little to disguise, how annoyed he was with himself. Orla vanished from his thoughts, gloom spreading like a dark cloud. How the hell had he ended up where he was? A single man, own home, expensive car. His chosen career, although difficult and dangerous, was well paid. Being with the woman of his dreams, despite her being someone else's.

He had poor discipline, a fact he had ignored for too long, and huge, mounting debts due to his suicidal gambling and loan repayments. The safety mechanism of ignorance to his self-created destiny, was no longer an option. This time he was playing for real and wasn't sure how, if at all, he could handle it. He wanted to talk with his surviving, adoptive parent, but was too ashamed. He was also ashamed that his weekly visits to her were being stretched out to months on end because of his necessity to work as much overtime as possible.

~

The sounds of happy revellers dispelled Smallwood's dark mood on nearing the towering inferno. It was a bizarre sight. Teenagers sat on a worn couch rescued from the unlit bonfire, gazing at the flames. Others meandered; the majority staggered. A woman with dark streaks of cheap mascara cascading down her cheeks painting a comical face, yelled at her equally intoxicated lover. The kids on the settee jeered from their auditorium. Along the periphery of the glare of the fire, supposedly hidden in ever changing shadows, many inebriated couples engaged in drunken romantic liaisons that would last as long as the blink of an eye. Smallwood noticed 'sensible' families doing the 'tour' of the local fires. Children gazed in awe at the size of the flames, their parents permitting they observe momentarily, carefully averting their attention away from the troupes of comical romantics, before moving on to the next street. He thought of his own family. His 'wee man', Jackie junior, or JJ as he was known by those closest to him. He would be sound asleep at this ungodly hour, his endearing mother Kate, waiting patiently for fourteen-year-old Shirley to return home. Kate never got angry with Shirley; she was simply worried for her safety. Kate was a wonderful woman and everything a man could ask for in a wife and partner. He recalled the image of their inaugural meeting, that was permanently imprinted in his mind. She was stunning, but in a simple way. Of slight build, with delicious dark hair, tied into a ridiculous beehive that the fashion of the time dictated. Her eyes were darker than the night; the feature he first noticed.

Kate had an aura, a strength that he couldn't explain, yet he felt a need to comfort and protect her at the same time. Maybe he had noticed a hint of pain in her eyes. Her mother had arrived in the Shankill from Cushendall, a tiny fishing village on the north Antrim coast. A single parent by choice, deciding against dedicating her life to a man she was sure she couldn't live with. Kate's father, a Catholic, in this republican village, pressurised her to engage in matrimony at every opportunity. As the 'troubles' began to simmer, the villagers took it as a cue to increase their intimidation. The intensified provocation occasionally gave way to sectarian acts of vandalism on her home. She deemed the time right to leave and be amongst 'her own.' Kate's infancy belonged to the Shankill. She progressed through the education system solidly, making many friends; her non-threatening demeanour was her biggest attraction. She had dreams of becoming an air hostess and travelling the world which her mother fully encouraged. However, those dreams evaporated when her mother developed a speedy form of Alzheimer's, which was then, a titanic mystery. Inheriting the rent book of their terraced home, she found a job in Gallagher's cigarette factory on York Road. Her mother withdrew into herself, before a care home, became a second dwelling to Kate, with the frequency of her visits. She never complained to anyone, how destiny had dealt her such a cruel blow. She often awoke alone, in what was now, her house, head on a pillow damp from tears. This was the hint of pain that Smallwood noticed. As he ambled toward Tennent Street, a hand on his shoulder dragged him from the warm thoughts of his wife and family.

'Fuck me big lad, you're hard to find!' The squat, powerful figure of Sammy 'Bulldog' Henderson, a natural born thug, walked past Smallwood to face him. Smallwood noticed how Henderson gave a side smile and spoke with his mouth at a ridiculous angle. Henderson wore his uniform of black leather jacket strained across his full frame, denims with absurd turn-ups, and bronze Chelsea boots with metal tips. Hard man boots. He was the other prominent member of the four-founding council collective, responsible for organising and controlling the east of the city.

Smallwood wasn't Henderson's greatest aficionado, due to his ruthless and vicious tactics in resolving conflict. He did, however, begrudgingly admire his organisational skills, albeit under an iron fist. Henderson abused his position to the point the ranks detested and feared him in equal measure. Many also believed that he would stop at nothing to become Supreme Commander. He in turn revered Smallwood, despising his natural popularity, never breaking eye contact during heated debates, and displaying disdain, rather than the fear Henderson had come to expect.

'There's something you need to see up at the band hall,' he snorted.
'Like you dipping into your wallet and buying me a drink?'
Henderson forced a grin onto his hardened pug-like features before taking the lead position, the sound of his steel tipped boots resonating off the deserted side streets walls. Smallwood considered the sight of his 'right-hand man'. He looked and sounded like a tap-dancing troll.

~

Against his natural grain, Patterson concentrated on his most immediate, and potentially explosive, problem. He dwelt on the same question that was constant in his mind; how he had spiralled out of control to reach his current predicament. The music of the Eagles singing 'Desperado' on the radio seemed to answer him.
'And it seems to me all the fine things have been laid upon your table, but you only want the things that you can't get...'
It was a summary of his life. Always pushing boundaries, never content with the status quo. During his five-year, part-time, Ulster Defence Regiment army career, he continually questioned authority, endorsing the fact he would never progress further than Lance Corporal. That compulsion to rebel, had been carried through to his current vocation, which, being linked to the Civil Service, would also guarantee a career on the bottom rung of the ladder. Six years into his job and it was obvious to his seniors, he was a natural asset to have on board, though none would recommend his promotion due to the hint of maverick he emanated.

He didn't walk the walk or talk the talk, a fact constantly pointed out by his 'mentor,' close friend and colleague, Andy Beattie. Beattie had befriended the young recruit after only two weeks of enrolment. Both from the same background in East Belfast, and loyally supported Glentoran football team. But more importantly, although sixteen years older, Beattie had the same sense of humour and tenacity. Patterson was akin to a younger version of himself. The son he never had. He too, was aware of Patterson's volatile and potentially self-destructive nature... more than Patterson himself.

The BMW crawled over Albert Bridge into the mayhem of early morning Belfast. Swearing unheard at any driver who dared comply with the speed limit, Patterson constantly surveyed the occupants of vehicles that drove beside, or behind him, or slowed in front. Clenching his thighs together, he felt the reassurance of the loaded Walther nestled there. Driving toward Carlisle Circus roundabout, a traffic sign lifted his temperament. The brown and white information sign pointing east toward the Antrim Road, an elephant with the legend, 'Belfast Zoo.'

'Some wee shite has turned that sign around again,' he mused with a grin on his face. Patterson accelerated up the Crumlin Road past the Mater hospital to his right, and the Belfast Crown Court building to his left. He took a sharp right into an opening that brought him to two mighty hydraulic gates made from steel, that had already started to open thanks to observation cameras. Patterson, nicknamed Paddy in his workplace, lowered his window when he noticed a stalwart, Bob Anderson, beaming at him with the remote control for the gates in his ancient hands.

Anderson's toothless grin, painted a bizarre picture of the oldest kid on the planet as he played with the controls.

'How's everything in the Zoo?' Patterson shouted to his soon to be retired colleague.

'OK Paddy…until you arrived,' he responded in a pretend, yet affectionate growl.

As Patterson speeded off into the massive car park, he shouted at Anderson.

'You're robbing some village of an idiot, you 'aul bollocks you!'

The oldest kid on the planet couldn't help but grin with admiration for the youngster. The only available parking space was at the furthest possible point from the entrance. After parking, Patterson raced through an exit gate, before haring down an open passage toward a corner. He veered left and sprinted in front of a series of block stone terraced cottages, that used to house employees. They were now deployed as training rooms, a gymnasium, a video library and the obligatory social club. Patterson ran back down the Crumlin Road, unseen because of the navy-painted corrugated iron that had evolved on once proud iron railings, thanks to the 'troubles.' A senior rank, a fortnight into his new role after a promotion selection, sauntered toward him. The blur that was Patterson raced toward him, providing an opportunity for the fledgling senior officer to flex his newly promoted muscle.

'Late again Patterson!'

'Funny, so am I!' Patterson replied without losing momentum.

The senior struggled to reply, frowning with confusion.

'Wanker,' Patterson whispered to himself through a satisfied grin. He skidded to a halt in front of another two gates, the right of which had a smaller, pedestrian gate ensconced in it. After ringing the bell of what appeared to be a giant's house, Patterson craned his neck to look up at the imposing site. The massive gates sat with pride in a solid, block, Victorian wall, encapsulating the entire workplace. It was the beginning of a city within a city. Seconds after ringing the bell, a muffled voice shouted from inside.

'Fire three.'

A loud buzzer was followed by a metallic click of the gate unlocking, and opening inward. A smiling face, crowned with a dark blue, peaked hat, welcomed him in.

'Hurry up, Paddy! The parades about to start,' explained the friendly guard.

'Tell them to start without me,' he replied, heading to the Tally Lodge; a hole in the wall protected by BRPP (bullet proof polycarbonate plastic) on the right-hand side of this massive vehicle lock. He dropped his security pass in the steel well and progressed on through an opening further along the wall, to the staff search area and the door to the armoury. He had learned that lodging his personal weapon in the armoury, meant a delay when finishing work, so he preferred to leave it hidden in his car in the secure car park. He had successfully entered through the first and second defence 'layers', of the Crumlin Road Jail.

Chapter 3.

The pair walked along a poorly lit street in the direction of the Band Hall. Most nights, due to its proximity to nearby catholic enclaves and erratic vandalised street lighting, the journey could be a harrowing experience. The eleventh night was different. Doors were wide open to accept the nomadic partygoers, projecting yellow rectangles of illumination onto the drab canvas. Drunk, but happy people, were singing or saying their goodbyes to generous hosts. Henderson held the door, as they entered the cramped shebeen, that was stifling due to the combined body heat. Blue smoke sat in a cloud a few inches from the plaster-swirled ceiling that had once been white before the onslaught of tobacco. A murmur of conversations, mixed with occasional laughter, unconvincing heated arguments and the clinking of glasses, filled the room. The crowds parted as Smallwood meandered his way through the sea of bodies. He was afforded Presidential reverence; nodding and smiling as often as he shook hands and embraced admiring drinkers. The invisible passage created for Smallwood remained open for Henderson, though not out of respect. On reaching the tiny but busy bar, the attendant motioned with a pint glass toward them. Henderson relayed his disapproval by leaning his head to one side. The barman disappeared, reappearing seconds later from behind a once locked door at the other end of the bar. Henderson took the lead.

Two evil looking Neanderthals, drinking beer and smoking, as they sat on two of the many beer kegs scattered in the back area, suddenly jumped to their feet. In an attempt to appear disciplined, they discarded the half empty tins behind the kegs, and in schoolboy fashion, dropped the cigarettes that they attempted to extinguish. Henderson's features contorted as he approached.
'Fucking security?' he growled.
Pushing past them, he travelled along a small concrete block corridor to a small set of wooden stairs. Smallwood grinned at the two guards, whispering reassuringly,
'Finish your beers lads, it's the eleventh night after all.'
The band practice hall upstairs, held an eerie silence in comparison to the bustle of downstairs, accentuated by the dark, spacious area. Distant walls appeared a deathly black behind manipulated lighting. Gloom lurked in the shadows not touched by the sparse illumination. Of the eight overhead single bulbs, equally spaced on a suspended wooden-panelled ceiling, only two showed signs of life. Both were fitted with restrictive shades, casting a sharper light on the wooden floor below. Under the first makeshift spotlight, the two remaining founder members of the organisation, sat at a rectangular table. Big, Willie Hamilton and Terry 'The Weasel' Montgomery. The table was bare, apart from a dice and a Webley revolver.

William Trevor Hamilton was born in the Newtownabbey area of North Belfast and settled in the Loyalist Rathcoole estate. His six-foot five-inch frame had practically guaranteed his role of protector to the people as the troubles gained momentum. Smallwood had an instant rapport with this giant, amongst the thousands of other shipyard workers. Hamilton's admiration of Smallwood's leadership qualities was apparent at every union meeting, qualities he mimicked, and adopted, when organising the growing, restless and suspicious male force of Rathcoole. Hamilton sought advice at every opportunity, strengthening a relationship that grew into a friendship. It was a natural progression as both men had similar traits. Solid, persuadable, quietly intelligent, happily married men. Equally important was their Loyalist beliefs.

The final member, Terence Montgomery, was classed as a low life by a majority of the association. His close ties with Henderson alone, guaranteed membership of this elite clan. His organisational and mathematical brain was universally revered, as much as his sadistic nature was despised. In Orangefield Secondary School, he'd been expelled in second year, apprehended during truancy, in the act of torturing and dismembering kittens. Continuous child psychotherapy, and promised support from a trusted relative, enabled re-admittance to the education system. During this period, Henderson took the young Montgomery under his wing. A product of an alcoholic single mother, Montgomery viewed Henderson as a father figure who in turn, admired the tenacity of the sickly youngster, marvelling at how quickly he worked out the intricacies of horse racing bets. From then on, 'The Weasel' sailed through school without fear. Six months after finishing education with only a Maths 'O' level, he was in a Juvenile detention home for attacking a known gay man single handedly, unaware of his latent, subliminal leaning toward homosexuality.

Ten feet into the heart of the hall under the remaining spotlight, slumped a half-naked man tied to a chair. A ripped shirt hung from his belt, indistinguishable in colour, due to the amount of blood, both fresh and dried. Though his head leant forward, chin on chest, it was obvious his face was swollen and disfigured. Bruises were scattered over his visible torso, cocktailed by a myriad of cigarette burns.

~

Patterson slammed the door on his grey metallic locker and raced back through the packed locker room toward the forecourt of the jail. He buttoned his tunic, checking his Ulster Defence Regiment service ribbon, was straight before tucking his rarely used whistle into a breast pocket. Patterson was all too aware of the strict dress codes demanded at the Recorders Court, such as the one in Omagh.
'A helluva drive,' he thought to himself, delighted that he would spend a day away from the jail, with the added bonus of extra wages in overtime and subsistence expenses. He tapped his trouser pocket, and realised his cigarettes, and money for the lunchtime card school, were still in the locker room. Sprinting back, he checked the top of his locker.
Nothing.

'Bollocks! Shite!!' he raged, digging out keys.

Within a minute, he located the valuables in an inside jacket pocket, tossing it unceremoniously, back into the locker. When Patterson reached the sprawling concrete forecourt, he dashed to the east corner and a BRPP covered grill at the entrance of Prisoners reception; the area where every prisoner in Northern Ireland's history began their journey. It doubled as a holding area for prisoners going out to court. The gate was locked from the inside until prisoners were in the location. Patterson hammered on the grill rather using than using the bell provided.

'Ok…hold your horses!' bellowed an annoyed officer.

Patterson raced past him along a narrow corridor, the left side of which, reminded him of a bookmaker's shop. From chest height to near the ceiling, was a strip of clear industrial plastic with 3 sliding openings, ready for new, or returning prisoners, to be interviewed, photographed and begin, or continue, whatever time the courts had appointed them. Already a few clerical grade officers behind the clear plastic, were busily checking the necessary documents required for the day. At the top of the narrow corridor, an opening to the right led into a cavernous, square holding area. Its mahogany-coloured chequered tiled, floor worn down by one hundred years of prisoners and staff. Wooden cubicles akin to changing rooms, adorned all four walls. These were waiting areas for inmates, prior to being escorted by Prison staff, or Police, to the court they had been summoned to. They were also the first taste of incarceration for new inmates.

In the far corner, a space led to showering, toilets and another door that held any prohibited prisoners clothing on their incarceration, which was most things. Leather jackets, steel tipped shoes and shirts that dared display a sense of fashion, hung on dedicated hangers for as long as the prisoners' sentence. A veritable feast for the cockroaches, mice and other infestations that plagued this aged place. Patterson then darted through the only other space available, to the left of the holding area. A senior officer sat on a slightly raised platform, with an enormous ledger open in front of him. It was a small area, holding only a set of scales and a height measuring device.

'Sorry I'm a bit late SO, the traffic was a nightmare.'

The grey haired, bespectacled Senior Officer was senior in every aspect, and widely respected. The ledger in front of him detailed any movement in, or out of the jail. He raised his gaze and tipped his head to peer over the top of his glasses.

'You're probably a bit more than sorry, kid. Do you want the bad news or the bad news?'

Patterson couldn't disguise his disappointment.

'I'll try the bad news first.'

'Omagh Court has been cancelled.'

'Shite!'

'And now the bad news. If you bothered getting your arse out of bed, you might have got here in time for the Enniskillen run, or the two Hospital guards you missed.' Patterson was devastated. A court run to Enniskillen would have generated more much needed income through travelling expenses, but Hospital Guards were the jackpot.

Twelve-hour shifts, guarded by Police, whilst guarding a prisoner usually unconscious for the duration of their stay.

'Tell me you're joking SO.'

'OK…I'm joking.'

Patterson's face lit up.

'Seriously?'

'No. Now get yourself up to C wing and report to the Principal Officer.' Patterson's chin lowered closer to his chest with each step, as he retraced his path back to the locker rooms. He was oblivious to occasional nods and 'hellos' from colleagues as he laboured against the tide of staff, in a trance like state. He realised how tightly he clenched his fists, attempting to control the shaking in his hands. The terror and rage building inside him, felt out of his control. In the, now empty, confines of the locker room, he became fixated on the metallic door of his locker. The ever-present dire thoughts of his dilemmas, were somehow, projected onto the anonymous door like an old-fashioned cine camera. He glanced around in a panic that someone else might witness his thoughts. He glared menacingly in defiance, blinking furiously with fire in his eyes, in a hope to exorcise the images, to no avail. He watched a collection of panoramic scenes of his living room. Red repossession Building Society letters, empty bottles, crumpled bookie dockets and unopened threats from a car finance company, covered the stained carpet. Filled ashtrays and discarded half smoked joints, flowed over a pathetic self-assembly, but, not self-cleaning, table.

Cheap curtains struggled to blot out daylight giving the scene a macabre, mausoleum air. The alien terror he'd felt, raced to the fore, as he punched the thin metal with enough force to leave a permanent indentation. The vision disappeared. His heart pounded and his limbs shook. He felt frightened, and alone. He was horrified that he couldn't contain his emotions, but more terrified of his predicament. Patterson stared again at the warped door, praying for a vision that would give him some hope, some answers. It didn't happen.

Chapter 4

The noisy steel tips reverberated around the room like gunshots, as Henderson entered. A leer crept over his face as he approached the others. Montgomery rolled a dice from side to side across the table, oblivious of his colleagues. The dice made a ghoulish sound. His features told a tale of frenzied activity, his gaze locked on the victim. Hamilton leapt to his feet when he realised Smallwood's presence. He looked straight at his natural leader, automatically adopting an apologetic gait, letting his glance drift to his shoes.

'What the fuck is going on here?'

Smallwood spoke with an emphatic urgency, simmering toward anger. Henderson's body language was feeding off the frenzy emanating from Montgomery. Henderson held his hand up to halt Smallwood.

'Hold on a minute. Terry, what are you doing?'

'Letting fate get involved,' Montgomery replied, thinking out loud. 'You see Mr. Wilson's show here is at its finale, and we haven't decided what it is yet.'

Smallwood's lips turned white, struggling to fight the disgust and rage rising within. Bile rose in his throat, as his veins pumped blood, escalating his adrenaline surge. Henderson, oblivious, was preparing to play out his rehearsed role.

'If we roll a one, he gets one in the kneecap.' Montgomery smiled and turned his devilish gaze toward the revolver. 'A two will be both kneecaps. Three, means kneecaps and one elbow, four -both elbows, and five is one in the head.'

Henderson grinned before delivering his rehearsed line.

'What if he gets a six?'

'He gets another go,' Montgomery droned, his tone falling flat. Henderson chortled as Montgomery turned his head toward him, his smile disappearing when his focus past his mentor's shoulder. With a frown, Henderson turned just in time to catch a ferocious back handed slap across the side of this face from Smallwood. The surprise more than force, knocked him off balance. Montgomery reached for the revolver, but was frozen by Smallwood's, 'I-Dare-You' stare, and that Hamilton had taken a step toward him. Montgomery accepted defeat, retreating back in his seat. Smallwood returned his attention to Henderson, who attempted to stand up and restore some dignity. He briefly inspected the torture victim with a feeling of disgust, before glancing back at Henderson, who had instilled defiance, breaking the eerie impasse.

'What was that for?!'

'Explain! Now!'

Henderson carefully mixed his defiance with conviviality. *'We're trying to make a living here Jackie, for God's sake.'*

Smallwood's dispassionate gaze, demanded his continuation.

'We have all worked hard, to establish this organisation. Can you imagine the Wild West show it would've been, if we hadn't controlled the Vigilantes?'

Smallwood folded his arms, a demonstration of impatience.

'Like it or not...we're leaders. But being a leader in this organisation doesn't put bread on the table. Don't try and tell me you find it easy on your shipyard pay to provide for Kate and the kids.'

Henderson sensed a deviation in Smallwood's demeanour, albeit a mistaken one.

'You've explained nothing yet!' was Smallwood's low, growled reply.

'Look, the hoods and the Provos are still out there. We've been getting stacks of requests from local businesses for protection from this scum. Protection they're willing to pay for.'

Smallwood's lips tightened and turned white as he struggled to control the anger that crept closer to the surface.

'Protection?!' Smallwood exclaimed, his tone rising. 'Are you serious?'

'Our organisation provides a service, and each business makes a donation in return. Weasel here,' nodding in the direction of the gargoyle like Montgomery, who offered a pathetic defensive smile, '...gathers invoices and such, then divides the payments equally between us and the organisation. Jackie we can make four hundred quid a month...each.'

Although emphasis on Henderson's last word was an attempt to appease, it had the opposite effect. Smallwood fought every sinew and muscle to remain calm. He nodded in the direction of the prisoner.

'Well Jackie...him and his brother... sort of...refused our service,' mumbled Henderson in a defeated tone.

Smallwood clapped a hand over his mouth in sheer disbelief, inhaling CO_2 to placate his inherited, fiery genes. He pondered the situation. Henderson attempted to regain control.

'But they threatened to tout to the peelers! Set us up. Slur the name of the organisation for God's sake!'

Smallwood stepped toward Henderson, his face leaning in to almost touching. Smallwood's chiselled features had never looked more menacing. It was the demon rage persona starting to reveal itself, a dangerous, unknown fact, to his oblivious opposite number.

'He doesn't have to slur the name of this organisation,' offered Smallwood in a tone unrecognisable to the others. 'You're doing a good job on your own!'

Smallwood held his position a few seconds longer than was natural. Henderson braced himself for an expected assault, glad it didn't arrive. Smallwood turned to face the prisoner. After two steps, he turned to face the rest.

'Leaders? That's what you call us? We're representatives...that's all! Do I have to remind you why we formed our organisation?'

Smallwood paced around, looking at the floor before returning his icy glare back to the hapless trio.

'We are engaged in a war. Indiscriminate attacks and assaults on any protestant! Our enemies are intent on urban genocide. That's why I took an active role...to protect our people! I never expected them to pay for it!'

Henderson listened, his mind racing. He had been embarrassed by the earlier assault, and the impudent form of treatment. His master plan was crumbling around him. His leader's mood hinted; he was in fear of being permanently deposed. Smallwood turned his attention to Hamilton.

'These two wankers don't surprise me Willie, but you....' his voice trailed off, a reluctance to persecute his oldest ally.

He shook his head and turned toward the semi-comatose prisoner. He addressed the group without turning around...

'It's over!'

Henderson had reached a monumental decision, realising this was a pivotal moment in his dictatorship. One that he must grasp with both hands. His face contorted into a snarl noticed by Montgomery, who slowly retrieved the pistol.

'Oh, it's over all right,' Henderson murmured, gliding on his toes, to prevent the steel tips on his heels causing alarm, toward Smallwood. A small, but sharp, kitchen knife, slid from Henderson's sleeve into a prepared grasp. Hamilton noticed, motioning to move, until he saw Montgomery's gun pointing directly at him. Montgomery held a finger to his lips, indicating silence. The last thing Smallwood witnessed, was the abductee being sprayed with a torrent of fresh blood. Before he could react and realise it was his blood, his last ounce of life escaped. Montgomery grinned like an insane inpatient, as he watched how forceful the blood projected from Smallwood's dying corpse. The thud of Smallwood's lifeless body on the wooden floor echoed around the band hall. In a demonic -like state, Henderson leant over his former colleague, wiping the knife clean on Smallwood's jacket.

'You're so wrong Mister big shot! It's not over. It's only just started!' Henderson snarled into a lifeless ear. He approached Hamilton, holding the murder weapon at his throat.

'And then there were three! And remember Willie boy, we're all in this together!'

'You know what to do,' Henderson barked at Montgomery before motioning toward the captive. 'And lose that arsehole too!'

Hamilton couldn't recall ever feeling this way before. Not only the feeling of being wracked with guilt that he hadn't attempted to save Smallwood, but the act of shaking with fear.

~

Kate was bereft. She wanted to kill those who took away her soul mate. Her blood boiled when the funeral minister advised that time would help her heal. It was nonsense. Her response was antithetical. With every second, minute, and hour that passed, she missed him more. Every day, week and month that dragged by, she became more distant and alone. Of course, Kate loved her children, but even that paled against her increasing love for the man who should have been by her side. Alone in the double bed, she announced to God that her love for her husband was greater and stronger than anything in her life. Including the Christian deity.

~

Ashen-faced, Kate sat on cracked leather seating on a double-decker bus. She embraced her two-year-old son tightly as he stood on her knees, peering out through the scraped glass windows. She gripped him as he struggled to balance, yet Kate's gaze was distant. Her daughter, Shirley, sat in the seat beside them, her face decorated with amateur teenage make-up, glittery lip gloss and clumpy mascara that did zilch for her eyes. She continually fidgeted in her seat, grunting with tedium.

'I should've been at the Matinee with Emma,' she scowled under her breath.

The sound of her daughter's voice dragged Kate into the present.

'Sorry love... what did you say?'

Shirley turned to face her, realising this could be her only opportunity of escape.

'Look mum, it's ok to take JJ to see Granny, but I have friends I want to be with. I'm fifteen! And anyway, Granny just lies there and doesn't move or speak.'

Kate took a calculated breath.

'I know it looks like that love, but the nurses tell me she hears our voices. They say she loves to hear her grandchildren...'

Kate's voice broke, an unexpected outburst of tears disrupting her speech. Shirley wrapped her arms around her and embraced her mother in a tight hug.

'Oh Mommy, I'm sorry, Mommy. Mommy please don't cry!'

They both hugged in silence, interrupted by occasional sobs. A fire engine squealed its intent as it rushed by the window.

'Fire regade!' squealed JJ, unintentionally helping lift the mood. Kate and Shirley shared a look of warmth, before blurting out laughter through their tears. Kate squeezed her children as much as affection dictated and kissed the top of JJ's head.

'I hope that you never remember these last few months, wee man,' she whispered.

~

A tranquil atmosphere hung in the old people's home. Everything was clean, yet had a stale freshness to it. Nurses and orderlies glided by in silence, unlike the incumbents who trudged around with artificial support, smiling at anyone who noticed. Kate was reminded of a library, whilst Shirley thought only of a funeral parlour. The only real sound came from a radio beside Kate's mother's bed in her private room. Jim Croce's 'Time in a bottle' did nothing to upset the enforced calm. Kate's mother was upright in bed, because she had been placed in that position for her offspring's visit. Her face looked like it had been carved from yellowish candle wax with sunken cheeks, dark rings under her eyes and a wisp of white hair covering her tiny skull. Her lips were colourless and lacked the life she once had. Although her eyes were fixed in a gaze somewhere behind Kate, she blinked every so often, her body maintaining involuntary muscle reactions only when necessary. Kate held her hand, and stroked it with the tip of her fingers. Shirley sat upright beside her, focusing on JJ on her knees. JJ's usual bubbly character, had succumbed to the forlorn surroundings. Jim Croce sang about knowing who he wants to spend eternity with before fading for the **hourly** *pips. Kate insisted Shirley and JJ take a walk in the grounds. The hourly pips gave way to the signature jingle of the Radio Ulster news.* 'This is Trevor Simpson with the Radio Ulster news. The badly mutilated body, recovered yesterday from a back street in Ainsworth Avenue in the Shankill area of Belfast, has been identified as missing twenty-two-year-old catholic labourer, Donal McAvoy, from the Falls area.

Mr McAvoy is the fifth catholic to be murdered in Belfast in the last 3 months. The Royal Ulster Constabulary are describing this latest murder as sectarian and believe it to be connected to previous killings. However, they refused to comment when asked, if this was a continuation of revenge killings following the murder of UDA leader, John Smallwood, in July this year. No organisation has yet claimed Mr Smallwood's murder.'

Kate leant across to embrace her mother's motionless body as tears cascaded down her cheeks.

'Mommy, I don't know if you can hear me, but I love you so much.'

Chapter 5

Principal Officer, Eric Wright, sat behind his desk in a converted cell office in C Wing. Like so many of the Principal Officers, he was a former English soldier who found the transition to Prison Officer, after demobbing, a natural choice. Few other employers had a need or want for a 'Brit' as the troubles escalated, and the Northern Ireland Office was desperate for experienced men. Consequently, good attendance during that hectic period practically guaranteed promotion. All the ex-soldiers were veterans of boring routine and danger. Wright also had the rare quality of leadership. He held a booklet and stroked his neat black beard in concentration whilst he read. Wright defied his years and was extremely fit. No grey hairs dared mingle with his short crop of neat black hair. His hat hung on a coat stand behind him, hinting at the informality of the meeting underway. The panel to the censor's office next door was shut, advertising the personal air. Across the table, Patterson sat in silence smoking a cigarette. He had reluctantly accepted his over generous share of the day's 'bad luck.'

'Eric, is this the Spanish Inquisition or my annual report?'

Wright looked up and smiled, before setting the report down. He lit a cigarette and sat back in a comfortable chair, as much a privilege as the white shirt he adorned. Wright nodded at the report and Patterson grabbed it.

'You'll notice I have given you another good report Paddy.'

He grinned his appreciation.

'Only because you deserve it,' he continued. 'You've adapted well to prison life. You're a good officer, with intelligence. You mix well. But off the record…'

'There's always a but!' replied Patterson, continuing to wear a pathetic grin on his face.

'…you have to lengthen that short fuse of yours if you want to achieve the promotion you deserve.'

Patterson's features hardened, his expression turning stone cold. He stared at Wright long enough to create wariness, before slamming his hand on the table,

'What short fuse?' he growled.

The adjoining censor's panel flew open at the sound of a raised voice.

Defiantly getting to his feet, Wright leant in close to Patterson.

'See? Exactly what I'm saying!' his tone measured.

Patterson's expression metamorphosised into a wide grin, accompanied by a cheeky wink.

'Got you there, PO.'

Wright's face blushed with oncoming embarrassment. He sat back down, smirking at Patterson and lifted the report, feigning writing.

'All other comments: *Can be a cheeky wee shite!*'

Patterson laughed out loud.

'Right, away up to C2 and help your sparring partner this morning. You'll probably be in visits this afternoon. They're always short.'

'Jesus, it just can't get any better,' he announced with sarcasm, before turning for the door.

The PO let a wry smile creep onto his face as Patterson left. When the door closed, Wright turned to the section of the report entitled: 'Recommendation for promotion.' He scribbled onto the paper and reread his praising words: 'Highly recommended.'

~

Autumn's long shadows created dark fingers the length of the tidy terrace street. Kate was at the front door chatting with Eleanor Hagan, a warm and trusting widow, often referred to as 'Auntie Eleanor' within the universe of their street. Shirley and young John were indoors and the cacophony of children playing football and street games, had been substituted for weekly baths and bedtime. Shirley was trying to convince John that there wasn't enough room in her leather school bag for all his toys.
'Look love, honestly there's no problem with the kids staying with me tonight,' said Mrs. Hagan, touching Kate's arm, 'They're good as gold. I'm always glad of the company now that big lad of mine is working over in Liverpool.'
She hesitated, leaning closer to emphasise her concern.
'You deserve a wee night out since...well, you know.'
Kate hugged her, fighting against oncoming tears that pooled her eyes.
'Thanks again Auntie E.'
JJ pushed past the both of them as Shirley engaged in a playful game of chase.
'Right, you two! Get over here.' Kate stated in an unconvincing growl.

Shirley stepped forward and lifted two worn toothbrushes from her school bag, presenting them to her mother with an 'I-told-you-so' smile.

'See…I didn't forget them.'

Kate conceded and crouched onto the footpath. She opened her arms and both children engulfed her in a tight hug. Kate glanced at Mrs. Hagan and winked, before redirecting her attention.

'You have to promise me you'll be on your best behaviour.'

'We promise,' bleated Shirley, JJ grinning beside her.

'I don't want to hear any stories…' she started, before Shirley interrupted.

'Mommy…listen…go out, have fun…we'll be ok.'

Kate again, fought the surge of inevitable tears while she hugged her offspring,

'And remember,' she said with genuine sincerity, embracing them once more. 'I love you both…very, very much.'

Shirley stepped back and JJ wriggled out of his mother's grasp to join his sister.

'And we love you too Mummy.'

Shirley took Mrs. Hagen's hand, JJ mirroring her actions. Mrs. Hagen smiled with eyes full of apology, before walking down the street. Kate folded her arms in a self-embrace, watching the trio disappear into the distance. Shirley turned and waved; JJ followed suit. Kate returned the wave before darting inside. She closed the door, leaning against it for strength. The energy drained from her body and her legs weakened.

Tears erupted and swamped her face. She slid down the door, scrunching into a ball as she sobbed into her lap.

~

The grill at the foot of the stairs in the middle of the ground floor, was unlocked by a uniformed officer, allowing Patterson to ascend. At the top of the stairs was another locked grill. Patterson registered the sound of cell doors being opened, and orders echoed through the angled ascending corridor. The noise always reminded him of his first day as a Prison Officer. He had never imagined a jail to be such a noisy place. But within the enclosed wings of the ancient Victorian building, any noise was amplified by the narrow living areas. Now that all the Republicans were safely locked in the dining area, the Loyalist inmates could begin their routine, in their self-imposed segregation. He kicked the grill in playful banter.
'Any chance?' Patterson shouted.
A familiar deep growl came from behind and above him. 'Do you want to wear that gate?'
Patterson turned to see his friend, Andy Beattie, on the thin walkway of the 2's. He smiled and replied, 'You don't have to use joined up writing you know!'
Beattie grinned before turning back to the inmate just inside the cell door. A grossly overweight loyalist, wearing nothing but tight jockey shorts. He listened to the prisoner's requests, ticking them off on his clipboard, before moving to the next cell. Beattie closed the cell door, his assistant already unlocking the next one. Within a few minutes, all prisoner's requests, including visits, Doctor, Tuck shop and Governor interviews had been noted.

Two cells were opened and locked back, allowing the first batch of Loyalist inmates to wash and empty the contents of their slop bucket deposits. They mostly contained urine. It was only the veteran prisoners who had learned to defecate into the mini portable toilets. As Beattie approached the locked stair grill, Patterson was joined on the stairs by a 'trusted' sentenced prisoner known as an 'orderly', who carried a pre-ordered cup of tea for his friend.

'Can I get you a cup mister?' the orderly asked through a toothless grin.

'Do you have coffee?'

'The Mister on the 1's forgot to get some, but I might have some in my cell,' the orderly offered with a fanciful smile.

A tight grin curled at the corner of Patterson's mouth as he lifted out his cigarette packet. He shook the box to free two filter tips, known as 'straights' in this underworld, handing them to the orderly, who grinned like a Cheshire cat.

'See what you can do, I'll take the old man's tea up for him.'

The orderly made the precious straights disappear with the guile of a magician, before shuffling back downstairs.

Chapter 6

The only light source in the living room was from a single lamp with a heavy shade, that emitted soft yellow light onto a pristine sideboard. A dying fire languished in the grate, no longer providing heat or illumination. The lamp's lazy rays rested comfortably on a single, pseudo-metallic, photo frame. A young, proud Jackie Smallwood, bedecked in swimming trunks on Crawfordsburn beach, could excusably be mistaken for a cover model of a 50's American body building magazine. Draped in his arms was a willing Kate wearing a confident smile on her face. The only other decorations on the sideboard were a half-drained bottle of vodka, an empty glass and a brown pill bottle. The weak light source, barely reached into the corners of the living room, giving it a comfortable, protective atmosphere, which was accentuated by the soft, crackly voice, of Doris Day whispering from the portable Baird record player. The retaining arm that held records in place on top of the turntable's spindle had been pivoted backward, ensuring that the record would play continuously.

When I grew up and fell in love, I asked my sweetheart what lies ahead.

Will we have rainbows, day after day, here's what my sweetheart said,

Que Sera Sera, whatever will be will be, the future's not ours, to see...

'The futures not ours to see,' mumbled Kate, with no hope of keeping in time with the record.

In a trance like state, she opened a small, round, make-up compact and lifted out a blushing sponge, so she could stare into the mirror in the lid. She applied blusher to her cheeks in a maladroit fashion, ignoring the muddy streaks of black eye-liner cascading from her eyes. It gave her the look of a macabre Pierrot. Blushing completed, she dropped the compact and assumed her preferred sitting position with her legs underneath her. It took a while to get comfortable due to having to bundle the endless yards of white dress out of the way. She held the framed photo in her hands before kissing it.

'Do you remember that record? That was the first tune we ever danced to. The Floral Hall, Antrim Road? Remember?'

Kate smiled so much that her cheeks ached after a few seconds. She was distracted by a loss of breath that came with a powerful urge to weep. She closed her eyes and threw her head back, face directed at the ceiling. She took many short breaths to regain emotional control, before taking one long breath and re-focusing.

'Why was I attracted to the only man in that dance hall with two left feet?' Her laboured voice, felt the hollowness of a one-way conversation, praying with all her might for a reply. She blurted out a laugh.

'Do you know if you hadn't been wearing those Teddy boy shoes; my shins would've been black and blue?'

Kate sighed, her tone changing.

'And don't think I forgot about that other wee hussy who was chasing you that night! I thought I would've ended up fighting for you! Oh awe, you thought you were gorgeous, Jackie Smallwood.'

She paused for a full minute and sat in silence; her eyes transfixed on the photo.

'And you were. You always were.' she whispered.

A hint of defeat and finality forced itself into her voice.

'I was so in love with you, my darling.'

Kate's shoulders spasmed and her breathing stuttered as she wailed into the photo.

'And I love you more than I ever have. I miss you.'

Tears fell onto the lipstick-stained glass of the frame that slipped from her weak grasp. Kate put her feet on the floor and it spilled off her knees, landing on the worn, fireside mat. She reached for the vodka bottle and gulped the burning liquid, careful not to make herself vomit. She entered the working kitchen and opened the back door. The cool evening air did nothing to dissuade her purpose.

~

The nursing home, except for an occasional cough, was deathly quiet. A night porter continued his mundane round, following a yellow torch light beam. All private rooms were open during the wee small hours. When he arrived at Kate's mother's room, he inspected her more closely than the others.

'This old dear must be pissing death off so much,' he thought to himself, 'Jeez, she looks like she died 20 years ago.'

As he turned to exit the room, the skeletal figure screamed at the top of her voice and bolted upright in bed.

'Fuck me!' yelled the porter, hunching into a defensive stance and dropping his torch. The old lady continued to scream.

The sound of movement from other rooms along the corridor, were soon drowned out by quick footsteps running. Expecting to see the grim reaper, the porter jumped as the duty nurse crashed into the room. She sprinted to the old woman and embraced her in an attempt to calm her down. The old woman sobbed and muttered the same word, over and over again.

'No... no... no...'

~

Patterson sipped at the bitter taste of cheap coffee, sitting opposite his mentor in the converted cell, known as the Class Office. Across the desk, Beattie recorded his achieved routine in the daily journal. 'Apart from being heartbroken at missing the court run, how are you kid?' he asked. Patterson felt awkward believing, without conviction, that Beattie was the only other living soul, who had an inkling of the shit he found himself in. However, that awkwardness soon dissipated.

'To be honest Andy,' he understated, 'Things could be better.'

Beattie reached out and touched Patterson's arm with the warmth of a knowing father. 'I have told you a million times before, I'm always here for you kid, whenever you want to talk.'

As Patterson's cheeks turned a little pink, he stopped fidgeting with the coffee cup and engaged in Beattie's welcoming gaze. Beattie studied the mist of despair in his friend's eyes and hardened his tone.

'And I mean, *really talk.*'

Without burdening his young charge, Beattie switched the conversation.' You heading off to your sister's place at the weekend?'

Patterson's Sister's place, was a neat and tidy terraced house on Albert Road in Blackpool, sandwiched between two guest houses. She lived as a single parent with her two sons for six months of the year, due to her husband's commitments as a deep-sea diver on oil rigs. Patterson realised they were the most important people in the world to him and without whom, he would've slipped a lot sooner into the maelstrom of self-destruction.

'Yeah…I'm looking forward to the break,' Patterson replied with a smile, but the devil of thoughts about the lost overtime sniggered in the deep recesses of his mind.

'Well, I'll tell you what. You go take a break from *everything,* and get your head sorted out.' Patterson noted an emphasis on the word 'everything' and acknowledged the knowing smile on Beattie's face. If it were anyone else, Patterson would be wary and perhaps aggressive toward them. However, it felt as if Beattie had wrapped an invisible comfort blanket around him.

'…and when you get back, we'll go and see the Glens hammering the Blues?'

A genuine smile formed on Patterson's face that Beattie was very much aware of.

'And don't forget to take over those football shirts for your wee nephews, I got for you.'

Before Patterson could reply, they were interrupted by a cacophony of panic coming from outside the Class Office. Shouts and footsteps abounded as they both got to their feet. An ashen faced officer filled the doorway.

'Quick Andy! Swinger in cell 12!'

Chapter 7

Shirley hugged Auntie E and thanked her for letting them sleep over. A smiling Eleanor Hagen, embraced both children before letting them race up the street to their own house. Shirley gripped her brother's hand as they skipped along the worn footpath.

'Do you know what wee man? I'll bet you she isn't even up yet. I wonder if she got drunk last night?'

JJ smiled back at her, totally oblivious as to what Shirley was talking about, youth maintaining his childish ignorance. When they reached their front door, Shirley put her fingers through the letter box to clutch the hanging string and retrieve the front door key. A puzzled grin crept onto her face, when she heard the crackling sound of Doris Day as she unlocked the door.

~

Patterson raced from the Class Office, closely followed by Beattie. Staff rushed frantically up the stairs, while audiences watched the drama unfold from above and below. The adrenalin rush surged through Patterson, as he reached the open cell door.

~

Shirley opened the front door, letting in daylight. The untidy state of the room still darkened by closed curtains was evident, lit solely by a dim lamp. Maternal instincts, yet to develop in a child so young, came to the fore. She held JJ close whilst surveying the room. Her stomach twisted; unaware the feeling was of impending doom.

'Mummy,' she whispered, edging into the room, as if walking on thin ice.

Content, but more alert of her mother's absence, she proceeded slowly toward the gap in the wall to the scullery where, to save space in such a tight area, a door had been replaced by a vinyl strip curtain. Through constant use, some of the vinyl strips had warped, allowing glimpses of the stairs at the back of the scullery. Shirley could see the bottom of her mother's wedding dress, draped from the highest spindle on the open staircase- she recognised it from the hours of pouring over photographs when her mum was feeling low. Shirley widened the gap of the vinyl strips. The dress, which should've been flat, had a shape to it. Shirley spied swollen, purple hands protruding through the long sleeves at either side of the lifeless dress. She glanced higher and seen the hideously distorted, lifeless face of her mother, that stared with bulging eyes. A leather belt tight around her neck, making it appear impossibly thin. Shirley shook, as warm urine flowed down her legs. JJ pushed his way through the plastic curtain, before Shirley grabbed him and buried his head in her midriff, denying him full sight of the horror. Shirley fell backward, and stumbled onto the worn settee, without releasing the protective grip on her baby brother. She squealed and shrieked, forcing her terrified and confused brother, to reciprocate.

~

Patterson slid to a halt at the open door of cell 12. An officer was attempting to lift a prisoner's deadweight higher from the hanging position, he had previously occupied.

Patterson bounded forward to assist, but blinked continually, platelets dancing across his vision, made him feel lightheaded.

His legs weakened as he grasped into thin air behind him, in hope of finding an anchor. Patterson looked up and accessed how he could assist, but his head spun out of control. He was close to losing consciousness. A few seconds later, his sight stabilised and the dizziness abated. The scene before him was no longer that of a prison cell, as multi-coloured strips, slowly opened in front of him. The hanging prisoner was replaced with a vision of a woman in white, floating above the ground.

'An angel?' he exclaimed, frozen in a trance-like state.

The image was shattered by the shouting officer supporting the hanging prisoner. Urgent hands behind, pushed him aside as more staff crowded into the cell. The prisoner's ligature was cut. He was laid on the bed, life having disappeared hours before. An ashen-faced Patterson was transfixed on the area where the 'vision' had appeared. His entire body trembled. Beattie took him by the arm onto the narrow landing and away from the scene. Patterson hadn't reacted to any of Beattie's encouraging words, still thinking about the apparition. Beattie trundled him into a corner in the Class Office and gripped him by the shoulders.

'Are you ok, kid? Talk to me!'

Patterson blinked, his eyes surveying the office with the look of a stranger. Recognition and normality oozed over his features as he became aware of his surroundings. He broke free from Beattie's grip.

'I'm ok Andy,' Patterson whispered.

'What the hell happened to you in there, you looked like you seen a ghost?!'

The phrase, '*seen a ghost,*' echoed through his vacuum of thoughts.
'I understand kid,' continued Beattie, 'it's never a nice experience to witness something like that for the first time. Shock affects everyone differently.'
Patterson clung to Beattie's reassuring words, as a means of escape.
'Yeah mate, that…that was it. Horrible to see. Never, eh…seen anything like that before …in real life.'
Patterson's words were laboured, punctuated with gaps of internal thoughts. Quickly, his normal, controlled, self-reliance returned.
'I'm sorry mate, I thought I could've handled it. The shock.'
'Don't you worry kid. Away down to the mess and get yourself a cuppa. Take a few minutes out. I'll explain everything to Eric.'
Patterson patted his arm with affection before heading down stairs. Beattie smiled and watched his young confidant disappear. However, his unseen smile evaporated and was replaced with a deep frown, full of concern and worry.

Chapter 8

Harry McDermott, was a slim wiry man with a lived-in face, semi-disguised by a well-shaped, neatly trimmed beard and moustache, the same colour as his salt and pepper hair. It was the Northern Ireland regime to label everyone with a nickname. His had been *Captain*, for nearly 30 years, after some quick-witted constable noticed a passing resemblance to Captain Edward John Smith of the Titanic, after reading a magazine on the ill-fated liner. Not a welcome nickname, but McDermott had reluctantly agreed that it 'stuck like shit to a blanket.' McDermott sat at his desk, in the back quarter of Criminal Investigations Department section of Hastings Street, Royal Ulster Constabulary station, enclosed by half glass/half board surroundings. His area had also two windows, one on both adjoining walls, of the corners of the room which had been locally nicknamed: 'The Goldfish Bowl.' Stubbing out a cigarette in the glass ashtray on his desk, McDermott ran his fingers through his hair and sighed. He looked to the far corner of his office, at a metal filing cabinet packed with different coloured folders with wrinkles of old age. The incline of the door portrayed the sign: 'Ongoing Investigations.'

'Why in the name of God do they not replace that sign with a 'we haven't got a clue' one?' he mused with a touch of annoyance. He was three months from retirement after thirty-five years' service. The thought of this year, 1988, had seemed wildly preposterous, even Orwellian, when he'd first entered the Police College. But the years had flown by and he'd peaked at the rank of Detective Sergeant.

He and his wife, Molly, were planning an active retirement in Scotland. They had found a delightful two-bedroom bungalow in Monifieth, just outside Dundee on the east coast. Their plans were twofold. They would be near their only daughter, who was married to a successful vet, and had two children. Equally as important, they would be far away from the everyday security threats to RUC members. He could relax at last, but not completely, thanks to the thirty-five years ingrained security awareness. McDermott's job had changed. Modernised. *Everything* was being modernised. His generation, were reluctant to accept change. He looked out at the three rows of desks. There were eight grey computer monitors, and miles of cabling, that disappeared through a hole in each desk to be connected to, what could only be described as, a suitcase with flashing lights. The black, curved screens were either filled with lines of luminous green type, or a tiny luminous rectangle, that sat flashing in the top left-hand corner. He was told that was the cursor. He thought it was because it made you curse when it didn't work properly, a regular occurrence' if like him, you didn't know how to operate it properly. McDermott surveyed a few staff currently on duty. Two Detective Constables, recently 'promoted' to plain clothes duties. He hated their style of dress. It was too flashy, but what really riled him, was the lack of neckwear. He had donned a jacket and tie for the fifteen years of his plain clothes era. These new mavericks grew their hair, wore bright, fashionable, open necked shirts and snazzy jackets. McDermott begrudgingly accepted that to blend in and make the public feel comfortable, when talking to non-uniformed policemen, plain clothes had to be the clothes of the day.

He was old fashioned. Or just plain old. The latest fad for fashionable young detectives, was a cellular phone, or *mobile phone*, as they called it. They reminded him of the black rubber brick he rescued from drowning, to gain his silver lifesaving badge in Templemore Avenue swimming baths, all those years ago. He was convinced they were a fad that would pass. The RUC radios and phone boxes with *real* phones, were irreplaceable. The cost of those monstrosities he hoped, would leave them out of reach of the people he protected.

'Protected,' he contemplated, glancing again at the metallic cupboard.

He'd joined the police to uphold the law and protect his city's citizens. After thirty-five years, and staring down the barrel of retirement, he felt like he had failed. No-one had ever dreamt how difficult Belfast would be during the troubles, still gathering speed and ferocity. The last decade had been brutal, innocent Catholics and Protestants being slaughtered. Soldiers, terrorists and RUC, suffered heavy casualties. The violence spread like an airborne disease to the mainland, where the government had been targeted, and to the Republic of Ireland, where it seemed anyone was a target.

'When the hell will this madness end?'

McDermott strolled to the cupboard, and retrieved a random batch of 'unsolved' files. What upset him was that every file in that cupboard had a report of someone, or many people, losing their lives.

Murdered. The rate of the paramilitary violence was breath taking. There were not enough police in Northern Ireland, to cope with the workload.

On many occasions when investigating an atrocity, it had to be shelved as another had occurred. Faceless terrorists. Cowards who shot from a rooftop. Bastards who pushed a button to explode a bomb that may, or may not, have killed security forces, but on most occasions, had obliterated the lives of innocents. He flicked through the folders, pausing at an incident he had witnessed first-hand. The city centre store was being evacuated after a bomb warning. The timings and construction of the device, were seriously lacking. As staff and shoppers were evacuating, thinking they had 30 minutes to preserve their lives, the whole bottom floor, where they headed, had exploded. He recalled the force of the blast and the deafening explosion, before the building was replaced by a spiralling plume of grey smoke. McDermott arrived at the scene, ready to assist, but where do you get training to assist a scene of carnage? The image that haunted him most, was that of the young woman, decapitated by a flying shard of front window, lying like a broken doll on the footpath. He clenched his fists as his body heated with anger, ignoring the files on his desk and stared at the open cupboard. 'What the hell did that girl, *any* of these people do, to deserve this!' His feeling of failure was almost complete as he tidied the files to return them to their dark, lonely, resting place, before noticing one on the floor, that had slipped off the uneven pile. The front flap was open, and an emotionless police photograph of John 'Jackie' Smallwood stared back at him. This was a case he'd been assigned to, and he recalled it well. His police instincts convinced him there was something erroneous with the inquiry.

It was assumed Smallwood, the UDA leader, had been murdered by the Provisional IRA, such was the lack of forensics. All interviewees had seen Smallwood enter the band hall that night, but only three saw him leave. No-one between the band hall and Smallwood's home, his supposed intended route, had witnessed anything. Par for the course on a drunken bonfire night. Smallwood could've been abducted in any number of places on his final route. However, there wasn't a hint of a proposed abduction from the grapevine, provided by Special Branch 'informers' on both sides. A few of the informers went as far to say that the Provos, had a modicum of respect for Smallwood, unlike the other three. The flimsy assumption he'd been abducted and murdered by the 'opposition', was loosely based on where his body was located - a local waste ground area where the Provos displayed their 'kills.' McDermott could never accept that. The Provos had never cut anyone's throat as a final punishment. And although their bullish macabre practices continued throughout the remainder of the most severe unrest, they had not been accredited with a similar slashing. Period. McDermott sighed and closed the file, setting them all back inside their metallic grave. He found it difficult to accept that Northern Ireland, was on a *genuine* course for *a type of* normality. A normality built on the graves of the unsolved murder victims. He realised the status quo had to change, for the benefit of the younger generation. A more cosmopolitan environment and attitude, would give them that chance of normality. Normality that had passed him, and many others, by. The weighty thoughts of the 'unsolved', couldn't help but make him feel closer to his adopted namesake. He now understood how Captain Edward

John Smith, must have felt on that tragic night of April 15th, 1912, when 1524 innocent souls were lost. McDermott, like Smith, realised there was absolutely nothing he could do.

~

Shirley sat in silence in the parlour room of a neat terrace house in east Belfast. A brass floor lamp provided dim light that spilt onto a pristine, patterned carpet. A fake animal fur rug sat in front of the hearth of a clean fireplace. The room was decorated with intent to provide comfort for guests, paradoxically creating the opposite to the children of the house. It was essentially, a forbidden place. Shirley was immobile. She had sat quietly, under sedation, for the last six months. Her mind fought between the memories of her mother, and the hideous image of the hanging woman in the wedding dress Occasionally her father's image appeared in her consciousness, gentle and soothing. His image comforted her until it fell back into blackness. A blackness she knew would never be lit. She and JJ had been formally adopted a few years after the death of their mother by a cousin of their late father, and her husband. They now lived in Cherryville Street off the Loyalist Woodstock Road in East Belfast. Although only 5 miles across the city, it was an entirely alien world. The malleability of JJ's young spirit meant that he quickly adapted, made new friends and became settled in Nettlefield Primary School. Both their surnames had been changed by deed poll, ensuring prying neighbours made no connection with the history of their parents.

JJ had briefly witnessed the death of his mother, but was oblivious to the ramifications. There were other things such as football, street games and friends, to fill his mind, and suppress any memories that may have harboured within. Shirley had remained as alien to her surroundings and 'new life' as they were to her. The trauma of deep psychosis in discovering the event, caused her to withdraw from the world around her. She'd spent many hours with psychologists, psychiatrists, welfare and social workers, who all attempted to wipe the stain of the past from her mind. She had been prescribed sedatives and had begun to self-harm and suffer bouts of crying, desperation and depression. No amount of care, compassion or medicine succeeded in helping her. A breakthrough occurred when a social worker arrived, accompanied by a student trainee from Lancashire. Shirley attempted engagement with the girl with the English accent, though months of withdrawal made it a slow, cumbersome affair. The social worker filed her report to the consultant psychiatrist who arranged experimental therapy, that included the trainee. In time, it become obvious that any sound of a Belfast accent was detrimental to any progress toward the far edges of normality for Shirley. Her aunt, Elsie Patterson, reluctantly admitted defeat. With a breaking heart, convinced she was acting in the girl's favour, she signed foster adoption papers, allowing Shirley to be relocated under the care of Mr and Mrs. Westcott of Blackpool, England. The Westcott's ran a modest B&B in Albert Road, close to the golden mile. They were perfect parents, who had been plagued with the dilemma of a childless marriage. On their inaugural meeting, they fell in love with Shirley. The same sentiment was *awkwardly mirrored by Shirley, her first positive interaction with adults since **that** time.*

Shirley sat in the parlour, a meagre bag of clothes at her feet. She once had more make-up than skin, and would cost her mother weekly fortunes for hairstyles, but now wore a plain smock and a padded raincoat. Her once gleaming, wavy golden hair, hung limply from her roots and her pale face, accentuated the dark rings under her eyes. The engine of the black minicab grumbled outside. A mixture of adult voices in the hall. The door to the parlour opened, and JJ entered. He had a plastic football under one arm, an untidy mop of black hair, and a smile that lacked two front teeth. Shirley opened her arms and smiled, an action that brought tears to her aunt Elsie. JJ rushed to her before emanating an impish growl, indicating that he needed to be outside playing football. Shirley hugged him and kissed the top of his head.

'You're going to come and visit me, aren't you?'

An unconvinced JJ reluctantly agreed, pinching his lips together and glancing toward the parlour door.

'And we'll go on all the rides at the funfair?'

JJ's grin widened for a second, but rides at the funfair would never match the importance of football.

'Off you go wee man,' she whispered, fighting back tears and using her mother's pet name for her brother. JJ needed no encouragement and sprinted down the hall. Robotically, Shirley lifted her bag and entered the hall.

Her Aunt Elsie sobbed in the embrace of Mrs. Westcott. Shirley waited, and took the hand of her new mother, before walking to the minicab, that sat outside. Shirley never looked back as the taxi drove off toward the docks, the Heysham overnight ferry, and her new life.

Chapter 9

Patterson had accepted defeat, as he swirled the last dregs of coffee in the cup. He'd cursed his luck. The incident of the suicidal prisoner still disturbed him, the vision of an angel leaving an imbalance in his confidence. It was the second account of a 'vision' today, and deeply distressed him. He questioned his sanity. He returned to assist Beattie. The routine of running the landing with his friend was a welcome distraction. To an onlooker, if may have appeared uncouth to resume normal duties immediately after a life had been lost, the cell door now locked until RUC investigators arrived, during the lunch period. The familiar routines, however, were the staple diet and back bone of prison life. Inmates relied heavily on them. The automatic mode helped to divert any other problems, or stress, that officers may have harboured. Just before midday, there was a lull having fed the self-imposed, segregated Loyalist prisoners in their cells. Staff were redundant, awaiting the returning Republicans from the dining hall, using strictly controlled movement. Patterson, Beattie and Beattie's original number two, killed the time with a game of cards, but it was interrupted when a voice bellowed from the 1's.

'Paddy! Paddy!'

Patterson poked his head out of the class office.

'Yo?'

'P.O. wants to see you.'

'I'll be down in a second,' sighed Patterson, expecting the inevitable.

He learned that he was to assist in A wing Visits, that were running late because of the bus bringing visitors from West Belfast, breaking down. When this happened, management expected staff to work during the lunch break. It was essential to provide the privilege of visits, a well-known bartering tool between Prison Governors and inmates, to maintain smooth running's. A Wing, the largest within the jail, held remanded paramilitary prisoners of both denominations, and also practiced a self-imposed segregation regime. At one time, the Visits area of A wing and C wing, the other paramilitary wing, were universally recognised as neutral ground. The different factions, programmed to attack their enemies at every opportunity, would observe those unwritten laws. Hints of collusion between the opposing forces, came in the shape of delegating the morning and afternoon visits, ensuring only one faction would fill the visits area at alternative times. Arriving at the desk in the visits area, Patterson was handed a blue visiting pass and the name of a 'red book' prisoner, located on A3. 'Red book' prisoners were deemed the most dangerous, their red book logging their every movement. When he reached the A3 class office he was met by Herbert McIntire, a loud, witty, overweight officer, who ran, what was described as, the most demanding landing in the jail. Patterson admired his style as he cleverly disguised the enormous responsibility on his shoulders. 'All right kid? You've hit the jackpot here, my boy. This scumbag, McGuigan, is meant to be one the biggest fish we have in here.' 'Think I'll handle him ok,' replied a confident Patterson.

As he signed the red book, McIntire continued. 'Apparently the thing that comes up to visit him is a cracker. Makes you think you're married to a man!'

Patterson chuckled and asked one of the landing patrols officers to unlock the prisoner. Padraig McGuigan emerged from his cell. Roughly the same height as Patterson, he possessed an aura of power. The overhead lights reflected off his shaven head, his beard carefully manicured. Piercing green eyes took in the surroundings as he strode toward the grille. The shaved head, once an intimidation tool for the Provos, had paled within the jail, due to a saturation of them. He was very demure, not exhibiting aggression, the norm for commanders. Patterson exuded total self-control, although well aware this monster wouldn't hesitate to destroy him on the outside. He smiled at Patterson before heading down the two sets of stairs to the 1's.

After being registered in the movements book at the end of the wing grille, McGuigan was escorted downstairs toward the tunnel, that ran under the road to the Crown court. Just short of that, they veered right, into A Visits search box. Normal practice for red book prisoners was a strip search at every visit, a potential flashpoint between inmates and staff. As always, the red books diligently agreed to the humiliating process, without any hint of complaint. Through another 'airlock' (double grille) at the prisoners' end of the visits area, McGuigan was allocated an open booth opposite the grille, enabling the officer in a high observation chair at the back wall, to maintain careful vigilance. Patterson, still clutching the visiting pass, walked the length of the visits area, through the exterior manned grille to a wicker gate in the large iron gates that led to the forecourt. He headed to the right of the enormous metal gates of the vehicle lock, to what was described as the 'well.' The officer on duty, akin to bingo caller. There was a grille between him and the forecourt. Behind him a white, waist high wall, created a chicane to the visitor's exit grille. The grille to his left led to the 'well' itself, where all visitors waited after stringent security checks, including the inevitable random searches. All grilles were electronically operated by an unseen officer behind a two-way glass frame in the wall. On the visitors' arrival, their passes were checked and sent to the well officer, who then relayed them to the visit's areas. When prisoners were safely located in their visit's areas, staff using the same pass, would collect the visitors from the well, escorting them to the waiting prisoners. These staff were known as 'runners'. Patterson was joined by a few other runners clutching multiple visits passes, outside the well in the forecourt. When all passes were handed through the grille, the officer systematically called out the name of the prisoner. The visitors assembled out of sight of the runners at the adjacent grille before entering the airlock, to be finally spewed out into the forecourt. There was a lot of light hearted banter amongst the runners, about the forthcoming Glentoran/ Linfield derby football match. When the grille to the forecourt buzzed, the officer on duty started to announce the visitors. 'Visitors for Vernon, Delaney, Thompson, Blair and McGuigan.' Already aware from the visiting pass that McGuigan was expecting one female visitor, Patterson didn't get embroiled in the stock exchange of sorting out who was going where, and visiting whom.

Instead, he waited for the arrival of this supposed 'beauty queen' McIntire had described. His facial features froze, when he spotted her at the back of the throng of incoming visitors. She had her head tilted down. When she looked up, she spotted him. Orla McGuigan's expression turned to shock recognition. Patterson didn't hear, nor register the farewell banter from the Linfield supporters. He walked what seemed like a mile across the forecourt to the wicker gate, as she tailed behind him. To extrapolate things, the forecourt officer, who was in conversation with a dog handler, had the wicker gate unlocked and open. This left him no opportunity to whisper to her, aware every male in the forecourt had locked their gaze on this stunning woman. Patterson tried to ignore the woman he'd left behind in the Hotel this morning. With legs like lead weights, he mounted the few steps up to the already unlocked entrance to the visiting area. All memories or thoughts of the previous beautiful occasions they had shared, were shattered. Occasional glances proved; she too was struggling. The ramifications for both were unbelievably dangerous. On entering, he had to act normal, but was sure at least one other visitor, or inmate, would notice his heart beating outside his chest, the pallor of his expression or the shaking of his hands. He dropped the visiting pass on the desk of the time keeper close to the entrance, before trailing behind her toward the furthest box in the corner, a route she was obviously used to. Every step he took, he felt eyes watching from all other booths. Unnoticed, he inhaled again and again, praying that the extra oxygen would be an ally in the war to control his nerves.

He half expected McGuigan to race from his booth in a rage. Orla's deceptive charade gave him strength. The constant staccato of ridiculously high heeled shoes, increased in pace as she neared the booth. McGuigan stood to greet her, oblivious of Patterson's demeanour. Orla rushed forward and threw her arms around him. Patterson's apprehension, now mixed with jealousy, a potentially toxic concoction. He averted his gaze lest his feelings rise to the surface, betraying them both. Instead of standing beside and chatting to the observation officer in the high chair, he exited through the search box, heading for the entrance hall staff toilets. On entering a vacant cubicle, he locked it and sat on the toilet lid. He held out his hands, attempting to control their involuntary shaking, his attempt proving fruitless. He shivered as if someone had walked over his grave, and worked at controlling his breathing before exiting the cubicle. He splashed water on his face, followed by a few fierce slaps to each cheek, to encourage blood flow. He decided to take ownership of the dilemma he found himself in. His main instinct, self-preservation. *'Was I to be a victim of entrapment?'* he thought. He would do *anything,* to avoid any more contact with Orla. He knew the relationship had to end, and out of character, he was determined to fulfil this self-imposed promise. For the first time in his life. His legs trembled on re-entering the noisy visiting area, deliberately avoiding looking to where his former lover, was visiting her dangerous husband. When he reached the front desk, the Senior Officer smiled, handing him a visiting slip.

'It's your lucky day Romeo. You get to escort the beautiful Mrs. McGuigan back to the visitor's well.'

He motioned to another officer who had arrived from Legal Visits, where McGuigan's barrister had insisted on an urgent meeting, in relation to his defence case.

'Davy here, will sign over his red book and take him to Legals. You get to take Mrs. Scumbag back over.'

He winked with false confidence, before making his way back to her with trembling limbs. Feelings of dread and discovery haunting him. She was on her feet in a deep embrace with McGuigan, pushing her groin against his whilst they kissed. It was the most erotic thing he thought he had ever seen, fuelling his jealousy, although his survival instinct took care of any wayward feelings. McGuigan opened one eye and looked over his wife's shoulder to see the two escorting officers. He broke the embrace and whispered, 'it's time to go', before giving Orla one final full kiss on the lips. She turned, looking directly at Patterson. The universe froze for a brief moment. He was helpless, as she now held all the cards in their dangerous liaison.

'What the fuck are you looking at?!'

Patterson widened his eyes, stunned. Not just by the words she spat, but by her venomous tone.

'Have you nothing better to do than stand and stare at a husband and wife having a private moment?! I don't know how you people can live with yourse ...'

McGuigan intervened, lightly grabbing her arm to cut the tirade short.

'Orla, it's alright. These lads are only doing their job.' He hinted at a smile, nodding towards Patterson, who felt those dangerous eyes bore through to his soul.

Orla stormed off in a strop, her heels emanating around the visits area, that now focused its attention on the outburst. Members of staff were at a high state of alert, aware of the Provo tactics of distraction, for ulterior motives. McGuigan shook his head and whispered to Patterson as he was led away, 'Women...what can you do with them?' Patterson followed after Orla, every republican watching him.

'My God! They know. Catch yourself on. How could they know?' he argued with his thoughts.

Eventually escaping the suffocating atmosphere of the visits, Patterson walked behind Orla to the large iron gates, manned on the forecourt side. Without looking in her direction, he moved beside her pushing the bell for attention. 'I'm so sorry,' Orla whispered.

Her lips barely moved, on a face that still held a mask of hatred. Patterson looked down and needlessly attended to his breast pocket. 'You did the right thing. You were convincing. Have I been naive all this time? Are you setting me up?'

Orla parted her mouth to speak, but the sound of the exit gate opening, stopped her. They strolled across the forecourt in silence, but she wanted to scream. She was frantic that he'd questioned her about him being a target. She wanted to reveal her undying love for him, but had to retain the facade of annoyance, as any deviation could spell a death sentence for them both. On reaching the well, the grill opened. Orla deliberately dropped her purse, a few contents spilling out. They both plunged to their knees to round up the errant items. As he handed her a lipstick, Patterson's fingers brushed against hers.

'Please ring me in a few days,' she whispered.

Orla stood and marched into the well, but had to wait for the airlock allowing her to exit. As the incoming grille was open, more visitors assembling in the caller's area. She stared at him through the grill, his gaze locked on hers. As the visitors slowly moved into the forecourt, a metallic clunk signalled the opening of the exit grille. Before she turned to go, she mouthed the words, 'I Love you.' Patterson was distraught by her actions. He shook his head and turned to walk away, contemplating losing the most perfect woman he had ever known. Neither of them had noticed the bald-headed, aged republican visitor, at the back of the incoming throng, who had witnessed their silent encounter. More importantly, they were unaware of who he was - a highly intelligent Republican strategist who was deaf…and an expert lip reader.

Chapter 10

Due to his enormity, Willie Hamilton lay on the only Queen-sized bed in all of the Rathcoole estate. Being less active than the remaining two founders, meant limited cash flow. He was glad he hadn't descended to the 'depths' of his former 'comrades.' His meagre existence comprised of quietly controlling the estate, working nine to five and having a normal life with his devoted and diminutive wife, Susan, who helped the big man suppress the guilt feelings that never left him. He spoke to no-one about Smallwood's murder, wary of the ructions it would cause, more so, because of eternal shame. He was disgusted at how Henderson, and his evil side-kick Montgomery, had prospered at the protection rackets his mentor vehemently opposed. Henderson now lived in a mansion in the desirable Helen's Bay area of North Down with his Catholic wife, flying in the face of everything he was meant to stand for. Montgomery led the life of a rich playboy, commuting from the Spanish villa he shared with his many boyfriends. He only returned to the court of Henderson, and to watch his beloved Glasgow Rangers. His reputation had plummeted to a level, lower than ever thought possible. The arrogance toward men below his self-imposed rank was impossible, harassing and attacking anyone he didn't like the look of, confident that his close relationship with Henderson and his PIRA contacts would nullify any form of retaliation. Currently, both were feared more than loathed, a situation Hamilton knew was not infinite.

The fear was evident as long as the unholy alliance Henderson had initiated with the PIRA, existed.

He'd negotiated a deal with the enemy's ruling council to 'carve up' the City of Belfast. Both profited from racketeering, thinly disguised as 'door security' firms for the entire city centre pubs and clubs. Each side hand-picked gangs of thugs to act as doormen, that establishments were then forced to employ. The licensee had to pay each thug a handsome wage, and 25% of their nightly takings to the respective organisation. Hamilton recalled the start of the enterprise when owners first refused. The same thugs loitered outside their premises, 'convincing' punters not to enter, or run the risk of facing the wrath of paramilitaries. It was a loss/loss situation for the vendors. The remainder ceased reporting activity to the authorities, after the treatment received by the first objector. He'd spent months in hospital and would never walk unaided again. Hamilton felt it like dealing with the devil. Henderson and Montgomery, oblivious to internal hatred, felt invincible. Foot soldiers in Rathcoole frequently approached Hamilton, questioning why the organisation had to fund raise for loyalist prisoners, buy their own uniforms, pay for travel to a visit, amongst a myriad of other complaints, whilst Henderson and the 'psycho faggot,' as Montgomery had now been labelled, could change their cars and swan off to Spanish villas, at the drop of a hat. Hamilton was admired as remaining 'one of the people', but a revolution was forming.

Neither Henderson nor Montgomery realised, the PIRA's patience was cigarette paper thin. The high-profile antics of the two mavericks could affect their standing within their own communities. They were becoming dangerous and uncontrollable. It couldn't, and wouldn't, continue.

Where possible, Hamilton spent all his free time with Susan, strengthening his standing within the estate. They held hands wherever they went, a picture of endless love. Hamilton's reasons, unbeknown to Susan, were also for safety and reassurance against his inner demons. Many people thought they looked like characters from 'Of Mice and Men', because of the height difference, but never dared breathe their thoughts out loud. Religiously, once a month, Hamilton would make a lone pilgrimage to Carnmoney Cemetery. He would sit on the same bench, focusing on the black marble paramilitary headstone dedicated to his former leader. Long ago, and without city council's permission, a series of privet hedges had been erected in the corner of the sprawling burial ground, that catered for the UDA 'fallen.' An 'offer' made by the paramilitaries to voluntarily maintain the area, persuaded the council to allow it. The headstone screamed a lie, its tribute etched in golden script. 'In memory of The Founder of the UDA, Jackie Smallwood, a true Loyalist. Murdered by the cowardly enemies of Ulster.' Susan never complained, in fact, was proud her husband paid homage to a life-long friend, content to leave him to his inner thoughts. Had she ever insisted on accompanying him, she would have witnessed something she had never seen before. Her husband crying.

Susan slept like a log as Hamilton tumbled again, into his frequently visited nightmare. Smallwood under a spotlight. An horrific slash across his throat, his skin, chalk white. Two grey Gargoyles danced, darting in out of the light, cackling and grinning around his feet. Smallwood reached out to Hamilton, repeating, 'I'm so, so, very disappointed in you...so very disappointed...'

Hamilton bolted upright in bed, groaning and panting in a pool of sweat. Susan, now used to his routine, reached over and held him as she squinted in the darkness.

'It's ok Willie, it's ok...I'm here.'

~

The weather, for a change, was kind in Blackpool. A rare Autumnal sun, brought out the crowds. Candy floss, kiss-me-quick hats and teeth breaking confectionery rock, were in abundance. There was a lively buzz as the cacophony of excited tourists strolled and roamed along the Golden Mile, attire heavier than in summer. The massive, untidy looking beach, was interspersed with deck chairs and picnickers. Even brave bathers, who dared enter the freezing, oily brown water, of the Irish sea. Straw-hatted, tired and over worked donkeys, ambled along with squealing children on their backs, their owners squeezing out the last remnants of income before hibernation. There was noise everywhere. Laughter, to distant screaming from the white-knuckle rides, to the irritating and tuneless music from the countless amusement arcade machines.

Patterson loved every minute of it. These were the distractions he needed from his personal quandary. His mind was filled with the surroundings: the water, sunshine, the company of his beloved sister, and his two treasured nephews, albeit they had a silly English accent. His multitude of personal problems were forced into a cupboard at the back of his mind, forgotten for the meantime. Unfortunately, it was a cupboard that could never be locked.

The four sat, well wrapped up, on a bench in the low sunshine. Patterson and Shirley enjoying the hint of heat, whilst the boys attempted to eat their massive candy flosses from the bottom up, managing to cover their faces and hair with the sugary, glue-like substance. Shirley had worked hard to find a happy place. A place where she could cope with her tragic past. The Westcott's had been perfect parents. Never shying away from questions of her past, emphasising that she was adopted. They also gave their love unrequitedly, giving Shirley an existence. Growing up, she helped out in the cosy B&B, 'Seaview' as a waitress, cook, receptionist and most importantly, a daughter and part of the family. Working in the Westcott's pride and joy helped to fulfil the emptiness she had experienced. During the time as receptionist, her caring attitude shone through to the degree, she was encouraged to go to the University of Nursing and Midwifery. It was a natural fit and she had excelled. In a befitting paradox, she settled into Geriatric care, working in a home for the aged. She devoted all her love, and professional attention to Mrs. Westcott, who had succumbed to accelerated Dementia, and 'lived' under Shirley's care for the last few years of her life. Although deeply saddened by her passing, Shirley felt strength in how she had helped, repaying the kindness, unreservedly afforded to her. Mr. Westcott passed away in his sleep a few years later, when his heart decided to stop. Because of his better than good health, local doctors were baffled. Only Shirley understood his heart hadn't suddenly stopped. It had been badly broken a few years before. Shirley now had an inner strength, never once thought possible, and it helped her cope with the passing of her adopted parents. Not only their love and dedication, but the strength of her marriage to David Grantham, and the birth of her two boys, Patrick, and his younger brother Richard, gave her a solidity to cope with anything. They inherited the B&B, reverting it to its former usage as a townhouse. Although it was unfortunate that David spent months away at his deep-sea diving job in Scotland, Shirley got used to her quality time alone with the boys. There was one missing point of closure she had reconsidered for years. She couldn't decide when to cross that bridge.

She sat beside her younger, handsome brother on the lukewarm bench. He was far divorced from the giggling boy, then spotty teenager who visited her every summer. The Westcott's had reserved his own room, treating him more like a son than Shirley's brother. Although they were occasionally annoyed at his penchant for the brightly coloured gaming machines at the amusements. On more than one occasion, they had to rescue him after kicking the penny push machine, because it refused to offload a multitude of coins into the winning tray. During these incidents, one stern look from his big sister brought out the bright side of her brother. He would apologise for his behaviour with false promises of non-recurrent performances. And the Westcott's, like everyone else, couldn't resist that cheeky innocent grin. Shirley smiled inwardly and stole a glance at him. His eyes hidden by tinted Aviator sunglasses. She was confident, he was eyeing every eligible female parading past. Two pink, sticky faces shouted.

'Uncle John, can we go to the Pleasure beach?'

Shirley made an attempt to nullify the request. 'No Boys! We're not made of money!'

Patterson reached into his trouser pocket and produced a £10 note. He motioned to Shirley.

'Sure, I haven't given the lads their pocket money yet, but I need to get this changed.'

He glanced at the expectant boys whose jaws had dropped at the sight of the £10 note.

'Now lads, where is the best place in the whole of Blackpool to get this thing changed?'

'The...Pleasure beach?' whispered a nervous Patrick, his voice trailing off in disbelief.

'Exactly! Now let's go.'

Both boys punched the air. 'Yes!' they shouted, with wide grins.

Shirley and Patterson followed behind. Shirley unconsciously took her brother's arm, as she had done for as long as she could remember.

'You spoil those two you know!'

They both smiled.

'When are you going to get married John? Have kids of your own?' Shirley asked.

Patterson raised an eyebrow. 'Me? Married? Do you realise the sadness that would cause?'

For a second Shirley was unsure how to reply. She looked at him, head cocked to one side.

'I mean, the combined Global sadness of the world's female population, who would be robbed of the opportunity to sample my many delights!' Patterson lifted his sunglasses, fluttering his eyelashes, before winking and giving her that cheeky smile. 'You're full of it!' Shirley laughed, as they walked toward the Pleasure beach, holding his arm tighter.

~

The bustle and vibrancy of the Pleasure beach was absorbing. Patrick and Richard struggled to contain their wonderment and excitement, as they bounced through this Land of Make Believe. Their innocence was not lost on their mother, or uncle, who both sported wide, tender grins.

'Wouldn't you love to be that age again?' purred Shirley.

'More than you'll ever know.'

A few paces later, Patterson beckoned his nephews. 'Right lads! Over here and watch a master at work.' He pointed at a rifle range, boasting an opportunity to win a Teddy bear. They were encapsulated.

'There's something I have to tell you lads, and its top secret. Can you keep a secret?'

Both nodded their heads in unison, mouths agape with excitement.

'I was selected by the top boss in 7th Ulster Defence Regiment (army) to become a sniper. All the best snipers shoot left-handed,' he continued.

'Why are left handers the best?' enquired Patrick, cocking his head to the side.

Shirley stifled a smirk knowing that the inquisitive minds of her children, wouldn't accept anything unless explained.

A slightly perplexed Patterson dipped his eyebrows and thought for a minute. 'They just are.'

Both boys rolled their eyes before turning back to him.

'Anyway,' he continued, 'I went on to be the best sniper in the army and once got a call from Batman, to help catch the Joker!'

The boys were completely hooked at the mention of their favourite superhero.

'I shot him, not with a bullet, but with a dart that made him sleepy, so that Batman could take him off and put him jail.'

'What was Batman like Uncle John?' asked an amazed Richard.

'Well...I really shouldn't tell you…but he looked a bit like me...only far bigger and far stronger. And do you know what football team he supported? Glentoran!'

Shirley had to cough to disguise her giggles.

'Wow,' echoed the amazed boys.

He learned that it was £1.50 per pellet. 'I don't want to buy the effing thing, only shoot it!' he moaned, and was met with an innocent look from the vendor. Leaning on the counter, Patterson broke open the barrel of the air rifle and inserted the pellet. Both boys, having never been this close to a gun, were spellbound, and stood to his side watching his every move. Patterson clicked the barrel home and nuzzled the butt into his left shoulder, whispering to the boys through the side of his mouth, without ever taking his eyes off the target.

'Your weapon has to become a part of you, so you control it. Breathe deeply...in...and out...'

The vendor stifled a chortle, watching the boys imitate their uncle, over exaggerating their breathing and looking like puffer fish.

'...and when you breathe out fully...you don't pull the trigger.... you squeeze it.'

The crack of the exploding pellet snapped the boys out of their hypnotic state. Patterson growled, his shot finishing four inches from the bull's-eye.

'Unlucky sir,' announced the portly vendor.

'Unlucky my arse! You couldn't hit a barn door with this bloody thing! Bloody rip off!'

'Tell you what sir...I'll give the two lads a free shot each if that'll make any difference?'

Patterson exhaled to calm himself, and nodded in agreement. Patrick followed his uncle's instructions to the letter, and regrettably, the same result. Richard was more unorthodox, closing his eyes whilst breathing. Patterson shook his head in playful disbelief as he turned to his sister. The crack of the rifle was quickly followed by a loud shot of 'Hurray' from the vendor. Shirley's face lit up simultaneously. Patterson turned back to witness Richard being handed a giant brown teddy bear, that was half his size. Shirley grinned with pride and smirked at the look on Patterson's face.

'Old lucky arse,' he whispered with a warm smile.

'If you've got it, you've got it' Shirley teased.

'Always thought that husband of yours looked like Wyatt Earp'

'Aye...as much as you look like Batman!'

They burst out laughing before joining the children in their wild celebrations.

Chapter 11

Patterson left Shirley to take the boys home, fancying a pint on this warmish day. He had been warned not to be more than hour, or he'd be dining in the corner chip shop. And not to be drunk either, as he had babysitting duties later, whilst she covered a shift at work.

He found a bright spot outside one of the many pubs along the strip, and ordered a pint of Harp from a young waiter.

'Harp?' questioned the bemused youngster. 'Yes, Harp? Not like the instrument, but like the beer,' he replied with a sarcastic tone. 'Oh, you mean lager!' 'No, I mean Harp. The lager will do,' he sighed. He had hoped that over the years, Blackpool would invest in some real beer, like the real beer he drank at home. Blackpool evolved at its own traditional pace. He opened a packet of Embassy Regal cigarettes, retrieving one using his teeth. It was an irregular habit for most, but one that Patterson had adapted from an early age. He was 11 at the time his best friend at school, had introduced him to the evil weed. His friend lived alone with his alcoholic father. It made it easy to steal packets of his No. 10 cigarettes, as his father in the mornings could barely remember his name, never mind where he'd left money or cigarettes. Patterson smiled remembering them both sitting on a threadbare settee watching a gangster film on the portable black and white TV. When offered a cigarette, a gangster on the TV had pulled one out of the packet with his teeth. His friend persuaded him that was the cool way to do it. Erasing the fits of coughing, followed by the dizziness and ultimately, the vomiting, from his mind, Patterson had removed cigarettes from packets in that manner ever since.

'Wee Danny...the boy who showed me how to ruin my lungs,' he mused to himself.

His mind inevitably drifted to the wreck his life now was. No matter how much he ruminated, Patterson knew, he was the only one to blame for his predicaments. He needed money to pay his debts, because the Prison Service wasn't creating enough. He couldn't go to the bank as he owed them as well. He briefly thought about Orla, but the morsel of control he thought he had, quickly skipped past it. He was convinced the IRA were aware of his duplicity. *'Where the hell am I going to get help from?'* his inner voice screamed, feeling an urge to up end the table and do as much damage as possible. The sight of clenched tight fists, brought his thought process to a halt. He was terror struck at becoming so angry, so quickly... again. He was worried this was becoming something that might consume him, as if he had any more room in his life for travesty. Struggling successfully to rid any sour thoughts, Patterson thought about his Aunt Elsie who had outlived her husband, Bobby. She had been the rock in his life. A kind gentle woman, who had adored and cared for him. He made a mental note to call and see her within the next few weeks. Quickly finishing his pint, he ordered 2 double Vodka and cokes. He always bought doubles in England as their spirit measures were a mere spit in a glass compared to back home. The only saving grace, was the free coke. At the end of another Embassy Regal, and finishing the second of his drinks, he strolled toward Albert Road, now possessing the Dutch courage to complete his mission.

He meandered through the crowds, checking his pocket for loose change, relieved he had enough to complete his task.

~

It had taken Orla days to get over her visit with McGuigan. She had been in close proximity with the two men in her life. One she was scared to be with, and one she was scared of losing. Unbeknown to her, she mirrored the same thoughts as Patterson that day. She was convinced *they* knew something. She was sick with worry, panicking every time the doorbell rang. Up to now, it had been the postman or her friends, or family, the fear gradually dissipating. Any distraction was good for her, and she spent two days a week helping out in a charity shop on the Falls Road. She had privileges of being the wife of one of the organisations generals, that included a two-seater sports car. Her only real friend in life was her Yorkshire Terrier, 'Gleoite', Irish for cute. Her privileges also served as bars in a cell. She was trapped in a loveless marriage. She felt useless, realising at an early age she was infertile. The only possible escape from her situation, hadn't called her since she last seen him in jail. She feared she may never hear from him again. He may have been frightened off, knowing who she really was. She needed John, but she was unsure as a man, or as an escape to a normal life. During the long lonely days at home, she'd constantly looked at the phone, urging it to ring, crying herself to sleep at night when it hadn't. The warm sun reflected off the leaves on the trees, and she had taken to ironing in the modest back garden of her semi-detached, immaculate home.

Thick fencing surrounded the borders of her property, acting as a windbreaker. Gleoite chased butterflies in the meagre heat, barking incessantly.

Orla never cared about the barking; she was immune to any complaints from neighbours due to her 'status.' As she folded a blouse, a voice came from inside the house.

'Hello? Orla?'

She crept back into the kitchen and encountered Barney Nugent, one of McGuigan's 'minders.' Nugent was a full framed man, renowned for his kick boxing training regime. The physique was evident, through his sports top. His raven black hair was jelled into place, and his tanned skin gave him an Italianesque look. They embraced briefly.

'What brings you here Barney?' Orla asked, glad of some human company, though her suspicions re-surfaced. Before he could answer she continued.

'Jeez, where are my manners. Do you want a cup of tea, or maybe even a wee beer outside in the sunshine?'

Nugent declined; his face stoical.

'Thanks, but I can't. I've a bit of news for you.'

Orla's stomach twisted, as she felt her resolve of acting the devoted wife, was starting to crumble. She tried to appear casually nonplussed.

'News? what news?'

Before he could answer, the telephone in the hallway rang. Nugent moved to one side, letting her enter the house, before following her into the living room. The door to the hallway was left ajar. Nugent watched and listened.

'Hello?'

She listened for a few seconds, before looking toward Nugent.

'How many times do I have to tell you? This isn't a taxi firm dickhead!' she yelled into the phone before slamming the receiver down.

'Does that happen often?' Nugent asked with an icy tone.

'Maybe, once or twice a week. I think our number must be close to one of the taxi firms in town.'

'I'll get that checked out and make sure that company changes its number.'

'Oh, Barney that would be great. Anyway, what's the news?'

'It's about Padraig's case. Seems a lot of witnesses have changed their minds about giving evidence. We reckon the case for the PPS will crumble at the next hearing in three weeks, and you'll have your man back in your life.'

Orla's eyes filled with tears as she struggled for breath. She put hands over her mouth, as if in shock. She bounded up to Nugent and threw her arms around his muscular frame.

'Oh Barney, that's great news!' she sobbed into his shoulder.

The big man untangled himself.

'Enough of that missus, somebody might get the wrong idea if they're looking in the window!'

She blurted out a laugh and apologised.

'No harm done,' said Nugent as he turned to leave.

'Wait,' he said, turning back. He handed Orla a pink envelope. 'Nearly forgot to give you this. It's from your husband. I'll let myself out.'

'Oh,' Orla muttered. 'Bye.'

When the door closed, she collapsed onto the leather settee. She fought to catch her breath, torrents of tears following. Not cheerful tears, tears of dread, and a realisation she only had 3 weeks to escape. She opened the envelope and lifted out the white card with 2 red hearts on it. Inside there was a simple but poignant message…

My one true love, be true to me

'Oh my God,' she exclaimed under her breath, terror invading her expression. 'He knows.' Dropping the card, she ran to the telephone and kneeled in front of it, praying as if it were the Virgin Mary. She dialled the operator.

~

Patterson pondered on how he was going to deliver his message. He'd edited and rehearsed it many times before picking up the receiver, slowly inserting the coins. It rang 3 times before a voice he recognised, and loved, answered.

'Hello?' said Orla

He panicked, thinking for a second, he couldn't do this or wanted to do it. In the same second, he ridiculously imagined they could work something out.

'Hi. It's me,' he said sheepishly.

'How many times do I have to tell you? This isn't a taxi firm dickhead!'

Patterson automatically replaced the receiver, understanding their code that she wasn't alone. He stood looking at the phone trying to reassure himself, and failing, that they could have had a life together. He opened the door and walked away. As the slow closing door moved back into place, the phone rang. Patterson stopped, turned and ran back. His legs became heavier, his steps shorter, until he ground to a halt. He listened to the muffled ringing before turning and walking away. He was saddened, but accepted it was over...for good.

Chapter 12

Imogen Henderson was alone in the cavernous conservatory to the rear of her house on Church Road, Helen's Bay. The Georgian house had previously been two splendid semi-detached houses. The neighbours quickly moved out when the Henderson's arrived. She wasn't surprised the neighbour had sold them their house at a price well below market value, allowing them to create one mansion. Bulldog always got what he wanted, including her. She was his 'illicit pleasure' way back when, overwhelmed by his generosity in gifts and holidays. It was a whirlwind romance and a wedding at Gretna Green, that her staunchly catholic family refused to attend. She never realised how completely ex-communicated she would be by friends and family, for marrying a protestant. One with a reputation. He'd lied he was a property businessman, sating her inquisitiveness for their first three months of wedded bliss. Then the violence began. Any questions about his day to day, and often nightly business, would be met with intimidating silence. Her first probe too deep, was met with a right hook, knocking her to the floor and crashing against a solid glass table, leaving a hideous scar on her cheek bone. Realising she was trapped in matrimonial hell with a gangster and a terrorist leader, she attempted contacting her family. Their refusal to acknowledge her existence quickly taught her to obey her new master, in an attempt to exist at all. Loneliness and abandonment, propagated to the point of depression when she tried to take her own life, cutting her wrists in the bath. Unexpectedly, Henderson returned home early, and saved her.

He metamorphosised back into a caring, loving husband for the next few months during recuperation. They again shared the passion she had once known in the bedroom, but it was only one of the many masks he could adorn at a whim. She tried to do, and say, the right things, to make the mask at least semi-permanent. It led to the birth of their son, Matthew, providing a more defined reason for continuing life. It wasn't long before Henderson slid back into his previous persona, avoiding Imogen, who devoted herself to Matthew. Matthew developed into an intellectual, sensitive young man who she was proud of, but created conflict with her husband. Henderson wanted to know why he had to go to a Grammar school? Why he didn't like football? Why he played the guitar and wanted to go to the School of Music? Why he never brought a girlfriend home? Truth was, Matthew was ashamed of his father, vowing never to bring friends, male or female, into the toxic atmosphere of their home. In fact, he wasn't interested in girls. On finishing college, he informed his mother he was heading to Europe, to 'discover' himself. Tears welled in Imogen's eyes the day she drove her only son to the international airport, repeating promises of sending him money if he needed it, and to take care. She would never forget her last embrace with her scraggly-bearded hero, and the sight of him walking through the security gates into the departure lounge. He glanced over his shoulder with his guitar strapped to his back, offering her a small wave and a broad smile. That was 5 years ago, but Matthew constantly kept in touch. He made money playing guitar in pubs and restaurants across Europe, whilst working as a waiter. He eventually settled in Fuengirola on the Costa del Sol, having saved enough money to rent a beachside Chiringito, where he would play Spanish guitar for the locals every night. He explained to his mother over the phone, that it was only with the financial help for his soon to be life partner, that he could've achieved his dream. When Imogen asked her name, she was taken aback to learn it wasn't a girl, but Simeon, a Dutch national he'd met during his year in Amsterdam.

Nevertheless, she was happy that he was happy, but downhearted in the realisation that Matthew and his partner could never come home, as long as her husband was there. Imogen raced to the back door on hearing scratching, a smile painted on her face. 'Matthew!' she exclaimed in a soothing voice, bending down to pick up the stray black and white cat that had 'adopted' her. She produced a bowl from under the sink in the utility room, and poured some dry cat food into it. Matthew attacked it with a purpose. She stroked the soft hair of the cat's back, wishing it were her son's head. Feeding over, Imogen headed to the conservatory, illuminated with soft up lighters, and sat at the end of an enormous, fawn, Italian leather couch. Matthew sprang onto her knees, purring for attention. She loved the fact that her husband hated cats, because he couldn't control them. But she hated everything else. Her controlled life. The scar on her face. This monstrosity of a house decorated after her husband's fashion. Most of all, she hated Montgomery, or 'weasel' as he was rightly known, her husband's business associate. He was a scrawny armed, long-haired demon, whose beady eyes disturbed her. To the outside world she had everything, but she felt the exact opposite. When Matthew rolled onto his back to offer his tummy, Imogen heard the sound of the front gate being opened and the barking of a dog. She lifted

Matthew and set him outside the conservatory doors, quietly whispering, 'Shoo! Go away!' before racing from the lounge into a palatial kitchen. She grabbed some goat's cheese with shaky hands, and put it on a marble topped island, before washing lettuce at the sink at speed. She heard the noise of her husband entering the utility room, having locked their white Alsatian, 'Snow', in a pound off the rear gardens. The solid mahogany door to the utility room swung open. Henderson was sweating under a Gabardine jacket. Age had not been kind to the 'Bulldog', whose reddened and bloated face, made him look more like a Pug. A clump of fine grey hairs clung desperately to his balding head.

'Is that fucking cat back annoying you?' he growled.

'No, no,' replied Imogen, turning away from the sink. 'It must be a rabbit or badger or something.'

'Never feed the wee fuckers or they'll torture you. Talking of feeding, what's for dinner? I need it quickly, I've a meeting in a couple of hours.'

'I thought we would have a nice Goat's cheese salad for a change.'

'Salad? Are you out of your mind? This is your husband you're feeding, not that excuse for a son of yours.'

She turned back to the sink in terror as Henderson approached.

'Put a steak on for me...*now!*' he yelled before marching off toward the cloakroom.

Imogen squeezed her eyes shut tight, seeping out tears.

~

Shirley parked, and looked toward the house. The soft light struggling through the curtains of the boys' bedroom, suggested they were still awake. She didn't expect anything less during Uncle John's visit. She considered telling him off for keeping them up late, but had already planned on telling him something else. Quietly opening the front door, Shirley hung her coat on a peg in the hall, before tiptoeing up the carpeted stairs. Halting at the door of the boys' bedroom, she leant her back against the corridor wall, listening to her brother talking. He was sitting on a chair in between the bottom end of the two single beds. The drowsy children, bedecked in Glentoran shirts, struggled to stay awake.

'Look lads, it's ok,' came the soothing voice, 'Wee boys argue, and even sometimes, get so angry they want to fight. But fighting is no way to sort anything out. The arguments start when one… or another …' he glanced at each in turn, '…starts telling a wee white lie. But one wee white lie can quickly grow into lots of lies… and then a huge lie! *So* huge, it makes you look like you've grown another head!'

The boys giggled. Shirley couldn't prevent the warm tears running down her face.

'So, lean over, shake hands and promise me you two hallians will be best friends in the morning.'

The tired boys reached across and touched each other's hands, then answered their uncle with laboured voices,

'We will, Uncle John,' they promised before rolling over and snuggling down.

'Night, night,' Patterson replied, turning out the bedside light. He kissed each boy on the forehead and studied them, drinking in their innocence. Envious of their futures, a path he would love to start all over again, he prayed that God would keep them safe. A teary-eyed Shirley stood in the neat kitchen as Patterson entered. He raced to her and held her shoulders, while looking into her worried eyes.
'You, ok? What's wrong?'
Aware speaking would only come after the grief Shirley was feeling, she threw her arms around him, nuzzling her head into his shoulder.
'Oh John! God forgive me...' her voice trailed off.
Patterson experienced dread as they separated, and Shirley regained her normal decorum. She motioned him to take a seat at the breakfast bar, then lifted a bottle of Bushmills whisky from the glass-fronted drinks cabinet, along with two crystal tumblers.
'God, this must be really serious,' Patterson whispered with caution in his tone.
Shirley poured them two stiff ones, immediately gulping down half her own, before coughing and sitting opposite him.
 'I've done exactly what you told the boys not to do, John. I've told you lies, for a very...*very* long time.'
Patterson frowned, his stomach flipped and twisted. His mind racing through anything his dear, sweet sister would have lied to him about, for all these years.
'I guess...' she struggled. 'We should start at the very beginning, and I swear, John, I will tell you everything!'

~

Twenty minutes later, Patterson fixated at the last drop of whisky in his glass, swirling it around in circles. Shirley had heart-wrenchingly unfolded his real life in front of him. She stuck to the details and timeline, including revisiting the time they discovered their mothers' body. Patterson convinced her she hadn't lied in a bad way, but in a protective way and for which he was thankful. He hadn't said much more, causing Shirley to await a further reaction, with trembling hands and a racing heart. She was terrified he would be angry at her, or worse, not want to see her again. She could only guess what detached, deranged thoughts he was wrestling with. He looked up slowly.

'You done the right thing, big sis.' Patterson said.

She raced around the breakfast bar and held him again, the inevitable tears reappearing.

'Oh John, I'm so, so sorry!'

Patterson broke their embrace, reassuring her he was on her side, before lifting the almost empty whisky bottle, and sharing the remainder. Shirley sat back down, facing him.

'It's so...weird. To think my Da was the leader of the UDA. If that gets out, do you think I could lose my job?'

'Nobody except me and Auntie E knows, John, I swear to you. They couldn't sack you...even you didn't know.'

Patterson gave her a wry grin.

'As usual, you're probably right.'

'And our poor Mummy. '

The mention of their mother made Shirley's eyes glisten again. Patterson placed his hands on hers.

'I'm sorry. But... what was she really like?' said Patterson in a sincere tone.

Shirley fought back the tears, sucked in some air and began.

'Mummy was beautiful. The most beautiful, loving mummy in the world. I don't even have a photograph of her to show you!' she blurted loudly, tears flowing like rivers on her cheeks.

Patterson motioned to stand before she stopped him, holding his hands tighter on the counter of the breakfast bar.

'I'm ok John, honestly. My tears aren't only for her, but for the lost time we didn't talk about her when growing up. That's my biggest regret. She really was beautiful, with eyes as dark as yours. She was going to be an air hostess. But her mummy became ill and she had to look after her in a care home. She used to take us up every Saturday to visit. Do you remember that?'

Patterson returned her question with a puzzled look. Shirley smiled.

'Of course, you wouldn't. Her and Dad, were devoted to each other and loved being together. Although, dad worked long hours ...even longer hours when he got involved. But everyone admired him. He was nothing like the scum in Belfast nowadays. Paramilitaries? More like gangsters. No matter what is written in the history books about Dad, he was a good, honest, hardworking man.'

She paused, eyeballs turning heavenward and then smiled.

'He used to carry me on his shoulders and call me his Princess. And you always remind me of him, John.'

Patterson returned Shirley's smile with a grin.

'He used to say that you'd be the next Sammy Hughes, and play for the Glens, the way you tell my two.'

Her smile dissolved as her expression changed with a grim twist to her mouth.

'I saw a documentary on TV about his murder a few years ago. The reporter is *convinced,* that he wasn't murdered by the IRA, not only because they didn't claim it, but because...'

'Because of the way he was killed...because they never done that. Holy shit! I *saw* that documentary!' interrupted Patterson.

'Yes. They were sure it had to be one of their own.'

Patterson struggled with the anger rising within. After only just learning who his father was, he already felt a duty to discover who had killed him. The person that robbed him of a normal childhood and torn his sister and him apart for so many years. They had also killed his mother Shirley noticed his demeanour.

'You ok John?'

Patterson unclenched his fists, returning to the present.

'Yeah...I'm fine'

'One other thing. You must *never,* let Aunt Elsie know you have learned this. She and I have spent a big part of our lives protecting you from the awful truth. It would destroy her.'

Having regained control of his inner fury, he held his sister's hands once more.

'I wouldn't dream of it.'

Chapter 13

A black Mercedes Benz with tinted windows, crunched over the gravel driveway of the house. At the automatic gates, it indicated right, driving off in the direction of Crawfordsburn. It was difficult to discern the driver during daylight hours, impossible at night. The unmarked blue Ford Capri, sitting 100 yards back along Fort Road, lowly growled to life, tailing the Mercedes, keeping as much distance as possible. Henderson lifted the plain, brown envelope that had 'Occupant', and his address written on it. Inside it, a piece of A5 paper with a message.

'3. 8:30pm. Kerry's great for fishing this time of year. *Only if you own a boat*'

Henderson knew where he had to be and at what time. This was a message from the IRA. He double checked the map adorned with numbers in his study, that pinpointed over 20 establishments in the north Down and Ards area. He turned out the light in the living room before peering through the blinds. 'Go get 'em boys' he said out aloud. He grinned, watching the officers from the Organised Crime branch, prepare for a hot pursuit in their Capri, as Imogen drove away from the kerb. He knew where she was headed: The Spar store in Crawfordsburn. Locking the front door, Henderson hurried to the Junction of Fort Road and Kathleen Avenue A none descript, Ford Escort reversed out from Sheridan Drive and drove toward him. It pulled up and the back door of the car opened.

'Evening lads,' he said to the other two passengers. Without waiting for a reply, he continued, 'When will those monkeys ever fucking learn? Ah?'

The preposition at the end of Henderson's sentence, demanded a reply, and the passengers dutifully laughed. 'Wankers.' The driver, Trevor McIntyre, forty-nine years old, had served eight years in the cages at Long Kesh Prison, and was renowned for leadership and organisational skills. He also headed the Security firm Henderson had established. The other passenger, younger by ten years, was a giant of a man with jet black hair and constant facial stubble. No surprise that he been nicknamed 'Desperate Dan'. He was the coordinator for the doormen teams, distributing rotas and shift patterns at the behest of McIntyre. His secondary role was akin to a sergeant major, patrolling the clubs and pubs where his men were acting as security, ensuring calmness was the order of the day. He always suffered disappointment if no fracas had erupted during his tours. It denied him the opportunity of 'busting a few heads' or 'keeping in shape' as he preferred to call it. After a 20- minute journey over Craigantlet hills, they arrived in Dundonald; a small town often referred to as greater East Belfast. It was a heartland of Loyalism. Henderson had a satisfied grin on his face as they drove past Ballybeen estate. He was amongst his own people. They pulled into the empty car park of the Quarry Inn, a faceless, block concrete pub and a favourite haunt of Paramilitaries. The interior of the place contradicted the car park, heavily populated with groups of men intertwined with couples. On entering, most heads turned in fear of an attempted sectarian attack, but were sated by the barman's announcement.

'Ok, Lads. What can I get you?'

Few of the females recognised Henderson and his entourage, although the males were alert. The married men turned to their partners, striking up inane conversations to maintain ignorance, and not make eye contact. Groups of other men who the three noticed, nodded and returned to chatting in a lower tone about their hatred of his leadership.

'Jimmy, how are you?' asked Henderson offering his hand to shake. The bartender reciprocated with false enthusiasm.

'I'll have a brandy and…' he turned to the others, 'what do you want?'

'A couple of pints of Guinness would go down well,' McIntyre replied

'Oh, drinking and driving Trevor. You might get in trouble with the police,' mocked Henderson in an adolescent tone.

'Fuck the peelers,' McIntyre sneered.

The trio laughed amongst themselves, before Henderson pulled a thick roll of twenty-pound notes from his jacket pocket, a move he had rehearsed to impress, many times before.

'I'll get these.'

The barman, already resigned to a drop in profits, dare not challenge the code.

'It's ok, Bulldog, these are on the house,' he replied, a false grin covering his true feelings.

'You're a good man, Jimmy.'

The bartender's false grin turned to a false smile, as he went to serve other patrons.

Shortly, a young female emerged from behind a closed door at the end of the bar and whispered to Jimmy, who then looked toward Henderson, who was already staring at him. He motioned for Henderson to go out the previously closed door. Henderson found himself in an untidy office, comprised of a filing cabinet, desk and chair. The desk was covered by reams of invoices and purchase notes. A cream-coloured trim phone sat atop the pile; the receiver detached from the main housing.

'Kerry's great for fishing this time of year.' said Henderson.

'Only if you own a boat,' uttered a heavy Belfast accent, with a hint of southern brogue intermingled.

'Listen, and listen carefully,' continued the alien voice.

~

A furious Henderson reappeared from behind the closed door and walked toward the others.

'Right,' he scowled. 'We're leaving!'

Desperate Dan complained about his unfinished pint. Henderson halted him in his tracks.

'I said we're fucking leaving! You have a problem with that?!' he bellowed.

McIntyre grabbed the big lad by the arm, marching him toward the exit Henderson had stormed through. There was a muted silence in the pub at the outburst. When the doors closed, Jimmy, the barman addressed the shaken crowd in a sarcastic tone,

'Thanks lads, good to see you! Pieces of shit! Happy days are here again, everyone, Elvis has left the building.'

A cacophony of laughter erupted.

An apoplectic Henderson, marched back and forth in front of the two others, who stood beside the car.

'We have a problem,' snarled Henderson. 'These fucking associates we deal with aren't happy about how we run our security.'

The others frowned in confusion as they looked on.

'Do you know why? I'll tell you why! We're letting underage kids into the bars. And the reason?'

Both men looked at the ground in embarrassment.

'So that our doormen can sell them those fucking, space tablets, or whatever the fuck Weasel got from the continent are. Don't get me wrong, this is a money maker, but dis-fucking-cretion is the order of the day! The peelers have started sniffing around the pubs more often, which is exactly what those other fuckers don't want.'

There was a heavy silence as Henderson let the others digest his tirade before continuing.

'Here's the way it is. We knock that selling on the head for a few weeks to let the dust settle, so I can talk to these people and convince them of the money-making potential. And no kid who hasn't got ID, gets into to any of the places. Understood?'

Before McIntyre could stop him, Desperate Dan spoke.

'But Bulldog, I've one lad who has booked a holiday for his family on the back of those tablets.'

Henderson raced over to him; his face uncomfortably close.

'I don't give a flying fuck about a holiday!' he hissed, spittle bouncing off his minder's face.

The big man, although controlling his anger, relented, wiped his face, and went to sit in the car. Henderson turned to McIntyre.
'I'm fed up with his attitude T. Get rid of him.'
'I'll talk to him mate, he'll be fine…' His voice tailed off as he witnessed the unchanging look of determination on Henderson's face.
'Ok then,' McIntyre huffed with reluctance.

Chapter 14

The Belfast derby between Glentoran from the east of the city, and Linfield from the south, was the biggest game in Northern Irish football. Although on a much smaller scale, it had been compared to the Glasgow derby of Rangers and Celtic, such was the maniacal fervour. However, due to the religious make up of both sets of supporters, it was more like Rangers versus Rangers. Linfield were by far, the better supported, mainly due to their red, white and blue kit that mirrored the colours of the Union Jack, and of the Rangers kit. For the last decade, they had also been the most successful. Glentoran fans seethed at the money made available to them, due to the fact of their leasing their stadium for international home games, and could buy any player at any cost. Glentoran were managed on a shoestring budget. It was a glorious sight, to witness the throng of supporters, from both sides, descend upon the Oval ground from opposite ends of Mersey Street, separated by a few hundred yards, and two thin lines of policemen. A cacophony of flags and scarves, accentuated by chanting fans full of hope, confidence and dread, spread in equal measure. Amongst the Glentoran banners and flags, a green, red and black Union Jack, let the opposition know they were as British as their adversaries.

Within the ground separation was instantly prevalent. The main stand, and standing section to the right of it, stretching around the back of the goalmouth, was dedicated to home supporters.

Large gaps either side, filled with police, led to the Linfield encampment, encompassing the smaller stand, that backed onto the Sydenham bypass and the standing area behind the goal, at the city end. Patterson and Beattie shifted in their uncomfortable fold down seats in the main stand. It gave an unbridled view of the game and Patterson loved to look beyond at the cityscape. He focused on the Shipyard. The giant paint hangars were dwarfed by the two yellow, monolithic cranes, Goliath and Sampson. He now knew this had been his father's place of work. His thoughts continually drifting to that path.

'What do you reckon?' asked Beattie, interrupting his train of thought.

'Oh,' replied Patterson, taken unaware. 'I'm not sure Andy. The blues are on a run at the minute.'

Before Beattie could speak, a supporter with a green, red and black sombrero, endeavoured to rouse the supporters, by banging on a drum and chanting 'Ga-len-torn!' Within seconds, the majority of the supporters, not only in the stand, but the entire Glentoran side of the ground, hypnotically followed his lead. Beattie laughed out loud and shouted to Patterson, 'We'll discuss it later.'

~

Patterson and Beattie, jostled among the hordes of supporters spewing out of the Oval, and meandered through the tiny streets, towards Ribble Street, where Patterson's car was parked. It was insane to park closer to the ground, as it would take an eternity to escape.

Due to the intensity of the frenetic match, they both felt drained as they, and countless others in the stands, headed every crossed ball and challenged every decision. The game had ended in a draw, thanks to a late, re-taken penalty goal by Glentoran, a result that pleased one side and deflated the other. The biggest winners were the police, as hardly any supporters goaded their rivals in a drawn game, ensuing peace amongst the supporters. Patterson was still enthusiastic about the outcome, no longer thinking melancholic thoughts.

'Some match!' he declared through a wide grin; his eyes gleaming. 'Brilliant! I thought the way we played in the first half they were going to score a bucketful after the break.'

'Billy McGaughey's volley was unbelievable.'

'That was the turning point kid, the blues started to crumble.'

'I'll tell you what, if those three shots hadn't have hit the post, we'd have destroyed them. And the penalty?'

Beattie laughed in disbelief.

'God love that referee, he must be a Glenman. When have you ever seen Tommy Hill hit a penalty over the bar?'

'And God love their keeper, for moving off his line before the kick had been taken.'

Before they realised, they had arrived at the car. Putting the key in the ignition, Beattie touched Patterson's arm to stop him starting it.

'Look, we've got to talk Paddy.'

Patterson's senses were on high alert. Recollections of his 'talk' with Shirley at the forefront of his mind. He stared wide-eyed, nostrils flared, at his friend, without reply.

Instantly recognising Patterson's facial expression, he continued. 'Don't get your knickers in a twist, this is just a talk. Mano y Mano...and it goes no further than you, me and this car. Agreed?'
Patterson considered Beattie's sincere tone.
'Ok. Talk.'
'Look, I'm only telling this for your own good. And I want to help you if I can. You've become...well...easily irritated of late. And you get angry, I mean *really* angry, like that...' he clicked his fingers.
Patterson contemplated what he knew was the truth and looked down to the floor of the car.
'You're right Andy,' before returning his gaze back to his passenger. 'And to be honest...it scares me a wee bit.'
There were a few awkward seconds of respite before Beattie continued.
'Have you ever considered Anger Management classes? They can help you.'
Patterson thought he needed Alcoholics Anonymous and Gamblers Anonymous, never mind Anger Management classes.
'I've considered it.' he lied.
'That's a good start kid. I'm now going to ask you a question, and I hope you're truthful with me. Ok?'
Patterson nodded with apprehensive agreement.
'I don't want to know anything about your private life, no details, nothing. But I do think you have problems outside of work. I'm not looking a confession or anything, but I think the problem you're having with holding yourself together boils down to a couple of things.'

Patterson struggled to respond and returned the key to the ignition. 'Fair enough, if you don't want my help, go ahead, drive off and we'll forget we ever had this conversation,' Beattie finalised, putting his seat belt on.

Patterson stared at his hand on the key and ruminated what Beattie had said. Slowly, he took the key out.

'I'm sorry Andy, I didn't...'

'You've nothing to be sorry about, kid. But you can't keep running away from any issue you're faced with,' he advised.

Patterson sighed with helplessness. Beattie touched his arm in an act of reassurance and continued.

'Look at me and answer this one question.'

Patterson nodded.

'The way I figure it, is that it's not the job causing you this...problem. You can do that standing on your head for God's sake! I think it's one of two things, and hopefully not both.'

Patterson stiffened in his seat, Beattie holding eye contact with him.

'It's either a woman problem...'

Patterson's expression remained blank.

'...or money.'

Patterson's eyes flaunted this understanding, before returning to the blank expression.

'Ah! So, it's money problems.   "What are you, a mind reader!?' Patterson replied in his usual derisory tone, a sign of humour to his friend. He regained his agitated state as Beattie rubbed his forehead with his fingers and thumb, contemplating.

Turning to his younger colleague, he had a grave look on his face. A beaming smile evaporated the dour look, as he spoke.

'Thank Christ for that! If it had been a woman, you were own your own!'

Patterson unsuccessfully stifled a blurt of laughter. In the following minutes, Beattie explained of his unexpected windfall. A great uncle, who never married, and the last sole survivor of his immediate family, had died two months ago. He'd been a successful engineer, working all around the world, and lived alone in a mansion on the shore side of the Carrickfergus Road out of Belfast, six miles from where Beattie was born. The only people named in his will were his carer, two nieces and Beattie, his only nephew. There was a substantial inheritance due to all, according to the letter he received from the solicitor executing the will. As they drove along the Albertbridge Road, Patterson spoke.

'I'm really glad you care about me, but...I can't take money off you.'

'Who said I was giving you money? It's a loan, kid, that's all. You pay it back when, and if, you can.' They turned onto, and drove up Castlereagh Road. Patterson grinned like a Cheshire cat, pondering a future without debt. A future where he could change, become real again. He vowed to Beattie that he would attend anger management classes, only this time he meant it.

On reaching Montgomery Road, they drove down to Stirling Avenue. When they pulled up in front of his house, Beattie turned again to Patterson.

'Don't worry about money, kid, just promise me once more you'll sort yourself out.'

Patterson unbuckled his seat belt and leant across to hug him. An unexpected tear trickled down his face.

'Ok, ok, that's enough,' said Beattie, breaking the embrace. 'Anybody would think we're a couple of shirt lifters!'

Beattie opened the door to get out of the car before leaning back in. 'Between me and you?'

Patterson formed a Cub Scout salute with his two fingers and said, 'Scout's honour.'

'You look after yourself, kid, I'll see you on Monday at work.'

Beattie closed the door, and stood on the pavement before his house, a well-maintained semi, with a bay window, and a tiny manicured front lawn. He sighed, hoping, but not convinced, that his offer would sort his young friend out for good. He watched and waved as Patterson drove off.

'Happy Fucking Days!' Patterson shouted at the top of his voice, while slapping the steering wheel. He noticed Beattie waving to him and smiled. 'You're a life saver amigo,' Patterson thought with warmth.

Then his rear windscreen imploded.

Patterson crashed into a parked car when Beattie opened the tiny, ornate gate to his house. setting off a booby-trapped bomb, obliterating his friend, and destroying Patterson's Road to salvation.

Chapter 15

McDermott left the Goldfish bowl, and walked toward another table in the middle of the sprawling office space. It was early Sunday morning and he should've been at Church. His tranquil thoughts of being in a building full of hope, love and prayer had been shattered. On an adjacent wall was a map of Castlereagh with Stirling Avenue highlighted. He dropped a file on the desk before sitting and looking at the two Detective Constables facing him. Roy Jackson filled every inch of the chair he sat on, and then some. The stitching on his brown pinstriped jacket held on for dear life, with his every movement. At the age of thirty, this black haired, swarthy colossus, was captain of the RUC rugby team. But because he pondered and deliberated in his mind, any question he received, to the uninitiated, could be considered 'a bit slow.' However, Jackson had one the sharpest minds on the force, and an equally dry sense of humour. Beside him was William Douglas, looking more diminutive than normal, due to the proximity of Jackson. Wiry thin and wrinkled, more due to chain smoking than being closer in age to McDermott, he had the worst dress sense in the room. His clothes always creased and shabby, the colour schemes cataclysmic. He had spiky hair that refused to bow to the Brylcreem he would administer. His Roman nose and large glasses reminded everyone of an owl. McDermott, however, was thankful that Douglas had the sixth sense of Policeman's intuition, a priceless commodity.

'Ok Jacko, what have Castlereagh got?'

Jackson and Douglas poured through their notebooks, and the assembled photographs on the table.

'We know the device had to be planted between 2pm and 5:30pm after the victim left for the football, and due to the manufacture and success of the device igniting, forensics are practically writing off any finger prints.'

McDermott grimaced and pondered.

'How the hell does anyone get to plant a device in the middle of the afternoon, a *Saturday* afternoon at that!? Beattie's poor wife, had a massive stroke after the event, and is in intensive care. It could be a while before we can talk to her.'

'We have... *something*, Captain,' interjected Douglas. 'A few uniformed boys talked to a Mrs. Stewart who lives ten doors away. She noticed a Post Office van pull up at the Beattie residence around 3:30pm. She remembered it driving up, but took no further notice, as she had her back garden to tidy. It's not an unusual occurrence.'

'She didn't see the driver?'

'Sad, but true,' replied a solemn Douglas.

The grim atmosphere was interrupted by a uniformed officer bursting into the room. He nodded apologetically to McDermott.

'Sergeant, we got a tip off on the Confidential Line about farm outbuildings, off the Stoneyford Road. near White Mountain. The E4a (specialised police group) lads found a civilian gagged and bound, in a bad way.'

'And?' replied McDermott.

'He works for the General Post Office, and takes his van home with him at the weekends because of his shifts.'

All three detectives suppressed their delight at the breakthrough, yet became more animated.

'Has he been interviewed?' said Jackson.

'Yes,' replied the constable. 'He was hijacked by two masked men on Saturday morning, while driving home on the Hannahstown Road. It was about 2am. He claims that he couldn't describe them, except for the masks and the camouflage jackets. They blindfolded and beat him. He's in a state of shock.'

McDermott nodded toward the constable who dutifully left the room. He left the other two to reflect, whilst he figured out a strategy.

'Ok, listen up lads. I'll contact the Detective Chief Inspector at Castlereagh, and we go public on this. I want an appeal on television, radio and the papers. Get the licence number of the van from the GPO, to run alongside it. I need you two to revisit the scene, and re-question everyone in the street again. Concentrate on the van. Distribute pictures and get the beat boys to set up patrols, to question anyone that drives along there. When this poor sod becomes compos mentis, I'll need you both to question him. It's a long shot, but we have to try. Is there anything else?'

'Yes Captain,' said Douglas. 'The other Prison Officer who dropped him off, will get out of hospital tomorrow. We'll interview him later in the week.'

McDermott nodded again, sighing with resignation. Both detectives gathered their photographs and paperwork as McDermott headed to the goldfish bowl, slumping into his chair.

'Cowardly bastards,' he thought. His desk phone rang and he snatched it up in hope of a breakthrough. His soulful demeanour re-appeared, as he dropped the handset into the cradle.

He shouted to Jackson and Douglas, who were about to leave.

'Lads! They found two burned out vehicles at 4am in Poleglass. One of them was a Honda Civic...the other one was the van.'

~

It was five days after the bomb. During that time, the police had called to get Patterson's statement, the reason his house was unusually clean. He had spent hours on the telephone with his sister Shirley, who convinced him he wasn't to blame for the atrocity. Every conversation Patterson attempted; sentences crumbled to tears. Shirley had pleaded with him to come over and let her take care of him, but he refused. He was frightened Shirley might see through his false persona and satisfied her with the fact, that the Prison Officers Welfare department called on him frequently. His doctor had prescribed him medication to sleep and relieve any pain, but Patterson had never given the full details of his state of mind to the doctor. He didn't want to appear as weak. He had been excused from work, for three weeks, to help cope with the trauma he had experienced. A few bald patches on the back of his head, served as frames for the stitches and scars the exploded windscreen had gifted him, yet he was immune to any trivial physical pain. Patterson's mind demanded attention elsewhere. And now, like every day, he was alone with dark thoughts as his only companion. True, he had a lot of 'friends' in the service, but most were married with a family and had busy lives to lead. The well-wishing phone calls soon tailed off, as their normal lives took precedence. He walked miles during those few days, mainly in the lounge or back garden, and now he lay on the settee feeling destitute.

The fingers of his left hand played subconsciously with the philtrum below his nose, squeezing the two sides together before releasing. He was aware of the stubble on his face, but didn't give a thought to shaving. He stared at a blank ceiling.

'Where do you go now kid?' he asked aloud to the empty room. 'You had a chance. A way to sort this fucking mess of a life out...and some Provo bastard stole it from you.'

A prang of guilt pierced Patterson's heart, realising his statement intimated Beattie was more than a friend. He sat up and he put his head in his hands before focussing again on the ceiling.

'Andy, please forgive me,' he whispered. Patterson sobbed hard at the thought of his lost friendship. He lay face down on the settee, his head buried in a cushion, eyes shut tight. He had a persistent buzzing in his ears that the doctor assured him would pass. The buzzing acted as a force field, restricting his darkest thoughts from escaping. He knew he had immediate problems to solve, dreading getting out of bed each morning to face another day. He had contemplated, albeit briefly, driving his car off a bridge, making his litany of pandemonium disappear forever. His physical body demanded rest. He was soundly asleep within minutes, only to be engulfed in a troubled, vivid dream.

Patterson was in a black hole that looked like the bottom of a well, although the dense blackness, wasn't as constrictive as he imagined it would be. It was more intimidating and infinite. A pinprick far above him was the only available light source, but faded to grey as it reached him. As he walked toward it, in what felt like an upward diagonal path, the pinprick of light remained constant.

Realising this was his only escape, Patterson started to run toward it, but no matter how fast and how long he ran for, it maintained the same distance away. Panting and struggling for breath, he fell to his knees and screamed at the top of his voice, 'Help me! Help me!' He closed his eyes and wept in the same position. He had no conception of the time that passed while his eyes were shut, but when he opened them, the light source had grown in size. Patterson rose to his feet, approaching it with caution. A muted vision of a man appeared at, what was now, a wider, brighter space. The vision was two dimensional and monotone. Patterson recognised his father from the television documentary. He steeled himself once more, stretching for all his worth at a ghostly hand reaching down to him. No matter how close he imagined he got, the distance between his, and the ghostly hand, remained constant.

Patterson sat bolt upright in distress. Throughout the next few hours, he survived on coffee and cigarettes. He tried to recreate his father's helping hand, to no avail. He was convinced he now had a goal, an atrocious one, but a goal nonetheless, during the remainder of his miserable life. He was utterly fixated with thoughts of his father. Patterson re-commenced his conversation with the ceiling, as he resumed his normal position on the settee.

'Dad, I'm sorry if I've let you down. I understand you, not being here for me, wasn't any of your doing. You probably know how the bastards killed my friend. As much as they are evil, the ones who murdered you, are the scum on the bottom of those evil bastards' shoes.'

He was ignorant to the tears rolling down his face.

'I know you would have kept me straight, taught me self-discipline, and ensured I never got to where I am now. But pure evil denied us all that. The bonding. The love. I would have made you proud.' Patterson paused to control his emotions.

'They were responsible for the death of our mum, too. Shirley told me how much of an angel she was. I pray to God you are both now, re-united in heaven. I hope someday, and that may be sooner, rather than later, I will join you, and become a family once again. I can almost imagine your protests, Dad, please don't get angry... but I will, ... *I have to*, avenge your death...no matter what it takes.'

His lonely speech had bolstered his determination, an impetus for retribution.

~

Beattie's funeral was delayed for days, giving forensics a chance to gather any sliver of evidence, on anything. Though it was mainly about the bomb construction and an attempt to identify the ballistics value, to discover if there was a pattern with other deadly devices. There wasn't much of Beattie left to be buried and his remains were accompanied by sandbags in the closed coffin, giving it the weight of a cadaver. It was cold, and the incessant rain, seemed befitting of such a tragedy to Patterson. He tossed his weatherproof Barbour jacket onto the backseat of the tiny red Vauxhall car his insurance had sponsored. Devoid of emotion, he thought of how cruel and fragile life was. He considered life as one whole entity, all humans merely it's sum. Life was incessant, and whenever a single cell was damaged beyond repair, that spent life was automatically extirpated.

The space in the structure covered, the soul and its existence, gone without trace, for eternity. It was the only true equality in the scheme of things. When life was over, it was *truly* over and existing in its place, a smattering of memories and photographs, that would be diluted over time. It made Patterson angry, as he never had that speck of reminiscence to dwell on, and draw comfort from. Patterson's parents had been taken from him, without him being able to register, or store, any precious memories. He drove away from Carryduff, over the Castlereagh hills towards the city's biggest cemetery, Roselawn.

~

The massive car parks surrounding the crematorium were filled to capacity, leaving Patterson to park at the side of an arterial road, en route. Throngs of mourners, mainly Prison Staff, making their way to the site, made Patterson assume the Crumlin Road Jail must be running itself. Low rumbles of conversation, were interspersed with complaints about the rain, as a medley of black umbrellas bobbed above the hordes. Patterson pulled his Barbour jacket over his black suit and made his way up. Neither the rain, polishing and flattening his black hair, or bouncing on his face, seemed of any significance. Above the melee, he could hear the tortured notes of bagpipes, the piper tuning up for this important performance. Staff couldn't understand why he refused to be part of the colour party and honour his friend's final journey. But Patterson wanted to remember Beattie as a friend, not a colleague. He managed to retain his calm, as increasing numbers of the congregation asked about his well-being.

Others turned with curiosity, when he entered the jam-packed place of worship, offering smiles of sympathy. Patterson stood at the back wall, ignoring offers of a seat near the front. He didn't want to be ensconced by false sympathies from the Hierarchy. The Lord mayors of both Belfast and Castlereagh, were joined by high-ranking NIO officials, attending as a duty, and not for remembrance or reflection. The tedious, low volume, organ music that had been running on loop tape, came to an abrupt halt. Silence descended over the assembly. The first strangled note from the bagpipes, emanated from the hall entrance, before a series of other notes created a reverential noise, thinly disguised as a tune. The piper slow marched into the hall toward the pulpit. All heads turned in Patterson's direction, more to gauge his reaction than in sympathy.

He wanted to shout, *'Fuck off everyone! This isn't about me!' This is about my friend*!

The piper and six pall bearers, were dressed identically, with polished black boots matching the gleam from the peak of their hats. The dark blue, silver buttoned uniforms were pristine, with razor sharp creases and proud medal ribbons on show. All wore white gloves. The coffin was placed on plinths at the head of the aisle, an impressive array of flowers at its base. Patterson noticed the gap in the pew, amid the remaining relatives of Beattie. A space where his comatose wife, Doris, should have occupied. Patterson hated this part of any funeral. The officiating minister would spew out sparse details of the stranger in the coffin, working solely on fractured advice from friends and relatives. He understood it was a difficult task, as it was akin to reading a shopping list, while trying to sound emotional and caring.

It was the continuation *he* really hated, when the minister would enthusiastically glorify the only thing, he knew. Or thought he knew. The existence and powerful all-embracing, of our Lord Jesus Christ. The descriptive nouns were plentiful, all encouraging and resplendent. Aware this fanciful tirade would dominate the remainder of the service, Patterson quietly slipped out into the packed hallway, and wormed his way into an open space outdoors.
. At least once he heard a female voice whisper, 'God love him, it must be too much for him.' For the first time that day, his facial features afforded him a brief smile as he thought… *'You've no idea how right you are missus.'*

He thought about God, as he lit a cigarette, glad of the shelter that announced the hallway. He had conflicting views. He wanted to *believe*, the image of his happy parents together. Yet, this so-called God was ruthless, and blind, to the terrors that the human race had to experience. Floods, avalanches, famine, war, and the killing of those *he* held dear. Shortly, the funeral cortege wormed its way toward the prepared hole in the ground that was his wife's family's plot. Beattie was from the Carrickfergus area and had, in life, supposed he would be finally interned there. His wife's family made that decision for him. Patterson walked to the side of the collection of mourners, his mind elsewhere, continuing to brave the rain. Suddenly, he was under the shelter of a black umbrella. He glanced sideways to see his Principal Officer, Eric Wright. 'We're all going to miss him Paddy, he was a good man,' said Wright, a deadpan look on his face, eyes pooled with the tears he fought to contain.

He put his arm around Patterson's shoulder.

'Yes Eric, I know,' replied Patterson in a matter-of-fact fashion. When the final prayers were said, and the coffin lowered to its new and eternal, subterranean resting place, the crowd started to dissipate.

It wasn't long before Patterson was alone again. He peered into the grave in contemplation. A cemetery workman hinted that it would be better to fill the hole, as the water would ruin the coffin. *'Do you think he cares?!'* Patterson thought, but instead, he nodded and walked back to his car. He left the cemetery, ignoring the prepared post funeral gathering at a local hotel, before turning right, toward Ballygowan. He felt numb and drove instinctively, not remembering how he had reached his turn-off. Instead of turning right at the junction to Carryduff, he turned left and drove past La Mon Hotel toward Gransha. Patterson had no idea where he wanted to go, but he didn't want to be alone in a house that had been serving as a prison. He just drove.

Chapter 16

An air of tension within the jail, lasted for almost a week after Beattie's death. Staff reinforced security; movements heavily restricted. It was a collective display of strength from the prison staff, the only retaliation they had against their colleague's murder. Though it was a lop-sided retaliation, reserved only for republicans. During the course of each day, the routine for one faction would be, slopping out and washing, before heading down to the canteen for breakfast. The remainder, would be served breakfast in their cells. After returning from the canteen for a headcount, the same faction would be given access to the exercise yard for most of, what remained of the morning. This period, gave staff an opportunity to control the movement of the remaining prisoners, two cells at a time, to slop out and clean their cells, wash and shower, if time permitted. On completion of the exercise period, the opposing faction would return to the canteen for lunch, whilst the incarcerated ones would be served theirs on a tray, and locked back in their cell. After all prisoners were locked and accounted for, the staff broke for lunch. In the Afternoon, the roles were reversed. However, in the evening, the faction who had the yard in the morning, would be allowed to assemble, or 'association' as it was referred to, once more in the canteen. Whilst their adversaries, two cells at a time, could perform ablutions, clean up and collect their supper.

Each faction had agreed to this regime, taking it in turns to have the association day. It was a self-inflicted segregation, as all prisoners were legally entitled, to two exercise periods and to eat all their meals in the canteens.

Another daily practice, was random cell searches. On occasions of suspicion, entire wings were locked down for 24 hours whilst dedicated search teams carried out an entire search of the wing including wash houses, yards, store rooms and even the class officers' bunks.

A Wing was different.

Practices were the same, but due to the high level of principal inmates, there were separate canteens at the end of each landing, and more frequent cell searches.

~

The day after the assassination of Beattie, McGuigan had briefed his two Commanding officers on A1 and A2 as they walked together around the exercise yard. During the walk they occasionally laughed out loud to advertise a normal 'day at the office,' aimed at the officer in the towering observation post, and for the cameras. They conversed in whispered tones, using their mother tongue. McGuigan was glad the Prison Service hadn't yet realised how effective it would have been to teach their staff, his language. When he had important information to deliver, the group would narrow their walking route until they were in the middle of the yard, out of earshot of listening devices, secretly placed around the toilets, shelters and in the walls. He explained to them what to expect, as it had happened before on many occasions, ordering them to ensure that no soldier of theirs complained, and he *meant* no-one. He had already passed the message to C Wing, via visitors.

This was a Cathartic process the jailers were undertaking and to rebel against it was to lengthen the duration.

'Let them think we are respecting them, and allowing them their dignity. That makes them weak.' were his final words before the tannoy system had spewed out its first command to 'Lock up.' For whatever reason, the first call had evolved into an appetiser for both factions, and it was only after five minutes that the second course repeated the command. However, no prisoner, in these opposing armies, returned to their cells before their commanding officer had given the order.

~

McGuigan, like the majority of the republicans, was awake when A3 night guard staff handed over to the day shift. This meant two headcounts. The night staffs making sure they were all there, and the day staff making sure the nights were correct. It was only when the numbers were returned from each landing, correlated and confirmed, that the day would begin. McGuigan couldn't see outside his locked cell door, yet he, and all other republicans, listened intently. It was a time for gold digging, listening to any loose chat amongst staff, mistakenly assuming their internees would be sound asleep. It often provided nuggets of information about their collective personal business, essential for future operations. Each team on the three landings, knew of some staff's families, their wife's names, where their children went to school, which pubs they frequented, and much more.

He heard McIntire, the Class Officer, shout down to the 1's to unlock the orderlies.

Orderlies were low risk sentenced prisoners, referred to as the ODC's (Ordinary Decent Criminals) and menial task units of the jail. The staff had a modicum of trust with them, much to their detriment, as a select few were unknown republicans without a criminal history. They were offered, or forced, to commit secondary crimes such as hi-jacking vehicles, to let the seasoned Republican offenders establish a communications and information network within the jail. The A3 orderlies, clamoured up the stairs to begin their first task of cleaning toilets and brushing landings, whilst the staff updated journals, checked cell and index cards, and filled in the red-book takeover times. As the orderly quickly brushed the landing toward the toilets and canteen end of the wing, he hesitated briefly, making sure that during his brush stroke, the end of the handle knocked quietly twice, on McGuigan's cell door, before resuming his task. McIntire appeared from the class office and shouted to the orderly, 'Any chance there? We've a prison to run sometime today.'
'Nearly done Mr McIntire, just want to check the loos to see if we need any paper.'
'Quick as you can kid.' replied a satisfied McIntire.
The orderly smiled and raced into the toilet area, removing a thin sliver of clingfilm from his mouth, that contained a coded message in miniscule writing. Ensuring it was tightly wrapped and waterproofed, he placed it up inside the cold water tap of the sink furthest from the entrance. He had already been assured by the Republicans, first out today, that this sink was 'out of bounds.'

~

McGuigan lifted the book from the shelf in his cell, forcing open the weary spine, where he had hidden the message at the start of that day. It was 20 minutes until lights out. The headcounts had diminished, as bored staff were happy everyone was home. He digested its contents, sat back on the bed and rolled a cigarette using the message as cigarette paper. McGuigan quickly puffed his way through it, making sure the ashes were mingled with other discarded butts in his aluminium foil, makeshift ashtray. Lying on the bed, he closed his eyes, his subconscious automatically bringing the message to the forefront of his mind. It read a few words, but had colossal undertones,

tru. no loc yet. 2 wks mx.

In the privacy of his surroundings, McGuigan uncharacteristically, allowed himself to be angry. He thought of Orla and the bastard screw. He wanted to howl at the moon such was his vexation. Through self-taught meditation techniques he used for police interviews, he quickly regained composure and formulated a plan.

Chapter 17

For the first time in 20 minutes, Patterson consciously blinked. The realisation of that basic human function, catapulted him back into the present reality. Rain laden clouds dictated the world he was in, would be one of achromatic, making every vibrant colour appear miserable, with its varying muddy shades of grey. He was in an empty car park, staring out over a dull, muddy, green area and a paltry strip of grey sanded beach, towards Belfast Lough. His head jerked left and right as he drank in his surroundings. He noticed the sign that read, *'Seapark. All dogs must be kept on leashes at all times.'*

'Seapark?' he questioned, before a spark from his memory alerted him. He'd been here before as a cub scout with 18th Willowfield pack. They had a field outing to this place years ago, off the Bangor Road near Holywood. There was an absence of dog walkers as Patterson exited the car, meandering slowly toward the beach. He held his hand over his mouth, blinking his eyes rapidly, understanding that he had subconsciously navigated his route here. He tried, without success, to recall any of the journey. Unbeknown to Patterson, his subconscious had led him back to one of the few places of abject joy, he had experienced in life. A life without fear, worry, drink or gambling. A life of innocence. His mind had evaporated all that was dull in his childhood. Standing on the pathway, he overlooked the beach, hypnotised by the murky, choppy waters of the Lough. It dragged him back to the present. The present being his only solace, as any future, was a dream of pure fantasy, in his current state.

He could feel the magnetism of the dark water, beckoning him. The waves seemed to softly whisper,
'Come, rest in my arms, and all will be calm.'
He took one step toward the beach, before a yelping dog and it's complaining owner entered the car park. Their fracas served as a slap across Patterson's face, bringing him back to his senses. Back in the car, his thoughts became more defined. Thoughts and responsibilities. He twisted the key in the ignition, the lukewarm engine spewing hot air throughout the vents, clearing the windscreen. Patterson's thoughts of his father discerned that this day of mourning was yet to be fulfilled. He drove, fully reactive and determined.

~

Although on a very personal mission, Patterson was guided by security awareness. He stopped at a garage in East Belfast to buy flowers. Their best offerings were mediocre to say the least, but would suffice. Due to their gangly stems, he purchased a pair of household scissors for trimming to fit in a graveside memorial vase, he assumed would be present. He toyed with the notion of breaking the stems, but this would be his one and only occasion he would honour his true father.
It had to be right.
After a few reconnaissance trips along the Carmoney Road in Glengormley, he focused on the entrance to the graveyard. His trained mind persuaded him to park in an adjacent street, and enter the cemetery on foot. His career could be over if anyone seen him, and what he was about to do.

Patterson retrieved the flowers from the passenger seat and slipped the scissors into the right-hand Barbour Jacket pocket, his regulation Walther pistol into the left. He took the separate hood of the jacket, buttoning it into place, as the inevitable rain had recommenced. It would deny his features to any onlookers. He scanned the deserted street, before setting off toward the cemetery. The persistent rain was annoying. No longer constant and heavy, but infrequent, with no hint of the force it chose to fall with. His features, buried in the monk - like hood, Patterson walked past the groundskeeper's offices, before continuing to his right where he spied the dense privet hedges, indicating the entrance to the Loyalist memorial plot. A few pensioners paid homage to a gravestone 100 yards to his left, too immersed in grief to notice him. A few visits to the library to pour over old newspapers, made identification of his goal simple. As he approached the opening in the hedge, he glanced behind and around, confident he was unseen. The entrance dictated a left toward another wall of Hedge, before turning into the inner sanctum. The assembly of pristine graves was impressive. Their layout, a replica from above, although hard to distinguish from ground level, was of an Ulster Flag. A rectangular, black tarmaced path served as a border, the cross paths in the middle, constructed of burgundy gravel. A mosaic made from miniature marble tiles sat in the middle of where the paths intersected. A six-pointed white star with a red hand inlaid in its centre. Above the point of the star and the hand, was an intricate crown. The entire construction was so striking it would have graced a Pharaoh's temple. Patterson noticed all the headstones, bar one, were white domed marble. Constant maintenance from volunteers had kept any green mould at bay and the stones were replenished annually. The only irregularity in this immaculate symmetry was a tall black marble plinth facing the path that led to the crown. The grandeur of such a resting place had intoxicated Patterson, but his fascination dissolved, when he noticed a giant of a man, sobbing into his hands at the plinth gravesite. Patterson froze considering his options. Should he leave unnoticed or stay and pay homage to his father? His hand tightened around the pistol grip of the Walther in his pocket, giving him comfort in his choice.

As Patterson crept to the last length of the path, he whispered to himself, fear seeping into his psyche.

'Why am I doing this? Why am I doing this?'

Before he reached the end to turn right toward the ogre, the anger inside him grabbed the fear and crushed it, throwing it far back to the inner recesses of his consciousness.

'Because I want to do it! I need to do it!!' Patterson growled through gritted teeth.

Clicking the safety catch off his pistol, he strode forward. Hamilton reacted to the sound of footsteps and turned his head. His peripheral vision registered someone interrupting his genuflection to his lost leader. Patterson's expression was chameleon-like, offering him a sympathetic expression.

'You ok, big lad?'

The giant rose, fists clenched. Red, tear-stained eyes gave a demonic look as he sucked in air, his full frame now displayed. He took steps towards Patterson.

'What the fuck's it got to do with you?' he bellowed.

Patterson whipped the pistol from his pocket and aimed. Hamilton froze.

'A lot more than you think, arsehole!'

For a brief second, Hamilton felt recognition of that face, that growl.

Chapter 18

Experiencing wrath and resentment, McGuigan remained calm in the presence of his barrister after learning of a witness willing to testify against him, prolonging his stay in jail. This episode was out of his hands. As the cold-blooded killer shook the hand of his legal counsel, he tilted his head to one side.

'Well, what can you do, only hope and wait?' he said.

The barrister nodded, and scurried down the narrow corridor, to another of the four contained legal visiting areas, to deliver the same message to McGuigan's co-accused. As the barrister disappeared, an officer holding a pink visiting slip informed McGuigan that he had a visit. Walking out of Legals, the officer spoke to him.

'That meeting didn't last long Padraig, did it?'

'He hadn't much to say.'

'Awe, and he'll probably be even quicker with the next 7 on his list. Those whores earn a packet for each visit with each one of you, no matter how long it lasts?'

'Really?' McGuigan purposed, raising his eyebrows, feigning a look of surprise.

'Fuckers know how to make a killing!' grunted the officer.

'Oh, I know what you mean,' replied McGuigan, aware the officer wasn't cognizant of the irony he had delivered.

They made the short trip through one search box into the A visits search box. The searching officer requested a strip search, his second within two minutes and three yards. McGuigan sighed and began to remove his pullover.

'For goodness' sake, give him a break, Tommy! He's only after having one coming out of Legals,' retorted the escort.

'Fair enough.'

Oozing innocence, McGuigan shrugged his shoulders and offered, 'Are you sure?'

'Awe, head on in there.'

'Thanks lads, I appreciate it.'

On entering the visits area, he headed straight for the booth he knew was his destiny, furthest from the visitor's door, beside the officer in the high chair. 'My usual penthouse suite I take it,' McGuigan offered the observing officer, who couldn't disguise a smile, completely unaware McGuigan was using a technique to make the officer relax. Each Provisional prisoner had identified the officers who preferred non-confrontation, and continually acted in this relaxed fashion whilst in their company, diluting their vigilance and creating a slight advantage to surprising and overpowering them, if and when, it was required. McGuigan sat at the nearest point to the officer on the long-fixed bench at the prisoners' side of the fixed table, and waited. Nugent strode toward his boss, who stood up at the end of the room. Shouts of 'Mo Chara' echoing from all the other booths. Not only in display of honour to McGuigan's right hand man, but hoping their false association with this Adonis, would make an impression on their girlfriends or wives, many of whom were open jawed and awestruck. Nugent simply smiled and nodded at the adoring throng, until he reached the end of the room. A brief masculine embrace ensued, before Nugent spoke the customary words.

'Mo Chara.'

McGuigan's terse expression melted into a genuine grin as he replied in English,

'My friend.'

They slid along the opposing benches, positioning themselves close to the wall, as far from the observing Officer as possible. The officer strived desperately to eavesdrop the conversation, realising it was futile when he heard their mother tongue.

'Well?' McGuigan began.

'Shouldn't be a problem, Padraig. His granny lives alone in Hilltown in County Down. Next week she'll go missing until the witness sees sense.'

'Good, but make sure you send ringmasters and not clowns. If anyone insults, shows discourtesy or physically harms the old dear, I want their kneecaps. Understand?'

'Crystal. Do you want an update on the whore?'

McGuigan's malevolent eyes hardened and bore into Nugent's heart. 'Don't ever her call her that!' he hissed through bloodless, thin white lips.

His forceful request was answered by Nugent's chin dropping to his chest in defeat. In essence, he had mistakenly challenged the leader of the pack, and knew it was time to yield.

'Sorry Padraig,' said Nugent in his most apologetic tone.

McGuigan continued to hold his aggrieved facial expression, wide-eyed and a corded neck, letting Nugent know who was in charge, before slipping into a coherent demeanour.

'Up to this moment in time, Orla remains as my wife. Understand?'

Nugent nodded over enthusiastically.

'I want you to gather as much information and observe him at all times. Where he goes, what he does and especially...' he paused momentarily,'...who he's with.'

'Consider it done. But we could apprehend him and take him down south.'

'Are you fucking deaf? Nothing happens to him until I am out of this shithole. I want my face to be the last thing he sees. By the time I finish with him, he'll wish he had've died a long time ago.'

~

Patterson sat as far away as possible from Hamilton on the bench that faced the black marble plinth. The Walther in his left hand, remained pointed at the pathetic giant. Hamilton had spent 20 minutes explaining every last detail of Patterson's father's life. Patterson had taken some comfort from his admiration, of the man he now knew, to be his father. His father's achievements and leadership, fed his comfort the most. Hamilton watched Patterson lifting the flowers and walking to the vase in front of the plinth. He used scissors to delicately cut each flower short enough to sit neatly inside the urn, before standing upright, looking to the sky, then drooping his chin onto his chest, fighting with all his strength to stem the flow of tears that were forcing their way from his eyes. He thought about his father for a few private minutes, before resuming his position on the bench.

'What happened the night he was murdered?' he requested in a tone Hamilton had been dreading. He replied with a soft tone full of compassion.

'Are you sure you want to hear this son?'

'Don't ever call me that! Ever!' And we never met!! Do you understand?'

Hamilton nodded and paused. He took a deep breath before relating his account.

Pipes of anger rolled through Patterson's conscious mind, heating to a dangerous level, as he digested Hamilton's story. On completion, Hamilton realised how agitated and disappointed the young man had become.

'If you were so close and loyal to my Da, why the fuck didn't you stop them?! Or even attempt to stop them!' barked Patterson, his tone racing from a low growl to a demonic falsetto.

Hamilton looked deflated, tears cascading down his tilted face, merging into drops on his nose. 'I don't know, I don't know. I've lived with the shame all of my life.'

Patterson's anger remained fuelled. Still looking at his shoes, Hamilton continued speaking softly, more to himself than Patterson. 'Those two are dangerous bastards. Henderson has turned the UDA into a company! *HIS* company, and he's the managing director. No-one trusts him.'

Hamilton paused to align his thoughts before continuing, 'Everybody's too scared to do anything. Including...me,' he stuttered with shame.

Before Patterson could intervene, Hamilton continued his monotone monologue.

'Anybody who challenges him, simply disappears and the Provo's are always conveniently blamed.'

He slowly rose to his feet, as did Patterson, his security awareness at high.

'It means, he's either working with them…or...'

'He's still doing what he did to my Da!' snarled Patterson, unaware he was drifting to a place beyond his control. He turned to walk away before Hamilton lightly touched his arm.

'I...'

Patterson spun around and pressed the Walther between Hamilton's eyes.

'Don't ever touch me!'

Patterson's hand trembled, as he applied more pressure to the trigger. Hamilton closed his eyes in submission. For what seemed like a lifetime, Patterson held his position, thoughts racing through his mind. Forensics, attracting attention. Somewhere in his deep subconscious, a truth emerged. He took the pressure off and stepped back, engaging the safety catch, before nestling it back into his jacket pocket. He turned again to go, but Hamilton called to him in a pathetic tone.

'I can help you to get to those bastards.'

Patterson pivoted to face the plinth. Hamilton's tone became more sorrowful as he continued talking.

'I owe it to your Da.'

Hamilton plunged his face into his hands and sobbed.

'I see his face every night. This is killing me,' he cried.

The pipes that heated his anger, exploded in Patterson's mind like a blinding flash. He felt he had entered an ethereal state. Everything was calm and he could no longer hear sounds. He raised his head to the grey sky, instinctively nodding in agreement. Every movement was in slow motion, as he dug into his pocket, feeling the grip of the scissors. He gradually spun round, surprised at how laboured his voice sounded; like a record being played at the wrong speed.

'It's fucking killing you alright!' Patterson bellowed. What was once slow motion, became hyper speed. Patterson stabbed the scissors into Hamilton's neck, severing his jugular vein. He jumped back and into reality, as blood spouted from the wound. Hamilton turned to face him before the blood loss disabled his balance, causing him to collapse. His forehead emanated a sickening crack, as it split on the black marble. What unnerved Patterson the most, was the look on Hamilton's face. It was one of contentedness.

Chapter 19

Jackson sat uncomfortably, on the edge of a settee. A uniformed female officer sat beside him. The diminutive figure of a shell-shocked Susan Hamilton, sat opposite. Jackson had agreed with McDermott that it could make Mrs. Hamilton feel more at ease, due to his build being similar to Hamilton's, a deliberate ploy that appeared to be paying dividends.

'So, Mrs. Hamilton,' stated Jackson

The lady with a puffy face and reddened eyes interrupted, 'Please, please call me Susan.'

'Ok Susan...do you know of anyone that had a grudge against your husband? Had he been threatened in any way in the past?'

The doll-like figure looked down at her hands, her trembling fingers trying to knit together as she contemplated.

'I don't think so son,' she struggled, her voice barely audible. 'We kept ourselves to ourselves...'

Before she could continue, she lost the fight of containing emotions, and buried her face in her tiny hands. The female officer disregarded the rule book and rushed to sit on the arm of the chair, enveloping the delicate widow in her arms.

'It's ok, it's ok,' she consoled.

Jackson ignored the desire to get evidence and stood up, respectively suggesting they call another time. Susan looked up at him with desperation in her eyes.

'Please stay. I'll be ok.'

The female officer returned to the settee as Jackson slowly sat down.

'Are you sure?'

'Yes, son, I'm sure. I want to help you as much as I can, to get whoever did this.'

Susan took a deep breath to aid recovery of her composure.

'My Willie was good man. He looked after as many people in this estate as he could. I've never seen him harm a fly. He wasn't the monster they sometimes made him out to be in the Sunday papers. They didn't even know him.'

Although rivulets of tears began rolling down her face, Jackson was astounded at her determination.

'The only time I ever seen him angry, was years ago when *those two* called at our house.'

'I take it you mean Henderson and Montgomery?' replied Jackson, having done his research prior to the visit. Susan's tone turned ominous.

'Yes, that's them,' she said, holding onto a tiny gold cross that hung on a fine chain around her neck.

'If I weren't a Christian, I would tell you what I thought of those nasty people.'

'What happened the time they called?' enquired Jackson.

'Willie wouldn't let them in the door! They started arguing and raising their voices. I never told Willie I heard everything. They threatened him, and told him to keep his mouth shut and that he wouldn't be a part of their set up!'

'Set up? What did that mean?'

' I don't know, and I never asked,' replied Susan. 'But I was glad he wouldn't have anything more to do with them. We never heard from them again, or at least as far I knew.'

She was drained, slumping back in her seat after her revelations.

'Susan, you've been very co-operative and helpful, thank you. If you remember anything else, please give me a call,' said Jackson handing her a card.

'I will, son, I promise. Are you sure you don't want a cup of tea before you go?'

'Thanks, but we're fine. We have to get back to the station.'

Jackson and his partner headed for the door out of the living room, reassuring Susan, they would let themselves out, before she got up to see them out. After farewells, they walked down the path towards their car.

'Oh,' shouted Susan. 'Did I mention his nightmares?'

The pair stopped in their tracks before rushing back, the female producing her notebook.

'Nightmares?'

'Yes. He's had them most of our married life. He refused to look for medical help. He talked in his sleep sometimes when he was having them.'

'Can you remember anything he said,' asked Jackson, his detective intuition kicking in.

'He kept saying he was sorry, and he should have done more to help.'

Jackson waited for more, but when he realised that was all Susan had to say, he reluctantly pressed further. 'Do you know who he was talking to...or about what?'

'Oh yes,' she replied with an air of confidence. 'That poor man Jackie Smallwood, who's grave he would visit each month.'

~

Back in Hastings Street RUC a few hours later, McDermott sat with the other of his deputy sheriffs. They had regrouped outside of the fish bowl, using the larger tables to accommodate pictures, files and notes.

'Like I was saying Captain,' said Douglas over the brim of his glasses. 'No trace of a murder weapon, although there were specs of blood on the gravel.'

'Did you get a match?' inquired McDermott.

Douglas sighed without responding.

'Hamilton's blood?' McDermott suggested.

Douglas wore a tired grin of confirmation.

McDermott's frustration spilled over. 'Jesus Christ! We need a break here...somewhere!'

Douglas retained silence as McDermott opened up the yellowing file with the name *'Smallwood'* emblazoned on it. He sat for a few minutes pouring thoughtfully through the decaying documents. Douglas broke the silence.

'Penny for your thoughts?'

'There's something not right here, Doug. I mean, of the three remaining UDA founders, Hamilton was the *last* one I would've put money on to be murdered. But why him? Why the twenty odd year gap?'

'I think we can rule out a serial killer?' proposed Douglas.

'At this minute, we can't rule anything out.'

The dour mood was interrupted by Jackson entering the room. McDermott looked at him in anticipation and hope of a breakthrough.

'Anything Jacko?'

Jackson deliberated, as usual, and made himself comfortable, before opening his notebook.

'For a change, the locals in Rathcoole estate were very helpful and talkative. He was well respected. I was even invited into the lair of Hamilton's second in command, Trevor Richards.'

Douglas whistled through his teeth. 'You're taking a chance there, big lad.'

'You would think so, Doug, but there seems to be a determination to help apprehend the murderer. I asked about rivalries, long running feuds, even extra martial affairs. It seems Hamilton was a decent godfather.'

'What about his wife?' interrupted McDermott.

'God love her, although she was understandably upset, she was very helpful.'

Jackson paused and flicked through his notebook, re-reading a passage inwardly before addressing the others.

'There was something Captain, although I'm not sure if it's any help?'

'Try me.'

'It seems he has had nightmares for years. Talked in his sleep and was always full of remorse. He kept saying he was sorry and that he didn't do more to help.'

Douglas asked, 'Did she know he was talking to?'

'Yeah. One of the founding fathers, Jackie Smallwood.'

'The grave he was at!' said Douglas.

McDermott flicked through Smallwood's file reacquainting himself with the case. On each yellowed page there were a series of his original notes. Jackson leant his head to the side, his brow furrowed. 'Does this mean anything?' he questioned.

For the next 10 minutes, McDermott and Douglas related the murder case of Smallwood, explaining how it was blamed on the Provos and how Hamilton was one of the last three people to see him alive.

'Jesus, you might have been right all along,' mused Douglas. 'Unfortunately, there's no way the Superintendent would reopen an historical case on the strength of an emotional widow's testament to her husband's sleep talking. But bring those two clowns in for an interview regarding Hamilton's murder. They'd better have good alibis.'

There was an uplifting air in the briefing room with this revelation.

'If we're all done here lads,' said McDermott gathering up his paperwork.

'It'll be a few days before we get a full forensics report and the autopsy will be longer,' Doulas said. 'But I managed to talk to their team leader at the sight. His early estimation is that we're looking for someone between 5' 6" and 5' 10".'

Jackson smiled before replying. 'We're so lucky to have modern technology on our side. We've narrowed our suspect down to half the population.'

McDermott couldn't resist a wry grin.

'Lads, I know it goes against the grain to use precious resources to trap some lunatic who has done the population a great favour, but it's our job. In the words of Baden Powell, *'we will do our best.'*

The others nodded in agreement before Jackson made the scout salute. 'Dib-fucking-Dib.'

'Doug, put him back under his rock for the night,' McDermott said, still grinning.

When the others left, McDermott remained at the large table, surveying the room in its semi gloom. The concrete block walls, thinly disguised by layers of sickly green paint, were starting to peel, as they had, since they first felt paint. Despite the gloom, McDermott felt a strength in these familiar surroundings. However grubby, they remained constant. And for what felt like the first time, in a long while, his trained instincts and acumen were reignited. He could *feel* that something was about to happen, that may lead to an historical tidying up. He had an itch he was determined to scratch.

Chapter 20

It was lonely in Patterson's meagre home. Unusually, he had maintained the tidiness and cleanliness of the place, and hadn't given a thought to drink or drugs. He stepped outside the back door to have a smoke; another sign that he was becoming more disciplined. On entering the garage from the side door, he was confronted by a mound of old clothes, pillows sunken in defeat, half used paint tins and hardened brushes, amongst a plethora of other items he would never use again. He dug into the pile and retrieved his Barbour jacket.

'Jeez, this bloody thing cost me a fortune!'

He laid the jacket on the concrete floor, examining it carefully. He'd undertaken this process every day, since the day at the graveyard. The look on Hamilton's face still haunted him. Why had he seemed content? Did he truly believe that his death and sacrifice, would absolve him of all guilt and crimes? Not likely. His mood turned darker, recalling the scenario of his father's death and Hamilton's cowardly role. His body tensed, fists clenched and fury grew. His recently installed, self-discipline kicked in. He took a deep breath and exhaled, oblivious as to how much he had genuinely become his father's son. He thought incessantly about death and the existence of heaven. As much as he was a heretic, he wanted to believe that his mother and father were there together, and in time, they would be all reunited. He understood the appeal of Christianity. Even though it was man made, the hope it emanated, could help make people better than they were, *or* had been.

'But...', he thought. 'After what I've done... will I be accepted? '
He inspected the coat for the hundredth time. He had considered burning it, dismissing the idea, as he may have to explain his actions to someone. Therein, lay a confidence he would never be arrested for his crime. Although that wasn't apparent directly after the event. Patterson plunged into extreme paranoia, glued to the news reports on Hamilton's death, waiting for the phone to ring, or a knock at the door. He imagined everyone staring at him, as he bought newspapers, any newspapers that covered the story. Combing through the Sunday World, a paper synonymous with paramilitary activity, he was delighted to learn of their flimsy undercover theory was one of an internal feud. There wasn't a story anywhere, mentioning sightings or identities, or motives, and more specifically, anything appertaining to him. He focused on the coat again. Any spots of blood, had been covered with gloss paint, mimicking an accidental spillage, rendering it useless to workers at Carryduff Dump.

He re-checked the pockets, ensuring they were empty, before cramming it into a black plastic bag. The other used clothes, were layered on top of it. After filling the remaining bags with the other defunct items, he loaded up the spacious boot of his repaired car. Donning a pair of marigold latex gloves, Patterson moved to a messy workbench at the back of the garage. He opened the top drawer on the bench, to lift out a clear plastic bag sealed at the top. Very carefully, he 'shuffled' the item onto a piece of newspaper. Lifting it by its plastic handles, he examined it.

The handles, and any part of the metal structures that weren't soiled with dried blood, had been diligently cleaned with vinegar, methyalted spirits and baby wipes.

Satisfied, he dropped the scissors into the bag and resealed it.

'Your day will come,' he announced to the closing drawer.

~

'Don't worry about that John, I can help you,' a delighted Shirley sang into the telephone. Patterson had contacted her regarding a visit back to Blackpool during the last ten days of October, prior to returning to work. He confessed he would struggle financially.

'It'll only be until the Insurance money comes through, and some other insurance the Prison Service and MoD have. I'll book the cheapest crossing this week.'

'It's no problem. I'll ring and transfer some money through the building society to your account.' There was a brief but significant pause. 'Is everything...ok with you?'

His reply was calculated.

'I'll be honest Shirley, sometimes I struggle, but am beginning to feel stronger...I think. I miss Andy.'

The last syllable died in his throat.

'Oh, John.'

'No, no... don't worry. Everything's going to be ok. The POA Welfare people have been out, and they're very good. I've also been seeing a counsellor,' he lied.

'God love you. Why don't you transfer to the English service, and live over here? What about Liverpool, or Preston? You'd be able to see the boys every...'

'No Sis, I'm sorry. I can't.'

'But it's dangerous over there. The murder in the news of that man at the graveyard. It was awful.'

There was a longer than normal pause before Patterson replied.

'It wasn't awful.'

She was aware of a distinct change in her brother's tone.

'I have a few ex-police friends, and a guy whose father was a journalist. The one at the graveyard, was one of the last three people to see our father alive.'

Shirley was stunned.

'Are you sure?'

'No doubts. I hope he rots in hell.'

She was shocked at his statement, struggling to reply. She quickly changed the direction of the conversation.

'Look, just make sure you get those tickets booked, ok?'

'Sorry Sis...I didn't mean to sound...'

'It's ok John. I understand. We'll talk more next week. Look after yourself. Love you.'

'You too.'

Patterson replaced the receiver and stared at the phone. Not for the first time in the last week, an image of Orla crept to the fore of his conscious. The sleepy, beautiful Orla he had woken beside. Not the hellcat in prison. He toyed with the idea of ringing her one last time, to finalise the end of their relationship. There was still a part of him that clung to the ridiculous notion, they could somehow make this work. The realisation that she 'belonged' to the most dangerous terrorist in Northern Ireland, beggared belief.

Extraordinarily, he deemed the continuance of their affair as a challenge. Like the challenge when gambling, where he was always sure he would win. His newly discovered discipline, created through adversity, nudged him toward logical assimilation. Albeit warped ideology. He was now on a mission, a mission he was determined to achieve. A mission that, if it included Orla, could be insurmountable. He made his final decision. It was over for good.

Chapter 21

Imogen struggled to occupy herself in the kitchen with the door closed. She worried for her own safety. Her husband had been in a foul mood for days, since being questioned by police in relation to the Hamilton murder.

'Cheeky bastards!' he'd complained relentlessly.

Henderson was holding court in the conservatory with Montgomery, the 'weasel'. Imogen hugged herself tightly for warmth, as even thought of that 'thing' in her home, chilled her to the bone. The sun-tanned wiry frame of Montgomery was almost lost to view on the monstrous couch. Henderson paced the floor, a reddened face and sweat, advertising anger. He stopped in front of his number two, leaning in menacingly.

'What the fuck is going on here? Well? Well?' he roared, his pitch rising.

Montgomery had lost the feeling of being intimidated by Henderson.

'I haven't a Scooby Do,' he replied nonchalantly.

Henderson returned to pacing up and down the arena of the conservatory, getting angrier by the step. Montgomery pulled a packet of Spanish cigarettes from his faded denim jacket, placing one in his mouth, before patting his pockets in search of a lighter. Henderson increased his pace toward him, slapping the cigarette from his wiry lips.

'You're not smoking that funny stuff in my house...you...fucked up faggot!' Montgomery considered explaining it was normal tobacco, but thought better of it.

He glared with narrowed eyes and white lips at the back of the parading Henderson, because of the reference of his sexuality. As he continued pacing over the tiled flooring, Henderson's frustration grew. He stopped and turned toward Montgomery, from the far end of the room.

'Was this anything to do with those UVF wankers?!'

Montgomery, sitting on the edge of the couch, had hands held open in submission.

'I've already spoken to their people. Nothing was sanctioned. The only possibility could be a wild card. But for what reason?'

Henderson regained a modicum of control, sitting in an oversize chair facing him. His face reclaimed its off red colour, and the sweat that 'glued' his sparse clump of hair to his head, dissipated.

Henderson tilted his head to one side, reflecting his curiosity, before questioning his underling.

'Did that big bollocks have a run in with anybody?'

'No, not that I know of. All his brigade commanders in Rathcoole seem to respect him.'

Henderson flopped back in the chair, his feet barely touching the floor. His eyes turned skyward in thought.

'There's another...outside possibility,' Montgomery interrupted Henderson's machinations.

Henderson leaned forward, glaring at Montgomery, his mouth at the usual distinct angle. He replied from its lowest corner.

'Like what?'

Montgomery hesitated, aware of the ramifications of his next remark.

'Maybe...he talked to someone. You know...about…'

Before he could finish the sentence, Henderson leapt from the chair and grabbed him by the lapels.

'No!' he snarled. 'I told you both, that that would never be mentioned again. Understand?!'

He flung Montgomery, who tumbled backwards onto the edge of the couch, and proceeded to bounce off it, colliding with a solitary table that supported an ornate lamp. The lamp shattered when it met the tiled floor. The door to the kitchen burst open and Imogen rushed toward the melee.

'Oh Samuel. Look what you've done!'

Moving toward the debris on the floor and attempting to rescue the fragments, Henderson grabbed her arm tightly, and spun her around to face him. 'Get the fuck out of here!' he growled with an intensity that announced his request was non-negotiable. She obliged without protest, aware of the pain in her arm and fearful of further treatment later. Montgomery picked himself up and tried to re-establish his decorum. He re-took his seat as Henderson resumed pacing. After a short bout of nervous silence, Henderson stopped in front of the seated Montgomery, who braced himself for any further assault.

'Here's the way it is.'

Montgomery was acutely aware this was not going to be a discussion.

'We have a problem here. A problem that needs to be fixed. Change the focus of attention. You *know* what has to be done.'

Montgomery's jaw dropped in amazement.

'Holy shit Bulldog...you're not serious? The Provos will go apeshit!'

'They're our fucking business partners!'

Henderson adopted a calm resolution.

'I'm deadly serious. Fuck the Provos. Fuck business. This is survival. Organise it.'

~

Tuesday was normally a quieter night in both the Republican and Loyalist enclaves, scattered across the city. This one, quieter than normal. Thanks to ridiculously sized television aerials, the citizens of Belfast could access RTE television from the south, including sporting events not available on BBC or ITV. Celtic were playing CS Hobschied of Luxembourg in a third round, second leg, European Cup qualifying match. Paradoxically, the number of viewers in both camps were close to equal. Every Loyalist bar and Rangers Supporters Clubs, were at full capacity, the patrons supporting any team that might cause Celtic's demise. Unable to properly pronounce the name of the obscure team, the Loyalists had adopted the name *Hob Shite*, screaming the name when they scored a vital away goal in the last five minutes. At this point, Celtic were going out having lost the away game 0-1, making their current accumulative score of 2-2 irrelevant, because of the away goals. Fingers nails of both religions, were whittled to the core. An eerie hush descended upon both camps, as the tension mounted. Loyalists shouted at the television for the referee to blow the whistle, whilst Republicans prayed for a miracle. In the Shamrock Bar on Flax Street, a sea of green and white jerseys rose like a tidal wave, every time their team went forward.

In the ninety-first minute, as the referee glanced at his watch, a long hopeful ball was latched onto by a Celtic forward. He danced through two defenders and sized up a shot as he entered the penalty box. The opposing centre half slid in to clear the ball, but accidentally took out the attacker. Every Celtic supporter in Belfast erupted into an ear shattering crescendo of 'Penalty!'

Hearts sank in the loyalist areas. However, the noise abated over the city, when the referee blew his whistle, and walked over to confer with the linesman. The commentator suggested, as the referee pointed to his watch, whilst in deep conversation, that the whistle may have been for full time. Instead, he blew his whistle again, pointing to the penalty spot. The noise levels went stratospheric as Celtic supporters screamed *'yes'* whilst jumping up and down hugging each other. The noise abruptly vanished as the Celtic forward placed the ball on the spot. Some turned away, crossing themselves repeatedly, whilst others closed their eyes, unable to withstand the drama unfolding on the box. Rosary beads were held and kissed, pleas to Jesus, Mary and God were muttered incessantly, by the brave remainder transfixed on the action. The forward blasted the penalty, the keeper saved it, sending the Loyalist side of the city into raptures. Stopping the ball from entering the net, he managed to push it onto the post. It rebounded straight back, hitting his shoulder and rolled over the goal line. The euphoria of the Celtic players celebrations and the heartbreak of the Hobschied side, were mirrored in each faction's drinking dens. 'The Fields of Athenry' erupted in a semi-shouting attempt of singing, in the Shamrock, the drinking resuming with aplomb. The barman grinned as his till became bloated and the pipes drained. He spied a few younger clients of a disputable age swallowing pints like they were going out of fashion. He gave them a one more pint, leeway. The cacophony died down as the happy patrons drifted out.

Three of the underage drinkers hugged and said their final farewells at the corner of Ardoyne Avenue, before staggering their separate ways. The youngest of all didn't notice how quiet it was at this time of night. He tried to formulate a plan of getting home and into bed, before his mother knew he had been drinking. He struggled to stay on the pavement as he weaved along Flax Street toward Herbert Street, mouthing the words to 'Athenry' in a, now, broken voice. A car pulled up beside him, it's colour indistinguishable under the yellow street lights. The youngster contorted his features, struggling to focus. The driver, wearing a Celtic top wound down the passenger window. A slow wide grin spread over the young lad's face.

'Here, mate, how did the match finish?' enquired the driver. 'I'd to take my bloody wife into work!'

The young lad staggered over to the open window, leaning in to talk.

'Ah no way. No way. You missed it? Let me tell you... it was brilliant!'

The driver produced a pillow that he held in front of him. The young lad laughed.

'Pillow? What's that all about?' he continued, before jolting backward as four rounds rattled into his chest.

~

McDermott was at his desk in the fishbowl. Jackson faced him while they read over reports about the shooting.

'Take it the Doug's up at the scene Jacko?'

'Yeah', Jackson replied with a glum sigh. 'And the car they found burnt out, over in the Shankill, we're assuming was the one involved.'

McDermott wore a grave expression, with eyes that looked serious.

'That lad had only just turned seventeen for Christ's sake!'

They sat in silence for a while, ingesting the information.

'I'm confused, Captain'

'Why so?'

Jackson exhaled before lifting the evidence files.

'The UDA have claimed the killing in response to Hamilton's murder. I have spoken to all the handlers, and not one of them has reported anything. Their insiders haven't even heard a rumour about it.'

The return to the vacuum of solutions settled in again. McDermott stroked his beard, calculating his thoughts. He grabbed the yellowing folder from the cabinet and placed it open on the table.

'Smallwood, the closed case we discussed before.'

Jackson looked confused, as he nibbled his lip before pouring through the file.

'That's right Captain, Hamilton is mentioned here as well. Do you think there's a connection?' McDermott hesitated before answering.

'I have a hunch Jacko. Police intuition and all that.'

He paused for a second and thought it could well be frustration, and that his time in the service was running out.

'Your report of Hamilton's behaviour at night, his nightmares and apologies, convince me he didn't murder Smallwood. Which leaves Henderson, and, or Montgomery, though my money's on Henderson. Who coincidentally, inherited the UDA leadership, soon after Smallwood's murder around twenty years ago. His position means that only he, could sanction that horrific, senseless killing of an innocent teenager.'

Both became embroiled in animated conversation, focusing on the two remaining founder members.

'I need to speak to the Superintendent about surveillance, especially on Henderson.'

'Bad news Captain. I was speaking to one of the E4a guys yesterday. They've had a team shadowing Henderson for almost a year now.'

'And?'

'Nothing. In the eyes of the law, he's as clean as a whistle. They've checked business accounts, savings, you name it. He doesn't come across as a book keeper, but everything is in order.'

'I know he's something to do with this!' McDermott replied, slamming his fist into his other hand. 'I'll talk to the Super anyway.'

Jackson sighed; aware he was about to deliver a stumbling block to McDermott's ambitions.

'E4a were relieved of their babysitting duties, due to further terrorist activity. They were also made aware, it was 'inefficient usage of resources'... on the Super's recommendations.'

McDermott pushed his chair back in disgust. 'Prick! Too involved in trying to climb the promotion ladder! Licking the arse of the paymaster for his own benefit, and bollocks to any poor sod who seeks justice or protection!'

Jackson nodded respectfully before standing to leave. McDermott lifted his head from the cradle of his hands and eyed him with desperation. 'We need a break, Jacko......or a miracle.'

Jackson's face was resolute as he turned to walk away. When he got closer to the door, he started to hum the song *'I believe in miracles.'* McDermott momentarily glared at him, before blurting out laughter.

Chapter 22

Homework was complete. An article in the Irish News, had covered the formation of the UDA, and where the leaders were now. They had also hinted at a link between his father's and Hamilton's murders. It provided the smoke screen required. More importantly, they had sent a reporter to the home of Henderson, who was practically set upon by a large white Alsatian. Patterson had driven the route past his house on a number of occasions, happy to learn Henderson's feeling of invincibility, bar an electronic gate, had led to minimal security.

The BMW wasn't out of place as Patterson parked under the shadow of a tree in Kathleen Avenue. It was 8pm and the October sky had already succumbed to the night. Patterson took a deep breath, acutely aware of any pedestrians. None appeared. A few items stuffed into a small dark backpack. Everything about him was dark. His coat, trousers, shoes and gloves. Prior to leaving the car, he filled his lungs with air. Not to instill courage, for he felt no fear. He thought about his father, and those thoughts had brought him back to life. He still smoked on occasions, but all other former vices had been shelved.

'You have given me a purpose, Dad,' he uttered, looking up to the inside roof, before exiting the vehicle. There was a few hundred yards to cover, before he reached the junction to Fort Road. Surveying the surroundings, Patterson edged past Henderson's mansion, only the roof visible, due to the height of Laurel hedging. He passed the entrance gate, before turning into Grey Point. With no street lamps, this was a place was safety.

On carrying out reconnaissance in daylight, he noted the first two houses on the left were for sale, and also shared a hedgerow with Henderson's place, meaning they too were in darkness. Patterson bolted across the large lawn of the second of the empty houses, and nestled himself in the Laurel hedging. As this house was perpendicular to Henderson's, he found easy access to the far left-hand corner of Henderson's huge lawn. He surveyed the house from a distance. It was enormous, a conglomeration of huge colourless blocks. A garage to the left with a wall attached to the main building, and a door at its end. The only illumination upstairs, was a landing light creeping through an open bedroom door. On the ground floor was an enormous conservatory, and a brightly lit modern kitchen. The lights failed to extend to Patterson's hiding place.

He eyed a squat, pug like Henderson, pointing in anger at a thin woman, before she disappeared into what appeared to be a giant couch. Henderson stomped away from view. Moving slowly to remove his backpack in the confines of the hedge, Patterson froze. An animal brushed up against his leg. He returned to breathing, as he shooed the cat away. Within seconds, angry incessant barking came from behind the wall. The side door of the house behind the wall opened, as the motion detection light at the front of the house came to life. 'Fuck up barking!' Patterson heard Henderson holler at a dog that ignored him, increasing its intensity. He heard thumping sounds followed by whining. The door in the wall opened, and Patterson caught a glimpse of Henderson's silhouette, before he stepped onto the back lawn. Four motion detectors light up the lawn like a football stadium. Patterson covered his face with his black suede gloves, peeking through fingers. The combined light stretching to the giant hedge.

'You! You wee bastard!' Henderson growled.

Patterson was seconds away from fleeing, but noticed that Henderson was shouting in the direction of the black and white cat, that sprinted for cover. He watched Henderson go back through and close the door, before hearing him shout into the open door of the house.

'That fucking cat is back again. I'm going to shoot it! I'm taking the dog out for a walk. Have my dinner ready when I get back!'

The door slammed and the gravel beneath Henderson's feet crunched, as he and the dog left. Patterson made an instant decision. He raced over to the shadow of the wall, through the brilliant lights. Leaning back against it, he clung to the wall, as a door opened in the conservatory. Oblivious of his presence, the woman called out to the hedges.

'Here Matthew,' she repeated in the same tone as a Sunday school teacher. 'C'mon boy!'

The cat trotted across the lawn and the woman knelt to stroke it, before picking it up and returning inside. Patterson advanced through the door in the wall and opened the side door to the house. He found himself in a huge utility room. Ignoring it's grandeur, he removed the backpack, retrieving the scissors from their plastic coffin, whilst scanning the room for a hiding place. He assumed the door to his left must be the entrance to the house. A series of cupboards attached to the walls surrounding him, and worktops with sinks and cupboards sat below.

Quietly setting the bag down, Patterson eased his frame onto the worktop that faced him. He reached on top of the wall-based units, and groped for a flat space. The amount of dust on his glove advertised the perfect, untouched location. He offloaded the scissors, then came to a frightening standstill. The woman's voice grew louder as she approached from the kitchen. Realising he was about to be caught, Patterson scoured his options. Make a run for it or hide? The decision was made for him, when the door to the utility room opened. Now behind the door, Patterson stood statuesque without breathing. The woman turned on a light and motioned to her right, before getting to her knees and opening a lower cupboard door.

'I know what you're after Matthew,' she purred.

The cat that had followed her in, ambled past the opened door and stared directly at Patterson standing motionless on the opposing workplace. Patterson thought he'd been caught by nothing but a mere feline, until the cat dismissed him and returned to its provider. The woman produced a box of dry cat food and filled a bowl, setting it on the kitchen floor. It munched greedily on the crunchy treats. The woman replaced bowl and ushered the cat out, before finally closing the door.

Patterson, now in darkness, took a few controlled, nervous breaths, fighting the urge of gasping for the air his lungs craved. When the woman's voice was barely audible, he grabbed his bag and kept to the shadows. He crept out of the utility room, and on through the hedge of the 1st unoccupied house. Patterson felt calm as he drove home, paranoia a distant memory.

His plan had begun for real. And tomorrow morning, he would revisit his sister and have some quality time with her and his nephews. He ignored the part of his brain that hinted, that this would be for the last time.

~

McGuigan sat in his own personal visiting area, conversing with a downbeat Nugent in Gaelic.

'Barney, I fully understand the lack of information coming through. It's always the way after an 'event'. These wankers increase their security awareness for a couple of days before the boring routine once more relaxes their tongues. I can wait.'

Nugent shrugged, feeling he had failed his leader.

'At least we know he'll back to work soon,' he stated.

'I know' replied McGuigan, his network of 'supposedly trusted' orderlies, overhearing that information.

'How's she doing?'

Nugent had been dreading being questioned about Orla.

'Everything seems ok. She doesn't go out much mind, apart from her Mum's. She's doing a few extra shifts in the charity shop and the occasional run to the supermarket. '

'Does she have visitors?'

'Yeah, sometimes. A few of the other lads' wives called round for a girlie night in.'

'Anything else?' McGuigan asked. Nugent was fully aware of what he was talking about.

'No. Nothing.'

He was answering the question that referenced the phone tapping, and hidden microphones McGuigan had insisted upon. McGuigan hated himself for knowing he had to do this. How isolated and frightened he knew she must be feeling. He was also walking a tightrope, using group funds for personal domestic problems. He would sort it out with her in a fortnights time, when his case collapsed. Sitting in silence, a silence Nugent dare not interrupt, he contemplated the other side of that deadly coin. She had betrayed him by sleeping with the enemy. These were the more predominant of his thoughts. His disciplined training knowing full well, he would have to ensure she hadn't betrayed him as a soldier. It was expected from the senior council, and he would deliver. He prayed that after interrogation, she would learn to love him again.

'Have you called with her?' he asked, breaking his silence.

'I was there this morning. She was hoping for a visiting pass for Saturday. She looks broken my friend.'

McGuigan paused for a few, long seconds.

'No. No visitors pass. Continue to make sure she is under scrutiny whenever she leaves the house.'

Nugent nodded in agreement.

'Any other business?'

'Yeah, the army council are planning retribution for the shooting on Tuesday night.'

McGuigan was calculated in his response.

'About time. '

The two stood, as an officer approached with a visiting slip, embracing briefly but long enough for McGuigan to whisper, 'keep her safe.'

Nugent nodded as they shook hands, before walking their separate ways.

Chapter 23

Orla felt she was in a prison cell, sitting on the settee with the dog asleep on her lap. She had discovered that she was being monitored every minute of the day. When she went to the local shop, the same bunch of teenagers were there. The car parked constantly outside her house that would follow her to the charity shop, her mother's house, *everywhere*. Did they think she was stupid? Or had they deliberately made it obvious? Was this part of the psychological torture she had to endure, prior to the physical she knew would eventually follow? The refusal of visiting passes concreted her assumptions.

Her thoughts drifted back to the early days of her marriage. She had won the golden ticket in Padraig McGuigan. The young firebrand destined to rise through the ranks. The envy of many. Then she recalled the mysterious meetings, having to walk the dog, and being temporarily ex-communicated from her own home. The absences that dare not be questioned, and the constant police searches. She had been reduced to a trinket on McGuigan's charm bracelet. He was once a great lover, but his marriage and loyalty to the organisation, reduced her to nothing short of an occasional mistress.

Inevitably, she thought of John, regretting not holding him for every second they had spent together. Making love every minute they had had. Why did he have to be a Prison Officer?! If he had been a soldier or policeman, they could have still been together. She accepted it was fanciful to think it could have worked out; existing in two polar opposite worlds. There was an iron clad probability, that it would have been doomed in the end.

She clung onto the premise of the typical American screenwriter's rom-com formula, like the film she loved the most. *Sleepless in Seattle*. Boy gets girl, loses girl, secures girl and lives happily ever after. But her life wasn't a film. And this wasn't America. She would never meet John at the top of the Empire state building. They wouldn't run away and live together in that huge expanse of a country.

'This is tiny fucking Ireland!' she hissed through tears.

Her dreams were in tatters. Her life in danger. Any aspirations, disappeared like water on a beach. Not only had she lost the man she truly loved, but had lost her slim hope of escape.

She looked to the phone in the hall. She had sat for hours, dedicating herself to the plastic- moulded god, praying for it to ring. She now despised it, having never been more alone, concluding that her only hope of survival was to plan her own escape.

~

An agitated Henderson, walked his dog down to the seafront, and along a path toward Crawfordsburn. It was mid- Saturday morning, the sun offering light more than heat, sitting low in the sky. Still no response from the Provos. He had an excuse already compiled, hoping the lucrative side to their joint 'business' partnership could convince them, it remains intact. Some innocent within his organisation would be knee-capped, and blamed for the killing of the young Catholic. He would solemnly swear it had been a renegade and nothing like it would ever happen again.

'Yeah,' he thought to himself, 'that'll keep the bastards happy.'

Other dog walkers turned and moved away from Henderson when he unleashed the dog, running and barking like it was possessed. There had been many incidents of Snow attacking other animals, but although some were naively reported to the dog warden and the police, there was no follow up proceedings, due to witnesses retracting their statements. Henderson produced a rubber ball, the dog whining and howling for him to throw it. Thus began the constant process of retrieval and throwing, as they moved up the beach to its natural end, an outcrop of rock adorned with grass areas on top, and the path to Crawfordsburn. Henderson struggled for breath, as the dog dropped the ball at his feet constantly. Long. Sticky, strands of saliva swinging uncontrollably from its impressive jaws, its tail flailing in anticipation.
'Right! Last one.'
He threw the ball over the edge of the outcrop toward the whin and gorse bushes and the grass area. When the dog chased the ball, he sat down regaining his breath whilst looking across Belfast Lough. It was eerily still, with occasional white triangles of yachts dancing in time, with the meagre breeze. Belfast as a whole, appeared normal and peaceful, and not the beast it had become, due to the troubles. His tummy rumbled for food. He called the dog.
'Snow! Here boy!'
Without as much as a barked reply, Henderson resorted to whistling. Two fingers curled his tongue, as he exhaled an ear-piercing sound. Some joggers on the path above, jumped back in fright and looked at him in surprise.

'What the fuck are you looking at?' Henderson growled toward them. They moved on hesitantly.

Henderson clambered onto the tarmac path from the beach and took a few welcome gulps of air, before heading to the top of the outcrop. 'Here boy! Here boy!' he continued to shout. He moved onto the grassy area toward the sea, careful not to stand in one of the many hidden ravines covered by the grass and bushes. A few yards further on, he noticed the hind legs of Snow, protruding from behind a whin bush.

'Getting too old for all this running about, are you boy?'

With no reaction from the dog, Henderson hesitated, self-preservation thoughts dominating his mind.

'Snow?' he barely whispered.

After a few more steps, Henderson spotted the dog in the prone position. Its tongue hung out, it's eyes glassy, and a dark red dot in between its eyes, where a bullet had entered its skull. Blood trickled down its furry face. The ball lay beside its head.

'What the fuck...' Henderson started to say, before his speech was interrupted by the feeling of cold steel against the back of his neck. One of the former joggers walked in front of him, pointing a pistol fitted with a silencer, into his face.

'Don't make a sound. Do exactly what I say, and your miserable life will last a little while longer,' explained the gunman in a deadpan, Irish accent.

Outraged and unfamiliar with being ordered, Henderson retaliated, his mouth growing into the ugly sloping shape, as he hissed through his teeth, 'Do you know who I am?'

Henderson's bravado was cut short, whenever the gunman reversed his pistol, ramming the metal handle directly into Henderson's nose, that depressed with a sickening snap, as cartilage beneath the skin ruptured. Blood flowed in torrents from both nostrils. Henderson bent down in panic and pain. Whenever he raised his head, the gunman pressed the silencer hard against his skull. His tone, more menacing than before.
'Don't test us!'

~

Shirley sat with her brother at the breakfast table. The boys, still in pyjamas, were glued to the children's television programme, *Going Live*, squealing with laughter at Trevor and Simon clowning around, whilst Philip Schoefield tried, unsuccessfully to restore order.
Patterson smiled with admiration at the boys.
'They're going to make you proud someday Shirley.'
Without turning her attention away from them, she placed her hand on top of her brothers. 'I know. Hopefully as proud as you have made me, wee man.'
Patterson's smile grew wider.
'Wise up wee girl,' he teased in his roughest Belfast accent.
'We're going to miss you when you go, you know that don't you?'
Patterson nodded.
'John...you've changed.'
Patterson ordered his thoughts before replying.
'You think so?'

'Not in a bad way or anything. I feel… there is a peace in you now, where there once wasn't, …if you know what I mean?'

Patterson looked straight into Shirley's eyes. 'I know exactly what you mean. It's because, well... I think so anyway, because I now know who I am. My life feels more structured. I have definitely got a better sense of self-discipline. I've got the drinking and gambling under wraps.'

She smiled and moved to hug him. 'All we need now, is to get you a beautiful English woman, who will persuade you to move over here.'

'She'll not be handsome, she'll not be pretty, she'll not be a girl from Belfast City,' he sang.

'Away off with you.' Shirley replied, playfully punching him in the arm.

Patterson leapt to his feet and shouted to the boys.

'You too hallians better be ready whenever I count to one hundred, or you'll not be up at the top of Blackpool tower with me today.'

The boys looked at one another. Richard raced to turn the TV off, whilst Patrick shouted to his uncle. 'Count slowly, Uncle John.'

'Too late', he replied, uttering a deep throated growl. 'One...see it's already started'

The boys squealed with excitement, clambering over each other in their race upstairs. Patterson shouted upstairs. 'Two.'

'You torture them,' Shirley said, through a smile.

'Sure, they love it.'

'Aw, and it's me that has to bring them back down to earth.'

Shirley turned to him.

'I wished you didn't have to go home tonight.'

She began to ascend the stairs before pausing and turning. 'John, there's something I've been wanting to say to you.'

He looked at her with his eyebrows scrunched downward, his senses heightened.

'When we spoke last week on the phone, and I mentioned the murder in the cemetery, your reply scared me a wee bit.'

Patterson took time to ingest what had been said, before replying.

'And I meant every word of it,' he stated in a steady, low-pitched voice

Shirley hesitated.

'God forgive me for saying this, but I've done nothing but think about it since then. If he were party to our father being murdered...then I would agree with what you said.'

As tears welled in her eyes, Patterson rushed to hold her in his arms.

'Don't get upset. It's only human to feel that way. Let me be the angry one.'

Chapter 24

The once proud dictator, was in the back seat of a black Audi, sandwiched between two gunmen with pistols on their laps, aimed toward him. In the front beside the driver, was the gunman responsible for his restructured nose. His only luxury, a once white handkerchief, now dyed red with his own blood. Henderson was engrossed with what had gone before.

They had dragged him off the path and into the thick forest, before stopping at a shallow grave. He'd been convinced, it was the end, but it was for his dog, not him. He had stood in disbelief and sorrow, as his prized animal was cast into the hole, unceremoniously covered by dirt and branches. Selfishly, he was glad it was the dog, and not him. Frustration had somehow rendered him oblivious to the danger he was fully immersed in. It was too surreal to be *actually* happening. He was more familiar to getting his own way. He understood the psychology of being a permanent aggressor. It weakened the opposition or those with any doubts. He was a true General. Nobody had ever stood up to him. Except once, at the earliest stages of his campaign. He had adjusted and immediately solved that problem, as powerful Generals do. He was aware of a spark in his subconscious, that the historic individual act of defiance, might be returning to haunt him.

His journey past Holywood toward the city centre was a living example of the juxtaposition he was immersed in. *This is my kingdom*, he mused driving past Palace Barracks toward Sydenham. The two giant, yellow monolithic cranes of Harland and Wolfe shipyard, came into view on his right.

The entrance to East Belfast. He had been furiously devising opportunistic attempts at possible escape along the route, before accepting the futility of it. Yet, he also had a growing inner confidence.

'If they intended to kill me, why am I not already dead?'

He was self-assured he would be given an opportunity to negotiate his way out of trouble. He had danced with these devils before, and treaded on their toes. He could do it again. Irrespective of their political values, they couldn't exist without heavy funding. This was his bargaining chip. They drove past Short Strand onto the Queens Bridge, before turning left onto Oxford Street. At the next Junction, past the Royal Courts of Justice, the car turned right onto May Street, taking them past the back of the City Hall. When they halted at traffic lights with the junction of Adelaide Street, the front passenger turned around.

'Look at me, and listen very carefully. When I tell you to get out, walk to the first bench on your left through the front gates of the City Hall. You then sit on the far-left end of it. Do you understand?'

A defiant Henderson nodded.

'Get out!'

The two minders in the back seat rushed out of the car, and disappeared in opposite directions, quickly swallowed up by pedestrian traffic, on a busy Saturday afternoon. As soon as Henderson disembarked, the car drove off. He crossed the road to the south-eastern corner of the city hall Grounds, walking along Donegall Square East, oblivious to the strange looks, because of the dried blood on his face.

His demeanour determined, no-one glanced for too long. Turning left onto Chichester Street and through the black wrought iron gates, he located the bench he had been directed to. The grass areas that enclosed the city hall were crisscrossed with marble paths, allowing visitors and citizens to gaze at the myriad of statuesque artworks, dotted throughout the grounds. Sitting on the bench, he witnessed the maelstrom of the public, as hordes of shoppers rushed and bustled along Donegall place. Only a scattering took respite in this magnificent rest haven. His senses were on full alert, observing as much as he could. Teenagers arm in arm. Pensioners on a bench opening flasks of tea. Turning back to look toward Donegall Place, he was aware of an older gentleman, now seated at the far end of his bench. He wore a dark over coat, and a black fedora was perched on his head, allowing glimpses of his sterling silver, manicured hair. He held a plastic bag full of bread crumbs causing the pigeons around his feet to coo their approval.

'Continue to look down Donegall Place and nowhere else. You are being observed.' stated the old man with a gentle, yet determined, tone.

'What's this all about?' replied Henderson, now locked on the main shopping thoroughfare.

'I'm sure you're aware,' was the resolute reply.

Henderson had dreaded this impasse, but was glad he had rehearsed his speech.

'I can explain...'

'NO, YOU CAN'T!'

There was a lull in the conversation, as a proud young couple wheeled their new born past, oblivious to the dire circumstances of the situation they had stumbled upon. The old man smiled with warmth in his eyes, at them, continuing his tirade when they were out of earshot.

'We have categorically no involvement, at any level whatsoever, in the murder of one of your gorillas!' the old man continued. 'Unlike yourselves, and the sectarian execution of an innocent teenager.'

Henderson grasped the severity of the conversation. His whimsical 'alibi' now useless. The old man took his time between speeches, letting the enormity of their importance sink in.

'The cold-hearted British Press are labelling this murder as… a 'knee jerk' reaction. How convenient for them. I wonder if that's what his grieving parents will put on his headstone. *'Death by knee jerk reaction?'*

The old man's focus returned to feeding the birds. Henderson was bereft of a new strategy, *any* strategy.

'We are well aware that this isn't the first time your organisation has created a 'smoke screen' by murdering innocents to disguise your own barbaric actions.'

The blood drained from Henderson's face. He turned deathly pale, in the knowledge that the enemy might have known of his past demeanours. One in particular.

'We never forget, and are now better prepared and equipped than in the 60's. Your debt will be repaid in full, …sometime. Only there will be no innocents.'

He paused for full effect.

'You and the rest of your gangsters, are under surveillance 24 hours a day. Be careful to look over your shoulder.'

Driven by the potential loss of income Henderson pleaded. 'What about our...you know...arrangement?'

The old man stifled a hint of a laugh.

'*Former* arrangement you mean!' he snapped. For the first time, he stared at Henderson, with intimidating pale grey eyes. 'Any agreement that once existed is now formally terminated. We will assume all of your interests. You will then have time to put your house in order. Do it, and do it quickly.' The old man folded the plastic bag and slipped it into a coat pocket. He rose to leave in silence, and looked skyward, before turning to walk away.

Henderson struggled to raise his heavy frame.

'Wait! How am I meant to get home?'

The old man stopped, without turning to face him. 'At this moment in time, I would suggest, that is the least of your worries.'

~

'Oh my god! What happened?' cried Imogen, as Henderson burst through the front door. She eyed the mess where his nose once was.

'Never mind that! I need money for the taxi.'

'A taxi? Samuel, what's happened?' she repeated.

'Just get me some fucking money!' With trembling hands, she clawed two £20 notes from her purse, and Henderson snatched them off her. Even after all she'd been subject to, she felt frightened and worried. He was still her provider and protector. In fact, he was all she had.

On returning, Henderson walked to the conservatory and slumped into his favourite chair. He plunged his head into his hands and stared at the floor. Imogen approached him with caution, and sat across from him. She had so many questions, and fears. Without looking up, he spoke.

'Don't ask me anything Imogen. I...I...have a few business problems that I need to attend to.' She frowned at Henderson's apologetic tone. He sounded frail and sad, almost defenceless. Raising his head, he spoke to her as tears swamped his eyes. 'The dog ran away. I couldn't find him.' He buried his head into his hands once again, and sobbed like never before. Imogen had witnessed, for the first time in her marriage, that her husband was frightened.

Chapter 25

The Sealink ferry was 90 minutes into the four-hour crossing of the Irish Sea. The 'graveyard' crossing, was headed for Larne. The inky black sea melted into the sky; the horizon indistinguishable. From a distance, the ship was merely a collection of uniformed yellow dots, gliding over a calm sea. Montgomery was sitting, gazing though a porthole at the black sea, fighting the urge to sleep due, to his alcohol intake. It had been four days since the teenager incident, and the lack of response had been palpable. Nothing from the other side or of the sacrificial lamb that Henderson had intended to deliver. 'Maybe Bulldog has already talked to them and agreed something?' he unsuccessfully suggested to himself. He wished this ship was faster so he could get home and talk with someone, *anyone*, to gauge *any* reactions. He had contemplated the idea that their 'doormen' agreement may well come to an end. In fact, more than likely. He had already prepared for that, knowing it was on the horizon. He gave no thought that his life may be in danger, such was the gusto Bulldog has instilled in him.

'The Untouchables,' he said with a smile.

His back-up plan was for their team to go it alone on a different venture. He had already contacted a supplier in Spain, of Turkish descent, who would guarantee him as many tablets and blocks of dope as he wished, along with a safe passage via the Bilbao - Cork route. It was amazing how many of the wee money spinners could be crammed into the inner tube of a spare tyre. And more often than not, when the southern security learned you were en-route to the north, they quickly hustled you through, glad to see the back of you.

There were so many arterial routes on country roads, that made crossing the border, child's play. Montgomery shifted his attention from the porthole to survey the bar area. Like the seating areas throughout the ship, it was depressing. He had intended to get the 5:30 crossing because the Rangers match had had an early noon kick off. Unfortunately, after stopping with his entourage in The Grapes pub in Glasgow, he'd been recognised by the staunchly loyal protestants in attendance, elevating his temporary status to celebrity. They had no idea how he was despised by the majority of the ranks who were 'over there, taking the fight to the fenians.' Everyone wanted to talk to him. Or have Polaroid photographs alongside him. He had illicit proposals of quick sex, with at least three inebriated women, the thought of which made him nauseous, although, he delivered each a passionate kiss on the mouth, protecting his status. His entourage attempted to drink the pub dry when offered a free day. When he gave the signal to leave, his hosts insisted they stay on for a while, so they could be fed and would order a minibus to get them to the ferry on time. Montgomery had to concede to his followers in the name of public relations, although seething inside. The inevitable occurred, even though the minibus driver attempted to break the land speed record, the wait for the later ferry was spent in Custom House Bar in Stranraer.

As his attention flitted around the bar on the ship, he could see his compadres at different stages of inebriation, ranging from paralytic to unconscious. Some slept on the seats of the round cubicles they were in. Others slept on the floor, faces sticking to the rancid carpet. The bar had closed and other passengers quickly moved out, and far away from, this rabble and their farting and snoring and swearing. Lone passengers sat as far apart from the human race as possible, whilst couples remained close, in a protective mood. Any conversation was whispered. Apart from the engine, it was eerily silent. Montgomery needed the toilet again; because of the number of pints, he had consumed throughout the day. He supplemented marijuana for booze for the most part, keeping him within touching distance of reality. He shook as he stood, stretching in between yawning, occasionally bouncing off chairs at the edge of the aisle.

~

From his seat, the stranger carefully monitored Montgomery. He had been patient, waiting until he could be approached alone. He knew everything there was to know about him. The stranger was wearing a reversible jacket, and carrying a micro back pack. The toupee he donned would have been undistinguishable, apart from the different colour of his locks. He alighted from his seat in silence, in order not to disturb the sleeping passengers, and followed Montgomery along the narrow corridor to the toilets. Inside were four urinals. Montgomery occupied the one closest to the corner, with one hand leaning against the wall for stability. The stranger immediately made his way to the one beside him. Montgomery glared at him with one eye wider than the other.

'Can you get any fucking closer?' he snarled.

The stranger smiled, replying in an effeminate voice. 'That's your decision, not mine.'

Montgomery turned to face the stranger, flaccid penis still hanging from his trousers.

'Do I know you?' he asked in a more moderate tone.

'Well...not yet, although you may have bumped into me in the Kremlin bar.'

Montgomery smiled at the mention of his favourite gay haunt, and leant into to kiss the stranger who stood back in protest.

'Whoa, big boy, not here. What do you take me for?'

Montgomery squinted his eyes with a hint of anger.

'Is there nowhere else more private?'

Montgomery's features morphed into a devilish grin.

'Top deck. Two minutes.'

~

Montgomery stood in shadows of the top deck, after making his way back along the length of the ship's walkway to an underpass section. He leant back against the safety railings and produced a marijuana cigarette as the stranger approached.

'A little something to get you in the mood.'

'I don't need anything to get me in the mood,' the stranger purred.

Montgomery lit the cigarette nonetheless, beginning to speak, before the stranger put a finger to his lips. Montgomery inhaled and leaned back as the stranger unbuckled his belt. He lowered his trousers and Montgomery looked to the black sky with a sigh.

'A great end to a shite day,' he thought.

In an instant he felt elevated, almost as if he were in flight. By the time he realised he was, the back of his head crashed against the side of the boat and his unconscious body tumbled into the black abyss of the sea.

The stranger tore off the toupee and hurled it overboard, creating a bald head ringed by auburn hair threatening to grey. He took off his back pack to retrieve a pair of glasses and a cap, before finally reversing his jacket. He looked at the sea for a few minutes, wearing a broad smile full of menace. Once he was satisfied with his act, he relocated to a different, much quieter seating area.

Chapter 26

Patterson felt like a recruit, climbing the concrete stairs from the forecourt toward the corridor, the beginning of the artery that led to the inner world of the jail. He'd been contacted on Sunday by the duty office, explaining that he had a 9am start, and to report directly to the number one Governor's office. He didn't know what to expect, as he walked along the black and white tiled floor that hinted of former grandeur. Directly ahead of him was the 'glass door', the airlock to the 'Circle', and access to all other areas, albeit via other 'air locks'. Circle was a crude description, as it more pentagonal in shape. The officer on duty looked as bored as Patterson had, during his 6-month stint on that accursed grill, a preserve of new recruits. To his right was the key room, where every key had to be signed in, and out of, every day, and be fully accounted for, before anyone could leave. The keys were as important as the numbers of the prisoners' tally. Each class officer, of each landing, in each wing, including the hospital, had to report their numbers, to include those still at court, during the end of the day shift parade. Those numbers had to correspond exactly with the key and control rooms numbers. Patterson stopped at a wooden door opposite the Key Room and tapped on the frosted glass pane, admiring the intricately painted gold serif legend, 'No.1 Governor's Office.'

'Enter,' came a bellowing response in an educated, Yorkshire accent. Patterson obeyed, the Governor alighting from his seat to shake hands. Oliver Bleasdale was a giant of a man, who left an impression on anyone meeting him for the first time.

His cropped black hair, was complimented by his august beard.

Although wearing a casual tweed jacket, simple white shirt and regimental tie, the influence of his career as a major in the Grenadier Guards was obvious. His attire was immaculate. He radiated control and power. Patterson's maverick side that defied authority, had despised the last two Governors he had served under. Pencil pushing Civil Servants, promoted through their mundane regime, demanding to be saluted, and who had no experience, or idea, of the real Prison Service world. Their tenures were short lived. However, he had an immediate respect for Bleasdale, who was fair, honest, and led from the front, during any major incidents. That, and the fact he hated Civil Servants as much as Patterson did.

'Good to have you back young Patterson.' Bleasdale stated.

Patterson was impressed with his vice like handshake and nodded demurely.

'Take a seat,' he invited, as he returned back to his chair around the impressive walnut table.

Patterson nodded a hello to Chief Officer Ramsden, who was already seated at the end of the table.

'You are a sterling Prison Officer and a credit to our Service,' Bleasdale continued.

Patterson's mouth turned down at the corners, as he struggled to ingest the compliment.

'You've come through an awful lot in the last few months. Chief Officer Ramsden and I were unsure if three weeks would have been enough time to recuperate after such a horrendous episode. I could give you a list of so-called officers, who would have 'swung the lead' and made excuses, to be absent to the far side of Christmas.'

'I needed to get back to work, sir. I need to be among people and return to a normal routine. Welfare agreed with me that, therapeutically, it was the best thing I could do.'

Bleasdale nodded in agreement whilst Patterson spoke, more than a hint of admiration on his face. Ramsden spoke, in what appeared to be a rehearsed routine.

'I have suggested to the Governor that your return be phased, two days a week, to let us analyse how you're coping.'

'With all due respect, Chief, I would like be back on a full-time basis. If I find I am struggling, which I doubt, I will report to you straight away.'

The two senior figures glanced at each other momentarily, appearing to have a telepathic conversation, before Bleasdale spoke.

'Ok. However, the next part is non-negotiable. You are being transferred to B wing, where you will undertake general duties. You won't be running a class; you'll be an assistant to the censor and the parcels officer. We're minimizing your contact with paramilitary inmates as much as possible for the interim. Principal Officer MacLean has already been briefed.'

Patterson sat impassively, as he received the news, his thoughts of the loss of added revenue, no longer important. He had a plan which overruled any fears or doubts.

'Thank you, Sir... Chief,' he replied to both as he stood up.

Bleasdale remained seated, his fingers interlocked as his arms rested on the table. He looked contented, his nod announcing the meeting was over. When Patterson left, Bleasdale turned to Ramsden a trace of anger in his voice.

'Why the hell is he not a Senior Officer yet?' he demanded.
'Well Sir, he has a...'
'I don't give a shit about what he has, or has not. I'm using my privilege for the next round of promotions. He *will* be promoted on my recommendation, without having to go through those useless boards!'
'I understand, Sir,'
Bleasdale stared into the middle distance of the office, toward the painting of Queen Elizabeth II, but he didn't focus on it. Ignoring Ramsden, he spoke out loud.
'I know a bloody leader when I see one.'

~

Henderson was frantic with frustrated rage holding the handset of the phone. The caller continued. 'Bulldog, we haven't seen him. He was on the boat with us, and because the stewards had to waken us after the crossing, we just assumed he got off on his own. He must have got picked up by local taxi men.'
'I'll break his back when I get him! Keep looking, and when you find him, make sure he knows the importance of getting over here!'
He slammed the handset back into its cradle. Montgomery was his puppy dog, who never defied his master. It wasn't like him not to keep in constant touch when he was home. He recalled the 'speech' from the senior Provo on Saturday.
'Just be careful to look over your shoulder.'
'Is this the start of it ...or am I being paranoid?' he thought.
Arrogance overtook his mindset, as he decided Montgomery would appear sooner rather than later.

Retrieving a notebook from his pocket, he leafed through it, until he found the number he was after and drove to the payphone at Helen's Bay shops.

'*Malcolmson*,' was the announcement at the other end of the line.

'Bobby it's Sam. We need to have an urgent meeting. The combined council.'

'Why? What's happened?'

Henderson took a calculated breath before replying.

'The leadership is under threat from the Provos, and I don't mean just me.'

'How do you know?'

'I'll explain it at the meeting. We need to bring the Ulster Volunteer Force and Red Hand Commandoes (Loyalist Paramilitary groups) on board.'

'Surely we can sort this without inviting those lunatics to the party?'

'Just do it!' Henderson ordered, 'Thursday night!'

He slammed the receiver back into the handset before Malcolmson could reply.

On the drive back, Henderson pondered the threat. He was more than aware that he, his position, and his Organisation, were teetering on the edge of chaos. He would ensure they were prepared to fight.

~

McDermott was alone in the outer office, unconsciously running his fingers through his hair as a sign of frustration. He had received the full autopsy and forensic reports from the Hamilton murder, earlier. He had taken a break, sitting alone with his thoughts over a coffee, hoping it would help him focus more. He'd found this routine advantageous when tackling a cryptic crossword. If he left it for a while, he would look at the clues with fresh impetus and solve a few more, annoyed they had escaped him in the first instance. One clue often helped open another. But not this time. The forensics were minimal, the autopsy and profile of the assailant, covering too large a catchment. Within the full report was more gloom. No sightings. No unusual behaviour. No reports of cars driven away at speed. No information from informants...on either side. All investigations into Hamilton and potential enemies, had been fruitless. And to cap it all, the only two brought in for questioning, had iron clad alibis.

'Must have been a ghost', he hopelessly thought.

His police instinct hinted, that Henderson and Montgomery had something to do with this, but couldn't request to the Superintendent that they be recalled again for questioning because of his hypothetical claims. He had narrowed down the profile of the killer to one of two types. He, or she, was either a professional, due to the lack of forensic evidence and their disappearing like smoke on windy day. Or someone got lucky, *very* lucky.

'What I am missing here?'

He returned his attention back to the reports

Chapter 27

Coat over her head, protecting the hair she had spent an hour coiffeuring, Orla held the basket that contained Gleoite, close to her chest. The rain was incessant. At a brief glance, she was able to define the dark shape of the car, waiting to follow her. She was tired of being baited. Her desire to run and complete her escape was growing steadily. There was now a time limit. Her husband was due in court next week, when he would be released, because of the lack of witnesses. She needed to get away. The continuity of tracking her movements, was making opportunities disappear by the minute. She considered running away at night, but as she peered through her curtains in the dark, she saw a car with two glowing cigarettes inside, was parked facing the house. Again. She placed the basket on the passenger seat of her Peugeot 205 Gti, before racing round to the driver's side. The windscreen immediately misted because of body heat, but quickly dissolved when the engine ignited, the heaters kicking in. She loved her little car, as much as her dog. They were the few constants in her life. She was certain her car would easily outrun the battered Ford escort of her constant companions, although convinced, she wouldn't get far. The organisations communications network would be there at some stage along the route to capture her. Her punishment would then be sealed. Window wipers flicked back and forward mercilessly, to clear the windscreen as she drove off towards the Charity Shop on the Falls Road.

~

'Here we go again,' grumbled the spotty teenager in the front passenger seat as their car followed Orla's. 'Never knew the IRA had a babysitting service.'

The older recruit offered a stern look.

'I want to be involved in active service, not this shite!' he continued.

The driver spoke in a grave tone. 'Look son, here's the way it is. We're ordered to do a job and we do it. No questions asked, no complaints. Do you understand?'

The youth heeded the information, nodding in agreement.

'Good. Now stop your gurning.'

~

Orla watched her 'tail' pull into its reserved parking space, on the right-hand side of the Falls Road, directly across from the Charity Shop, facing against the traffic. Turning left into Brighton Street, she parked in a reserved space, immediately to her left that belonged to the flower shop on the corner. She rightly assumed this space, and the reserved one for her 'minders', had been commandeered by her husband's comrades. It also assured that her 'minders' could keep an eye on the tail lights of her car as well as a grandstand view of the shop. At the onset of their watching duties, she'd visited the bakery they were parked in front of, deliberately avoiding eye contact by walking around the rear of their car. When she exited, a bus had pulled up at the stop in front of her shop. She froze momentarily before walking past the front of their parked car, to cross the road.

By doing so, she realised *their* view of her car was blocked, as the bus pulled in. It could be her chance of escaping. She spied unseen from upstairs every time a bus stopped, but was devastated when the view of her tail lights was blocked, one of the 'minders' would walk the short distance past the obstacle to monitor her car, before the bus drove off. She was resigned as to how flimsy her escape plan was, but couldn't conjure an alternative.

Today she was different. Choices no longer an option. She had to escape. Orla raced from the car carrying the dog basket, around the corner, onto the Falls Road, and unlocked the front door to the charity shop. She hung her coat up in the small back kitchen, before retracing her steps into the shop. Flicking on the lights, the weather imitating nightfall, she randomly checked the railings of second-hand clothes on display. She glanced at her watch. *'Two minutes,'* she whispered. Outside, grew darker as the bus blocked any hint of watery light. Orla was now upstairs in a gloomy, converted storeroom. From the second window she observed, unseen, a youth alighting to keep an eye on her car. He didn't look happy in the rain. As soon as the last passenger boarded the bus, the youth rushed back to the car. The bus took a few seconds to re-join the legion of traffic trundling its way toward the city. Orla checked her watch. 'Oh God...30 seconds!' She was terrified at the thought of such a small window, but accepted she'd no other choice.

~

'Jesus Christ that weather's getting worse. We going to have to start using a boat if this keeps up!' the young passenger playfully complained, not wanting to upset his partner further. 'How many buses are on this road?'

The driver chortled, 'Too many. Anyway, skin's waterproof!'

They observed the shop closely, during the following 45 minutes. Only two customers had entered, probably to get out of the rain. The younger passenger, making his scouting trip on three more occasions. Occasionally the light would go in the room above the shop.

'What's up there?' he enquired.

'Storeroom, extra stock and office, along with the safe.'

The driver glanced in the rear-view mirror.

'Stand by for action, Tonto, there'll be a bus along shortly.'

The youngster's mood downturned, knowing he would be re-drenched in a few minutes. He glanced over at the shop window, where he spied Orla talking to a pensioner. She was pointing upstairs. Seconds after disappearing from view, the light went on upstairs. He became mildly excited turning to the driver.

'Hey look! She's away upstairs again and the bus is on its way down the road.'

The driver looked at him with a dead pan expression.

'And your point is?'

'Ok, ok,' the youngster huffed, zipping up his coat.

~

Glancing through the front window, Orla spied a few potential bus passengers taking shelter under the awning of the flower shop next door. She knew the bus was imminent, two minutes at most. Twenty minutes earlier she had made preparations. The back doors of the kitchen and out onto the backstreet, were all unlocked. Gleoite was content in his basket. She deliberately exaggerated her hand gestures to the old woman in the shop, explaining she had to look upstairs, positive there was a coat that would be perfect for her. With less than a minute to go, Orla left the shop and darted into the corridor, before sprinting upstairs and flicking the light on. Hopefully her minders would be convinced enough, although it didn't matter, this was her throw of the dice. She hurtled downstairs out of view of the customer, pulling on her coat as she ran. Grabbing the dog basket, she traversed the two back doors, not caring to close them. Had she had time, she would have panicked, but this was her leap of faith, and she concentrated on nothing but execution. On entering Brighton Street, she hugged the wall to her car and unlocked the passenger door, before leaping in with the dog basket, and quickly shuffling over to the driver's seat. Her conscious, constantly repeating the mantra, *'you need to be ready to go. One chance.'*

Shuffling down in the seat, content she was invisible from the rear, her hand darted up and manoeuvred the rear-view mirror, enabling a vista of the main road. She battled against adrenaline to control her breathing, imagining her 'watchers' would hear her through the rain and traffic noise, from fifty yards away. She started to gain control with short sharp breaths. There was no fear, only determination. And then she saw him.

~

The youth inwardly complained as he raced through the deluge to catch sight of the car. He had the hood of his parka jacket fully zipped up, creating a tunnel vision. A fleeting glance cemented what he already knew.

'This is fucking ridiculous. Where *else* was the car going to be? She's upstairs. What does your man think this is, a James Bond film? '

His attention then turned to the bus.

'C'mon...c'mon driver. Get the gravy dribblers on board.'

Without taking any further notice of the car, he heard the hydraulics of the bus as the doors closed, the indicator light clicking and blinking. He sprinted the short distance back to the car.

~

As soon as the youth turned to run, Orla sat bolt upright, turned the key that was already in the ignition and drove at speed along Brighton Street. Shifting into second gear, she heard the cacophony of car horns directly behind her. For a split second she feared the worst, before glancing in the rear-view mirror.

~

The youth leapt into the passenger seat, slamming the door shut.

'Whoa! Look at that eejit!'

Both he, and the driver, witnessed a black taxi overtake the bus as it moved off. Irresponsibility turned to calamity, as a car parked opposite, and facing up the road, decided to pull out. The black taxi swerved to avoid collision, while nearly clipping the front of the bus.

The driver slammed on the brakes and passengers on the bus stumbled forward. The combined horns of the bus and the car, lasted longer than polite reminders, angering the taxi driver who leapt from his cab, followed by the bus driver and car owner. Unheard arguing and lots of finger pointing, rescinded after a minute or so. The youth laughed out loud, delighted that at least *something* had happened during his monotonous tenure.

'What a wingnut!' he shouted, jumping about in his seat.

The driver appeared calm as he smiled back, his peripheral vision locked on the upstairs light in the shop. When all three had returned to their vehicles, the road began to clear. The driver suddenly yelled at the passenger to get out, as he was in the act of doing so.

'What?' the youth responded, his mouth agape with confusion.

The driver roared back at him. 'The fucking car's gone!'

'Holy shit!'

Chapter 28

Patterson embraced the sedate B Wing routine. He had impressed the censor officer with diligence in all that he did. He was fastidious in censoring letters, organising visiting passes and completing tuck shop requests, throwing himself wholeheartedly into any allocated task. This was the new Patterson, a more driven and focused person, unbeknownst to his colleagues, involving himself in everything, and anything, to fill his day. His new Principal Officer was pleased to see him offering breaks for the staff stuck on the grills leading in and out of the wing, as well as volunteering to run errands, or help out in B visits area. At lunchtime he would visit the canteen and watch TV or play snooker, no longer drawn like a moth to a flame, to the many card schools taking place. Before the end of lunch, he returned to the wing, which was quieter than normal. In fact, the entire Jail's volume was turned down during staff break times. No closing of doors, shouting to one and other, bells ringing or incessant chit chat.
'Paddy,' came the shout from the PO's office as he walked past.
He entered and sat in a chair across from Tommy MacLean, a rotund man with a face stuck in a permanent grin. He exuded wisdom and warmth. Patterson had taken to him immediately, and thought he was an archetypical, happy grandfather, from a Norman Rockwell painting. He was joined by the security PO.
'All good kid?' he enquired.
Patterson smiled, nodding his head in affirmation.
'Norman's here to talk to you.'

The security PO looked solemn. 'There's a general threat out at the minute. Your name, amongst others, has been mentioned in the Intel reports.'

Patterson sat, expressionless, waiting for the PO to continue.
'We're not sure of the level of threat yet, but you need to be extra careful. I've organised with the Trades to install security measures at your house.'
Patterson ingested the information before commenting.
'Thanks for the warning,' he said unperturbed.
'I'm sorry this has happened kid,' MacLean offered.
'It's all part of the job Tommy, don't worry about it.'
'The Trades boys will be at your house tomorrow morning. I'm giving you a special leave day to get things sorted. Ok?'
'Ach Tommy, you're my guardian angel. Means I can get full tonight.'
'Now fuck away off out of here,' MacLean replied with a huge grin on his face. MacLean admired the way Patterson ignored the etiquette of addressing rank, glad to witness a glimpse of the Patterson he'd been used to.

~

Orla's car hurtled along the M2 motorway toward Londonderry. Whatever had happened was a godsend. A sign that everything, *might,* work out. Her initial plan was to drive toward Dublin and Wicklow where she had relatives, but reckoned that's where *he* would expect her to go. She harboured a secret childhood memory that McGuigan was unaware of.

As a thirteen-year-old schoolgirl, she'd spent two summer weeks at a Gaeltacht school in Donegal, on the insistence of her mother, to learn the Irish language. She hated the thought of it. She wanted to chase potential boyfriends, listen to music and buy make-up. But Orla was pleasantly surprised to learn that the teachers weren't nuns, or grey spinsters with moustaches, but a lot younger and far more endearing. Instead of dreary classroom lessons all day, her tutor, Siobhan Bonner, was very interactive and would organise field trips to local areas, especially the breath-taking beaches. She recalled that the beaches were plentiful and immense, but always appeared to be desolate, the locals spoilt for choice. Her favourite was the one near the village of Annagry. It was hidden to the occasional tourist, as there were no signs or pointers, as well as being a good three-quarter mile walk across fields. It was worth it. She would never forget Siobhan explaining to her, whilst pointing out to sea, that if you could walk in a straight line, you would end up in New York. She smiled, remembering the song on the minibus that Siobhan would encourage them to sing. They used the Irish word for beach, Tra, repeatedly to the tune of *'Busy doing nothing'* from *Snow white and the seven dwarfs*.

Driving non-stop for a few hours, Orla's paranoia dissipated, and her adrenaline levels stabilised. Successfully traversing Londonderry, she headed for the village of Burnfoot, barely into the Republic, and a small B&B off the beaten track, hoping they accepted dogs, and sterling, being so close to the border. Her cover story of being a journalist for National Geographic, impressed the elderly owners, who would normally refuse pets, but were keen to reap the publicity.

~

Patterson detested these parts of his commutes. In and out, from home and the jail, were the only unalterable legs of his journey. In essence, killing zones. The loaded Walther pistol, loosely nestled into a buckskin shoulder holster under his unzipped jacket, retrievable in seconds. His awareness paramount, after receiving the news he was now, officially, a target.

Twisting his way through the concrete chicane, and out onto the Crumlin Road, Patterson scoured right, to the junctions of Agnes Street and Cliftonpark Avenue. A line of traffic on each, impatiently waiting for the lights to change, allowing them to join the choked line he was bound for, during the rush hour. His car slipped out into a space in front of an oncoming Nissan micra. He noted a white van had 'jumped the lights' behind the Nissan. Patterson was at a high state of alert, as the traffic crawled toward Carlisle Circus roundabout, registering the first three cars that exited Agnes Street and fell in behind the van. A two-tone Ford Fiesta, a blue VW Polo, and a large grey Saab Estate. The gun was now placed between his legs as he moved along at snail's pace, checking mirrors for any overtaking motorcycles. He feared them most, because of their ability to manoeuvre, even in traffic jams. The white van disappeared at the roundabout, toward the Antrim Road, and by the time he had reached High Street, only the Polo and Saab were still directly behind him. He had noticed the Saab was a woman alone, whereas an elderly gentleman was in the Polo.

Relaxing somewhat, he returned the pistol to its holster and drove onto Oxford Street, heading for the King's Bridge and into East Belfast. At the Woodstock Link Junction, he waited for the lights to let him journey onward up the Woodstock Road. His direct route was via the Ravenhill road, yet he preferred the Woodstock. It had sentimental value, giving him a feeling of security. He was also paying the promised visit to his adopted mother, Elsie. He understood how infirm she was, and wore a hearing aid the size of a match box. He felt guilty at not sharing more time with the woman who had given him everything in life. He had changed, now feeling more patient and disciplined. Still scrutinising the following traffic, he noticed another two-tone Fiesta. It wasn't unusual as they were popular, but he was almost sure, it was the one that had pulled out of Agnes Street, earlier in his journey. Calculations raced through his mind.

'If it wasn't behind me going over the Kings Bridge, how was it here now? Or was it behind me all the time?'

Before dismissing his fanciful thoughts, he realised how it *was* possible. The Fiesta could have crossed the Queens Bridge, then up through Short Strand to re-join the link.

'Is this really happening?' he thought out loud, almost chuckling at the seemingly outrageous scenario. Annoyed that he would be late to visit his adoptive mum, he decided to put his theory to the test. He moved at the docile speed the traffic dictated, watching the Fiesta, now four cars back. He drove past the junction of Beersbridge Road and Cherryville Street and witnessed the Fiesta stopping at the lights.

The outbound city traffic dictated his snail like pace. As he reached the next junction of My Lady's Road and Willowfield Street, he turned left, and slowly drove the length of Willowfield Street, toward Castlereagh Road, a parallel arterial route, away from his intended destination. He focused on the rear-view mirror, hoping to see the Fiesta drive past, putting paid to his theory. On reaching the end of Willowfield Street, his fears were affirmed, as the Fiesta also turned. He couldn't move out onto Castlereagh Road due to a few stragglers' city bound, whilst the Fiesta crept closer. Within seconds, he enraged another driver by accelerating out in front of him. The Fiesta followed, now only one car's distance between them.

He had a decision to make. There were two lanes at the Junction with the Beersbridge Road. Left, to return to the Woodstock via the Beersbridge Road, or right, to join Castlereagh Street back toward the City. Patterson chose left, confident that he could lose his followers in the area he had been raised. On nearing the junction, the car in front drove through the lights on amber. Patterson slowed and stopped at the red light. The Fiesta was still sandwiched one vehicle back. As the traffic from the Beersbridge road started to move in front of him, Patterson accelerated through the red light and round the bend of the road, to the sound of multiple car horns and angry shouts. A few hundred yards past Templemore Avenue, he turned right into Calvin Street, racing to the end. He knew of the gap at the end of the terraced houses, just before the Church, an entrance to a wide backstreet that doubled back and parallel to the houses, out of sight. He never flinched from checking in the mirror, content the Fiesta was still stationary on the Castlereagh Road.

He parked, and sprinted back, barely glancing up the long Street, without leaving the backstreet. From the distance of the Beersbridge Road, Patterson was invisible. A few minutes later, the Fiesta drove past the entrance to Calvin Street, on a hopeless journey. Patterson remained in the back street for 30 minutes before venturing toward Cherryville Street.

Chapter 29

Nugent sat in silence, opposite McGuigan in the visiting box. He had never witnessed his commander physically fighting to control his anger so intensely, closed fists shaking. He dared not interrupt. After a few strained minutes, McGuigan regained control.

'Have you alerted Dublin?' he stated, fixating Nugent with his demonic expression.

'Of course, and Newry and Armagh as well. They've all got her car registration and are out driving the roads as we speak. I've a few contacts at the airports and sea ports on lookout as well.'

McGuigan silently contemplated before replying

'Good, though I can't imagine her flying, because she's probably got that stupid wee dog with her.'

He looked directly at Nugent, a hint of sorrowful eyes,

'Barney, she loved that dog more than me, did you know that?', he questioned, not expecting a reply. Nugent appeared nonplussed.

After a few awkward moments, he spoke,

'Padraig…please let me state the case for our surveillance team.'

Initially McGuigan's features hardened as he reacted to the request, but soon morphed into a more compassionate, leadership guise. He nodded.

'Sean Cronin, who ran that team, was meticulous. It was a pure fluke. But she had to have planned it. She must have already been in the car before the lookout approached. They couldn't have avoided it.'

Ingesting the information, McGuigan exhaled a breath, showing control.

'You're right, Barney. It couldn't have been avoided. We'll find her.'
Nugent nodded animatedly in agreement.
'What about the screw?'
Nugent thought carefully, before replying. 'He knows we're onto him.'
McGuigan tilted his head slightly, demanding continuance.
'Two of our best men tailed him yesterday in the rush hour traffic.' Nugent informed. 'He gave them the run around before going through a red light and disappearing. This bastard's good.'
McGuigan worked through his thought process before replying. 'Leave off him for a few days. It'll make him lackadaisical. Then start again next week. I want relays, multiples, CB radios and motorbikes. And make sure the drivers are women on their own. No tail for more than a mile. Overtake and alert the next pursuer.'
'Consider it done!'

~

McGuigan lay on the bed in his cell staring at the bare ceiling, struggling to remember when he and Orla were last *truly* in love. He'd lost her a long time ago. Not through frequent incarcerations; she'd been nudged out of his life to make way for his active service. He hadn't cared, merely expecting her at his beck and call. He understood her wanting to escape from the life he had built for her. He was sadly confident that she was aware, her actions had condemned her. All he would ever have, were the hints of memories from their early days together. He hoped that when she was captured, he wouldn't be ordered to be part of the interrogation team. He understood why she sought comfort in another's arms.

He tried to imagine what she was doing now and how she was feeling.

'I pray to god, that wherever she's trying to get to, she makes it. She deserves it,' he whispered out loud, as a silver tear crept from the side of his eye.

~

On the journey, Patterson became lost in his own thoughts. He wanted to hurt Henderson as much as possible, and get him in jail if he could. Then, and only then, could he implement his final strategy, although at this stage of planning, he was unaware of what it would be, and how he would execute it. His utter conviction that this was his destiny, put paid to any forward planning, unaware he had entered a dystopian universe. A few hundred yards later, he slipped two envelopes into the post box. One was addressed, '*Manager, Berlin Arms, Shankill Road Belfast*', the other was for the Sunday World newspaper offices.

He stepped inside a phone booth to make a few calls.

~

 Orla had risen early, and sat down to a hearty breakfast. Gleoite received a miniature version in a bowl, assuring the owners they would be featured in her fictitious National Geographic reports. She drove to Letterkenny and parked on the deserted fourth floor of a multi-storey car park, before walking to the station to catch the Dungloe bus.

As the bus worked it's through Cresslough and Dunfanaghy, heading for the Rosses, Orla petted her dog, smiling all the while, blissfully ignorant of the other passengers. She had a deep feeling of calm, as the ragged countryside flashed past her window. Occasional twisted trees, murky lakes and moss type grass, failing to engulf the outcrop of stones that had been there for a millennium. The mighty Atlantic glistened, when it snuck into view between the rolling hills. She observed the farmers scattered attempts of creating boundaries for 'their' land with stones, or rusted barbed wire, enhancing the wildness of this beautiful place. Everything appeared sporadic and ruffled, unlike the pristine and regimented fields of the north. It felt untroubled and welcoming. Gleoite was fast asleep on her lap as the bus moved through Falcarragh, toward Gortahirk. Orla was as impressed, as the first time she had seen Mount Errigal, whenever it crept into view, waking Gleoite by moving to the opposite side of the bus. Errigal was the queen of the seven sisters of the Derryveagh mountain range. The tallest mountain in Donegal, had a pinkish glow emanating from Quartzite, confirming her superiority. Orla felt like the schoolgirl she once was. Fifteen minutes later, the bus stopped in Annagry at Bonner's Pub. Disembarking, a smiling Orla looked at the pub sign with the same surname as her Irish teacher, before walking to the field that led to her favourite beach. Gleoite bounced through the wispy grass chasing birds he would never catch, excited at being in a strange place. Orla continued to follow the barely visible, beaten track to its end. Before descending the ramshackle steps, she stopped, and drank in the vista. It was everything she'd remembered. An arena of rock to her right, and in front, a curved beach with dampened sand near the shore that appeared red, making it look like Mars. Orla stepped onto the beach, heading for the first, of two, outcrops of Monolithic Stones. They resembled the fingers of a giant buried below. She watched the sea lick the beach, before moving back to the drier sand, away from the shore, and sat down. Gleoite raced barking at the meagre waves as they fled, yelping a retreat on their return. Orla was alone, yet happy, as she studied the soft sand drizzle from her grasp through open fingers. She was mesmerised at the beauty of God's creation. She felt safe… and free… at last. Gleoite panted heavily, trotting toward his owner, exhausted at chasing waves that receded further each time. Orla picked him up' and hugged and kissed him. 'You're the best wee dog ever, aren't you?' she whispered as Gleoite struggled to keep his eyes open, unused to such lengthy periods of exercise. Orla set the sleeping dog on the sand, removing its collar and lead, before draping her coat over her pet. She took the car keys from the coat pocket, and the parking ticket from her jeans pocket, as she walked up the beach to the sole, dilapidated rubbish bin, depositing everything. Turning to go, she remembered her wedding ring. It meant nothing to her, as she twirled it around her finger. She slid it off and tossed it into the bin. Standing over Gleoite, Orla felt a lump in her throat, and though her placated smile dictated differently, an involuntary tear rolled down her cheek. She turned to face the water. The tide was definitely going out, as the stone monoliths had grown in stature. She walked toward it, humming the same tune from all those years ago. It made her smile. She didn't feel the cold when her feet met the ocean, and continued to stride ahead, re-imagining the line to New York. The deeper she went, the harder it was to walk, although the outgoing tide assisted by pulling her, which she welcomed. Immersed to her neck, her body swayed as if dancing, the current setting the tempo. She started swimming to no avail, the weight of clothes dragging her underwater. Her head bobbed above the waterline for a fleeting glance of the brilliant, blue sky that met the dark, mysterious blue of the ocean at the horizon, and mouthed the words, *'I'll meet you at the top of the Empire State Building, John,'* before disappearing for the final time.

Chapter 30

Henderson was amongst six regional commanders, on the constructed stage at the back of the band hall. It wasn't his physique that made him stand out, it was the white plasters across his face where his nose used to be. The noise levels of the assembled paramilitaries milling about in the audience, were unusually muted. There was a collective awareness that something 'big' was about to be announced. As Henderson motioned to take his seat at the centre of the folding wooden table, a UVF commander, with a hint of cynicism, enquired about the plasters. 'I cut myself shaving, OK?!', he barked in response, a little disconcerted that his growl had no effect on a commander out of his remit. As Henderson waited for the others to join him, he surveyed the assembly of amassed volunteers, before focusing his attention on the lights hanging from the ceiling near the entrance. This place had barely changed since the night he took control. When the commanders were seated, he rose, sending an anticipated hush across the audience. He stood in silence, deliberately glancing in all directions, in turn, before addressing them.

'Fellow commanders, brother organisations and collective volunteers,' he stated, purposely acknowledging the powerful stake holders at the table.

'I have called for this meeting, as we are approaching the threshold of a crisis.'

The audience shrugged their shoulders and grimaced, but were eager to learn more. The leaders at the table cocked their heads to the side, and narrowed their eyes in doubt.

'This started as long ago as the 1960's, when *our* organisation was formed to protect our people.' Henderson deliberately paused for effect. 'They assassinated our glorious leader, Jackie Smallwood, God rest his soul, in an attempt to weaken us. To destroy us. Yet, through the determination of our volunteers, we have become stronger. We showed the resolve the protestants of Ulster have. We struck back with such force and determination, we put them back where they belonged!'

The enthusiasm from the audience started to simmer.

'They mistakenly feel they are stronger, and are on a course seeking our elimination. And I mean *everyone* in this room. A few weeks ago, began the start of their campaign, with the cowardly murder of another of our founding fathers, Willie Hamilton. And it is with great regret, I have to inform you that the whereabouts of Terry Montgomery, missing since last Saturday, are unknown.'

'Bastards!' someone shouted from the crowd. Other angry insults ensued, as the tension and hatred started to boil over. Henderson, stood in silence, contented, until the UVF commander rose.

'Enough!' he shouted waving his arms to deflate the passion, 'Let him finish!'

He gave Henderson a suspicious look.

'I firmly believe Terry has been abducted by the enemy, and is more than likely, already dead.'

The noise from the audience calmed, a deathly silence filling the room.

'They killed my dog. I have received death threats in the post. But let me tell you this!' Henderson snarled, banging his fist on the table for effect, 'I may be under threat... but these fenian bastards don't scare me!'

The younger volunteers in the audience erupted with cheering, creating a flood of enthusiasm that couldn't be quelled. Henderson drank in the plaudits of the audience, now dancing to his every note. 'This isn't just about me,' he shouted, turning to the commanders who sat either side. 'They are trying to destroy our organisations from the top down! But we will not let them do that! It is our collective duty not to run, but to fight! We will not allow them to leave our people defenceless, to be slaughtered physically and politically, and be dragged into the clutches of the Republic. We are now officially...at War!' The uproar of support was deafening, blood thirsty young guns already conceiving plans for future atrocities. Henderson nodded to his driver, McIntyre, at the far end of the hall before talking to the leaders on the platform.

'I'll be in touch early next week and we'll make arrangements,' he stated without waiting for a reply.

Henderson disappeared into the crowd with the presence of a hero. The remaining commanders, were a far cry away from the animation and support of the crowd, as they rose to leave.

The UVF commander walked past Malcolmson and whispered quietly, 'I wouldn't trust that fucker as far as I could throw him. It's him's up shite creek. Who knows, Bobby, maybe the Provos are going to do you all a favour?'

Malcolmson didn't respond.

~

In the unlit bedroom, Patterson peered through a gap in the curtains, surveying the cul-de-sac, looking for anything that appeared alien, or out of order. It resembled a housing graveyard, the feeble dawn light, suppressed by cloud cover, turning everything colourless. He didn't expect much at this ungodly time of the morning. He was leaving earlier than normal for his commute to work, planning on driving toward Lisburn to enter the city that way. A different variant on his route, essential due to the tail he'd shaken off the previous evening. He didn't need to bring anything with him, and would grab breakfast in the canteen. He was working the split shift system, prior to a night Guard that included a 5-hour day shift. He would return later that evening to commence the 11-hour overnight shift and concluded with a late start, evening duty on Sunday. Grabbing his overcoat, Patterson slipped out the back door. Keys in one hand, loaded pistol in the other as he surveyed the horizon directly facing him. His back garden was bordered on two sides by hedges and a garage, giving him privacy, although the far end consisted of a small picket fence, behind which were fields and rolling countryside. He had always taken his personal security seriously and adopted the safety mechanism of 'thinking like a terrorist.' He reckoned this part of his routine would be the most vulnerable, although any terrorist would have to stand to shoot and be framed in silhouette against the skyline, hence the loaded pistol.

Keeping his view toward the back of the garden, he entered the side door to the garage, flicking on the stuttering fluorescent light, before dropping to his knees and examining under the bottom of his car and its wheel arches. Content, Patterson turned off the light, retracing his steps back into the house, checking through the blinds of the lounge windows to make sure any pursuers weren't waiting for him to open the garage door from the inside. He opened the door from the outside and headed to work.

~

McDermott sat quietly at a gleaming, black wood effect, table opposite the Superintendent, who studied the files he'd presented. He surveyed the room and its artefacts that the seniority of promotion afforded. The walls a creamy grey, illuminated by chrome up lighters. The door high windows leading into the office were draped with expensive wooden blinds, isolating them both from the outside world. It was efficient, organised and authoritative. The Superintendent lifted his head and gazed at him before exhaling a sigh.

'Harry,' he began, pausing to consider his thoughts. 'I realise there was a call to the confidential line pinning Hamilton's murder on this thug, but there's no evidence.'

'But...' McDermott began, as the Superintendent interrupted, raising his hand.

'You've double checked his alibi, and it's rock solid. Have you considered that maybe there's an internal feud going on amongst these gangsters, and he's being set-up?'

McDermott paused momentarily before responding. 'Although I'm convinced, he has something to do with the murder, it's his safety I think we have to worry about. They shot his dog for Christ's sake.'

'I agree Harry. It's our job to serve and protect the community. Which unfortunately, includes this low life, but why did they shoot the dog and not him? I propose that act was a warning, which convinces me more, that this is a feud. Or just some nutcase who hates dogs.'

McDermott realised he was fighting a losing battle.

'Furthermore, we don't have the resources to protect him.'

McDermott was decimated.

'Look Harry, I know this is more to do with you wanting to tie up loose ends before retirement. But you're building bridges that don't exist.'

As he spoke, the Superintendent gathered up the loose files and handed them back.

'That'll be all Sergeant.'

Before he could rise, the door behind him crashed open, and Douglas raced into the room with a sheet of fax paper. The Superintendent glared angrily at this unannounced interruption, his face contorting, but Douglas ignored him and addressed McDermott.

'This is the ballistics report on the pistol used to kill the dog Captain. They've traced it back to the Provos!', he exclaimed.

Both turned to face the Superintendent. His anger replaced with a solemn frown.

'I'll have to talk to my superiors,' he replied.

McDermott nodded and left the room, Douglas giving a two fingered salute to the blinds that hid his superior.

~

Joe McDonald sat at his desk in the Sunday World newsroom, mulling over the letter he had received that morning. It was from an alleged, serving RUC officer, and had described that Samuel 'Bulldog' Henderson, was a police informant who he had frequently witnessed being interviewed by Special Branch handlers. He was also being implicated in the murder of Willie Hamilton. McDonald rubbed his bald head in frustration before leaving the office to address his journalists.

'Listen up everybody,' McDonald barked, attracting their attention. All eyes focused on the former rugby international, his frame filling the door to his office.

'You've all got copies of this letter.'

The gaggle of hacks nodded in anticipation.

'If it were more solid, this could be our breaking news story of the year, and I for one, would be glad to go after this scumbag. But...having contacted our insider in the RUC, he knows nothing about it, and trust me, he is reliable.'

There was a collective groan from the crowd.

~

Bobby Malcolmson sat with his second-in-command, re-reading his version of the same letter in the upstairs office of the Berlin Arms. The main difference in the content was the introduction.

'ALTHOUGH I AM A POLICEMAN, I'M A LOYALIST FIRST, AND ALWAYS WILL BE.'

He handed the letter to his comrade, before losing himself in thought. Malcolmson had many run ins with Henderson over the years and was aware that Henderson was getting the lion's share of the profits from the protection rackets. He despised his heavy-handed methods on innocents. He had never fully trusted him. He thought about big Willie Hamilton and how his poor wife was now permanently alone after his murder. Maybe this was the time to change? Time to have a new leader. The sombre-looking, second in command, handed him back the letter.

'What do think?' Malcolmson asked.

Without replying, the second in command nodded. 'Fuck him. Do it!'

~

McDonald continued. 'I would run with this, but our Dublin offices are gurning about the number of hits we've taken in the courts over false allegations...'

Before he could finish, a phone rang at one of the desks. Although annoyed to have been interrupted, McDonald waited patiently for the journalist to answer. He realised it was an important call, as the journalist hit the button on the recording device on his newly fangled phone counsel. Silence ensued in the room as the journalist hastily scribbled down what he was hearing as back up to the recording device. A few seconds later he replaced the receiver.

'Well?' McDonald roared at him.

The journalist's face morphed into a beaming grin.

'I think we just won the football pools!' he replied. 'They used the UDA codeword. They're claiming the same!'

Cheers, laughter and high-fives filled the room, along with hands eagerly being drummed on desks.

'Gentlemen,' began McDonald, 'I think we've got work to do!'

A scrubbing brush couldn't have removed the smile from his face.

Chapter 31

McDermott entered the house and hung his coat in the hallway. 'How did it go today, Harry?' chirped Molly from the kitchen. He strolled up behind her and kissed her cheek.

'A wee bit frustrating. Things didn't go quite the way I'd hoped they would,' he replied, 'but there's still time.'

Molly gave him a reassuring smile before turning back to her potatoes. They had an unwritten rule, that he would never discuss work whilst at home. He didn't want his sweet Molly to relive the traumas he had had to endure. She was content not to pry.

'Away and get your slippers on, I'll bring you a nice cold beer,' Molly suggested.

'You spoil me woman,' he replied through a grin, as he ambled into the lounge. His automatic routine would have been to flick on the TV, remove his shoes, and relax onto the sumptuous cloth settee, with his feet on the pouffe. But tonight, although disguising it from Molly, he felt irritated as he stared at the fire flickering in the hearth. He didn't hold out much hope from the Superintendent, who prioritised finances over policing. McDermott recollected the good old, bad old days of years ago, before the word *budget* entered the police vocabulary. You were not only allowed, but encouraged, to react to your hunches. It seemed that the police force was turning into a business rather than a public service. The comforting smell of warm chips cooking in the kitchen, brought him back to reality. This was their Friday night special, as Molly called it. Chips, fried eggs and two rounds of bread and butter. McDermott smiled, thinking, *'It's great that some things never change.'*

'Jacqui was on the phone,' interrupted Molly carrying his glass of beer, 'the wee one rode his bike today without stabilisers!'

McDermott grinned. 'That's brilliant, he's such a determined wee lad.'

'Bit like his Granda. Do you want the TV on?' she questioned, moving toward it.

'No love, it's ok. Sure, there's nothing on. I'm a wee bit tired,' he replied rubbing his eyes.

'Ok then, but there's a wee film on later I want to see. It's a romantic comedy.'

'Can't wait,' he replied, sarcasm in his tone.

'Doesn't matter, you'll fall asleep anyway,' she laughed.

As Molly turned to retrieve McDermott's slippers, he leant over and pinched her backside, making her blurt out a surprised giggle.

'Maybe we'll have an early night,' McDermott said with an expectant look, twirling the ends of his moustache.

'Well, Mr McDermott, you'd better not fall asleep during that!' she retorted, wiggling her rear end ridiculously, as she headed back to the kitchen.

McDermott pulled off his off his shoes, his thoughts jumping to family affairs. He'd realised years ago, that he'd became more of a replacement for their daughter, when she left for Scotland. Molly pampered him relentlessly, ironing socks and underwear and unceasingly cleaning the nest that was their home. He loved her with all his heart.

The phone in the hall rang and before McDermott could react, Molly shouted, 'It's ok, I'll get it!'

McDermott had a wry grin as he thought to himself, '*Point proven.*'
She entered the lounge with a more serious demeanour.

'It's work love.'

McDermott assumed something major had happened, compounded by the background noise of people running about, and phones ringing. He spoke with the Superintendent.

'Harry, have you seen the news?'

'No,'

'The local news will be on in a few minutes, watch it, and then be in here before 10. We've a lot of organising before daybreak.'

'Ok,' he replied understanding the Super didn't want to give important information over a landline.

'And by the way Harry....I was wrong.'

The line went dead, and he raced to turn on the TV. Molly deliberately didn't inquire about the call.

'Our breaking news story. The police have released the name of the body that was washed up near Whitehead in Belfast Lough, late last night. He is 58-year-old Terence Montgomery, a known senior loyalist, last seen on the Larne Stranraer ferry last Saturday night returning from a football match. Police are appealing...'

McDermott clicked the TV off.

'Holy shit!' he whispered, his mind racing through probabilities.

~

Patterson drove into Belfast via the Castlereagh Hills and the Rocky Road, listening to Van Morrison's, *Them*, singing *'here comes the night.' 'You're right there, Van,'* he thought as dusk crept to darkness. He had a great affinity with this tight winding road, and the serious decline at the end of it.

It was a popular courting spot, because of the views over the city, even from the back seat of the car. He briefly thought about Orla. They had driven here on more than one occasion, before migrating to indoor pleasures. As he neared the dangerous bend that announced the decline, Patterson braked, drinking in the vista. Glimmering, white and yellow dots highlighted the housing estates and main centres of population. To the left was a splash of white light bigger than the rest, signifying the rugby match at Ravenhill. To his right, the giant Harland and Wolffe cranes stood proud and yellow, illuminated by up lights. The sparkling white flashes of busy welders, seemed as fireflies, briefly hinting at the vessel they repaired. He loved this view, this city. The jingle announcing Downtown Radio news, interrupted his solace. Patterson's grip on the steering wheel tightened, on learning of Montgomery's death, his mouth in a snarl, growling through gritted teeth.

'I had should have a chance to kill him. I *deserved* to kill him!' Patterson adopted a ghoulish expression, rage surging through his mind. Gradually, he calmed and contemplated his next move. He was now convinced; he was in a race of death with someone else. He prayed his plans for Henderson would bear fruit, understanding they were dubious.

He needed Henderson in jail, his arena, and by some means or another, he would watch him die, knowing it was the son of a reputable leader he thought would never threaten him again.

Chapter 32

A cavalcade slipped silently through the darkness toward Helen's Bay, the occasional streetlight, the only illumination. Three vehicles, two unmarked patrol cars and one unmarked Mobile Support Unit van. The van came to a halt, unseen in Kathleen Avenue, as the cars headed onto Fort Road. The first car contained Detective Inspector Ernest Tumelty and McDermott, along with two uniformed officers. McDermott had respect for Tumelty, and didn't care at being overlooked as the leader of this taskforce, convinced it was the Superintendent's intentions. Jackson and Douglas were in the remaining vehicle. When both cars came to a halt in front of the house, McDermott alighted as Tumelty spoke.

'I'm only here as a back-up, Harry, no matter what that prick says. This is your baby.'

McDermott winked.

'You're a good man Ernie.'

Both Tumelty and the uniforms waited, as McDermott continually pushed the buzzer on the outside of the electric gates for attention. A light in the upstairs of the house came on before a window opened and Henderson leant out.

'What the fuck do you think you're doing?' he shouted in an act of bravado.

McDermott reacted. 'Hopefully saving your life. Now let us in!'

When McDermott, Tumelty, Jackson and Douglas entered the house, McDermott spoke to Henderson for at least 10 minutes, the uniforms standing guard outside the gates.

Henderson had pleaded innocence, in relation to Montgomery's death and genuinely looked saddened, his macho persona a distant memory. His wife arrived as McDermott spoke.

'We're not here about Montgomery, it's about you...' he turned to Imogen, '...and your wife.' We have reason to believe that your lives are in imminent danger.'

'But how do you know!?' Imogen squealed, visibly shaking.

'*A long-seated, inevitability to her deepest fear,*' McDermott thought.

She started to wring her hands before sobbing. Henderson put an arm around her shoulder for comfort. Both Tumelty and McDermott were aware of the awkwardness of the action, obviously not commonplace.

'We can't go into any details I'm afraid, but can confirm it is a top-level threat.'

Both officers watched him as he pondered the situation.

'So… what's going to happen, or more to the point, what are you going to do about it?'

'We have organised a safe house, under protection, for the time being,' McDermott started.

'Safe house!? Are you out of your mind?' he interrupted. 'I'm not going anywhere. Your lot will have to protect me! It's your fucking job!'

His bullishness reappeared as he discarded his tearful wife.

'That is our future intention, but your house, as it is, is nowhere near basic safety levels. Maybe you don't understand, but an assassination attempt is imminent, and we need to protect you elsewhere until your home is secure.'

McDermott stared at Henderson, who huffed, defiance battling survival in his mind.

'We're staying!' he finalised.

'Ok, if that's the case, I need you to draft a letter saying that you refused our protection and exonerating us from blame...WHEN THE TIME COMES!'

The emphasis of the certainty of McDermott's statement, hit Henderson hard. His wife rescued him.

'We're going,' she stated with a determination Henderson was unused to. As she rose to leave the room, Henderson's brittle confidence returned.

'We're only going because of her. You get that!?'

McDermott nodded before replying. 'Pack clothes and toiletries for a week. Quickly, we need to be out of here.'

'I've a few phone calls to make,' demanded Henderson.

McDermott grabbed his arm forcibly, spinning him around to face him.

'No phone calls, or any communication whatsoever, at this moment in time. You can catch up when you return. Understand?'

A hapless Henderson nodded without complaint, whenever Tumelty and McDermott shepherded them back upstairs.

~

5 hours later, the mansion was sealed off from the outside world. Two uniformed officers in high visibility vests, more for protection against the cold sea air, shielded the wrought iron gates, advertising, visitors were unwelcome. The two unmarked cars and the MSU van were abandoned in front of Henderson's precious black Mercedes on the white gravel driveway, mirroring the actuality of Henderson's plight. Backed into a corner with nowhere to run. Both guards had been pacing back and forth in front of the gate attempting to maintain a modicum of heat, whilst carefully surveying their surroundings. A Ford Cortina rounded the corner, slowing down, at the sight of the officers. This wasn't unusual, as every nosey neighbour was anxious to discover what was going on. However, the occupants of this car, didn't remotely fit the profile of a local resident, the rundown car advertising the fact. Both guards automatically placed their hands on their holsters, unbuttoning them for quick release. The car increased its speed to drive past the gates.
'I knew there was something going on!' growled an angry Bobby Malcolmson from the passenger seat, before smiling at the officers as they drove past.
'Right, get round to McLaughlin's house. He'll find out,' he ordered the driver.
'Wasn't that your man Malcolmson?' the younger guard asked as the car disappeared from view.
'Yup,' replied the other, 'Looks like the scumbags are worried.'

~

Behind the gates, the four-man search team, bedecked in blue overalls, diligently combed the garden area armed with metal detectors, iron prods, trowels and shovels. McDermott's brief was, to recover any sharp metal objects. Jackson and Douglas had joined him and Tumelty in the kitchen. Jackson looked like he was wearing a leotard.

'Do they only make these overalls for midgets?' he announced.

'Nothing a few hundred years of jogging wouldn't solve, Jacko,' replied Douglas.

The big man dug his hand into his pocket.

'Something here for you Doug,' he replied, pulling out his hand with the middle finger extended.

'Captain, it'll take a year to search that attic alone,' he addressed McDermott, 'It's enormous!'

'We've only got to midnight Jacko,' McDermott replied, deflated. Jackson lifted his coffee and wandered to the settees in the conservatory. Douglas went outside for a smoke, leaving McDermott and Tumelty alone.

'This is a big gamble, Harry.' exclaimed Tumelty.

 McDermott nodded in agreement before Tumelty continued. 'I had to crawl over broken glass to get the MSU search team from the Super. God forbid, we don't find anything, or he'll have our bollocks for breakfast. You could be retiring sooner than you thought!'

'I know Ernie… and I thank you for getting me the team, but I'm convinced we'll find something here, even if it's been planted. And if we do, it's Henderson's problem, not ours.'

'We better my friend…'

The conversation was cut short as Douglas interrupted, crashing in through the door.

'Captain, we've got visitors!'

McDermott walked down the gravel driveway to the gates that were still closed. He noticed the irate features of the local Councillor and UDA sympathiser, Trevor McLaughlin, between the shoulders of the guards standing side-by-side facing him, and blocking his path. McDermott had unresponsive feelings for this loudmouth who abused his meagre powers. He also noticed the newspaper photographer across the street.

'How can we be of assistance?'

'You can bloody well tell me what's going on here. I would like to speak with my constituent...straight away!' roared McLaughlin.

McDermott diverted his attention to his finger nails for a few seconds, gaining control of the conversation, before slowly looking up and staring directly at the councillor.

'Ok,' he started with a steely voice. 'First of all, your constituent is not in residence, and may not be for quite a while.'

McLaughlin was flummoxed.

'Secondly...what's *'going on'* here, is a Police investigation, of which you are not privy to. And if you don't have a judicial document giving you access to the said Police investigation, I would suggest you piss off, and crawl back into the slime from whence you came. Do I make myself clear? "How dare you talk to me like that! I want your police number; I'll be lodging a complaint!' McLaughlin bellowed in an uncontrollable rage, before addressing the uniformed guards, 'You two are witnesses!'

The guards had their lips in a downward smile as they opened their hands to each other, before the senior spoke.

'All I heard was the Detective Sergeant explaining that this was a Police investigation. What about you?'

'Same,' the younger replied shrugging his shoulders.

'Why you...you...!' McLaughlin shouted, the fury dismissing his ability to finish the sentence, before turning and marching back to his car.

'Cheer's lads,' McDermott said before turning to walk up the driveway.

Chapter 33

Patterson couldn't believe the time when he stirred. 1:30pm. 'My god!' he thought, 'I never lie on this long after a night guard.' He stretched and yawned, before snuggling back down under the warmth of the blankets, staring at the ceiling. He felt calm, way beyond anything he could recall, convincing himself this 'sign' of total relaxation, further quantified his newly discovered, sole purpose in life. He'd never been more determined to complete a task. He attempted to envisage, what would happen after the event he was planning. If he was lucky, which definitely wasn't part of his makeup, he may be able to escape. Go on the run. Head to Dublin, and fly to Australia. He smiled. 'Who am I trying to kid?' He was fully aware that his actions would most likely be the final ones of his lifetime. The subconscious drive of avenging his father's death, convinced him it would be better to control his own destiny, rather than be caught and tortured by the IRA, and suffer a slow, humiliating death. His mind wandered to Shirley and the kids. If he upped sticks and moved closer to them, they could be in danger, as IRA death threats didn't have sell-by dates, and weren't restricted to Northern Ireland. Although deep in his heart, he knew he would miss them. Nonetheless, he would attain a modicum of honour. Everything would be sorted. No more hassle from the money lenders or the bank. This single act of revenge would wipe his slate clean. Having no longer dismissed Christianity, but embrace its ethos, he was further convinced he would be reunited with his parents, when this was all over. That thought cemented his warped determination.

~

By 5pm, all police officers on duty, were scattered between the kitchen and the conservatory, feeding on local fish and chips. The television blared out football results, intermingled with cheers and jeers in a form of banter.

'Seven hours Harry,' a dejected Tumelty said, before returning to attacking a chip sandwich.

'Don't remind me, Ernie. We've only got two rooms upstairs, and down here to do.'

Within half an hour, the MSU searched downstairs, whilst McDermott and his crew finished off the 1st floor. McDermott checked a make-up table, laying the drawers contents out in a meticulous line on the floor. Using a mirror and torch, he checked inside the now, blank spaces, rather than run his hand along blindly, potentially slicing a finger by hidden razor blades. Convinced there was nothing, he lay on his back, shining the torch up to the underside of the table. 'I'm getting too old for this,' he grumbled, his bones aching in the effort of ascent. He noticed one of the downstairs team had entered the room.

'Sergeant, you need to look at this. Might be nothing, but I thought I'd better check.'

McDermott tried, unsuccessfully, not to groan as he slid himself out to stand. His eyes grew wide with excitement, when they focused on the item the officer held between two latex covered fingers.

'Found these on top of one of the cabinets in the utility room.'

McDermott struggled to conceal his delirium at the sight of the scissors. They appeared to be pock marked with rust.

'Bag those and get them over to the forensics lab straight away. I'll ring ahead, they'll be expecting you.'

When the officer left, McDermott struggled to raise enthusiasm in the continuation of the search, but kept the information about the scissors to himself, not wanting the remaining staff to take their 'foot off the pedal'. Four hours and two coffee breaks later, he received a message on his police radio, requesting the phone number of his location. Seconds after he replied, the phone rang.

'Sergeant McDe...' one of the MSU officers began to shout, but McDermott raced downstairs, snatching the receiver.

'Harry, we've had a look at these and it's very odd,' came the voice from the receiver.

McDermott wasn't sure whether to celebrate, or bemoan his misfortune. The voice continued.

'The majority of the steel on the blades, and the handles, have been cleaned with at least 3 different detergent agents, yet the *apparent* rust wasn't touched.'

'And?' bleated McDermott, evermore desperate.

'The good news is, that the *rust* is dried blood, and matches the blood group of Hamilton. Not only that, it is an exact match with puncture wounds in his neck, and the angle in which they were delivered. Although, and we're not completely convinced, but due to the lateral exit of the entry wound, we would be seventy/thirty positive that is more than likely to be a left hander.'

Stunned, McDermott held the receiver in his hand, and dropped his arms by his side. Eyes closed, he whispered, 'Thank you, God', before being interrupted back to the real world by the now, diminutive, voice in the receiver.

'Harry! Harry! You still there?'

'Yes. You're an absolute star. Thank you.' he replied before hanging up.

Paradoxically, McDermott felt alone and emotional, trying to grasp the magnitude of the information he had just received. He cared not, that this would be mud in the Superintendent's eye, or that it had the hallmarks of a set-up. For probably the last time in his career, he had caught a bad guy. His instincts had prevailed. He requested the MSU officer round up everyone in the house, and assemble them in the kitchen. For a few seconds, he rehearsed an internal victory speech, but the tide of emotion determined, he could make a fool of himself. With everyone present, an expectant hush fell over the kitchen. McDermott, eyes glistening with tears of relief, cut his victory speech short.

'We got him,' he stated, sending the crowd into hysterics.

Tumelty recognised how much this meant to his old friend, and rushed to hug him, allowing McDermott a few seconds, to lose a tear against his shoulder.

'At least we'll have our bollocks for the rest of our lives, you lucky old bastard!'

McDermott blurted out a laugh before Tumelty gripped him tighter.

Chapter 34

Sundays were always quieter, the parochial population putting their lives on hold for worship, the remainder, attempting to climb out of hangovers. Calm weather accentuated the feeling of tranquillity, the sunshine painting the landscape beautifully. The senior guard Commander briefed McDermott when he, Jackson and Douglas arrived at Palace Barracks. They were in tow with a grey police Land Rover, fully manned.

'He's not a happy bunny Sergeant, well… not since he received the Sunday papers,' explained the Commander. 'We've had to keep him under lock and key, because he insists on leaving.'

'Into every life a little rain must fall,' replied McDermott, the inkling of a grin on his face.

The Commander and McDermott stood in a street of a purpose-built, housing estate for soldiers' families. Although the majority of the houses in this particular street were uninhabited, set aside for Special Branch meetings with agents and informants, and within the security forces family, a safe haven when required. Jackson and Douglas parked two doors away from the house, that had two soldiers at its front door. McDermott and the Commander walked toward them. The occupants of the Land Rover disembarked, advertising they had been handpicked. Their individual, substantial frames, were covered in protective riot gear, presenting a menacing display.

'I was going to ask if you needed back-up but…' offered the Commander.

'I think we'll manage, but thank you.'

He briefed Jackson and Douglas. 'Ok lads, we'll go in first, and our colleagues will transport him to his new home. Jacko, you lead. Let's go.'

The seven strong contingent, arrived at the front door, alongside the Commander, who produced a key. McDermott rapped the door and shouted, 'We're coming in!'

The entrance hall was non-descript, an exact match of every other dreary dwelling in the barracks. To the left, a staircase, a door to the meagre lounge, on the right. Henderson bounced out from the lounge into the hall, grabbing a crumpled newspaper, his reddened face contorted with rage. 'What the fuck is going on!?' he demanded, holding the Sunday World newspaper for all to see the bold headline: **Senior Loyalist Supergrass in hiding,** with a photograph of the police guard outside his house.

'Have you read this shite! These fucking lies! I need to call my solicitor. You bastards are setting me up!' he ranted, spittle flying from his mouth.

Jackson moved forward, his colossal frame eclipsing the outside light.

"Calm down Mr Henderson, and move back into the lounge!" he ordered. Henderson backed off, as the ensemble followed him, the riot team filling the hall. Henderson sat on an inexpensive, regulation chair, near the window.

'Where's your wife?' McDermott asked.

'She's in bed, and hasn't stop crying since she seen this,' he replied, motioning toward the newspaper.

'This headline has absolutely nothing to do with us, we're here on a different matter.'

For a brief second, Henderson pushed his chest out and narrowed his eyes, his ire rising again. He stood up.

'Well, you can fucking talk to me in my house! I'm not spending another second in this shit hole.'

As he made to leave, Jackson extended his powerful arm, placing it on Henderson's chest. McDermott produced the arrest warrant they had procured early that morning, at a sitting of the special court, after presenting evidence to the Public Prosecution Service.

'Samuel Henderson, I am arresting you for the murder of William Thomas Hamilton on September 1st...'

'What the fuck!' he screamed, rushing toward McDermott. Douglas darted alongside Jackson, each grabbing an arm and pivoting him 180 degrees to the right, before slamming him up against the wall. Two of the riot squad, handcuffs at the ready, moved in to expertly cuff the now, hapless, Henderson. An angry McDermott put his face on the wall and glowered at Henderson, before he continued.

'...you have the right to remain silent and do not have to say anything, but what you do say may be given in evidence.... Arsehole!'

Henderson howled in anger and frustration as he was trundled away, and dumped into the rear of the Land Rover. McDermott knocked lightly on the bedroom door, before opening it. Imogen Henderson lay on top of the bed in a foetal position. He likened her to a discarded doll.

'Mrs. Henderson,' he whispered

She turned, and slowly sat up to address him. Her eyes bloodshot, her skin a deathly white, making the scar on her face more notable. 'Can I go home please?' she begged.

McDermott knew he couldn't oblige until the news of Henderson's incarceration was widespread.

'Tomorrow morning if that's ok?' he replied with sincerity.

She just nodded, reaching for a glass of water to swallow two more headache tablets, before bursting into tears. He rushed over and put his arm carefully around her, in fear of harming her delicate body.

'It's ok, things will be ok,' he whispered in a soothing voice, 'I have a female officer en route to stay with you, until the morning.'

He laid her on the bed and draped a blanket over her. She continued to sob into her pillow as McDermott headed for the door.

'Sergeant...' the diminutive voice croaked, stopping him in his tracks. He turned to look at the slight bundle that was Imogen, '...I can go and visit Matthew now...thank you.'

Chapter 35

At 4pm in the jail, every prisoner had been fed, watered, exercised and showered. This was the 'dead' hour. In fact, Sunday, was the dead *day*. No movements, no visits, parcels or tuck shop. A ghostly silence spread throughout each of the four wings, with only the slightest mutterings of conversation echoing quietly. The only staff now on post were the Evening Duty; they would be there until the place was officially secured for the night. The association staff were in the canteen, watching TV or playing cards, or snooker. Alone in the censor's office, Patterson was redundant of work, his attention focusing on the Sunday World newspaper. He was transfixed, as much as surprised, knowing that his plan had already started to bear fruit. He stared at the archive photograph of Henderson, inset against the larger photo of his house, guarded by Police Officers, hoping that his feelings of hatred would somehow, be conveyed. The noise of the wooden hatch between the censors and PO's bunk sliding open, jolted him back toward reality.

'Paddy, away up and get Tommy and Davey down for a wee game of Jack change it, I'm bored shitless.'

Patterson's focus was still drawn to the photograph, the SO's request a soft noise in the distance.

'Are your ears painted on? What are you doing in there?'

'Oh...sorry SO' he replied, stumbling back into the present, 'I was doing a bit of paperwork.'

'Aye, Sunday newspaper work, you lazy wee shite.'

'Yer girl doesn't think I'm a lazy shite,' retorted Patterson. 'Right, I'll give them two a shout.'

The SO sat back, giggling at *that* comment, which he always found funny. A few seconds later, his phone rang. As Patterson grabbed his cup to wash, and tidied the desk, the SO appeared at the entrance to the office.

'Forget the card school kid, there's a committal in reception they need a hand with.'

He glanced at the headline of the paper. 'What a coincidence, it's that wanker there!' he continued, pointing at the newspaper before turning to leave. Patterson stared at his nemesis; aware he'd need to adopt a stoical approach, when he was face-to-face.

'Soon.' he whispered.

~

Patterson made his way from B wing across the circle to D wing, before entering through a large open grill leading down to the base. All the while, mentally disciplining himself with the mantra, *'He's just another prisoner.'* At the bottom of the stairs, Patterson doubled back, and entered through the right of two doors that were painted in the same sickly brown. His route took him directly into the reception area, through the SO's logging area. A few of the RUC Mobile Support Unit, still in riot gear, were milling around in the cavernous reception area. Henderson was being processed in the corridor that led into reception from the forecourt.

'Ok lads?' he offered.

'Not too bad mate,' one of them replied, 'Watch this one, he's a bad bastard!'

Patterson smiled before replying, 'To be honest, we don't get too many good ones in here.'

The MSU officer held a wry grin. Patterson felt his confidence grow. This was his playground.

'Do you need us to hang around in case he kicks off?' offered the MSU officer.

'No need, he's not going anywhere. Anyway, if he does, he'll hope the dog handler's Alsatian finishes him off before he meets Grumpy.' Trevor Black, a bald headed, basic grade officer with gnarled features and a repertoire of profanities, emerged from the SO's logging area. He had one of the jail's longest service records, yet never tried for promotion, even though he constantly 'acted up.'

'If you're finished talking like a wee girl, go out there and help the fucking clerical staff.'

'Speak of the devil,' Patterson smiled before moving to the corridor. The MSU officer waited until Henderson was finished being processed by the clerical officer at the other side of the window, who then leant across and slid open a gap further down, handing a Polaroid camera to Patterson.

'Paddy, do the needful for me will you while I finish checking the warrant?' Patterson accepted the camera, preparing to take three photographs. One to be stamped and signed by the MSU as a body receipt. Another would go into his file, the final one being his identification within the jail, until allocated a cell card. Patterson had no idea of how he would react coming face-to-face with his father's murderer for the first time.

He understood that losing control could mean, he may never get to fully complete his plan. Reaction, would attract attention, especially in front of Black, who never missed a trick. Patterson was guided by his subliminal thoughts, adapting the character everyone believed him to be. He asked Henderson to stand against the wall of the narrow corridor, adjacent to the window.

'Don't tell me you were born with that nose? What happened to you?' Henderson contemplated the young, loud-mouthed officer, before replying. He was a total stranger, yet... there was something about him. Had they met before? He couldn't quite describe his feelings toward him. For the first time since his arrest, he had a remote feeling of trepidation, without explanation.

'Nothing! It happened before I was lifted,' he mumbled, not taking his eyes from this seemingly harmless individual.

Patterson proceeded to take the three photographs.

'Ok, we can do an 8 x 10 in a gloss or matt finish, framed or unframed. Or 1 big one and 4 wee ones like the school photographs,' he stated with an air of confidence.

'What?'

Patterson leant closer; his tone of phrase icy cold. 'Jail humour pal, get used to it!'

He led Henderson to a changing cubicle and closed the door. Patterson lit a cigarette.

He knew it would take Black a few minutes to log Henderson's details into the admissions journal. It gave him time to resume his normal persona, feeling it had slipped with his last remark. Extinguishing the cigarette, Black reappeared, carrying a prison issue blue towel. He advanced towards Henderson's temporary cell.

'Right son, get that on you,' he ordered Henderson, who fumbled his reply.

'What do you mean?'

'It's not rocket science. Strip bollock naked and put your clothes in that.' He pointed to a bag hanging from a coat hanger. 'And use that towel to hide your dick with.'

'Is that all I get to wear?' Henderson exclaimed, a hint of fire in his tone.

'What did you expect? A fucking dressing gown and slippers!? You're in jail now!'

Henderson threw the towel at Black in an unconvincing show of confrontation. He noticed Patterson approach.

'I'm not here to be humiliated!' Henderson protested.

Patterson moved sharply, to lift the towel and stand between them both, handing the towel to Henderson.

'Look fella, nobody's here to humiliate anyone,' he began 'What my colleague here is trying to explain, in his own inimitable way...granted, is the routine. The routine that every other prisoner before you, has, and every other prisoner after you, will, undertake, because this place runs on routines.'

Patterson paused for a second, letting the information sink in before continuing.

'To be honest, no officer in here gives a flying fuck if you agree or disagree, but...I can guarantee... you will go through this routine, one way or another. The easy way... or the hard way.'

He had Henderson's complete attention.

'If you continue to disagree, at least four serious, fuck off big guys in riot gear will assist you, using headlocks, and arm locks and other such shite. Now it's your choice.'

Henderson was speechless. He felt vulnerable. No one had ever reacted against him like that in his life, and he was powerless.

'Do you smoke?' Patterson asked, interrupting his thoughts. Henderson nodded.

He opened his packet of cigarettes, shuffling a single one from the box as an offering. Henderson didn't react, instead feeling like the puppet and not the puppet master.

'Go on, take it, it'll not kill you,' he continued.

As Henderson slowly raised his hand toward the offering, Patterson pulled it away.

'Wait! It probably will kill you, in years to come...who cares?' he presented again, this time letting him accept the offering. Henderson produced his lighter.

'Gas Lighter? You'll not have that for too long, they're not allowed in here.' Patterson continued, before producing his own petrol based, Zippo lighter. This was the acid test, focusing on his hand as he flicked open the cover, spinning the wheel designed to spark the flint, and ignite the petrol-soaked wick. Time had slowed, his actions appeared robotic. Patterson was aware adrenalin, or nerves, could cause his hand to shake, a sign he didn't want Henderson to witness. Inwardly, he was delighted, his hand statuesque and immovable, while he offered the flame. Henderson took a long puff and sat back, feeling more relaxed about his predicament, thanks to the wise words of the young officer.

'Take five minutes and think about what I've just said. Then it's Blind date time.'

Henderson's features crumpled in confusion.

'The decision is yours,' Patterson continued, mocking the delivery of the television announcer.

An inkling of a grin appeared at the corner of Henderson's mouth before he spoke. 'Jail humour again?'

'Now you're whistling Dixie!' declared Patterson, before closing the door.

~

Patterson walked to the Logging area, where Black was finishing, and checking his paperwork. Black had admired how Patterson had taken control and managed the situation, but never in his wildest dreams, would he ever admit to it. He offered his accolade in the usual manner.

'See you young fellas, youse are too fucking soft,' he stated as endearingly as possible.

'No Grumpy, too smart. Sadly, a feeling you'll never know.'

Black light heartedly clenched his fist.

'I'll dig you!'

'Sorry old man, but you're not ready yet,' Patterson responded. 'I would hit you so many times, you'd think you were surrounded. Now, whilst our newest non-paying guest is making his deliberations, please excuse me, but I need a shit!' Lifting the key off a hook, Patterson walked to the toilet area. The toilets and showers in this area, for the inmates, were open plan. Half door cubicles for the showers, and a half door, that sat in a perpendicular frame housing each, of the two toilets. No toilet seats or locks on the door. Patterson inserted the key and opened the solid wood door that housed the Staff toilet. It was a porcelain version of a padded cell, wall to ceiling white tiles, a white wash hand basin and pedestal toilet. He locked the door, leaning back against it. This was a sanctuary within the jail. There were no windows. No-one could touch him here. He started to sporadically hyperventilate, loosening his mask of normality. He was sweating, thinking of Henderson.

Patterson was proud that throughout his career, he had treated every prisoner he came in contact with, the same way, irrespective of their crimes. But this was different. This was personal, *very personal*. His stomach spasmed and cramped, and he became nauseous, racing the few steps to the toilet, dropping to his knees whilst lifting the seat. Grasping the porcelain rim, he leant over, convinced he was about to vomit. Instead, sour spittle dribbled from his open mouth. He worked harder to control breathing and the putrid hate rising in him, as he got up and sat on the toilet. Staggering to the wash hand basin, he ran the cold tap, scooping handfuls of water onto his face before staring at the mirror. His reflection, almost unrecognisable. Blood filled his cheeks and forehead, the veins at the side of his skull working hard to transport it, standing out like ropes on his skin. His eyes were wide in a frightening way, as he stared with his teeth gritted together. He wanted to scream, but fought the urge. Closing his eyes and taking deep breaths, a measure of calm spread over him. When he opened them again, he was happier with his appearance and spoke to his reflection.

'I have seen the Devil,' he said, visualising the pug like demon he'd met earlier. He unequivocally ignored the fact, there were two devils that day, and one had glared back at him from within the mirror.

Chapter 36

The Superintendent glanced back over his shoulder toward him. 'Take sugar?'

McDermott replied with a shake of his head. The Superintendent collapsed into his plush chair, sipping and absorbing the fresh caffeine. Interlocking his fingers on both hands, he leant across the table without a trace of superiority.

'I've got to take my hat off to you Harry. With all those years of experience and instinct that this proud force has bestowed on you...you've done it. It must be a good feeling to have wrapped up a case that has been bugging you for so long. Catching a murderer who was nearly lost to the winds of time. Not only have you made me proud, but the Chief Constable sends his congratulations.' He offered his hand to McDermott who only stared at it before crossing his arms and sitting back.

'Thank you for the accolades Super, but with all due respect, we've got the wrong man.'

The Superintendent was exasperated, withdrawing his handshake. He remained silent, urging McDermott to continue.

'Yes, I'm glad we've got this thug off the streets, but only because his life is in danger.'

'But the murder weapon was found at his house...hidden for god's sake. What other proof do we need!' he replied, his cordial tone gone.

'You called it earlier in the investigation...it's a set up. There is nothing about the forensics report that can tie him to it. He's the wrong height, the solvents used to clean the handles and parts of the blades, are not present in his house, and why the hell would someone not clean the blood off a weapon used in a murder? Henderson may not appear to be clever, but trust me on this one, he wouldn't be that stupid. And I haven't even mentioned his previous stonewall alibi. '

The disgruntled Super showed his bottom teeth in annoyance.

'We're charging him with murder, Harry.'

'And rightly so, because the evidence points that way. But it won't stick, and you know it.'

The Superintendent chewed on his bottom lip contemplating before adopting a different tack.

'What've you left, three weeks?'

'Two,' McDermott offered.

'Harry, you owe it to yourself. You owe it Molly. Take it easy, slide into retirement, you've enough outstanding leave to finish in a few days. We'll sort this out.'

McDermott's expression was pained, as he rubbed his eyes before speaking.

'I don't want to plead, sir, but I will if I have to. I just *know* I'm close to the truth. Let me revisit this, and the Smallwood case, for my last few weeks.' He sat back and opened his arms in submission. 'It's all I ask.'

The superior had an arm on the table and his fingers drummed incessantly. He covered his mouth with his free hand and exhaled a loud sigh through his nose, a tribute to deep thought.

'Ok. Here's the way it is. You and those other two Comanche's, have until the day of your retirement, to find something...*anything*. No theories, no hunches, only evidence. Is that understood?'

McDermott smiled and stood up, offering his hand as a gesture. The gesture reciprocated.

'Thank you!' he stated, turning to leave.

'Harry...' McDermott halted, turning round.

'Just to let you know, I'll not be contributing to your leaving present. You just got it!'

~

Henderson couldn't sleep on his first night in a prison cell. Not because of the lump that failed to pass itself off as a pillow, nor the stained mattress, or the blanket that had the consistency of a brillo pad, but because he was alone, in a cell with his thoughts. So many questions and suspicions, with no trace of solutions. 'Who set me up?' his overriding conception. He initially rejected the notion of IRA involvement. It was too elaborate, and they wouldn't have wasted so much effort. They already had opportunities to kill him. His deliberation swiftly moved to internal scenarios.

Was it a takeover bid from Malcolmson, his number two? Or something to do with the UVF or Red Hand Commandoes, who constantly pressed for more violent responses to the slightest glitch on the radar? Had he annoyed someone to the point of desperation? He was deliberately ignorant of the fact that he was unpopular within the Organisation...*his* Organisation. He also had fleeting notions of RUC involvement in this charade, but to what extent or reason? He drew confidence from the fact that *when,* he received bail, his sole purpose would be to get to the bottom of this and guaranteed, whoever was responsible, would have a limited time left on this planet. Inevitably his conscious drifted to the here and now. He had been stripped of rank, stature and leadership with ease, at his incarceration. He was powerless and it frightened him. He had become faceless, labelled as an equal under the banner of prisoner. None of his fellow detainees cared for who he thought he was. He was ordinary, just like them and would be treated in the exact same way. That was emphasised earlier, when he attempted to use his powers of intimidation to forcibly jump the queue for the washroom, before being thwarted by a persistent alcoholic offender, who told him to 'fuck off and wait your turn!' He was now nothing but a number. The plastic plate with the untouched grey breakfast, of over fried bread and worn-out eggs, sat on a small wooden table in the cell, his only meagre furniture. He longed to be back on the plush settees of his palatial home, flicking through the TV channels, Imogen jumping to his every whim. His sorrowful plight evaporated as the metal door opened. Two officers filled the space.

'Right Henderson, interview with the Governor!' stated the older of the two in a non-negotiable tone.

The morning melee of washing, slopping and feeding was over, his new compatriots locked away, as he was escorted the length of the empty base toward a makeshift office. The elder officer faced him, explaining the protocol.

'Don't sit until you're invited to. Address the Governor as 'Sir' and do yourself a favour by not fucking about, or you'll spend an awful long, lonely, time down here with us.' His face changed to a forced smile. 'Understand?!'

Henderson nodded and a spark of his former existence appeared, as he thought, *'If you talked like that to me outside, I would break your back.'*

The younger of the two, gently rapped the frosted plastic window in the wooden door before a reply of 'enter' followed. Henderson was impressed by the large, bearded, smartly-dressed Governor, amplified by the narrowness of the spartan office. The Governor glanced up at him, then at the empty chair, before nodding and returning his attention to the reams of paperwork at his side of the desk. In the seat, Henderson was aware of the close proximity of the escorts, perpendicular to him at each side. Ignoring his presence, the Governor continued studying the paperwork in a calculated fashion. Eventually, he tidied the mess and sat it face down on the desk before staring at Henderson.

'My name is Governor Bleasdale, and you are now a guest in my prison. You will be fed and watered, receive medical and welfare attention, and, dependent on your behaviour, association time and visits.'

Henderson stared back without response.

'I am duty bound to make you aware of important information in regards to yourself,' the Governor continued, nodding briefly at the paperwork. 'I can report, with authority, that because of external security forces sit-reps, and our internal security investigations, there is a live threat against your life, both outside and inside this establishment.'

Henderson's jaw dropped slightly at the revelation.

'...and for those reasons, you will be held on remand in B Wing.'

Henderson was outraged, growling a reply without invite. The escorts shuffled closer, ready to pounce.

'B Wing!' he yelled, 'You're not putting me in with those paedos... and sex offenders! I demand to be housed in A wing with my own people, and take my chances with those fenian bastards! They don't scare me!' In his fury he attempted to stand, but forceful arms pinned him into the seated position. Bleasdale glared at him as he stood up and leant on the desk.

'Listen carefully,' he ordered. 'Those un-sentenced prisoners are like you, innocent until proven guilty. They are your equals.' He paused for effect. 'No-one, and I mean no-one, demands anything in here! Do I make myself clear?' His tone had risen in sincerity. A furious Henderson glared back at him. 'And for your information, the threat is from, *your people!'*

Henderson gasped, the blood draining from his ruddy face. The statement acted as a preverbal slap in the mouth. The pressure on his arms eased, allowing him to stand. His legs felt weak as he turned for the door, halting as Bleasdale spoke for the final time.

'On a personal level, I want you to know, that I am of the Catholic persuasion.'

Chapter 37

The young recruit focused on the floor, taking quick breaths as he patrolled the narrow corridor in Legal visits. Only into his second month of duty, after graduation from the Prison Service College, he wondered if he'd made an horrendous mistake. The comfortable conditions of the family hardware shop, seemed a universe away. He'd joined the service on a whim, attempting to 'prove' himself to his father, asserting he would make his own decisions in life. But he was terrified of this place. Mingling with the worst of society, every minute of every day, amalgamated with the humane treatment these animals expected and received, sickened and frightened him. Carrying a pistol everywhere, that would be useless against an under-car bomb, the young recruit would never get used to it in his life. He promised himself to speak with his mother tonight, and begin the journey of returning to normality. For the time being, he was the sole member of staff working in Legal Visits. He could hear the others, including the Senior Officer in charge, chatting merrily, laughing or groaning at intended jokes, whilst the others worked studiously on their crosswords or today's racing bets. It highlighted his importance, and belonging, within the group. Bottom of the barrel.

The main area was a wider, but shorter, corridor. To one side, a long bench cemented into the wall for the waiting 'runners.' Opposite, a desk with a Senior Officer at the 'tunnel' side, directly facing the basic grade, 'Recorder and dispatcher' at the visitor's entrance side. Behind the Senior Officer, two narrow corridors extended left and right, that were used as observation walkways, of the four soundproofed cubicles in each, where inmates met with legal representatives. Transgressing the junction were holding cells, toilet and search box. Legal visitors were afforded the luxury of having their own private waiting area. They were escorted across the forecourt to an uncovered tunnel, wedged between the right-hand side of the main office block of the jail, and the reception area. They then entered another manned airlock, giving access to B Visits (right) or Legal Visits (straight ahead). Prison staff considered legal eagles as parasites on the government budget, reaping rewards for undertaking impossible cases they knew would run forever, without a care of success or failure. Their bank accounts benefitted either way. The young recruit rose from a plastic chair at the far end of the corridor, he was observing. He endeavoured not to appear timid as he walked by the 3rd, and only occupied cubicle, glancing through the toughened glass that filled most of the upper part of the door. The intimidating glare from the inmate within, determined he would not look in again during his tenure. His head was bowed, on the return journey to the sanctity of his plastic chair.

~

Liam Brennan, junior counsel for the defence, in the case against McGuigan, Toal and Flagherty, grappled to contain his excitement of being in the same room with Ireland's leading warrior, in the fight against British supremacy. Brennan, a republican from birth, nurtured by his Sinn Fein father, a counsellor in the small village of Moneyglass in Antrim. His father was an astute strategist, who remained loyal to the party whenever it split in 1970. He had recognised that force alone, would never repel the British invaders. The necessity to educate, and infiltrate, the corridors of power was paramount, and should run parallel to any armed struggle. He had his son's destiny mapped out. Liam always wondered how his family could afford to send him to Queens University, ignorant of the fact, he, and many others, were sponsored from party funds. McGuigan sat at the other side of the table and waited patiently. Brennan fumbled with his briefcase before producing the relevant paperwork. McGuigan noticed the young officer outside and made eye contact.

'Sorry about that, Mr. McGuigan.' announced Brennan.

'Call me Padraig,'

'Thank you. I have a mixed bag of news, I'm afraid. The Public Prosecution Service have successfully manoeuvred an adjournment until next Thursday.'

Fully aware of the reason for the adjournment, McGuigan tilted his head, a gesture for Brennan to continue.

'It seems their star witness in your case, has got cold feet, and no longer wants to give evidence. Even with the threat of contempt of court, the possibility of a three-month custodial sentence, along with a fine of up to £2500 for not doing so.'

McGuigan nodded with approval, Brennan impressed with his impassive demeanour. He galvanized his composure, before continuing.

' I also have other news, outside of your case,' he stated in a lower tone, nervously putting his arms on the table. Leaning forward, he clasped his hands together for fear of displaying his anxious mood. McGuigan reciprocated, mirroring Brennan's poise.

'Carry on.'

Brennan's mouth went dry, not just because he was interviewing a legend, but the ramifications to his career, if this ever became public knowledge. McGuigan realised the dilemma and reassured him. He captured Brennan's gaze and whispered,

'I know your father.'

Solace radiated from Brennan's face.

'I have a fellow sympathiser, who works for the Department of Driver, Vehicle and Licensing. I have an address for John Patterson, Prison Officer.'

For the first time during the interview, McGuigan's expression morphed from dispassionate, to content. He smiled at Brennan.

'This day has just got better.'

~

Although unaware, due to the facade he presented daily, Patterson slowly began to distance himself from the other members of staff. He didn't want close proximity to anyone. His 'mission', was a solitary endeavour. He didn't need distractions. That would only complicate things. Staff had been understanding, and sympathetic, at his changed personae. A fellow officer who had suffered, was ordained with ongoing respect and compassion. Patterson, on the other hand, had Henderson where he wanted him. It became obvious to him, the perfect scenario to execute his undertaking. Fully aware he needed fortune to smile on him during that period, Patterson was convinced it would be a success. After all, he'd been placed in B Wing, where his prey was now housed. He didn't consider this as a stroke of luck, but an omen. A justification. Patterson, unerringly believed, that destiny was already written for everyone on the planet and felt privileged, almost superior, to be the sole human aware of this 'fact'. He felt it his duty to assist the greater powers, ensuring he wouldn't deviate from the path chosen for him, endeavouring to ensure everything went according to plan. It had struck him like a lightning bolt, when he discovered the perfect scenario. He felt destiny at his shoulder, hinting at what to do and when, unveiling the next clue in his assignment.

Night guard.

The perfect scheme. Few staff. All other prisoners locked. There were obstacles of course, obstacles he had anticipated, and solutions he had formulated.

No one else, especially staff, would ever be in danger. Destiny owed him that. He accepted the canvas of his future, on completing his task, would remain blank, no matter how he strived to formulate any type of outcome. It had already been decided. He didn't fear the canvas represented the termination of his existence. The clock had already started ticking. He had considered applying for permanent night guard duty, confident his request would be honoured, still being considered vulnerable by the Governor and Chief Officer. But, on a permanent rota, he could be housed in other wings, as the paramilitary threat against him would be nullified, because *all* prisoners were locked up for the night. He put the word out to a few MGB's that were regulars in the wing. 'Money grabbing bastards', who hated night guard as they couldn't undertake any overtime. It worked like a dream, further convincing him, he was still on the dedicated route. He was aware that there were two projections to achieving his destiny. Attaining the deserved retribution, in the name of his father, and maintaining his high security awareness to ensure he stayed alive, robbing the IRA of the opportunity of meddling with his destiny.

Chapter 38

The class officer, and assistants, on B1 had been briefed by Security and the B Wing PO, about the volatile inmate they had received, and the high risk of assault that came with him. Henderson, therefore, was located on the 1's, in the furthest cell on the right-hand side of the landing, past the stairwell for the 2's and 3's, in the middle of the landing. It ensured lighter footfall as the only inmates in that area, apart from the ones already there, would be travelling to the Prison Hospital. Staff interned in the airlocks at each end of the wing, Circle and Hospital, were briefed daily, to halt prisoner movement, particularly Henderson, on the wing, whenever alien inmates were passing through. The Class Officer, Michael Galbraith, mid-thirties, had already interviewed Henderson. Galbraith prided himself in his work, being the protector of the most vulnerable inmates in the jail, affording them the privileges, security and care, that all other re-habitual inmates took for granted. It was his remit to protect them from all other inmates, and staff. Galbraith despised the way some of the staff flexed their muscles when dealing with his charges during cell searches, knowing full well it was an act of bravado on their part, as they wouldn't dream of reacting that way in the paramilitary wings. He was uninfluenced every time he confronted these charlatans and bullies, who never made official complaints about him, realising he had uncloaked them for what they really were. Galbraith had successfully fought a case to keep two sex offenders on his remand landing, as full-time sentenced orderlies, understanding they would have been destroyed in the mainstream of D wing sentenced prisoners

The orderlies and remand prisoners, were delighted to assist in the cleaning, and running of their section of the wing. Polishing brass handles of cell doors, mopping and cleaning shower areas, amongst other menial tasks. It provided purpose. Tasks that helped them combat the monotony and boredom of being locked all day in a cell. However, the entrance to the stairwell was their limit. In their half of the landing, the normal overhead metallic catch net, preventing attempted suicides, that stretched from one side of the wing to the other, on both the 2's and 3's, had been replaced by metallic plating. An extra form of protection for the most vulnerable, avoiding boiling water and verbal abuse, cascading from above. Any excursion past the stairwell toward the circle end, returned them to the kill zone, where they would be mere quarry to the vultures above.

For that reason, two sentenced orderlies were collected each morning from D wing, under the tutelage of the Censor Officer, to maintain this area of the landing and operate the Tea boat, delivering tea and toast to their uniformed masters, throughout the day. Galbraith had explained the routines to Henderson, as well as what was expected of him behaviourally, and assurances of protection afforded him. He made him aware that he had no time for bullies, and explained the consequences of such acts. He didn't really care if Henderson acceded to the rules, confident that a long period of solitary would eventually bring him round. It always did.

~

Henderson preened himself prior to his early visit. He had managed to reduce the nicks of blood on his face to three, sticking cheap toilet paper shards to his face, to prevent further bleeding. 'Stupid, fucking useless, Bic razors,' he mumbled to his reflection in the showering area, his notoriety demanding he washed alone. He loathed this place. Hated the fact the razors had to be signed out and in. Hated the fact he was surrounded by sex offenders, now his only friends. Hated that he had to piss and shit in a plastic slop bucket, that would be his cellmate until morning ablutions. And hated the news his solicitor had delivered him yesterday, that the RUC had successfully opposed bail. But more than anything, he hated that he was alone, and vulnerable. He couldn't pick up the phone and chat or demand. Startlingly aware, he was the lowest in the pecking order, in the eyes of that do-fucking-good screw, who ran this crap landing. Everything he said, requested or received was logged. Everything else was controlled, and out of his authority. He was told when to eat, when to exercise, when to visit and when to sleep. At night he would lie awake, trying and failing to visualise his way out this nightmare, struggling to accept he would no longer head the organisation. The realisation he may never again be a free man, was terrifying. Handing the razor back to the class assistant, he locked himself in the cell to prepare for the visit. He was annoyed it had taken so long for Imogen to visit, but *merely* annoyed. Gone was the fury that had been the norm during their marriage, understanding she had become the only rock in his sea of destitution, to cling to. He also rued the relationship, or non-relationship, he had with his only son and heir. When, and if, he was released, he would move mountains to cement that family bond, a thought he had never once imagined.

~

During the morning, Patterson read and censored a mountain of inmates' mail. He was interrupted by shouts up the stairwell, informing class officers to cease movement. After the racket of complaining inmates, and doors closing, the wing fell silent. A single cell door opening, disrupted the calm state, accompanied by more than one set of footsteps, getting increasingly louder. A staff member stopped at the opening to the censor's office, carrying a visiting slip.

'Paddy, that's your man going for his visit.'

'No bother,' Patterson replied, keeping his eyes glued to the frame presented by the Cell door opening. An uncomfortable Henderson looked in, slowing as he passed. He noticed the younger officer he had spoken to on his incarceration, at the messy desk. 'All right?' he muttered with a hint of a smile. Patterson stared at him for a few seconds, aware of not overdoing it, needing to have this monster's trust, to abet his downfall. He forced a false smile and nodded. Under the desk, his hands gripped his thighs in anger.

Chapter 39

Movement in the circle and D wing, was halted whilst Henderson was escorted down to B Visits. The escorting officer was as vigilant as all other staff, aware of the Governor's directive, that no harm should befall him. As Henderson passed the eerily silent end of D wing airlock, a prisoner from far down the landing shouted, ' Tout bastard!', before being bundled into his cell. The abuse spread like a plague from behind closed doors, led by the protestant ODC's (ordinary decent criminals). It was latched onto by the others of all persuasions, most of whom were unaware of Henderson's infamy, but enjoyed this, the safest form of rebellion, from behind a closed door. The rage raced through Henderson. He forced his mouth closed, exhaling through his nostrils, hands gripped in the shape of fists, fingers turning white. Although short lived, the cacophony of the chanting, 'Tout,' accompanied by rhythmic banging against cell doors, echoed in his mind. An unwanted reminder of his situation.

~

B visits area was the smallest, and least busy, within the jail. Due to the absence of natural light, it was by far the brightest, the ceiling festooned in tubular neon lights, flooding the area in illumination, at headache level. It was also the quietest. Shamed visitors, ignoring anyone walking by their booth, held whispered conversations. On entering, the recording officer indicated the second last, squashed booth on the right-hand side for the escort's cargo.

Henderson couldn't believe how small and compact the visiting area was, and how miniscule the booths were. It reminded him of Spence's chip shop on the Beersbridge road that he had visited many times. Inwardly, he prayed he would be given the opportunity to visit there again. Entering from the search box, there were five booths on the right and four on the left. An easy area to patrol. At the end of the walkway patrol area, was a purpose-built wooden structure, accessible at the side via a step. It was for the recording officer, who sat with his journal, along with wooden trays that housed visiting slips. He recorded every visit, and was responsible for terminating them after the requisite, allocated time. The visiting booth directly to the recorders left, had evolved into the Senior Officer's private space, as no-one in living memory, could recall this visiting area at full capacity. As Henderson was led to his allocated berth, SO Ricky Harrison rose to his feet in the last booth. At a glance, he could be mistaken as a boxer, his flat nose and broad forehead hinting in that direction, yet he was of high intellect, and revered for his leadership, and decision making. Henderson had a brief glance at Harrison, before sitting on one of the benches, either side of the table.

'Other side bad boy,' Harrison stated solemnly, towering above the dividing wooden partition.

'What are you talking about?' Henderson barked with a huff.

Remaining solemn, Harrison's tone had the addition of menace. He pointed to the opposite side of the table. 'Are those ears painted on? Other side!'

'What difference does it make where I sit?' replied Henderson, his vexation threatening to boil over. He'd had enough bowing and scraping in B wing already, and had reached the outer limits of tolerance. He folded his arms in an act of refusal. Without faltering, his focus locked, Harrison continued.

'Joe, I believe we have someone who is just about to forego the privilege of a visit,' he said, loud enough for the recording and patrolling officers, to move closer. A carrot had been dangled in front of Henderson. His bravado, could jeopardise a meeting he longed for. Depended on. He stood up and shuffled across to the appointed side of the table. Harrison continued to glower at him, before nodding discreetly at the other staff.

'There's a good boy,' Harrison patronised, his frame slowly sinking back down behind his wooden partition.

The visitor's door opened and Imogen was led in. Henderson was vexed at her appearance. Her skin was pale, with no hint of make-up, the scar on her face more prominent. Her frail hair looked lifeless. She *looked* brittle. As she approached the booth, Henderson rose, embracing and hugging her. She kept her arms by her side. When he faced her for a kiss, she turned her head, presenting a cheek. He motioned for her to sit, holding his hands out across the table empowering her to do the same.

'Baby, what's wrong?' he asked with uncertainty.

Imogen stared at him with ice, before replying.

'What's wrong?' she replied with indignation, holding her palms out and scanning the surroundings. 'Look around you. That's what wrong!'

Henderson's heart sank at how determined she sounded, a far cry from the feeble servant she had once been. He struggled to speak, unaware of what to say.

'I've put £500 into your account and lodged the parcel you requested.'

Henderson disliked the finality to her tone as she continued.

'I'm leaving you.'

'What!?'

'You heard. I'm leaving you, and the miserable existence I have endured for so many years. I'm going to live with Matthew in Spain.' A single tear, not of regret, but of contentedness, rolled down her face. Henderson reacted in an alien manner.

'Please love, don't say that,' he pleaded, his voice breaking. 'I need you more now, than ever. I need you, and I need our son. But…you don't have the money to go in live in Spain.'

'Our son? Our son? You hypocrite! He's *my* son, do you hear me, *mine!*' Her volume triggered awareness of the staff. Harrison exited his booth to stand beside the recorder's rostrum. Henderson tried to urge her, to keep her voice down, but she continued.

'You ignored that child because he wasn't a puppet you could control, like all those other scumbags!' She rose to her feet.

'Money? I've instructed the estate agents to sell the house and send the money to Matthew's account. Now if you'll excuse me, I have a flight to catch this afternoon. Good bye!' The thought of his palace being sold was too much to take, underlining his commitment to greed, rather than family bonding. He leapt from his seat and grabbed her arms from behind.

'You fucking sell my house and I'll...'

His reply was cut short by the two officers behind, as they applied Control and Restraint techniques on each arm, rendering Henderson defenceless. They brought him to his knees. The Recording Officer controlled his head, as he was carefully removed backwards, toward the search box. The usually reserved prisoners and visitors, peeked like meerkats from their booths. Extra staff flooded in from both entrances, in reaction to the wall alarm Harrison had activated. He guided Imogen into the safety of the booth during the fracas. Henderson tried, unsuccessfully to roar threats in her direction, but found it impossible.

'Sorry about that Mrs. Henderson,' Harrison offered, escorting her back to the visitors well.

'No need,' she replied, 'in fact I'm already beginning to look forward to being the *ex*- Mrs. Henderson.'

Chapter 40

He was content to witness the trailing car head onto the Saintfield Road. Going full circle, Patterson thought about the roundabout. In summer when it was attended, the centre was awash with colour. Splashes of white, orange, red, yellow and purple, as neatly prepared flower beds, shrubs and trees boasted their wares. During winter, the evergreen bushes dominated as sprawling lava, to engulf the withered delicate flora. They had grown untouched, providing a circular screen announcing the roundabout, making it impossible to view the opposite side from any angle. On completion of his 360-degree circular tour, Patterson re-joined the Saintfield Road for half a mile, before turning left onto Mealough Road, beside the reservoir, and into the countryside. He wasn't exactly sure what route to take, as there were quite a few options. He was used to alternating his route into work, making it almost impossible for anyone else to ambush him. He followed a sign at Ballylesson for Shaws Bridge and into Belfast, via the Malone Road. He was well aware that no matter what route he took, he still had to drive through the 'kill zone' around the entrance of the jail. That would never change.

~

At 7:30am, the Crumlin Road jail slowly came to life. Buzzers and bells emanated from the circle area, from staff wanting in, or out of their wings. Metal cell doors banged, keys jangled and the clip clop of steel tipped shoes and boots, emanating from each wing, amalgamating into a crescendo into the circle.

The noise was magnified by the remainder of the day staff gathering for the daily parade, some buzzing round the duty sheets that hung from metal hooks. Patterson was on the five-hour day shift of his night guard, and joined the 8am parade. A Principal Officer was charged with the task of carrying out the roll call. All Senior ranks on the day shift, stood to attention, or something resembling it, formed up beside the rostrum at the entrance to C Wing. The staff would form four or five ranks at the front. Most POs would race through the roll call, aware that staff at the back were calling out 'present' in different voices, for others who had yet to leave the canteen, or were running late. Today was different. An ageing bald-headed PO, notorious for his slow delivery, was on call. At least one member of staff, hidden from view, during this marathon session, would cough out loud before grunting 'arsehole' to the delight of all others. The indignation was complete when he attempted to dismiss the parade with his order of 'Shun!' All staff endeavoured to smash their foot down at different intervals, in an homage to Dad's Army. Patterson wasn't entertained, his mind focussed on what lay ahead. He was night guard tonight, but hadn't yet acquired all the elements he needed. His personal jigsaw was incomplete and would remain so, until his Aunt Elsie returned from her Ulsterbus excursion to the Dingle peninsula, in Kerry. After that happened, it would be time.

~

McGuigan, wrapped up against the bitter wind as winter approached, walked around A wing exercise yard in conversation with his appointed OC (Officer in Command) from A2.

'Just think Padraig,' the OC offered, his voice barely audible beneath the upturned lapels of his jacket, 'In a few days' time you'll be back out in the real world. I'll bet you you'll miss this place!' McGuigan displayed a wry grin. 'Yeah, like I'd miss an ingrown toenail!' As the two walked in silence, McGuigan reflected. Yes, he was excited to be receiving his freedom. To plan and to lead. But his thoughts were tinged with sadness at returning to an empty home. Orla had vanished into thin air, and he reluctantly accepted she would no longer share his house, or bed, again. He clung to the hope that the bastard screw had assisted her, and she was in hiding. If so, the screw would provide the information required during the last vestiges of his miserable existence, giving McGuigan his overdue retribution. The OC walking alongside, was aware his mentor was lost in his own reminiscences, and motioned he walk with other comrades. McGuigan nodded, admiring the respectability of the young gun, before returning to his plans for Patterson. Thanks to the junior brief, he had the registration of the vehicle, but more importantly, an address in Carryduff. He'd been in Carryduff a few times, its most prominent feature being the massive roundabout at the top of the Saintfield Road. McGuigan was familiar with the Muskett development, the last housing estate before Ballynahinch. Quite a few young families from the west of the city, had undertaken a mini exodus to Muskett, to escape the violence that stained daily life in the west of the city. McGuigan understood their rhetoric, but felt disappointed they had abandoned their roots. The Army council was, however, astute and had 'bought' a few houses in the estate to act as safe houses, or information gathering dwellings. It was common knowledge that police and prison officers were scattered throughout the area. Nugent had informed him, a volunteer was holed up in a house on Muskett Court, opposite the termination of Muskett Road, the entrance to the cul-de-sac that housed Patterson. It was a perfect scenario, Patterson having to pass it every time he left for, and returned from work. The volunteer's brief was to note timings; when Patterson left and returned from day shift, evening duty and night shift. Patterns were forming daily. Nugent originally suggested putting 'sleepers' at bus stops down the length of the Saintfield road to ascertain Patterson's favoured route, before realising he changed his route regularly. McGuigan had dismissed the notion, wanting Patterson in his own house. He longed to hurt him, to break every bone in his body in the duration of discovering information about Orla. He would have to be patient, as the Army council had a strategy in place. True, Patterson would be beaten close to unconsciousness, but he had then to be taken in an unmarked vehicle across the border to an isolated cottage, close to the Meath and Westmeath border, a secretive haunt of the IRA. On arrival, McGuigan would lead. He was well founded in interrogation techniques through regular schooling meetings within the organisation. Isolation, sleep and sensory deprivation, stress positions and water boarding to name but a few. By the end of his ordeal, Patterson would tell McGuigan everything he needed to know, and would be rewarded with a bullet between his eyes, before resting in a shallow grave in an anonymous and desolate area.

Chapter 41

Alone in the goldfish bowl, McDermott contemplated retirement, while waiting for his deputies to arrive. He knew colleagues who had re-enlisted after early retirement, due to boredom. He also recalled a few who had lasted less than nine months, before dying of alcoholic poisoning. They went from the overtaking lane to parking, instead of a gradual decline in activity, focusing on something else and keeping busy. He understood the move to Scotland and his darling daughter and grandsons, would be enough to prevent him from being another regretful statistic of that troupe. He was confident he could adapt to life outside of the force with consummate ease, although he realised that transformation would only be complete with solving this last case. He had nine days and a task force of three to do it, a mountain to be climbed. In the dark. *'No worries there then,'* he thought, in the typical Belfast sarcastic tone. Thoughts of bliss that could be achieved with success, was interrupted when Jackson and Douglas barged into his private sanctuary. Jackson flopped into one of the chairs across the desk from McDermott as opposed to Douglas, who quietly took his place.

'Well Captain, what's happening?'

'Welcome to the task force Jacko, let me introduce the only other member,' McDermott replied, his hand motioning in the direction of Douglas, who appeared puzzled.

'Task Force?'

'Yes Doug. Our all-powerful, and mighty Superintendent, has granted me the last of my three wishes by letting me, and you two, focus solely on finding the murderer of Montgomery and Hamilton. However, we work alone and have been given absolutely no resources. Well...that's what he thinks.'

They waited patiently.

'We all have friends in places and departments throughout the force. If you need to contact, avail of any information, require specialist equipment, or whatever else from them, ensure you let them know this is without the Superintendent's authority. and solely a favour to me. If the Super finds out, you tell him it was me that made you do it. I'll take the rap. Any questions?'

Jackson smiled before replying. 'Think you're safe enough Captain. Most of the boys would love to stick a boot up his arse.' The others grinned approvingly.

'The one thing we don't have, is time,' McDermott announced. 'We've got nine days, before I get a pipe and a rocking chair.'

Douglas blew out through his lips. 'Jeez, that's tight.'

'I know Doug, I know.' McDermott sounded deflated. 'On the upside, you'll make a few quid in overtime.'

Jackson danced his eyebrows as he spoke through a grin. 'Mmm...Money'.

McDermott shook his head, suppressing a laugh. 'It's a big ask lads, but trust me, it would be the best retirement present I could imagine.'

'At least you've got a part of it, with that monster in jail,' offered Douglas.

McDermott mused before replying. 'True, but the clock's already ticking on that. The murder charge won't stick because of the forensic evidence.'

The others nodded ruefully. McDermott then spent the next 20 minutes detailing his plan of action. He needed his troops to relook at every piece of evidence with fresh eyes. Spend at least two days on Hamilton, Montgomery and then Henderson. Any dust that had settled was to be disturbed. Anything that appeared trivial, needed to be re-examined. Think both inside and outside of the box. Look for patterns. Test theories. Uncover enemies. Be suspicious of associates. Get special branch to put their informants through the mangle and squeeze out everything they know, and weren't aware they knew. He would concentrate on Smallwood.

'Let's go to work fellas,' he announced.

They stood to leave, before Jackson halted and spoke. 'We could do this the easy way, Captain.'

The adrenaline that had been coursing through McDermott's body, increased in ferocity. He quickly thought that he'd missed something obvious. Mouth agape, he nodded for Jackson to continue. 'We could put an advert in the Belfast Telegraph job section. Wanted, a 5' 9"ish, left-handed, scissors killer. Previous experience essential. Immediate start.'

McDermott's eyes widened in disbelief. He felt an amalgamation of anger and mirth, biting on his bottom lip to suppress a grin. He quickly scoured the desk, searching for something to throw, and grabbed a yellow paged notepad, that he hurled in the direction of the colossus.

'Fuck off, Jacko!' he shouted in a growling laughter.

A cacophony of laughter filled the room. Jackson and Douglas gathered the loose leaves of paper and the remnant of the pad, placing them back on McDermott's desk. Douglas questioned him before leaving.

'Captain, you said this was the last of your three wishes. What were the first two?'

'To replace you two!'

'I'd get a new genie,' remarked Jackson, as they both exited with more than traces of grins still on their faces. McDermott looked at the closed door in contemplation, before whispering aloud, 'I'm going to miss you both.'

~

The movement of inmates to the 3 separate dining halls on each of the 3 A Wing landing's, was controlled by an officer in a secure box, protected by a locked grill. The officer controlled a smaller version of an airlock designed to make it impossible to open both grills at the same time, and accommodating a maximum of three people. The only route to the airlock, was on the opposite side of the landing.

Within the secure observation box, was a few wooden steps up to a small landing and a chair. During the dining period, an officer could observe from behind a two-way toughened glass window, and had a direct link to the class office, should anything out of the norm occur. The Officer on duty, unseen by the inmates during the association period, was engrossed in his crossword puzzle. Occasionally struggling to formulate an answer, he focused on the interior of the dining area, noticing that McGuigan sat alone. This was rare. No other prisoner approached nor disturbed him.

~

McGuigan had been in foul form for most of the afternoon. At a late legal visit, he was informed his case had been put back a week, due to personal matters, affecting the Crown Court judge hearing his case. With such a high-profile case, and so many costly hours already accrued, and evidence heard, it would take more than a week for a replacement judge to confidently adjudicate. He was told it was a family matter. McGuigan reckoned it clashed with a golfing trip to Portugal, and lounging about in the mansion he had on the outskirts of Lagos. Alone in his cell, McGuigan replayed everything he intended to do to Patterson, when the role of prisoner was reversed. It was his personal light at the end of the tunnel of being remanded. Frustratingly, his wait had lengthened. Nugent visited that morning, with the news that the army council were pushing to execute the mission, and hold Patterson until McGuigan was released, making apportioning blame in his direction, impossible.

But this was personal, and he stressed to Nugent how much he needed this. He needed to be involved from the start, to the grisly end. To be involved with the capture, torture and execution of someone who had interfered in his personal life. He made it paramount, that he would be at the wheel of this ship. He further explained to inform the witness who had retracted his statement, that the organisation would cover any cost he incurred for contempt of court, and that they would ensure a safe, care free time in custody, should that come about.

McGuigan sat at a table in the far corner of the dining area, showing no facial expressions of the mood, anger and frustration emanating from his soul. An unfortunate new, younger prisoner, had made an attempt to communicate. McGuigan's icy glare had the boy cowering away like a dog on bonfire night. McGuigan's presence, and silence, set the tone for the entire area. Some engaged in whispered chatter at other tables. The television at the opposite end, was barely audible. Even the card players and pool hustlers kept a low profile, such was the impact of McGuigan. In his mind, he discussed what had happened. Was it because the judge had another formal engagement? Or was it the PPS's last effort at turning the witness? He placated himself in the knowledge that it was only a lousy week, before he could get his retribution. His thoughts strayed to Orla. He'd been guilty of taking her for granted, aware she only stayed with him, because of his position. Not because of kudos, but because she knew she was trapped. She didn't dare leave him. Yet... she had defied logic. He remembered her at her gorgeous best, in head-to-toe tartan, returning breathless from a Bay City Rollers concert. He remembered her at her sultry best, wearing only makeup and his shirt, awaiting his return, with wine and candles. And the passionate love making in front of the open fire, that lasted for hours. Her throaty, sexy laugh. She was perfection. But the bastard screw, Patterson, had taken her from him. Had he shared all her delights? Had she cried with passion when he'd made love to her? He would soon know. He would also find her. One day.

Chapter 42

Pamela Wallace was the wrong side of mid-forties. She was a butterfly, who emerged from a marital cocoon, having wed her teenage sweetheart, Timothy McBride, who'd started a fledgling Property Service, in a difficult market. They lost the first few years of wedded bliss to working round the clock, and growing the business. Ironically, they could only afford rented accommodation, as any money earned, was ploughed back into their venture. Their breakthrough came when an astute bank manager noticed the potential for their company's growth, offering the loans they needed. Within 4 years, they started to show a profit, and hit the jackpot, when they won the contract for selling, from the biggest developer on the island. Focused on growth, Timothy became a paper millionaire by their 7th wedding anniversary. They bought their own house outright, and opened another branch. And another. He hired staff to give Pamela a break from her incessant workload, but mainly preparation, to be the perfect mother to the children they had started to plan. The relationship soured, when it became knowledge, she was infertile. He didn't want a child from a donor egg. They drifted apart. He worked longer, attended more meetings, worked weekends. She became a ghostly shadow, drifting through their palatial home. He tolerated her, which felt worse than if he hated her. She knew nothing but the property business and wouldn't accept the employment he offered from a rival company.

She suffered depression, which was entirely unacceptable to her pastiche 'friends' and neighbours, in their private development, close to the affluent Malone Road. She became a burden, waiting nervously each day, expecting he suggest separation. A beautiful olive-skinned secretary of Timothy's, came to her rescue one afternoon by announcing, at her doorstep, that she was carrying her husband's child. When the tears dried, she applied for divorce through infidelity. He thought nothing of it and gave her the house. It was a mere drop in the ocean. The eternal alimony however, created a bigger splash. She began to focus on herself, attending self-help and makeup classes, before enrolling with the Open University for a degree course in social work. Those she would help, would be surrogates for the children she could never have. The more confidence she attained, showed in her dress sense, leading to more admiring glances. She craved the attention men would afford her. She was always buxom, and carried a little weight. *Voluptuous,* she considered. An industrial sports bra, and sickeningly tight, hidden girdle, completed the package. She was now working in a place where the male attention would be never ending. She gathered her welfare package of income support, disability allowances and a plethora of other leaflets, designed to support the most vulnerable. She studied her reflection in the mirror. Her long black hair gleaming and immaculate, ringlets hanging to her shoulders. Her skin had the subtle artificial glow of tan from a bottle. Her eyes, accented by a hint of blue eye shadow, complimented by false eyelashes. She applied pillar box red lipstick, prior to checking her clothes. 'Never disappoint your audience,' she sang out loud. Her charcoal grey, two-piece suit, had a hint of pinstripe on both the jacket and pencil skirt. It made it a little difficult to walk comfortably, but advertised her ample posterior to the max. Finally, she undid the second button on her dark red silk blouse, exposing ample cleavage. Grabbing her packed attaché case, she headed down the narrow stairs of the cottage. Adorning a full-length black overcoat, she headed out into the cold air, turning to the left, and the entrance of the jail.

~

Patterson was sorry he wasn't present when Henderson kicked off in B Visits. He would have relished watching the animal suffer, yet paradoxically, was glad he hadn't been involved. It would have been a severe test of his self-control, a gamble he didn't need. Instead, he had been in the car park, collecting a forgotten packet of cigarettes from his car. Patterson was now, in a strengthened clear plastic box that jutted into the opening of B wing. He possessed one key that unlocked the B Wing grill, the opposing grille, controlled externally by the officer in the circle. Sitting in a moulded plastic chair, he was perpendicular to the PO's office behind, and the two converted cells, that were the medical dispensary and welfare interview room, to his front. His only company, the wooden sloped shelf that held the movements book.

He understood the majority of prison officer duties were monotonous, and that on the whole it was a boring way to make a living. However, he understood the violence that was never far from the surface, both inside and outside the jail.

Patterson utilised the opportunity, not to stave off boredom, but to plan. He looked down the wing toward where Henderson was housed. He was well aware that, when he executed his plan, the medic would be summoned and enter from the far end of the wing, being the only other officer on duty at night to have a master key, in case of medical emergencies. He fleetingly contemplated that, that could be his escape route, before chuckling aloud.

'Escape? Who am I trying to kid? And for what reason? To be hunted by the Provos and the police. To endure the miserable existence, I've created? No, you've created the mother of all fuck ups kid, and the only road to some sort of salvation, is a one-way street with a dead end....and you know it.' Patterson smiled before closing his eyes and glancing skyward. *'I'll make you proud dad.'*

His concentration was interrupted by an orderly tapping on the Wing side grille.

'Tea, Mister?' asked the bald, wiry, white-jacketed prisoner who looked older than his years. In the breast pocket of his jacket, was a steel knife from the staff canteen, a medal to the trustworthiness of the orderlies.

Patterson momentarily studied him before answering. 'Is there any coffee?' he replied

'Mister Galbraith has some in the class office, but he'll charge you 10p.'

"He should have worked in a bank! That's OK.'

'I'm doing toast for the PO. Want me to put some on for you?'

'No, I'm fine.'

Patterson watched the orderly disappear into the 'tea boat' cell, convinced there was a *vague* familiarity about him. The notion automatically left him when the circle grill opened. He spun round to face the circle officer, and Pamela from welfare, finishing their obvious flirtation. It was hard to judge how, if at all, she was beautiful, or sexy, as *any* female was automatically promoted to goddess, such was the deficiency of the fairer sex throughout the place. Still, Patterson liked what he saw.

'See you later,' she said to the officer, touching his arm longer that what would have been described as normal, before beaming a bright smile in Patterson's direction.

'Hello John,' she purred before moving closer and holding his hand lightly, her mood serious, 'everything ok with you, after that...well...you know.'

'All the better for seeing you Pamela,' he replied moving to open his side of the air lock.

He smelled her perfume and tried not to ogle her cleavage. Her radiant smile, framed by shocking red lips, automatically returned.

'I'm really glad to hear that you're doing ok. Oh, I never remember, do I need to sign your book?' she said pointing to the journal.

'Only if you're putting your phone number in it,' he replied with a wink.

'Oh, see you,' she giggled, hitting him playfully on the arm, before wiggling her way past into the wing.

She'd expected, and received, the wolf whistles from the prisoners on the landings above. Patterson watched her go, his previous confidence returned, realising had he not ended up in the mess he was in, he would have conquered her eventually. But, most of the staff, and the inmates, had the same dream, and to his knowledge, none had ever got close. Pamela leaned against the open door of the PO's office, explaining she wanted to see the 'new boy' first. MacLean reacted by entering the landing, calling to the class officer to unlock Henderson, then indicating to the officers on the two landings above to secure their wards. Pamela, walking toward the Welfare office, caught Patterson staring at her from the still unlocked grill. She offered a sultry wink, before entering through the wooden door, depositing her wares on the table. The noise levels rose, as doors on all three landings were slammed shut. Patterson stepped onto the landing to beckon the Censor officer.

'Eddie, have you got a minute?'

The censor appeared.

'You're not looking a break from a break, are you?'

'Wise up!' Patterson replied, 'I need a word with you.'

Henderson was unlocked, his safety now assured, and made his way along the landing toward the welfare office. The staff remained on high alert because of his earlier display.

'What do you call that orderly?' Patterson requested.

'Who, wee Mitchell? The baldy one?'

'Yes. I know him...from somewhere, but the name isn't ringing a bell.'

'He's only in two weeks of a six months sentence.'

'Mmm,' mused Patterson, 'There's something about him.'

Henderson passed the stairwell and walked with his shoulders hunched, toward the welfare office. He spied Pamela, who had left the office for a meet and greet, instantly lifting his spirits.

'I understand what you're saying Paddy. I'll get security to have a ...' The conversation was obliterated by squealing and footsteps. 'Bastard!' squealed the orderly, brandishing the steel knife in a raised fist, speeding toward Henderson, who grabbed at Pamela, bundling her round to give himself protection. The speed at which the assault was taking place, caught almost everyone out. However, Patterson, already facing down the landing, noticed the orderly as soon as he left the tea boat. His universe slowed. He seemed to have an age to remove the key attached to his chain from the lock, before pushing past the censor officer to intercept the assailant.

During this bizarre slow-motion event, he realised he was too far away from the orderly to prevent him dealing a lethal blow. Henderson had pulled Pamela, his shield, as far back along the landing as he could go. Instantaneously, Patterson leapt forward, making a grab at the orderly's legs. Then the world went to fast forward. The cacophony of shouting officers and high-pitched screaming from Pamela, did nothing to mute the noise of the orderly's skull cracking against the tiled floor.

The combined velocities of running, and Patterson's tip-tackle, served to make his fall onto terra firma, a rapid descent. Within seconds, it became a wildlife feeding frenzy. Staff piled on top of the prone orderly, grasping for any body part still available. MacLean moved to console Pamela, shuffling her into his office away from the scene, ordering the censor to keep an eye on her before returning to the landing. Henderson was deathly white, cowering in the corner, mumbling inanely.

MacLean shouted to the class officer. 'Get this cowardly piece of shite out of my sight!' Noise from the circle increased, as all available staff, security POs, and the Governor, raced to the incident. The hill of staff in the wing, slowly peeled away from the prone body, the head encircled by an ever-growing lake of deep crimson, accepted he was unconscious and allowing him medical help. Slightly winded, and unable to consume what had just happened, Patterson got to his feet as MacLean approached.

'Well done, Paddy, good job!'

Patterson stared blankly at him before re-entering the human race.

'Whew! That was close,' he smiled back.

Patterson was ordered to take a break in the canteen, as MacLean debriefed the Governor. He sat alone in the sparsely populated canteen with a coffee, contemplating the previous ten minutes. Before he could get lost in thought, he heard the click-click of her heels and looked up at Pamela, who rushed toward him.

'Oh John,' she whimpered as she embraced him. 'You saved my life.'

Patterson lavished the genuineness of her embrace. He felt her breasts squeeze against his chest, the smell of her soap and perfume filled his nostrils. Reality kicked in, realising being flirtatious in this situation would be pathetic, taking advantage of a woman who was vulnerable. He stroked her hair.

'You're ok. It's over,' he whispered in a reassuring tone.

She stepped back from the embrace and tried to smile, the seriousness and fear of her features fought against it.

'Thank you,' she replied before holding both his hands, slipping a piece of paper, unseen by onlookers, into his right hand.

'Thank you so much,' she repeated before one more brief hug. She whispered into his ear, 'I want you.'

Pamela offered a pitiful wave before leaving. He was certain her phone number was on the piece of paper. Why in the name of God had she entered his life now? He was on a schedule that would terminate soon, if the stars stayed aligned. He didn't need this distraction. He took another sip of coffee.

'Maybe, just maybe,' he mused, *'this is a part of my destiny. Maybe...it was meant to be. Maybe it was written that I should be on the grille when this occurred, enabling me to keep the prey safe until I could deal with him alone. And perhaps she is the prize. The last moments of pleasure before a nonexistence. Destiny is kind.'*

Chapter 43

It was nearing tea time on Friday evening, in Hastings Street Police Station. McDermott felt exasperated, after running around in circles. He had taken Molly shopping to get a break from his dilemma. They had a taste of normality, enjoying the breathing space, while dining in Marks and Spencer's cafe. He had hoped to return to his case with fresh eyes and a new impetus. Sadly, as he waded through the notes on A5, A4 and A3 paper, spread out over the table tops in the main office, it felt as if he'd been playing snakes and ladders, without the ladders. Every path was a dead end. Not a hint of information to send him in the right direction. He had read, and re-read, everything he had on Jackie Smallwood, but to no avail.

Lifting the yellowing folder, he opened it to stare at Smallwood's photograph. He sighed out loud before speaking. 'C'mon Jackie ...give me something...*anything*.' The stolid picture gazed back, not at him, but at the camera that had captured his image for eternity. His thought process was welcomingly interrupted by Douglas entering the room.

'Bit of news Captain, not that it's much help though.'

McDermott reached for the incident report that Douglas offered, briefly running his eye over it before handing it back to a now, confused Douglas. 'I already heard about the attempted assassination on Henderson in the Crum. A friend of mine, Principal Officer, Pete Clydesdale, contacted me.'

Douglas gave a nod of understanding before sitting down. 'I believe it was the Provos? Well, this time anyway.'

'Correct...and on top of the threat from his own crowd. It must feel nice to be wanted.'

Douglas sensed the frustration and disappointment in his leader's voice.

'Everybody's ignoring the Super's direction, and busting a gut to help you in this. You know that don't you?' he offered.

'I appreciate it Doug, you know I do. But I've only seven days left.'

'Oh, and by the way, Jacko's bringing an old mate of yours up.'

McDermott raised his eyebrows in a questioning manner, before the door opened. A white haired, portly figure, with a beetroot red face, almost half the size of his escort, stood grinning.

'Harry, you old bastard! How are you!'

McDermott's grin morphed into a beaming smile, as he rose from his seat. 'Herbie Long! I thought you were dead!'

The pair shook hands and embraced in a brief man hug.

'It's really good to see you again. It feels like a lifetime!' McDermott stated in a sincere tone.

'You too, mate. I know us Special Branchers are a bit sneaky-beaky, but we like to climb up into the real world now and then. You still hitting a golf ball?'

'My handicap's always been my clubs. Mark Twain was right. *A good walk spoiled.* Yourself?'

'Still a member of Temple. Walking those hills every Saturday keeps me in shape,' he replied sarcastically, holding his prolific stomach.

'Looks like more time spent at the bar in the clubhouse.'

'Might be some truth in that,' laughed Long.

'Ok Herbie, what have you got for us?'

Long sat across from McDermott, the others, sat either side with their notebooks at the ready.

'It seems the removal of this monster from society, has loosened quite a few tongues. One of my boys, provided some tasty info that Jacko reckoned you might be interested in.'

McDermott interrupted Long's flow of conversation. 'Herbie, you do realise the Super has blackballed me?'

'Prick that he is!'

A ripple of laughter radiated around the room.

'As I was saying, my boy is a reliable source, and I have never sensed more hatred for one person before. They're coming out of the woodwork, and pushing the rap on him for everything. A chance for the bad guys to clear their slates.'

Jackson interrupted. 'Kennedy assassination?'

Long grinned. 'Practically. Anyway, my source was at a wedding recently. A skinful of drink later, he got round to talking to the father of the bride, a fairly big player, who goes a long way back with Henderson. *Tucker Floyd* ring any bells?'

'Wasn't he one of the 'Imperial guards' for the four founder members,' McDermott asked. 'We were aware he was involved in numerous punishment shootings and beatings. But witnesses never came forward.'

'The very man!' Long concluded, leaning forward. 'It appears, he was 'on duty' the night Smallwood was, allegedly, apprehended and murdered by the Provos.'

McDermott's expression turned to stone as Long continued. 'You and I both know, that it wasn't the Provos. Floyd is claiming that he heard an argument upstairs whilst he, and a guy called Taggart, were downstairs, blocking the entrance way to the band hall.'

McDermott intervened.

'Taggart was found dead a few days after that.' He tumbled through his thoughts of long ago. 'Feud, or something, wasn't it?'

A steely grin crept over Long's face. 'That's the way it was painted, though no trace of a murder weapon, or suspect. However, the argument upstairs, was more of an interrogation and torture.'

'The shopkeeper who wouldn't pay protection money?'

'Yup, Eric Wilson. At that time, it was only Montgomery and Hamilton with him, and Floyd is certain, that Montgomery was leading the charge. Shortly after Henderson and Smallwood arrived and went upstairs, there was a lot of raised voices.' Long hesitated before continuing. 'Floyd, in his drunken state is convinced that Hamilton, Montgomery and Henderson murdered not only Eric Wilson, but Jackie Smallwood.'

The atmosphere was deadly still as this 'information' was ingested. Jackson broke the serenity. 'What makes him so sure?'

'Exactly. Being part of the inner guard, the muscle would be used, and trusted, to remove any bodies, as I'm sure you're aware. But that night was different. Floyd was tasked to stand in the shebeen at the other side of the door, and let no-one back there, whilst Taggart had to clear, and not let anyone near, the backstreet behind the band hall'

McDermott notioned for him to continue.

'At the same wedding party, Floyd was gurning about the state of the place upstairs, after the event. Blood everywhere, and he and Taggart were like two cleaning ladies sorting it out. He waxed lyrical about his former mate Taggart, but knew he had been spouting about two bodies being dumped in the car.'

'And then he disappeared,' stated Douglas solemnly.

'It has all the hallmarks of how those animals dealt with problems.'

Jackson whistled through his teeth. McDermott continued. 'With your blessing Herbie, I'd like to pull in Floyd, and have a good long chat with him. If it's all if's and but's, the Super won't re-open a historical case based on the speculation of a gorilla... and I can't tell him where I got my source from.'

'It's actually worse than that Harry. Floyd flew out yesterday to Tenerife, for two weeks in the sun.'

'A week longer than I have,' McDermott sighed. 'There's no way the Super would sanction flying us out to Tenerife with an international arrest warrant!' Jesus,' he continued, closing his eyes and throwing back his head, fumbling for inspiration. Long brought him back to his senses, by standing and offering a hand to shake.

'I'll tell you what Harry. I'll pull a few strings myself, to get this investigation re-opened, historical or not. Our boss reports directly to the Assistant Chief Constable. And I'll also request the assistance of your two comrades here, who have a working knowledge, to nail this bastard once and for all.'

'Lads?' McDermott questioned his deputies.

'We're doing this for you Captain,' stated Jackson, Douglas nodding in agreement.

Long continued. 'And just to eliminate some of the shite that always sticks to investigations, the 'Tout' label against Henderson, is a total fallacy. Not one of our handlers has had any informer dealings with him… ever.'

He left after an exchange of handshakes, and the promise that he would cost McDermott a fortune in drink money, at his farewell party the following Friday.

McDermott had an air of contentedness, knowing they were close to solving an historical case, the slack being taken up by his trustworthy colleagues, after he had retired. He felt he was giving something back to the innocents who had endured the troubles. Ironically, he was as far from solving the recent murders, as he was at the beginning of their investigation. This became his latest, and final, focus. He engaged with his deputies.

'What do you think?'

Jackson poured through his notebook until he reached the desired page. 'What Sergeant Long told us, fits in with the nightmares Hamilton was having. You remember, about being sorry and not helping Smallwood more?'

'Yes Jacko...you're right. And I'm confident you guys will tie Henderson up in knots after I've gone. But....it still doesn't solve the recent murder mystery. We've no idea who has been committing the murders, and no apparent motive. What I also don't understand; why are the Provos only after Henderson now?'

'Could be they've bought the 'tout' scheme. Or maybe they've become embarrassed at being remotely associated with him. Or is this their sick form of summary justice for all the innocents Henderson had 'removed?'

'True, the Band of Blood Brothers is officially terminated I would think. And his own side?'

Douglas took up the mantle. 'Let's face it, Captain, they aren't the sharpest tools in the box, but maybe they instigated the tout scenario. They've wanted rid of him for a long time.'

McDermott silently deliberated.

'There is another possibility,' interposed Jackson.

'With our new knowledge of the original murder, that fits with Hamilton's lamentations, maybe the motive is simply revenge?'

'But why so long after the event? And by whom?'

'Therein lays the problem Captain.'

'True. But I think this has to be our final line of inquiry. You guys sniff out everything you can about the fella Wilson. Wife, siblings, lovers, everything. Use the bloody Tardis if you have to. I'll focus on Smallwood. Remember troops, this is our last roll of the dice. I hope to Christ it works.'

Chapter 44

It had been a long, night guard duty. Patterson felt drained, the bags under his eyes as black as night, on completing his final stint at patrolling the landings. Checking vulnerable inmates on 15-minute observations, and registering with the pegging clock every half hour. The 'clock', not more than a box, was at the end of the third-floor landings. Night staff inserted, and turned a pegging key every half hour, registering someone was awake throughout the shift. His colleague, was snoring in the Tea Boat cell. Although Patterson's thought processes weren't fatigued, his physical state, acutely gave constant reminders of its need to rest and replenish. It was adrenaline propelling him on, aware he was within 50 feet of his prey. During the patrolling, he was fixated, staring through the glass slit in Henderson's cell door. He could have sworn he heard whimpering at one stage. Whether it was a dream, self-pity or disgrace at his earlier behaviour, using Pamela as a human shield, he couldn't tell. Perhaps it was the realisation that his empire had collapsed, and he was now public enemy number one. Or maybe it was because he was alone and frightened. Patterson didn't care, taking strength from the fact, the once almighty, Sammy Bulldog Henderson, was now his for the taking. He relished the thought of watching the scumbag experience terror like never before. He wanted to see begging, helpless eyes that would be futile. And most of all, he wanted him to know that this was payback. Payback for a man whose boots, Henderson would never have been fit to lick clean. This was for the loss of a father. The loss of a mother. The lost years of a sister's companionship, and the loss of a childhood that should have *included* his parents.

Had he have had access amidst those thoughts, he would have opened the cell door and strangled the whore with his bare hands. The anger and disgust that raced through him, made him feel that he could have the ripped the cell door off. Yet… he had to wait, but not for long. Patterson heard the proliferation of noise beginning to seep into the Wing from the circle. The 'early' staff were preparing for the new day, that would be a replica of every day before, and forever thereafter. PO Maclean, carrying his B Wing keyboard, was the first member of staff to emerge from the circle.

'Paddy, I need a word,' he said, beckoning Patterson into his office.

'You look knackered kid. You, ok?'

'What do you expect Tommy, sorry PO, sir? You're always going to be tired after a sleepless night patrolling your wing.'

'Patrolling all night my arse! Remember, I used to be a basic grade. Couldn't get to sleep maybe.'

Patterson's lips curled to an affectionate grin.

'Hope you're in no rush home kid, because the Governor and his entourage want to have a meeting with you at 8 o'clock. God love them having to come in at that ungodly hour.'

'A meeting? About what?'

'Not sure, but it's all good as far as I can make out. If you'd have been in trouble, those tortured souls would have been in at half-seven. Away down to the canteen and get yourself a bit of breakfast…if you can stay awake long enough.'

~

McGuigan's night had been restless. In the first instance, the ad hoc plan the Army Council had contrived to eliminate the UDA leader, had been an utter failure and stank of desperation. It was amateurish, and done nothing for the image of invincibility of the IRA. Had he have been informed, instead of being left out in the cold, he would have ensured distraction on a scale that would have facilitated, and produced, the result the council were striving for. McGuigan's anger slid toward paranoia.

'Why was I not informed? Is this a power struggle? Am I going to be stood down? Is it because I refused to sanction the capture of the bastard screw until I could lead the operational team? Why has the assassination of a UDA scumbag become more important than my plight for resolution?'

McGuigan reflected on his initiation, and the sacrifices he had made for the cause. He had been assured that no amount of incarceration would dilute the standing of any volunteer, especially those who had risen to the senior ranks. At this moment in time, he had his doubts. He remembered cajoling young volunteers, promoting missions that were of the highest priority, and how keen they'd been to 'strike out' against the foreign invaders.

His cold, and ruthless, massaging of their egos and aspirations, transformed them into puppets, keen to obey his every whim, with promises that they could rise through the ranks of the organisation. To go down in history. It pained him how gullible those kids were.

They were the Lemmings to his cliff's edge, merely cannon fodder, destined to lengthy prison sentences or a gun salute and a tricolour flag draped over their coffins. They would never be martyrs, there were too many already in this fraction of existence. He, with other senior volunteers, would dutifully mourn at their loss during the funeral services, praising their dedication to parents who didn't care. Parents who would lead a hollow existence until their deaths. For a few years after, there would be commemoration services and shows of strength, that would dwindle and fade, until the promised places in history, would only be remembered by those who had suffered personal loss. McGuigan had five days to wait. On release on Thursday, he would be driven to The Greenan Lodge on Black's Road in the west of the city, for a celebratory 'session'. Or so his 'tail' would think. Nugent had spelt out the schedule. As soon as he entered the establishment, he would exit out the back, into the boot of a Vauxhall car, driven by a young female volunteer. She would take the A1 outside Lisburn, toward Newry, diverting off at Banbridge, allowing him to lie on the back seat, before traversing cross country through villages such as Poyntzpass, Camlough, Silverbridge and Crossmaglen. One of the myriads of farmers paths, would get him across the border. Finally, he would be transported to a safe house in Dundalk to meet his team for the operation. Statements had already been memorised and rehearsed by sympathisers, and bar owners in Dublin, 'proving' he'd spent the entire time with them during the period of the operation, and that sometimes, he would walk and camp in the Wicklow mountains south of Dublin. All the while, trying to come to terms with the disappearance of his wife. The operation would commence the following evening when the information around Patterson's movements would be confirmed.

~

Patterson felt uncomfortable, yet calm, as he took his place at the war council table, in the Governor's office. Bleasdale was the centre of this mini universe, Patterson admiring his physical and psychological presence. Beside him sat a thin, pale civil servant, resembling a Dickensian bookkeeper. What little hair he had at the sides of his head, was as untidy as the drab blue suit draped over his skeletal frame. His expression was fixed in a disdained fashion, peering over gold rimmed half classes, inspecting and denouncing everyone, except the Governor, at the table.

'Gentlemen, you're all familiar with Officer Patterson,' announced Bleasdale. In turn the Duty Office PO, Security PO and the Chief Officer nodded acknowledgement.

'And I'd like to introduce you to Mr Tomlinson, The Justice Under Secretary from the NIO.' Tomlinson briefly raised his head, presenting a forced smile to the senior staff, affording Patterson a, 'what-the-hell-is-a-basic-grade-officer-doing-here' stare. Patterson smiled at the scowl, thinking, *'I'd love to see you in a riot situation whenever you have to face something other than pens and paperclips you trumped up piece of shit!'* Tomlinson's eyes narrowed as if he had telepathic powers.

'Mr Tomlinson has issued directives and suggested planning, after this assassination attempt on Henderson. And may I add, successfully dealt with by young Patterson.'

Patterson blushed.

'However, my instincts are, that this should be internally led, as…' he turned toward Tomlinson, '…with all due respect Minister, we have a better working knowledge of running this establishment. One prisoner will not disrupt the smooth running of my jail. I don't give a rat's arse who kills this scumbag, but it won't happen in here.'

Patterson bowed his head slightly to scratch an imaginary itch on his eyebrow, whilst thinking, *'hope I can prove you wrong Governor.'* Bleasdale continued.

'Chief Officer Ramsden?'

'Yes sir. The Security PO and I, have spent most of last night weighing up our options, and it boils down to two. Firstly, there's the Prison hospital with its secured wing. The main disadvantages though, are the amount of inmate traffic, and the potential access to drugs and weapons. Collectively we feel our best option is to reopen the Supergrass annexe under D wing beside the base.'

Before Bleasdale could react, Tomlinson abruptly butted in. 'That would be the option of preference for the Secretary of State. We can't allow…'

Bleasdale shook his hand toward Tomlinson as a sign of rebuttal.

'For once Minister, I have to agree.' He said, turning his attention to the Duty Office PO.

'Alan, I want a team of dedicated staff drawn up to cover days, nights and evening duties to 'mind' this monster, until he gets shipped out to the Maze.'

'Senior and Principal officers?'

'Ah, that's where young Patterson comes in. One full time SO and Mr Patterson as acting SO. It starts on Monday. Any questions?'

Patterson raised his hand enough to catch the Governors attention. Bleasdale nodded for him to continue.

'Ahm...sir...I've three days booked off from tomorrow to visit my sister in England. I've also booked a night guard for Friday, as I've hired an all-day session with a tutor, for my Open University criminality degree on Saturday,' he lied.

Bleasdale grinned with pride before again being interrupted by Tomlinson. 'Patterson, you will do exactly as you are told. You will be in attendance from Monday. You do not dictate...'

He stopped abruptly as Bleasdale's massive open hand, slapped down on the table, creating shock waves throughout the room. He glared at Tomlinson with wide eyes, indignation carved into his features.

'Don't ever treat MY staff like that again!' he roared. In a heartbeat, he addressed Patterson in a sincere tone.

'Enjoy your trip, and good luck with your degree. We'll see you Thursday when you can liaise with the other SO, and of course, your night guard will be babysitting the monster.'

Patterson smiled, not just in appreciation, but in the fact of destiny, in the shape of Bleasdale, had guaranteed the demise of Henderson. The annexe was smaller and less complicated than B wing in carrying out his plan.

'Thank you, Sir.'

' Ok, meeting over.' Everyone stood up to leave, including Tomlinson, but Bleasdale barked at him. 'You sit where you are! Thank you, gentlemen.'

In the corridor the security PO laughed. 'Somebody's in for a right bollocking!'

Patterson grinned as he headed out down the steps and across the forecourt. His eyes drooped from exhaustion, but he felt elated at the same time. Everything was falling into place. He reckoned he would sleep comfortably.

Chapter 45

SUNDAY

Driving off the ferry at Stranraer, Patterson veered north along the A77, that hugged the coastline toward Ayrshire, instead of his usual route, due south towards Dumfriesshire. The sun had already reached its Zenith. He pulled off the road to a car park on his right, before donning a scarf and buttoning his coat. Although bright, displaying everything in vibrant colour, the mere breath of wind, cut like a knife. He crossed the road and walked down a wispy grass verge. Standing magnificently, ten miles offshore, was his reason for the detour. The granite jewel of the Firth of Clyde, the Ailsa Craig, radiated in the sunlight before him. He'd learned at school that it was a volcanic plug from an extinct volcano. It had survived longer than all the sedimentary rocks that had been eroded years before, due to the hardness of its granite. He had always admired this beast. As a child, he had caravanned nearby, transfixed by the monolith when he first saw it. He'd imagined it was a spaceship, disguised and sleeping, until cracking open someday, revealing the space travellers. It had ignored strife, wars and weather, for thousands of years. It had never felt heartbreak, nor pain. He felt lucky to be witnessing this spectacle, aware the majority of the world's population were ignorant of it. Sitting on the cold grass, Patterson gazed in pure wonderment as its granite gleamed in the sun. Five minutes later, he rose and spoke to Ailsa Craig.

'Goodbye dear friend,' he whispered, turning back to the car park.

Another frustrating dawn for McDermott. Douglas and Jackson had telephoned in to explain they were at a dead end. The Civil servants connected to the health system, were all off on Sundays. The hospitals ticked over, while the pen pushers were meant to be having a day of rest on the Lord's Day. He had had the same negative feedback from City Hall in relation to births, deaths and adoptions. The only people that seemed to be working there, were security staff, and cleaners. *'God help us if any other country should decide to invade on a Sunday'* he thought. As so often, it was the parochial minority, wagging the tail of the dog of majority. He'd been embarrassed, as much as outraged, when they decided to chain up the children's playgrounds on Sundays. Denying traders and pubs revenue on the day, *they deemed*, to be the day of nothing, only worship. McDermott had dismissed his troupe for the day and decided to take Molly for a walk along the beach at Crawfordsburn. He knew she would make sense of it all and bring him back down to earth. He walked beside her, through the cold wind. Inwardly, he had mocked her 'Eskimo' coat, faux stitching making it appear comprised of seal skins and a ridiculously sized hood, the edges of which, were festooned with fake fur. When she pulled the hood up, her entire head disappeared, her voice sounding like she was in a tunnel. As his eyes watered, he wished he could pull his skimpy bobble hat down into a mask like Molly's coat. After a brisk ten-minute walk, they were back in the car. As usual, Molly had packed sandwiches and a flask of tea.

'Nippy enough out there, isn't it?' she cheerfully asked, while organising their in-car lunch, not waiting for a reply. McDermott had ignited the engine and warm air spewed out of the vents.

'I can feel my face again thank goodness.'

'Harry, I'm sorry you couldn't get any work done today,' she apologised, 'but it was nice to go for a walk. This could be the last time we walk on this beach.'

McDermott smiled for the first time that day, Molly's magic working.

'Yeah,' he replied, 'but I'm fairly sure Scotland has the odd beach.'

Her smile was permanent as they tucked into corned beef and tomato sandwiches in silence.

'Molly...do you think you'll be able to cope with me being at home and in your way all the time?'

'Don't you worry Harry boy; I'll have plenty for you to do. If we've made it this far, I think we'll manage.'

'Right as usual,' he replied, withdrawing back into silence and his thoughts. The effervescent Molly dragged him back to the real world.

'Harry, I know this case is troubling you. And I know you're running out of time. But, do you want to talk about it?'

McDermott gave her that awkward, you-know-I-don't-talk-about-work, look.

'Just this once love, I don't want you to be upset, especially on your last case,' she continued.

The words 'last case' hit him like a sledgehammer. That was his reality. Maybe talking to someone totally divorced from it all, might see something he hadn't?

'Ok, but you can't mention any of this to anybody…'

'Harry…it's me, not some criminal.'

Without any real detail, he skipped through the case, finishing with Wilson as the prime suspect. 'So, you see, we have a suspect, but I still sense something is missing.'

Molly drained her plastic cup of tea. 'It is weird, that there would be such a long-time lapse, before a revenge would start. But it seems like you're stuck on the Wilson fellow theory. It could be a lot of other people with different reasons.'

'For instance?'

'Could be someone else who has been hurt by these people. Goodness knows how many individuals could be holding a grudge against them. Maybe someone who had to flee the country, because of a threat by them. Or even a femme fatal.'

McDermott raised his eyebrows to hint at continuation.

'Or maybe one of these drug people you hear about, who want to own everything, and need these people out of the way.'

McDermott sighed with a slight grin on his face. 'Wow! You've given me so much to think about, and I've only a week left. You should have been a policewoman, Ms. Marple.'

'Sorry, Mr McCloud,'

McDermott grinned and leant over to kiss her on the cheek, 'It's ok. Tomorrow is another day and hopefully there will be *somebody* at work!'

They giggled like school children.

~

The Blackpool Tower and the Pleasure Beach's Big Dipper, were growing in size on the horizon. Patterson hadn't stopped smiling, all thanks to his brief sojourn at the Carleton Service Station, off the M6. He hadn't interrupted his journey to stretch his legs, nor sample the tasteless, overpriced delights, of the service stations kitchens. He'd bought cigarettes and a cup of coffee, requesting loose change for the payphone. He stared at the piece of paper with her number on it, before making the call, convinced she was a luxury destiny had provided. When he'd explained that he couldn't stay long on Wednesday on his return, because of work commitments the following day, she suggested he bring his 'jammies' for a sleep over. The smile remained cemented into his features, as he parked the car and walked into Shirley's home, his precious nephews, lovingly assaulting him with happiness.

Patterson hugged and kissed his sister, as the boys finished off their supper. He then chased them upstairs and invented a story in which, as usual, they were the heroes, and everyone lived happily ever after. Within half an hour, Patterson was downstairs on the comfortable, oversized couch Shirley had pushed closer to the open fire, that blazed and crackled. He felt warmth and security, becoming hypnotised by the dancing flames. Shirley entered, blocking his view for a second with the distraction of a glass of Brandy, before nestling down into a mountain of scatter cushions, curling her legs beneath her, at the opposite end of the couch.

'Were you listening to me?'

Patterson snapped out of his daze, 'What?'

'I said it's a pity you couldn't have come over next week. David will be back from Aberdeen.'

'Sorry sis, it had to be this week as I've a lot do when I get back. Maybe next time. Now, can I get back to staring at the fire?'

She grinned, copying Patterson. Neither spoke, their senses dedicated to the controlled inferno. Shirley broke the impasse. 'Penny for your thoughts?'.

Without averting his gaze, Patterson replied in a serene tone. 'Be a waste of a penny...I don't have any. Real fires do this to me every time. Every thought I have in my head, disappears into the flames. Worries, fears, triumphs, problems, dreams...all disappear into the dancing flames.'

Shirley, again focusing on the fire, purred her reply, 'I know exactly what you mean.' There was a comfortable moment of silence, as they resumed their entertainment vigil, before Patterson continued.

'What we're looking at, is the difference between us, and all other creatures on the earth. We discovered it, and embraced it. And then we created, and controlled it.'

Without deflecting her gaze, Shirley grinned in agreement, feeling not only the warmth from the fire, but inner warmth in that her brother was close and comfortable. In fact, he seemed more at ease with himself than ever before.

'A lot of early civilizations considered fire as a god. I wonder if they did that because it reminded them of life?'

'Listen to you, Mr Attenborough!'

Patterson faced her and continued. 'What I mean is… a lot of elements have to come together to create fire. It's then like childhood, as the sparks catch the kindling, then slowly matures, before bursting into a raging blaze that represents teenage and adolescent years. In time, it settles into the solid smouldering mass of maturity, and before you know it, the glow fades and becomes ashes. Just like us.'

She felt a slight chill at his analogy. 'Very philosophical, John, and if you don't mind me saying…a bit morbid.'

Patterson promoted a languid stare, before his cheek muscles contracted, announcing his irresistible grin.

'Are you ok John?' Shirley asked, a hint of caution in her tone.

Although his facial expression remained sated, thoughts flew through his mind. His grin grew wider, and more welcoming. 'Oh, I'm good sis, in fact...very good'

Shirley's kinesics advertised satisfaction. 'Well?'

'Well, what?' he replied in a playfully teasing tone.

'Well...what has you in such good form?'

After a genuine yawn, Patterson rose and stretched. 'I've a few bits of really good news, but it'll have to wait until the morning. I'm knackered!'

Shirley stood to embrace him, frustrated at his infantile secrecy, feigning a huff.

'Why won't you tell me?'

She received a hug and a kiss before Patterson replied. 'If I tell you everything, we'll have nothing to talk about for the next few days. Goodnight.'

She felt a mixture of emotions, retaking her position on the couch, and gazed back at the fire. She mirrored its warmth in her thoughts. Barely just disguising a niggling doubt.

Chapter 46

MONDAY

'What were the years you wanted to check Detective Sergeant?' asked the council worker.

McDermott had begun his historical paper chase into uncovering everything relevant to Jackie Smallwood, at the Office of General Register in City Hall that covered births, deaths marriages and adoptions. At one stage he thought the damn pen pushers would have asked for written permission, or even a warrant. However, the terminology 'Murder Case', had been the catalyst, the staff elated to have a sprinkling of excitement mixed into their otherwise, mundane existence. They assumed themselves as assistant detectives. 'Sixty-five to seventy-one please,' he replied, deliberately avoiding the exact time slot he required. As he sat at the visitors' side of the desk, the female council worker waddled toward a tower block of grey filing cabinets, and expertly removed the files. McDermott studied her. Her brillo pad-streaked grey hair draped onto her shoulders in a disorderly fashion, and her dark purple dress with a faded pattern, reached the floor. It was 'complimented' with a clashing, lime green cardigan, disguising an ample chest that had headed south an era ago. The picture was completed by a face that make-up had been a stranger to, and her cloudy eyes looked gigantic through thick lensed glasses. He considered she was born to be a civil servant. She dumped two thick folders onto the desk.

'There's nineteen sixty-five Sergeant, just to get you started.' She pointed at the cabinets. 'I left the rest of the files you need unlocked. So, I guess I'll leave you to it...unless...there's anything I can assist you with?' she offered, with a glint of hope in her enormous eyes.

'I'll be fine, thank you'

When the door closed, he ignored the files on the desk and recovered the sixty-seven files. Within seconds he found the entry for the Smallwood's. He scribbled all the details appertaining to the dynasty into his notebook.

The birth and death of John 'Jackie' Smallwood.

'Should be murder,' thought McDermott, despising how conveniently concise that one word replaced the actuality of the slaying, convinced more than ever, Henderson was the killer.

The birth and death of Kate Smallwood.

McDermott sighed, remembering the tragic suicide of an innocent woman, who had her life partner ripped away.

Adoption and deed poll name change of two children, Shirley and John, by a cousin, Elsie Patterson. A second formal adoption for Shirley, the elder of the children.

McDermott was confused by the second adoption, until he read the footnote from the Chief Medical Officer supporting the second adoption and relocation to England.

'After expert analysis, it is obvious that Shirley Patterson has developed increasingly severe trauma symptoms, following witnessing the suicide of her mother. Any programme of remedial medication has proven to be adverse, and there is the very real fear of total non-recovery. Following trials with junior therapist, Judith Gray from Lancashire, it was apparent the sound of an English accent, alien to her beforehand, showed an improvement in her behaviour, to a level of sustaining life, and a will to live it. Furthermore, the meeting with the possible adoptive parents, The Westcott's of Albert Road, Blackpool, has had a positive effect on Shirley. I therefore support the innovative idea of relocation to a part of the world, free from colloquial accents, that will assist in her recovery.'

McDermott was doleful, recollecting the aftermath of Kate's suicide. Distressed female RUC officers had arrived at the scene, attempting to help the distraught youngsters. He ingested the details of a family torn apart. Murder, suicide and adoption after adoption. No true history. Probably no original family memories for those poor children. A teenager disappearing into a catatonic world alone. Hopefully, the youngest, wasn't old enough to be scarred the way his sister was. A bell at the back of McDermott's mind started to ring. 'Patterson...John Patterson. Where do I know that name from?' he whispered aloud.

Then he remembered, the Prison Officer they had interviewed after the bomb that had killed his friend. 'God love that fella, he's had no luck in his life,' he continued with his solitary conversation, no hint that Patterson was remotely involved in his thoughts, about the recent killings. He underlined the address of Mrs. Elsie Patterson, before replacing the files and returning to the main office to announce his departure. As he opened the door to the main office, his female 'minder' turned with wide eyes. 'My Goodness that was quick!'.

'Oh, I guess I just got lucky. But then, your input was vital, thank you so much for your help,' he said through a smile. 'My pleasure, if it helps solve the case,' she boomed loud enough for her colleagues to hear, as she grew in stature in her seat. McDermott held his grin as he nodded and departed. The remainder of the grey clerks looked at his 'minder' with envy.

~

Patterson rose early, after an uninterrupted sleep, partially fuelled by his long journey and last night's brandy, but more so, a feeling of relaxation, and being comfortable in his own skin. He felt determined and confident, in the self-shaping of his future. He couldn't remember dreaming. Downstairs, he fixed breakfast for Shirley and the boys, whilst she was assigned to washing and dressing duties. Patrick and Richard were eager to get dressed, excited by the fact their favourite uncle was here, and that they were to be driven to school in his fantastic big car

They headed downstairs, in eager anticipation of receiving the call they were expecting from the kitchen.

'Soldiers!' bellowed Patterson in a distinct military voice.

The boys straightened their backs and adapted overly stern expressions as they attempted to march in sync, comically failing. Patterson stood at the end of the table with his chest out and a rolling pin tucked in under his left arm. He snapped the order...'Soldiers...halt!'

The boys stuttered to a halt, as Patterson shot his right hand up into a salute, lightly biting the inside of his cheeks to stop him laughing, as the boys mimicked his display by using opposing hands.

'Soldiers...eat!'

They leapt into their chairs, reaching for the thin strips of toasted bread, that they dipped into soft boiled eggs. Patterson quickly tucked tea towels into their collars to act as large napkins, protecting their school uniforms.

'Lads, please be careful not to get any egg on your uniform, or your mum will have my guts for garters!' The boys looked at him in an aporetic fashion. 'She'll be angry with me,' he simplified. Shirley dashed across the kitchen to the utility room with an arm full of washing, shouting as she loaded the washing machine,

'Uncle John will pick you from school today. I'll be home at four.' In no time at all, Shirley had loaded the machine, adorned her work coat, and then addressed Patterson.

'Remember, home, quick snack, homework and then TV.'

He saluted, suppressing a grin whilst both boys copied his actions. 'Yes Ma'am!' they barked in unison. Shirley blurted out a laugh, before ordering the boys to get their teeth cleaned. As each child passed, she held their heads, affectionately kissing the top of each, before announcing, 'Be good for Uncle John...love you.'

Both boys shouted 'love you too mummy' as they raced up the stairs. She turned her attention to her brother, addressing him quietly. 'And maybe Uncle John will tell me his good news when I get home?' He smiled and kissed her, whispering 'promise' in her ear. As she left, she began to reiterate the routine,

'Remember...' Patterson cut her off. 'I know, I know. Home-chocolate-Tetris-TV.'

She shot him a soft challenging glance, before sticking her tongue out and exiting. Alone in the kitchen, Patterson cleared the dishes of the table, a whirlwind of emotions swarming through his psyche. Soft warmth, at the open display of a mother and her children, emphasising their unbridled bond of love and togetherness. Mixed with simmering rage at how the bastard Henderson, had denied him, those experiences and memories. Placing the dishes in a basin of warm water, he glanced at the vanity mirror on the window ledge in front of him. The reflection had tears welling in its eyes.

~

Henderson sat across the table from his solicitor, in the makeshift office created in the Supergrass annexe. A converted cell with a wooden door, housing a plastic glass pane for observation by staff. He had come to terms with his incarceration, corruptly eulogising his status in his own mind. He misguidedly judged himself as the most powerful man in the jail, due to his 'exceptional status' of isolation, away from all other prisoners. Those feelings were balanced against alienation. He was under a threat from both sides, yet received no visits from his own 'people.' Paradoxically, his stubborn ignorance, created false hope in his solitary existence. He planned that after being released, he would rally a few of his closest allies, along with a gang of hapless, disillusioned youngsters, bred to hate Catholics, yearning to have a gun in their hands. They would help him create a new empire. He would make a titanic stand against the sworn enemy, with such ferocity, that would have disillusioned recruits from other factions, racing to join his ranks.

Henderson clasped his hands together, placing them on the thin wooden table, as he leant forward to get the attention of his court appointed, catholic solicitor. Nevertheless, he was glad to be represented by a firm who specialised in paramilitary clients. Someone who attacked the British legal system with the tenacity of a dog with a bone.

Henderson waited, while the solicitor waded through his bulging briefcase, before fishing out legal papers. His suit was sporadically dotted with coffee stains, and well lived in. He was always close to fully shaved, but his dark features would torment him achieving that goal completely.

His expression caught Henderson's interest. He was passionate about fighting against all odds, and his eyes had a steely resolve every time he spoke.

'Well, Mr. Henderson, the sun may well yet shine again.'

Henderson raised his eyebrows in a prelude to acceptance of good news.

'The PPS have until next week to present a case for trial. And, after their recent humiliations in the public eye, they will only proceed with a 90-95% projected success rate.'

Henderson tried hard to suppress the grin that wanted to dance across his face.

'On the back of that, my sources have informed me that the RUC case is less than watertight, and relies on the wafer-thin evidence, that blood samples from Hamilton were on the murder weapon that was hidden in your house. Though they can't explain why, if you were the murderer, which I know you're not…' he emphasised, '…presents no logical explanation for the body of the murder weapon, where fingerprints may have been cleaned with four different solvents, yet the blood remains are untouched!'.

'So, when's the court appearance then?"
They petitioned the court, and the judge has given them until Friday week to present a case, or all charges will be dismissed.'
The solicitor noticed a distinct downturn in Henderson's demeanour, advertised by his facial expressions.

He thought it better to leave the delivery of his final bit of news, until he packed his case and was about to leave.

Shuffling legal papers into the briefcase, he observed Henderson. His eyes looking at the table, whilst he mumbled and complained about the length of his incarceration. The solicitor motioned to the prison guard observer, showing two closed fingers indicating the number of minutes, before the interview was to be terminated. He stood in a rehearsed manner and addressed Henderson.

'By the way...as requested, I contacted the estate agent with reference to the sale of your home. At least you'll have shelter when you get out.'

Henderson's eyebrows lowered, his face a picture of puzzlement.

'The house is still there, and won't be sold because you are still married. The agents needed both parties' signatures.'

'What do you mean *shelter*?'

The solicitor took a deep breath. 'Well, although Mr Henderson couldn't sell the house...she sold everything in it. Fixtures, fittings, furniture, along with your cars, which were all apparently cash sales.'

Henderson smashed his fists on the desk. 'Bastard whore!'

The solicitor nodded to the observer, who opened the door to let him exit. Standing as close to the doorway as possible, he turned.

'You must have made her angry, Mr Henderson, because when she'd sold everything in all the bedrooms, she vandalised the wooden floors, by ripping up the floorboards. I'll be in touch.' Henderson's chin dropped like an anchor, colour racing from his face. 'No' he hissed under his breath, holding one hand over his mouth. 'She's known all along, where I hid the money.'

Chapter 47

The three wise men sat around one of the larger tables in the room that was festooned with a myriad of notes, photographs and sandwich wrappers. Jackson took a large swig of tea to wash down the giant bite of his Belfast bap with his favourite filling, Tayto cheese and onion crisps. The others looked on in wonderment, Douglas relating the scene to that of a killer whale in a frenzied attack. Jackson, oblivious of the others' attention, carefully lifted a napkin and wiped the side of his mouth, attentively dusting the remnants of crisps from the front of his shirt, before looking up in comical fashion.

'What?'

'If you don't mind..., can we carry on?' requested McDermott.

'Righto.' Jackson lifted a photograph of Trevor Wilson, that he offered for the others to share. 'Gentlemen, this is Trevor Wilson, the brother of Eric Wilson, who was murdered in the band hall on the same night as Smallwood. Unfortunately, it's quite old, and the *only* one available from Health and Social services.'

'The only one? Surely there must be updated photographs somewhere?' questioned Douglas.

Jackson picked up his notes. 'I've taken the liberty of checking with the DVLA, passport, and National Insurance offices. There is a total of fifteen Trevor Wilson's in Northern Ireland. Two are over ninety years old, and happy in their own world inside a nursing home.

Five are under the age of sixteen, one is twenty-five and has been in prison for the last three years, and one has been in Cyprus for two years with the Fusiliers. I'm going to spend the rest of the day ringing round the stations in Fermanagh and Tyrone, where the remainder are based, to eliminate them from our enquiries. In fact, the last record of *this particular* Trevor Wilson, was in the Ulster Bank in 1982, when he closed his business account, withdrawing all his money, including that which he had received from the insurance company, that had been lying gathering interest for fourteen years.'

'Any idea of the amount.'

'I thought for a minute that we would have to seek court approval for disclosure, however after lunch with the manager, he gave me an estimation that it was within the region of £150,000. Of course, he had to give them notice with that amount of cash, and dutifully marched into the bank with a suitcase a few days later.'

'Wow!' exclaimed McDermott.

'Yeah, I know. But here's the tasty bit.'

Everyone's attention was focused.

'This guy has been through hell and back. After the slaying of his brother, he went downhill rapidly, and was admitted to Muckamore Psychiatric Hospital in October 1968, after the authorities were contacted by his doctor, who had been treating him for depression, bordering on manic.

He had a long ten years in there, flying over the cuckoo's nest.'

Jackson hesitated momentarily, to recover his notes.

'From interviews and medical notes, he resisted treatment and was suicidal, being saved after two failed attempts, as well as being prone to violent outbursts for his first five years, a good part of which, he spent wearing a straitjacket in a padded cell.'

'Jeez...that would drive you crazy if you weren't already knocking at the door,' interjected Douglas.

'The picture then changed. He had some sort of epiphany in his sixth year, by, quite dramatically, settling down. He took yoga and fitness classes, freely engaged in counselling so much so, that his medication was reduced. He started to interact with staff and the other poor incumbents on the ward, to a point where he wrote, and recited, poetry for them. Almost like a pupa that became a butterfly.' Looking down at different notes Jackson continued. 'It says here in his psychiatric report,

'Having shaken off his cloak of violence and self-depreciation, the real Trevor Wilson has emerged. Mr Wilson displays strong traits of high intellect, and self-control, along with motivation. He revels at chess and cryptic crosswords. Given his former vocation as company accountant, it comes as no surprise he is bordering on mathematical genius, scoring in the mid 130's in his last IQ test. Although his recovery had been gradual for his first 5 years, his progress in the last 12 months has been remarkable. Most importantly though, is not to let his extraordinary progress overshadow the findings of his intense counselling, and voluntary hypnosis sessions. The panel has stated that there are still signs of a complex dissociative identity disorder.'

A confused McDermott rubbed his chin. 'What the hell does that mean?'

'That's exactly what I said to the nurse. She said it's a bit like Jekyll and Hyde, only that he controls it, turning it off, and on, when he decides. Realistically though, during his time in both institutions it never really surfaced.'

McDermott and Douglas ingested the information. There was a steely atmosphere in the enclosed room. Douglas questioned softly, 'Portrait of a serial killer?'

In the same trance like state, McDermott added, 'And it would, sorry, could be, the reason for the lengthy time period before seeking revenge.' There was an eerie silence in the room, as each policeman put the jigsaws in their heads together, coming to terms with the possible enormity of their findings. McDermott felt they were nearing finality. At last, they had a prime candidate. The only thing left was to locate him. However, he felt less than whole, understanding the pursuit of Wilson, after thirty-five years of policing, would be his final swansong, leaving the abyss of not bringing Henderson to justice for the murder of Smallwood. A branch he may never reach. He prayed the return of the goon, Floyd, from holiday, would be the lynchpin to reopening the case, confident his deputies would stop at nothing to bring, long overdue justice.

'Is that it, Jacko?'

'Sorry Captain. He was transferred to Purdysburn Institution on a roll out contract, meaning he would be assigned a job on minimum wage in various charity shops, but had to return back there after work. It was gradually increased to working a full week, that led to him being housed in his own one-bedroom flat on the Ormeau Road, although he still had to attend two weekly assessments back in Purdysburn.'

'How did that work?'

'Faultless. He had glowing references from the shops and never missed an appointment. Pity they never updated his photograph from Muckamore. Though he had an ID pass with a photograph.'

'Where's that?'

'Still with him I assume, or burnt or in a bin somewhere. Because he's been off the radar since March…'

'1982!' offered McDermott.

'Bingo! There was a radio and TV campaign to look for him, but it faded quickly as our daily troubles overshadowed everything.'

'Do you think he's still in this country Jacko?' McDermott asked.

'I'd be pretty sure he's still within the British Isles, or the south, as his expired passport has never been renewed. Nor does he have a driving licence, although that doesn't stop him driving.'

McDermott quickly scrutinised the notes he had taken whilst listening to Jackson.

'Ok here's what we've got. Trevor Wilson ticks all the boxes in our investigation. He has motive for revenge, and his history explains the lengthy time period before the attacks. We know, he is highly intelligent and resourceful. My only worrying thought is, why then, did he frame Henderson, when he could so easily have murdered him when planting the evidence in his house?'

Douglas responded 'Maybe, he wanted to publicly ruin him, before killing him? Remember, this is a highly intelligent person, with probably nothing in his life left, except to extract revenge. To humiliate a thug who thought he was untouchable. After all Captain, we know the evidence against Henderson won't stand up in court, but at least Wilson has destroyed his miserable reputation, and could be waiting for his return, to strike the final blow?'

'Possibly. Ok, I'll take the photograph, and beg our holiness to avail us an All-Points Bulletin, with TV and radio coverage. We'll play it as a missing person with mental problems. Jacko, you finish off stroking out the remaining Trevor Wilsons. Doug what's your next step?'

'Already ahead of you Captain. P&O have been trialling this new-fangled, CCTV security thing. They've retrieved the tapes from Scotland, and here, on the night of the murder along with a passenger list, which thankfully wasn't too large.'

'Brilliant Doug. Grab a cup of tea and wait for me. I want to go with you. Oh, and get a good photocopy of that photograph.'

~

After dropping the boys at school, Patterson made a few enquiries in the local area as to the whereabouts of a photographer, who specialised in portraits, before finding one on Highfield Road. He had persuaded the photographer to allow him, Shirley and the boys, attend outside of his daily working hours. To kill time, he walked along the promenade, nipping into Primark to buy a warm coat. He stood looking out at the Irish sea, restless in the wind, his collar up, in defence from the cold.

He looked down at the grey sand of the beach, and revisited the warm summers he'd spent there with Shirley and the boys. Tired donkeys, candy floss, screams of delight and deck chairs. A negligible hint of sadness wafted through his mindset, knowing he would never repeat those experiences. His mind was locked in on his destiny. Nothing would defer him from that goal. Patterson looked at the cloudy horizon, focussing on where he thought Belfast would be, before whispering the mantra, 'I'm coming for you.' Eventually, he wandered into a sparsely populated pub, picking over a plate of pie and mushy peas, whilst trawling through the horse racing pages of the Daily Mirror. The pub was comfortable, with soft chairs and an open fire. He granted himself a final flutter, careful to ensure he had enough money to pay for the portraits, and the Chinese meal he intended to provide for his 'family', on what *he* knew to be, their last evening together. Leaving his beer, he notioned to the bartender, that he was nipping into the bookmakers next door. He took the audacious attitude of sparring with destiny, by placing a £10 Yankee bet, consisting of six doubles, four trebles and a fourfold accumulator, that included one favourite and three outsiders.

On his return, he had smiled to himself as he watched the TV, and each selection, bar one, the favourite, came romping home, netting him £272 for his meagre stake, further convincing him, destiny had played a part in his success. Later that afternoon when he picked the boys up from school, Patterson noticed, how a few of the waiting mums had adorned make up, and smiled directly at him, instead of the careful glances of the morning. He wasn't sure if it was him, the car or the potential money spinner for these, obvious, single mums. When they arrived home, he asked the boys to stay in their school uniforms after they'd finished their homework.

'Why aren't Patrick and Richard out of their uniforms? If they dirty them… 'Shirley asked when she'd finished work.

Patterson cut her short. 'Because I asked them to. Now, will you hurry up and get changed?'

She frowned at him, whilst the boys played Tetris.

'It's ok, honestly. I've booked a family portrait photo shoot for us four. I'm getting a print for you, Aunt Elsie and me.'

Shirley felt a wave of emotion rush over her, and ran towards him, engulfing him in a tight hug.

'Ah John, that's so sweet,' she bleated, before stepping back to face him. Her mood changed to that of Matriarch.

'Are you sure you can afford this? I mean on a basic Prison Officer wage?'

He beamed that irresistible smile. 'Well Sis, that's the first of my wee surprises I've been keeping from you. I'm now, acting Senior Officer, on a senior officer's wages, which will become permanent in the very near future.' Although Shirley gleamed with pride, a small corner of her heart broke, knowing it would further cement him remaining in Northern Ireland for the rest of his career… and life.

Chapter 48

TUESDAY

Patterson's BMW, roared along the M6 toward Windermere with Shirley as his passenger. Low sun, highlighted the prepossessing array of colours of the dying leaves of deciduous trees, that looked resplendent. Patterson glanced at his sister; happy she still wore a contented smile. Her smile had been present from the minute she and Patterson dropped the kids off at school. They had arranged for friends to pick them up, in case they were late on their return journey. However, the *real* reason for her etched smile, was that she had her brother all to herself. Well, that and the fact they had both re-enacted the head banging scene from Wayne's World, whenever *Bohemian Rhapsody* was played on the radio.

'Have you got wind or are you turning into a Cheshire cat?'

Her smiled broadened. 'I'm happy John...that's all'.

'Why so?'

She leaned toward him, touching his arm with sweet affection. 'Because it's just you and me, for a whole day. It's been a very long time since we had that pleasure.'

'Yeah, like a million years! If it's any consolation, I'm happy we're doing this too.'

Shirley kissed Patterson on the cheek, before settling back into her seat. The motorway disappeared beneath the wheels of his car, as Patterson fought with internal thoughts.

They reminded him, that this would be the last time he would engage in a pursuit such as this with his sister. The previous night had been no better. He'd wanted to scream that he was on a course of antipathy, where he would reap revenge for the fate his father had suffered, but realised, it was better she didn't know, as it could complicate, even alter, the destiny he had come to rely on. Deep in her own thoughts, blind to the verges flying past her window, Shirley understood she would have to make the most of her time together with him, a rarity in their lives. She closed her eyes, attempting to plan what adventure they could undertake on their next day alone, whenever it may be. She sighed in frustration, continuing to draw blanks. *'I suppose it's just the euphoria of having him here today,'* her inner voice suggested… without conviction.

~

McDermott had assisted Douglas in the small offices of the P&O Ferry Company, the previous evening. They had trawled through the passenger list, both foot and vehicle drivers, and began to study and cross check the CCTV images, that were quite blurred. It had been a long, arduous challenge in the dark room, with only one TV set that had a recorder, enabling them to play and stop, video of the unwary travellers. They had worked through half the passenger list, and having access to the police communications database, were able to cross check, ring round and get confirmation from the actual passengers.

A few of Montgomery's henchmen were easily identified, all of whom had already been questioned as potential suspects.

Douglas had created a log, with identifiable timeframes and individual passengers, according to the ticket purchases. They had worked until 8pm, and were close to examining all the boarding passengers from the Stranraer CCTV side. McDermott had ordered Douglas to finish for the day, thanking him for his efforts. He was happy to leave Douglas to it this morning. Jackson had contacted, and successfully eliminated, the remaining Trevor Wilsons, and would join Douglas.

~

Molly had taken the bus into town, as she had done on a Tuesday, for what seemed like a life time, to meet her long-time friend Peggy. They would trawl through the shops for dear knows what, and finally have lunch in the cafe at Marks and Spencer's, in what Molly called, 'a little bit of opulence.' McDermott was aware she was on a cathartic journey, knowing that her meetings with Peggy would soon end, after they moved to Scotland. He had finished his staple breakfast of porridge and two boiled eggs, before moving to the comfort of the armchair in front of the television, with a large mug of tea. He kept the television off to avoid distraction of the pointless day time TV shows, where people bared their souls, or accused each other of something, or had their house fixed. He had decided to call with Elsie Patterson today. He struggled to understand the relevance of his visit, as he couldn't muster a thought as to how, or why, his visit would be beneficial. Ok, she had reared the son of Jackie Smallwood as her own. He was now a Prison Officer, who had narrowly escaped the bomb that killed his friend.

What more was there to know or find out? This was one of the stones that had yet to be upturned, even though he was convinced it was irrelevant. Still, it was what he had asked of his deputies. The phone rang in the hall.

'Morning Captain. There's something I think you should see,' said an animated Douglas.

'Doug, its only 9:30. What time have you been there from?'

'I started early to try and get this finished. Jacko's with me now.'

McDermott could sense the excitement in his friend's tone. 'Ok, what it is it?'

' You'd be better coming over and seeing it.'

'I'm on my way.'

He quickly rinsed his breakfast dishes before grabbing his coat and car keys.

'I'm sure Mrs. Patterson will be at home tomorrow,' he mused before leaving.

~

McGuigan briefed his second in command, in the A3 dining area during breakfast. He had emphasised the need for control, and to warn any mavericks who may think they could react independently after his release. Control was a two-edged sword, that gave the prison staff a false sense of security and the Republican prisoners opportunities.

McGuigan also promised he would visit within a month of his release, to get an update of any important developments in discipline and regimes, along with punishments that were to be dealt with. Having showered and dressed, he waited in the cell that had been his home for almost a year. As usual, his appearance was impeccable, yet another tool, in the psychological daily war against his captors. They would never see him frown, nor angered, no matter how humiliating it was to have his possessions rifled through, his home from home a mess, after daily cell searches. He hadn't dressed for the exercise yard, even though his comrades were wearing as many layers as possible, against the bitter winter wind of the open expanse. His visit was early, and after smiling and accepting the mandatory strip search, he was ensconced in his usual booth. Nugent and he conversed in whispered, Gaelic tones.

'The team has been assembled and they're making their way to Dundalk tomorrow.'

McGuigan nodded in appreciation, waiting for him to continue.

'Some big hitters in this squad, like we're talking the elite. They're coming from Limerick and Cork.'

'I should feel humbled… but I don't. Only thing they need to know, is that this is my operation, and I will lead it.'

'I understand, and am pretty sure they are aware too.'

There was a pregnant pause, before Nugent continued, dancing around the topic he knew would arise eventually.

'It's a pity you won't be staying for the party on Thursday, it'll be a riot.'

'Barney, there'll be plenty of time for plenty of other parties.'

Once more, the stagnant silence filled the air between them, as McGuigan focused on Nugent's eyes, making him feel uncomfortable. 'Any other news to report?'

Nugent felt deflated before beginning to reply. 'We've increased the number of members in the search. They're combing every square inch of the north, and right down to Wicklow. Her relatives down there haven't heard from, or seen her. I'm really sorry Padraig...'

McGuigan lifted his hand to display finality. 'Barney...you have nothing to be sorry for. It's that bastard screw who'll be sorry!'

~

McDermott stood behind the seated Douglas, in the cramped, dark room looking at a frozen, blurred image of a passenger on the screen. Jackson stood to the side with a video tape in his hand.

'Jacko and I have been through this a million times. We've cross referenced the foot passengers boarding the ship in Stranraer, with those who departed in Larne. And I have to say, it was my esteem colleague, Mr Jackson who noticed this.'

McDermott turned to glance at the hulk of a detective, grasping the tape like a Filofax, a comical smile of satisfaction on his face.

'Although it's difficult to make out, this passenger, we are sure, is a Mister John Smith, who purchased a return day ticket that morning. What we're looking at here, is him boarding in Stranraer on the return journey. However, there is no sign of him leaving the vessel when it docks at Larne.'

'John Smith? Not very imaginative, is it?' interjected McDermott.

'Keep that image in your mind Captain,' Douglas replied, as he retrieved the second video tape from Jackson, that had already been paused at the appropriate moment.

'Now this guy here…' as he pointed to the image, 'never actually got on the boat, unless...'

'He's in disguise!' blurted McDermott.

Jackson turned the light on as Douglas turned off the screen.

'Our friends at P&O have managed to get a print of both those images for us.'

The images were cello taped to the wall. McDermott looked at them, transfixed. Both 'people' appeared to have the same gait, height and weight. The main differences were the cap, glasses and different shade of jacket. Although the common denominator in both pictures, was the distinctive back pack, 'each' person wore.

'In my humble opinion, I think we've located the elusive Trevor Wilson.'

'Identified Doug, not located,' McDermott replied. 'Although, I'm proud of you guys for the work you've done on this. All we have to do is find him but, with Henderson in jail, it may be sometime before he resurfaces. And when he does, we'll be waiting for him.' He stopped short, 'Sorry, I mean ...*you* guys will be waiting for him…' his voice fading. Jackson wrapped a supportive arm around his boss. 'You are so right Detective Sergeant McDermott, and we'll be doing it for you!'

Chapter 49

It was frustrating, navigating through the small, but busy town of Windermere. Even at this time of year, the number of coaches ferrying tourists, mainly eastern Asian, was ridiculous, as the monsters trundled down narrow streets to the promenade, bringing the regular flow of traffic to a standstill. Patterson had foolishly exited the A591 to join the arterial, and most direct route into the town. The twisting roads and streets flowed like rivers tumbling down toward the promenade to join the lake. After ten minutes behind a coach, Patterson turned off into College Road and made his way back to the A591, convincing Shirley there was an alternative entry point further along, where the A592 joined it at a crossroads, according to his map. He successfully located and journeyed along the leafy, Rayrigg Road toward the centre and promenade. Rather than gambling on the availability of a car parking space, he parked on the road, a ½ mile before the town. They both wrapped up warm with scarves, coats and gloves before beginning their short exodus.

'It's a lovely place, isn't it?' suggested Shirley, hooking her arm into his.

'Yeah, but a nightmare to live in. Imagine having to put up with that number of tourists at this time of year? What must it be like in the summer season?'

'Yes...but without the tourists, there would probably be no town.'

'Fair point,' Patterson replied as he lit a cigarette.

'Are you ever going to give those things up?'

'My motto is, *if you're going to hang, you're not going to drown*. It's written how your life ends, and if these are culprits...' he raised and stared at the lit cigarette, '...well...Que sera sera.'

Shirley fought hard to disguise her panic at the mention of those words, that echoed from her past. The last words her mother had heard before....

'Your choice I suppose,' she managed to blurt out in annoyance, covering her true emotions.

Patterson felt hypocritical, already knowing it wasn't going to be cigarettes that ended his existence. They walked on in silence for a few steps, both hoping, without realising, they had successfully disguised their inner thoughts. The nearer to the promenade; the size of the pavement population grew. They entered into dance routines, stepping on and off the crowded footpaths, or forming single file, frequently stopping to let someone by. Shirley giggled, as she witnessed her brother's frustration, praying he wouldn't 'crack up' and turn on one of the hapless tourists, who had no idea of western etiquette, when it came to walking on pavements.

They crossed to the opposite side of Lake Road as they turned the corner downhill toward the promenade, as it was less heavy with footfall, being in the shade. They were both aware of the plethora of shops, selling a myriad of products. A cornucopia of metal, wooden and plastic trinkets with the name 'Windermere', or a swan adorning them, would be adored for minutes, and ignored soon after.

.Shirley had laughed out loud at her brother after he became annoyed, looking in the window of Atkinson's toys and hobbies shop. Captain Scarlett and the Mysterons had been re-released for the next generation of children.

'That's just not right. Kids nowadays wouldn't appreciate them!' he'd blurted, unaware that Shirley knew it was merely protective jealousy of a period of *his* life, that the younger generation, had no right to. They purchased two coffees in Styrofoam cups with a thin plastic lid, that struggled to hang on, before settling on a vacant wooden bench facing Bowness Bay, an integral part of the greater Lake Windermere. They smiled, watching the hordes of Japanese tourists battling with swans, for access to the shingle beach. Retrospectively, they looked past the chaos to the magnificent scenery and the calmness it exuded. The breeze was minimal, and the golden watery sun was reflected on the edges of ripples of the mighty lake. Patterson put his arm around his sister, appearing to by-passers as a perfect couple. 'It is a bit mental here, but look at that view!' He sighed.

'Makes you feel safe...feel privileged to be here...feel alive,' Shirley replied, gazing at the vista with admiration.

'Yup, it'll always be my new happy place,' Patterson said.

Shirley lifted her head off his shoulder and tilted it, her eyebrows sinking in confusion as she looked at him. Patterson smiled.

'Anytime I feel things are getting me down or feel under pressure, I think of my happy place. It was, for a long time, sitting in the caravan park with Aunt Elsie, watching the Ailsa Craig. Just watching, with not a care in the world.' He turned his head to look directly at her. 'But now...it's here... with you. I will never forget this moment.' Shirley failed to prevent a few tears of pride rolling from her eyes as she hugged him. 'Catch yourself on wee girl!' he whispered, in his most outrageous Belfast accent, holding her tightly. Wrapped together and struggling for thoughts as the display in front hypnotised them, they remained quiet. Shirley, try as she might, couldn't resist challenging him. She took her arm away and sat upright, turning to face him.

'Ok Mister...mysteron and the Scarlett's, or whatever they're called, you have more news for me?'

Patterson fought against a grin, at her inaccurate description of his favourite childhood toy, and displayed a look of surprise.

'Do you want to feel how cold that lake is?' she threatened.

The reassuring grin spread like wildfire across his features. He took a deep breath, and exhaled.

'Ok. Are you sure you really want to know?'

Shirley's scrunched up face reiterated.

'I've got a new woman in my life.'

Shirley rolled her eyes. 'And that's your surprise news?'

'Seriously sis, she could be the one. She came after me! I mean...she's a bit older than me, but she's loaded. She has a big mansion on the Malone Road and everything. In fact, I reckon, within a few years she'll be in an old people's home, and I'll be on her will to inherit everything!'

She hit him a playful slap on the arm. 'John, that's a terrible thing to say!'

Patterson giggled before adopting a more serious tone. 'She's actually everything a man could want in a woman. She's beautiful. Intelligent. Driven. In fact, I think she'll turn out to be my ultimate woman.'

Shirley, ignorant of the subtle hint Patterson had laid down on his future, smiled warmly and hugged him. 'I'm really happy for you John. I hope she makes you happy too.'

He uttered a child like 'thanks' and they rose to leave.

Shirley adjusted herself and asked, 'So… how long have you been seeing...sorry what's her name?'

'Pamela. It's our first date tomorrow night.'

'Ohh...she must be special if you haven't had your first date yet?'

'She is…but wait, there are two other things you need to know.'

Shirley's heart fluttered for a second.

'One. You're buying lunch, and two, my last surprise news, is that I'm taking you and the boys out to the swanky new Chinese place along the front, for dinner tonight.'

She locked her arm in his as they began their trek for lunch.

'Ok Mr Money-bags, you'll not get an argument out of me.'

Chapter 50

WEDNESDAY

A feeling of isolation, hung heavy on the shoulders of Henderson. He didn't know what time it was, except that it was early. Silence emanated from the greater section of the jail outside his world. No sound of metallic breakfast trolleys wheeled over tiled floors from the kitchens. All was calm. He hated these periods, wishing he was still sleeping, as he lay on the uncomfortable bed, under starched blankets. He was left alone with only his thoughts. He felt that *he* was nothing. Not helped by the thoughts that questioned him, teased him, creating bleak scenarios of his future. Worst of all, they troubled him. He was alone, based at the end of, and under, 'D' wing behind a full metal heavy door that opened from the inside, leading to an airlock resembling a cage. The difference between it, and the multitude of all other airlocks, was the all over covering of BRPP. Exterior cameras gave staff a forewarning of any potential trouble. Interior was, compared to the landings outside, narrow with eight cells, four each side with two other 'former' cells converted to showering and washing. There was also an interview room. The class office, a wooden compartment with all round glass for observation, was set centrally along the back wall close to the airlock. No stairs. No catch wires. At the opposite end was the 'virtual 'association area, containing a pool table and a television sitting on a shelf on the back wall. The first opening on the right, past the class office, was the entrance to the exercise yard.

It was barred by an iron Gate that led to an airlock consisting of two wooden doors, designed to keep heat in and cold out. Finally, passing through a second iron gate to the bijou exercise yard. A space of twenty by fifteen yards, closeted by four high, brick walls, one of which had an opening that served as an outside toilet. Instead of witnessing a clear rectangular vista of the sky, the opening now had a covering of weather resistant, clear polycarbonate, which, through time, had transgressed from a dull translucent to a milky opaque, such was the onslaught of the elements and grime of the city. Moss had stealthily spread from the edges, defying the efforts of the escorted orderlies, deigned to scrub and clean it each week. Henderson's isolation was manifest, with no-one to talk to. He couldn't discuss his past, present, or future with the screws, in fear of uncovering sensitive information that could prove detrimental. The screws were affable enough. They would chat to him whilst watching TV, played cards, and left newspapers when they'd finished reading them. They acted like friends, but not with any nefarious connotations. Simply put, they were as bored as he was. The only difference, a huge difference, was they went home at night. For a while, Henderson's ignorant pomposity had convinced him he was royalty within the jail, in his own suite, deemed to be the most dangerous person incarcerated. But that facade didn't last long. The constant tedium convinced him of the reality. He was the most wanted, the most hated. His only saving grace, freedom, only a week away. But what freedom? What was there to look forward to? His life, his business, his standing in the community, all lay in tatters. The power and fear he once possessed was obsolete. Universally.

He was despised, ever since the newspaper headlines declared him a 'tout'. He knew he would never get a proper opportunity to explain, or defend himself against the masses that were conveniently happy to have already made up their minds. It enhanced the Belfast saying, 'throw enough shite at a blanket and it will eventually stick'. He needed to reinvent himself. Start again. But where, and with whom? He'd heard of the emergence of a fledgling mid-Ulster terrorist gang, The Loyalist Volunteer Force. Surely such a small force would be glad to have someone with the clout he possessed? Or rather, *had* possessed. He had singular knowledge of multiple arms dumps, which could be used as bargaining chips to gain acceptance. Selling his house, or what was left of it, would create much needed capital in re-building a new empire. Henderson could count the people he could trust and rely on, on a few the fingers of one hand. Montgomery's closest contact and 'minder', had the phone numbers of the Russians wanting to introduce Northern Ireland to heroin. Another potential money spinner, that he would discuss with the current leader of this new force. A fanciful notion of using the revenue from his home and setting out on a quest to find Imogen and Matthew, briefly clouded his thoughts. Would he find them? Would they want to be found? Would they embrace and accept him…no, *respect* him? Could he accept what they had done? He decided to be honest, formulating questions, that his inner thoughts, masquerading as doubt, squealed, he *needed* to answer.

Did he still need Imogen? *Think so.* Could he forgive her for trying to sell, then destroy his home? *Absolutely not.* Did he still love Imogen? *Reluctantly, didn't think so.* Did he ever really love Imogen? He cowardly refused to answer this question, trying, and failing to dupe his thoughts...*ok! Ok! Probably not!* Could he accept Matthew and his sexual orientation...and his partner...live happily ever after... play 3rd fiddle in a family environment?... his thoughts mocked him.

'No! Fuck off! Never!' he shouted, bolting upright on the bed. A realisation that his biased schemes were close to fantasy, darkened his mood. In a moment of despair, he considered justifying the location where he was incarcerated, by adopting and embracing the existence he had been falsely accused of. 'Yeah,' he whispered, forming a broken smile, 'becoming a supergrass could solve everything.' He reckoned it could be the answer, *if* his fantastical theories bore no fruit. It would be a huge gamble, the courts reluctant to uphold such schemes after the last few spectacular Supergrass failures, resulting in zero convictions. There was outcry from MP's and the general public on learning of the fortunes in court costs, followed by compensation settlements for 'innocents.' But then, what he had on his side was the information of a former warlord, that could possibly cripple, even extinguish, the UDA and UVF completely. Name changed, new location, new life. But one he would spend dwelling in shadows. *'Be the same whenever I get released anyway,'* he thought, trying to convince himself.

He mentally listed the names of those who would face prosecution, a lot of whom were happy to see him locked up. This would be his payback.

He also knew he would have to confess to his own misdemeanours, making him feel uncomfortable. He honestly couldn't list every death he'd been involved in, or sanctioned. To the RUC, he'd offer up, in detail, the 'minor' misdemeanours during his tenure, that should sate their palate and strengthen his justification as a reliable witness for the Crown. However, there was one that Henderson could never admit to. The same one that troubled him every night, since the inception of his solitary confinement. The one that made him toss and turn as soon as he closed his eyes. The one that had become an ever present, horrific, recurring nightmare. The night he took control. The night he murdered Jackie Smallwood.

~

McDermott drove along the Woodstock Road to its junction with the Beersbridge Road and Cherryville Street, where the East of the City meets the South boundary line. He had fond memories of this area, having been posted here for two years at Willowfield Station, during his early career as a beat constable. Stopping at the lights, he noted the colossus that was once the Willowfield Cinema, known as 'The Winky', and the Unionist Snooker Hall, had been replaced by low level, non-descript retail hubs. Mirrored at the opposite side of the road, there was fencing with new builds in progress, replacing the Tramway Bar.

He recalled nipping in for a quick pint occasionally, after a shift back in the halcyon days, when youngsters playing football in the streets, ranked up alongside the most heinous of crimes. They would run at the site of any policeman. It had seemed easier in those bygone days in this area, and its village mentality. Everyone knew everyone, in all the streets. The youngsters' universe ran down the Beersbridge Road to Euston Street, back up to Willowfield Street, then back to the Woodstock Road. It had been a more settled place, not yet tainted by sectarianism. There had been quite a number of Catholic families, that were part of the fabric of the community. So much so, a chapel was built one street away from the Police Station, in this, which was regarded as a Protestant enclave. Catholic families had eagerly attended the 12th July celebrations. Their children sitting on the red, white and blue kerbstones on the Newtownards Road, as the magnificent sight of Bear skinned dragoons or Albert Foundry Works Steel Band marched toward the 'field' in Finaghy, at the other side of the city. People just lived their lives as people in those days.

Sadly, McDermott recalled the era when the tension between the opposing factions started to grow, as the disgruntled Marxist based, Official IRA, got fed up with being second class citizens in the north of the country, believing they should be whole once more. Across the city in both Protestant and Catholic areas, long standing friends and families were moved, or burnt out of their homes, as both sides underwent their local ethnic cleansing.

Having moved to Tennent Street by then, McDermott had watched the television with a broken heart at what once was a village community, unravel in front of his eyes. The Chapel had been ransacked, as the misguided hatred spread. The iconic image, was of the statue of the Virgin Mary, barely upright, in the middle of the deserted Woodstock Road, surround by broken bricks and marble. The troubles had officially begun.

Chapter 51

The chaotic breakfast routine was well under way. Bleary-eyed boys struggling to gain momentum, thanks to the irregular hour they had crawled into bed, after Uncle John's Chinese treat. Patterson was preparing cornflakes with hot milk and smiled, listening to his sister barking orders at the hapless souls upstairs. Patrick was first downstairs, his cow's lick like an exploded haystack, quickly followed by Richard, eyes still half-closed, even after being submerged to the point of drowning in the wash hand basin, by his endearing mother.

'Right! Get that into you. It'll put hairs on your chest!'

Both boys looked confused before digging their oversized spoons into the cornflakes.

'Ohh…warm milk!' purred a satisfied Patrick.

Richard replied, after attempting to take a large mouthful from the oversized spoon, most of which returned to the bowl. 'Mummy doesn't give us warm milk Uncle John!'

'That's because mummy doesn't have the same amount of time as Uncle John in the morning to warm your milk,' Shirley announced, entering the kitchen, constantly checking her watch, and rushing to organise all their lives at the same time. She lifted bread to put in the bread bin whilst eyeing up the dishes that hadn't already been placed in the dishwasher. Patterson stopped her mid-flow.

'Leave everything will you? I'll sort the place out after I've taken the Lone Ranger and Tonto here, to school.'

The struggle of maternal frustration from his agitated sister, wanting to do things her way and put her stamp on proceedings. But she conceded.

'Right, right…ok,' she acceded, pulling on her coat.

'Ok boys, mummy has to go to work. Uncle John will take you to school and I'll pick you up. Be good. Have a nice day!'

She maintained her routine of kissing the top of their heads, and telling them she loved them, before heading for the door to the hallway and motioning Patterson to follow her. For the split second she had before he arrived, she took a deep breath, trying hard to compose herself. Her emotions in turmoil. When he appeared, she held his arms at their side before looking directly at his face. She could do nothing to stop her lips trembling, as she presented a nervous smile, before giving way to a tearful outburst. Pulling Patterson forward, she wrapped her arms around him and buried her head into his shoulder, only just managing to restrain from howling uncontrollably. Patterson held her tightly, his Adam's apple pronounced, in his fight to regain composure. They stood silently in an embrace for what felt like hours, but was less than 20 seconds.

'What are you like wee girl?' he whispered into her ear before breaking the embrace.

She looked at the floor, embarrassed, drying her eyes with the help of a tissue.

'John, I'm sorry.'

'What for?'

'For being an eejit! For acting like a wee girl.'

'It's hasn't done my ego any harm,' he replied through a warm grin.

Occasionally, Shirley was frustrated by his deflection of serious matters through humour, but on this occasion, she was thankful for it. 'I think it's an age thing. As a child you take everything in your stride, without thought. The older you get; you worry about everything.'

'M word?'

'No, it's not the menopause, although I sometimes wish it was. Would give me an excuse to act this way.'

Patterson hugged her again for added reassurance. She continued. 'John, I've…, well me and the boys, have loved you being here. And before you say it, not just because of the free Chinese and the portrait photography… we've just loved you being around. And God knows when we'll do it again.' Patterson gave a wry, contented grin before hunching his shoulders and holding his hands out in submission. He delivered his rehearsed speech. 'With my new promotion and everything, I can't make a date, or promise anything right now. So, I guess I'll see you when I see you.'

Shirley ruefully had to accept the situation. 'Just promise me you'll look after yourself?'

'Course I will, but only if you look after yourself, and those two wee whippersnappers,' he replied.

They hugged for the final time, before Shirley glanced at her watch and became frantic. 'Shit! I'd better get going!'

She opened the front door before spinning round. 'Oh John! Don't forget to leave the print here, and put your front door key through the letterbox when you go!'

Using his eyebrows, each seeming to work independently, he gave her a look that confirmed he was well aware of his final duties. He pointed a finger toward the door.

'Go!'

She laughed and shouted, 'love you,' to which he reciprocated. When she left the house, unaware she would never see him again, she had an overwhelming feeling of emptiness. An emptiness that threatened to choke her. Her stomach felt cramped. Driving off, she put the cramp down to the Chinese meal. Though, it did nothing to fill the emptiness. When Patterson returned to the kitchen, both boys had their pullovers up, and shirts open, looking for the promised hairs the cornflakes would put on their chests.

~

McDermott indicated right, into Cherryville Street. Aware that Cherryville Street had evolved into a major thoroughfare, linking travellers to My Lady's Road, and giving access to the Ravenhill Road. He turned left after the Chip shop into Pearl Street, parking beside a gable wall.

As he alighted, he noticed one of the two wooden doors in the gable wall begin to open.

He smiled as he seen the sixty-year-old vendor of the shop on the corner of Pearl Street, skillfully manoeuvre his antique carrier bike, fully laden with newspapers, up a few steps and into the street.

'Frankie Shaw! Still doing the papers at your age?' he shouted over.

Frank took a few seconds, before recognition kicked in. 'Mr McDermott! Long-time no-see. Are you back over in Willowfield?'

McDermott adored the old-fashioned values of that generation. 'No, just a wee bit of business in this side of town. So, when will you retire?'

'Doing the papers is a retirement present to myself. Now if you'll excuse me, these papers won't deliver themselves. Nice to see you again, take care.'

'You too' McDermott replied earnestly, thinking that if Frank lived to be one hundred, and was still capable, he'd be on that bike every day. McDermott ambled down and past Frank's corner shop, turning left into Cherryville Street. At No. 45, opposite Sherwood Street, he rang the doorbell of an immaculately presented terrace house.

A few seconds later, he spied the shape of Elsie Patterson through the frosted glass of the vestibule door, shuffle down the hallway. When she opened the door, McDermott took note of her frailty, although like most women of her age, she had white, with a hint of blue, coiffured hair and bedecked in her finest jewellery, and a match box sized hearing aid. McDermott produced his Police ID.

'Hello Mrs. Patterson, I'm Detective Sergeant Harry McDermott, and if it suited you, I'd like a few words please?'

Her face marginally drained of blood beneath her make-up application. 'Is there anything wrong?'

'No, no, not at all,' he reassured her.

'Then you'd better come in,' she replied ushering him up the hall and opening the door to the parlour, 'Can I get you a cup of tea?'

'I'm fine thanks, I really don't want to keep you.'

McDermott sat on a settee he was convinced, hadn't suffered body weight for at least thirty years, whilst she sat facing him, on a matching chair. He noticed a collection of photographs on the pristine mantelpiece.

'I'm just checking on John, your son.'

Her defensive facial expression was immediate.

'No worries,' he continued, 'It's just a routine follow up on his health and wellbeing after, ah...the incident he was involved in.' McDermott witnessed how her demeanour became relaxed in the knowledge that Patterson wasn't in any danger, yet battled with hypocrisy, feeling pity for Beattie's fate.

'God love that poor man,' she began. 'That affected John quite a bit. For a while he was very quiet, and although he never mentioned it, I knew he was questioning how he had survived and not his friend.'

McDermott nodded a sympathetic, understanding agreement. He'd met so many police officers in the same situation.

'But he got a lot of help from those...' she struggled for the correct word.

'Counsellors?'

'Yes, thank you, those ones. But I think the whole episode has changed him.'

McDermott, with no inkling of suspicion asked, 'In what way?' He could see her formulating her next reply. 'I suppose ...in a good way. He seems more settled, more mature.' She smiled with pride, 'Do you know he's getting promoted at work?'

A genuine smile crept over his face.

'That's great news. Good for him!'

McDermott motioned to leave, but hesitated, already hating himself for what he was about to do. He settled back into the settee again.

Chapter 52

He dropped the boys off at the school gates and when they alighted from the car, he got them to stand side by side for a last-minute inspection. The boy's puffed out their chicken chests to impress. 'Mmm, not too bad.' His heart was bursting with pride at the two innocents. They were beautiful, adorable children, and he would never see them fully fledged. Perhaps that was a gift. This image, would be etched in his mind for his remainder. All the rigorous discipline he had exhibited to Shirley, felt about to crumble in front of his nephews. He fought wave after wave of emotion pushing behind his features.

'Right lads, one question before I go.'

The siblings enjoyed Uncle John's entertainment, and strained their faces as if they were already thinking harder than ever.

'Who do you both love more than anyone in the world?'

'Batman!' they shouted in unison.

Patterson shook his head in comic disbelief. 'Ok, fair enough. So, who do you love the second most?'

Patrick smiled and answered. 'Mummy.'

Patterson folded his arms and wore a mocking scowl. 'Third?'

'Daddy!'

Patterson tapped his foot to appear annoyed. He started to look over their heads in pretend frustration. 'Fourth?'

'Mmm…let me see,' replied a confident Patrick, comically mimicking rubbing his chin. Richard, by now, lost at sea. Patterson was smitten with pride watching the boy's behaviour. Patrick would be his legacy. He had all the traits and mannerisms that Patterson possessed as a child. All the attributes, to become a 'cheeky wee shite' just like his uncle. Patrick tried to whisper into Richard's ear, Patterson ignoring he heard every word. Both boys turned to face him. Patrick led the countdown.

'3-2-1…Uncle John!' They shouted and ran to embrace him, as he hunkered down to greet them. He wrapped an arm around each diminutive set of shoulders, whispering in their tiny ears, *'You know I will always, always love you both, forever and ever, don't you?'*

'We'll always love you too, Uncle John.'

He hugged once more before standing and addressing them. 'Promise me you'll both always do what's right. And you'll always look after Mummy when she's older?'

Patrick saluted and shouted, 'Yes sir!'… before they both turned, and bolted into the pandemonium of noise, amidst the sea of the other kids in the playground. Patterson held his breath as he watched them melt into the throng before returning to the car, he had parked round the corner out of sight. He erupted into a cascade of tears, struggling to catch and control his breath, unashamedly crying himself dry. The boys were worth that.

~

'I wanted to check on John's health, tie up any loose ends I have, because Friday's my last day. I'm retiring'

The last few words stuck in his throat in the realisation that the curtain call to his working life was imminent.

Elsie smiled, 'Ahh...that's nice. I'm sure you're looking forward to it?'

'It's like anything, I'll grow into it. We're moving to Scotland to be nearer our daughter. Baby sitters on tap.'

'You'll love it,' she replied through, what she thought was a safe and contended smile.

'Suppose so,' he shrugged, using his own subtle show of contentedness. 'There is *one* more thing, another case I'm trying to wrap up...but I haven't much confidence that I will.'

'Really?' Elsie said, becoming wary, wondering why he would tell her this.

'It's a case I've been working for a very long time, that feels so close to completion...and I'd sort of...hoped, chatting with you could have helped...even in the smallest way.'

'That I can help you with?' her tone with filled with trepidation and suspicion.

McDermott took a deep breath before dropping the bombshell. 'It's about the murder of John's father.' He was distraught, witnessing the doll like figure in front of him, implode.

She looked like she reached an idiom, a point where she had hoped the truth would never be uncovered, but struggled to accept the inevitability of it. She trembled, and relentlessly wrung her hands together. She wore a glass-eyed frightened stare whilst focusing on the dated, yet immaculate carpet. In a barely audible tone, she voiced a mantra of '*No*'.

Now that her head was bent forward, McDermott couldn't ascertain if tears had erupted from her tired eyes, that seemed to be caught in the headlights. When the Mantra became louder, McDermott defensively leant forward, worried her health was deteriorating in front of him. 'It's ok, it's ok,' he whispered in the most comforting tone he could muster, before recoiling backward as her head snapped upright, distraught features contorted in defiance, screeching in her loudest voice.

'It's not ok! It's not ok!'

The outburst seemed to drain her energy levels. McDermott correctly adapted a position of silence and submission. She began to plead. 'He doesn't know! He's never known! It was what his sister wanted, and we've protected him from the horrible truth!'

McDermott's thought process went into overdrive. *'Of course, they would have protected him, gave him a chance of a normal childhood.'*

'As far as he's concerned, he lost his parents in a car accident. He has no memory of them. The name Smallwood means nothing to him.'

She struggled to her feet, and held McDermott's hands in hers.

'Do you understand me?' she pleaded.

He nodded, feeling her grip on his hands tighten.

'You have to give me your word, promise me, that you'll never let him know. I'm begging you!'

Her resolve crumbled along with her grip. She fell back into the chair, emotionally and physically exhausted, before sobbing into her hands. McDermott retook his seat. There was a pregnant silence that he reckoned, would give her time to gain a modicum of self-control, before addressing her again. Her sobbing dwindled. She looked at him with a hapless expression.

'You have my word, Mrs. Patterson. I'm so sorry for upsetting you. I shouldn't have come.'

She studied him for a few seconds before replying, 'I know your sorry son.'

McDermott was humbled. She pulled a tissue from the sleeve of her cardigan and wiped her eyes. 'I admire you for your dedication of trying to do the right thing, even up until your final day, I really do. As much as I wished there was something I could tell you that could help, sadly, there's nothing. I wish to God there was.'

McDermott sighed. 'My apologies again. It's hard to shake off being a detective after all these years. But I can admit when I was wrong.'

Her demeanour had placated. He continued. 'It was because I knew John was in England, and I was running out of time.'

'Yes, that's right, he's over with Shirley. He gets home tonight I think.' Her tone became sombre. 'That wee girl went through hell growing up. The only place she could survive in...' hints of tears lined up on her lower eyelids, '…was anywhere but here.'

McDermott attempted deflecting her thoughts to regain some normality. 'Do you ever hear from her?'

Elsie's smile re-emerged. 'Oh yes! She always stays in touch.' She rose from the seat and collected a photograph from the mantelpiece. 'That's her and her two wee boys. They're beautiful, aren't they?'

McDermott smiled studying the photograph. 'Has she ever come home?'

Elsie's exposition instantly turned icy and serious. 'No. She's never been home. She never will be. It would destroy her. England's her home now… and it always will be.'

McDermott nodded sympathetically and rose from the settee. 'I understand...totally. Look, I'm sorry I bothered you.'

Elsie followed him down the hallway, hoping for further confirmation. As he stepped out into the street, McDermott turned back towards her. 'John will never learn the truth of his past from me. That's a promise.'

Her face lit up. 'Thank you, son. Enjoy your retirement.'

~

Patterson felt embarrassed, collecting the two, not three prints he had told Shirley. He'd lied to her, but had no other option. All through his journey to the boat in Stranraer, he assimilated his situation. Reality hit home, his subconscious racing through every scenario available to him after fulfilling his quest. All negative. Abandonment was the only hint of light for a future. For the first time, doubt seeped into his rationale.

'Do I really have to do it?' he questioned himself.

He scrutinised his life up to the moment of his epiphany, and the vision he had experienced of his father looking down into the darkness. He had made a promise. Yet, it wasn't just the oath to the vision of his father convinced him, he was doing the right thing. It was destiny that had cemented his future. Destiny had highlighted his life of feckless planning that had all but buried him alive in the shape of debt, serious, insurmountable debt. And of his dangerous liaisons that had made him a target, his longevity seriously questioned. The balancing act he had performed for most of his working life was a pre-set challenge. Walking on the edge over the ever-present abyss, gave Patterson a buzz no substance, or woman, could get close to. Pushing the boundaries was his drug. He was aware that he could never re-invent himself, discipline himself to a strict regime. He could only exist, in this world of chaos that he had exclusively shaped. Even if miracles were real, and he had an opportunity to re-start and live a life of safety, of hum drum, cardigan wearing, two point two children, economical hatchback and a garden with a shed… he would flatly refuse.

Patterson couldn't change, because he didn't want to change. He had experienced the highs and lows of gambling and drug taking and drinking. And even though the highs were sparsely scattered, they had the sweetest taste. He felt sorry for those who tiptoed through life, never experiencing anything close to that which he had. He had pleased so many women who were already betrothed, or in a loveless marriage, or pleaded to join him on his journey to sexual ecstasy. Not once had he begged any of them to escape, and be with him for eternity. He could never have married. Marriage would have nullified his zest for *his* idea, of living life to the full. During the darkest times whenever unpaid bills, gambling debts, or avoiding angry husbands created a challenge, he thrived. The challenge, merely survival, maintaining his shallow, yet exciting existence, fully aware his foibles had an expiry date. After driving onto the ferry, Patterson found a seat in a quiet area, closing his eyes feigning sleep, hopefully convincing any passer-by to lower their tone, whilst continuing his self-deliberation. He was more than determined to undertake his chosen path, fearful of his life ending in way that he had no influence over. He'd conceded the fact he would never reach old age, his ilk always seemed to die young, as if they had already played their role in society to the full. Fear was a stranger to him, strengthening his resolve. He mused between the meanings of revenge and vengeance. Revenge, the act of hurting or harming someone, in return for an injury at their hands. But his was the path of vengeance, inflicting harm in return for an injury on behalf of someone else. He was deliberately setting out to kill someone, on behalf of his father. He felt noble.

Unknowingly, Patterson had achieved the discipline that had evaded him throughout his life. He had compartmentalised his thoughts. Those of his sister and nephews had been locked away as he neared completion. He was where he wanted to be. Alone, and without distraction.

~

The light was fading rapidly as he pulled up outside an Art Shop on the busy Ormeau Road. He had noticed the first vestiges of Christmas, retailers limbering up for their best days of the year. Once more, destiny seemed to be pulling the strings as the vendor explained he could collect the framed prints any time after 12 noon on Friday, which coincided perfectly with the end of the 5-hour early shift of his night guard. Patterson successfully managed to join the sprawling, and trudging, rush hour traffic that crept at a snail's pace, up from the Ormeau to Saintfield road, climbing all the while. Any other given day or night, he would be agitated, annoyed by the lack of speed. However, a leer disguised as a smile, the thought of his liaison with Pamela later, etched onto his features. Those thoughts sat aside his eternal security awareness. Serendipity had triumphed again. It would be a quick turnaround, shower, shave, fresh shirt for work tomorrow, and spare underwear.

~

The house on Muskett Court that sat at the top of the main road through the development, was cold, very cold,

The non-complaining volunteer inside, was wrapped in as many layers as possible, providing limited movement. He was aware he couldn't smoke, sitting on a plastic chair in the shadows, staring out onto the poorly illuminated road that terminated in this cul-de-sac. He had two more hours of his shift left. He quietly clapped his hands, under the protection of two pairs of woolen gloves in an effort to stimulate circulation, then noticed headlights approaching. He slunk deeper into the shadows that became shallower as the lights briefly skirted in through the bay window. He recognised the car and the number plate.

'Welcome home scumbag,' the volunteer whispered, before reaching for the telephone, the only other furniture in the room.

The dedicated line in the offices shrilled for attention. The recipient held the phone to his ear without speaking. The answer he had anticipated bore fruit.

'Returned.'

The line went dead.

Chapter 53

THURSDAY

A long, satisfied, sigh, slithered from under the silk bedclothes of the Queen size bed in an enormous bedroom. Pamela Wallace had been teased into stirring by the sound of the shower, and Patterson softly singing. The oversized clock on the wall, told her it was just after 6am. She reached over to where he had been formerly sleeping, purring and recollecting the night before. She had spent her day unashamedly pampering. Nails, hair and had paid to get her make-up done. She knew how good she looked as she'd entered Ann Summer's shop; husbands being scolded for glancing a fraction longer than was necessary. She'd bought the sexiest lingerie combination the shop assistant recommended. The icing on the cake - suspenders and fishnet tights. She wanted to be the perfect hostess for this good looking, gallant, younger man, who had literally saved her life. Pamela had briefly considered the age difference, yet thought him a worthy suitor. After all, he was a great catch, irrespective of the gap in years. It was about time she had a relationship she hoped, would be long lasting. After dressing and preparing food, she studied herself in one of the many full-length mirrors scattered throughout her mansion. She thought it was as good as she had ever looked, the professional make-up giving her a sultry, sexy appearance. John Patterson had lit a spark that was almost dormant, and she was excited at the prospect. She grinned as she thought out loud, *'you're only as old as the man you feel.'*

She then playfully licked her finger before placing it on her backside, making a sizzling sound through her teeth. Apprehension toyed with her, when the doorbell rang. As soon as she opened it and looked into those dark eyes, she was immediately aroused, only just managing to contain herself. Her plans of a perfect erotic adventure seemed scuppered, when he announced that he hadn't brought his 'jammies.' Her face sparkled again, when he quickly added, 'I don't wear 'jammies' When they'd hugged, she'd pushed her groin toward him in an unrehearsed act of openness and acceptance. She swore, she'd felt him already aroused, through his thick coat. He'd been awestruck on entering her dwelling. Everything appeared huge and expensive, high ceilings and elegant cornices. Any furniture on display hinted at wealth, pictures and mirrors sat inside gold frames. The entire place was expertly decorated to give the feeling of warmth, security, and class. They sat on high stools, sipping wine from expensive, crystal glasses around the black, Italian marble island in the middle of the kitchen. They had engaged in verbal sparring, neither disclosing much about their histories, suiting them both. After a second glass, they began to relax. Pamela decided to complete her partially prepared meal. When she reached up to a higher cupboard for the spice she required, she felt him behind her. He lifted her hair, butterfly kissing her neck. She became hypnotic, ignoring the cupboard, resting her arms on the work surface below, pushing back and feeling him pushing forward. His hands reached around and massaged her breasts, causing her to wriggle backwards with more gusto. Patterson finally stepped back.

Her hands still leant on the work surface, her legs almost ready to give way, such was the erotic tension. When Pamela turned to face him, she gasped as he tore open her high-end designer blouse, its buttons resonating as they bounced off the tiled floor. Their love making in the kitchen was both a dream, and a blur. She craved more. After stumbling through a small plateful of food, she'd led him by the hand, two wine bottles in her other hand, to the amassed rugs and furs, in front of a roaring open fire in one of the pre-heated reception rooms. He sat against a settee with her in front of him, his arms wrapped around her, as they gazed into the fire. Pamela had never before felt so wanted and satisfied.

She'd happily permitted him to light what he described, was his last ever cigarette, as he'd explained he would never smoke again after tomorrow. Pamela was surprised it was self-rolled, and knew in an instant it possessed more than tobacco, yet without quarrel, she inhaled the smoke he blew toward her face. The world then became more beautiful, and the passion intensified. They made love in the room, on the stairs, the shower and in her bed, with increasing intensity each time. She never wanted it to end. He acted as a man possessed, as if it was his last day on earth. She was delighted to be his host. She lay in bed dreaming of a life together. Her alimony alone, was more than twice he could ever earn in a year. She had no debts. The house was worth the far side of 1.5 million. They could travel the world. Make love on white beaches in the Caribbean, in a mountain retreat in Switzerland, even in a rooftop lodge in the Serengeti. She was falling in love. Her dreamy state was disrupted when the shower finished. Patterson walked out of the bathroom, an Egyptian cotton towel around his waist, his head forward as he frantically dried his slick black hair. Looking up, he offered her that cheeky grin that melted her heart.

'Morning gorgeous,' he said walking over to the bed.

She smiled and sat upright, moving to the edge of the bed carefully, feeling tender from the night before. She was naked, her pendulous breasts, unashamedly hung freely as she sat on the side of the bed facing him, with no hint of inhibition. She immediately noticed the swelling beneath the towel round his waist and then took charge, motioning him forward with her finger before removing the towel, and accepting him. He stood and groaned, holding her head. On completion, he leant down and kissed her fully on the mouth, before breaking away.

'I've got to get to work,' he stated, extinguishing any possible further romance.

A few minutes later, they descended the bespoke spiral staircase, her arm in his. As he unlocked the front door, he turned to face her, to drink in the sight of her in a silk dressing gown. He smiled again.

'You are amazing.'

She gambled. 'You're not too bad yourself. John....when will I see you again?'

Patterson's expression changed for a millisecond, striking fear into her heart, before a reassuring a grin emerged on his face.

'One step at a time. Right, I'm off.'

Patterson kissed her again before exiting and pulling the door closed. The last kiss felt sterile.

Her joy evaporated, as she stared blankly at the closed door. She heard his car drive away and her legs felt weak. Leaning back against the door, a wave of emotion and doubt swept through her. *'Have I scared him away?'* Somehow, she knew that wasn't the case. The doubt turned to tears, that cascaded down her cheeks, and she could no longer stand. She slid down the frame of the door, her body shaking as she howled. She was convinced, through twisted intuition, she would never, ever see him again.

Chapter 54

A static angst hovered throughout the jail. Today was the showcase trial of its highest-ranking terrorists. Staff already knew how the trial would end, and because of the lack of witnesses, these three beasts would be released into the wild to cause mayhem and suffering. That wasn't their trepidation. Occasions such as this could create a backlash. Inmates left behind, would make a show of strength toward their departing leaders, from behind locked cell doors. The leaders dictated discipline, and kept the running of the jail as smooth as possible. Although hierarchy plans were set in place for the newly 'promoted' leaders by their former incumbents, it would take time for the remainder to settle into the new regime. This opened the door to mavericks who felt overlooked, reckoning they should have been instilled as dictators. The brief window of opportunity to stake a claim was the short period between the departure of the overlords and the acceptance of the new brigade. A successful attack on a Prison Officer, disruptive behaviour on the landings, or refusal to vacate the exercise yards, could escalate the prominence of a volunteer. The seasoned recruits however, performed exactly as their ex-commanders dictated, and accepted the new regime. It was the young guns who deemed themselves worthy, that caused any short-lived unrest. They would learn the hard way, and what it meant to disobey orders. Patterson was aware of the tension that crept as far as D Wing, home of the sentenced, as he made his way down to the Supergrass annexe. He met Senior Officer, Billy Lightbody, along with the exiting Night Guard officer and two other staff. Henderson's cell door was locked.

'What's up with the baldy troll?' Patterson asked of Henderson, using the nickname the staff had bestowed upon him.

'We let him lie on, catch-up on his beauty sleep. Anyway, it makes our job even easier,' replied Lightbody.

'A couple of century's beauty sleep wouldn't help him.'

They all laughed. Patterson asked if anyone fancied a cup of tea as he headed toward the showering area with the white plastic kettle. He grinned, when he thought about the nickname that Henderson had received. The mirth he was encountering, vanished on walking past the closed door of Henderson's cell, whispering under his breath, unseen by his colleagues, 'Time's almost up big boy.'

~

At 10am, the Loyalist paramilitary prisoners were in the exercise yards of A and C wings. Most were under the corrugated shelter (A Wing Yard) or congregated close to the walls near the toilet blocks (C Wing Yard), attempting to avoid the bitter winter winds and occasional sleet showers. The regime had come to a standstill within the wings. It was time to unlock Flagherty and Toal, in C Wing, and McGuigan in A Wing. An eerie silence dominated each of the wings, the only muffled noise was from B wing, sandwiched between both, more muted than normal. Not in respect of the overlords, but because it too, was practically on lock down, making extra staff available to assist in case of an incident. D Wing trundled along amidst the normal routines, but had restricted movement to one at a time during this fifteen-minute exercise.

An alcoholic recidivist, a regular guest whenever his release and clothing grants ran out, asked his class officer, who he had befriended over the years, what was happening?

The Officer cheekily replied, 'If I tell you, I'd have to kill you.' The conversation ended.

Governor Bleasdale insisted the prime motive during the removal of these men, was the overall security of the entire jail. Alien to his normal routine, he'd addressed staff at both the 7:30 and 8am parades. He'd emphasised vigilance and awareness, and to expect anything. Staff were aware of the risk and muted the rumour, that something big was going to happen. Staff from visits, legal visits, clerical and the duty office had been drafted into A and C wings to increase the amount of footfall, to enable snuffing out any threat. The telephone rang in the annexe, Lightbody answered.

'Ok, no problem. I can send two men.'

He addressed the other three people with him. 'Security need a few men to link up with those down at the tunnel, to escort the three Provos over to the courts. You two lads happy enough? It'll give me a chance to go through the staff rotas with Paddy.'

The younger and fitter of the two basic grades, eagerly leapt to his feet, turning to his comrade.

'Right Granda, let's go.'

The older officer, was in the last of his thirty years of service. He was well known in the jail. Reliable, wise, dry sense of humour, although almost skeletal, due to alcoholism, that served as nourishment. The duty office felt a duty of care toward someone as dedicated as he, and throughout the last few months, and up until his deserved retirement, he'd been detailed 'easy touches'. He had been a helper in the Tuck Shop, worked with front gate and vehicle lock staff, been 'on the book' in the quiet B visits. Basically, minimum contact with inmates. Patterson noticed the brief moment of apprehension on his face.

'Look Billy, we can go through this stuff later. We've all day. Sure, it's only for about a half an hour isn't? Jonesy, sit where you are.'

Lightbody gave Patterson a soft wink of appreciation, Jones gave a sheepish grin. Lightbody squinted at Patterson in a playful manner. 'You're really after my job aren't you, you wee fucker?'

'Not at all Billy. You're job's as safe as houses.'

Lightbody smiled, as Jones opened the manual grill to let Patterson and his fellow officer into the air lock, that would be sealed, before the outer metallic door buzzed open, whenever the coast was clear, after checking the bank of cameras facing into D Wing.

Patterson shouted from behind the grille. 'As safe as the straw house that one of the three little pigs lived in!'

~

Bleasdale was at the front of the Chief Officers bunk in the circle, directly opposite the glass door. His No.1 and No.2 Chief Officers, either side. He had dictated that each of the prisoners be escorted by two staff, and be withdrawn from their respective wings individually. The C wing two had to take the journey across the circle, led by the Golf 6 officer who possessed the keys to each wing. After leaving the circle, they entered a narrow corridor, the end of which was the completely boarded entrance to A wing. This compact area, was patrolled by Golf 8, who guided the court bound prisoners to an opening half way along the corridor, and the grill he had keys for, that led down stairs. Their journey would be to the left through the unmanned legal visits search box, then secured in holding cells to the back of Legal Visits, close to the mouth of the notorious tunnel. As Flagherty, the second of the C wing inmates, made his journey across the circle, there was a distinct lack of noise. The bristles on Bleasdale's neck sat up. He'd expected a racket as Toal left C wing for the last time, *this* visit. The silence unnerved him. The nervous tension was palpable amongst the escorting staff. Golf 6 was now redundant as C wing was clear. McIntire unlocked McGuigan's cell. He was dressed in a fawn jacket and white shirt, both of which had been retrieved from the Property store in the base area. Completing the ensemble, he wore pressed jeans and dark brown shoes. His remaining property, would be bundled into an industrial strength large brown paper bag and left at the visitor's exterior entrance, to await collection at a further date. McGuigan felt comfortable in his attire. He wasn't like the Loyalists, who wore their best suits and acknowledged the judge, in hope that their respect would shave years off their sentences. He and his army, flatly refused to recognise the court, which, ironically, didn't make a button of difference to their sentences. Their aim however, of making a protest against the court was achieved, serving as a marketing tool for their misguided admirers around the globe. Especially the catholic Americans. McIntire reckoned McGuigan's relaxed attire, made him look more dangerous.

'Well...are you going to miss us Padraig?'

McGuigan allowed himself a brief smile. 'Like an ingrown toenail, Mr McIntire.'

Two escorting officers met him at the grill nearest the circle. One of them had signed him off the landing and had McGuigan's tracking device, the red movements book, in his breast pocket. Unusually, the grills on A2 and A1 were unlocked, as the trio descended the stairs. McGuigan was acutely aware of the number of staff mingling on the 1's. He deliberately inspected each officer, as he strode the twenty paces toward the inner grille at the end of the wing. Some bullishly engaged his stare without fear, whilst others deflected theirs, mostly because they didn't care, and a few who felt intimidated. The first escorting Officer was given entrance to the wing wide airlock, to sign the movement's book, whilst the other one remained inside the wing with McGuigan. McGuigan knew the routine off by heart. As the grille to the airlock was opened for him, he turned to the remaining escorting officer.

'I'm really sorry Mister, but I've forgotten something,' he pleaded in a false apologetic tone.

The officer, looking irritated, replied. 'What have you forgot?'

McGuigan glared directly into his eyes, his face bordering on demonic. 'This.'

He turned back to the Wing, leaning slightly backwards and taking a deep breath. At the top of his voice he shouted, 'Tiocfaidh ar la!' (Our day will come) It was the catalyst for unrest. Bells and buzzers went off in every locked republican cell. Banging of doors, accompanied by demanding requests. Urine from slop buckets was spilled under the doors, the staff on the 1's dodging the cascading yellowy waterfalls. The activity was reciprocated in C wing as soon as the noise levels spilled across.

'Right! Let's go,' ordered the inner officer.

The remaining escort in the airlock spoke directly to McGuigan, with a huge amount of sarcasm. 'Thanks for that!'

McGuigan, didn't reckon him worthy, replying with the grin of the devil painted on his face. 'Sure, it'll break the day up for you. Give you something to do.'

Chapter 55

McDermott felt deflation on the penultimate day of his career, still embarrassed after the debacle of his visit with Elsie Patterson. He hadn't mentioned it to Molly, such was his shame. He compared himself to a Marathon runner. Twenty-six hard miles of a career, and unable to complete the remaining three hundred and eighty bloody yards, that would give him completion. In a sense, he had drifted off the path of righteousness in the past few days. He didn't care about tying up the Smallwood case as a service to the honest, taxpaying, normal people of this diminutive dot on the globe. No, it had become desperately personal. He was being selfish in his efforts. Yet another feeling of shame. Molly's marital caring instincts were to the fore. She knew more about him than he did. She could see the pain in him, could almost feel it. She wanted to make it better, as always, but accepted he was on a lonely path. Not of self-destruction, but of disappointment.

'Harry,' she asked from across the breakfast table. He looked up from an untouched breakfast. She seen hopelessness in his eyes.

'Look love. Don't focus on this last case. Think of the many you have successfully been involved in over the years. Think of the potential lives you've saved.' She reached across the table and held his hands. 'Focus now on our future. Think of your grandchildren, and our new life together.'

McDermott was stunned. There was so much Molly didn't know. So much mayhem he never told her about. She continued.

'You know the investigation will go on after you've left. Your two partners have sworn to that. And they're doing it for you.' She paused. 'I don't want our new life to be tainted with unsolved crimes. You have to accept that, Harry. For our sake.'

For the first time in his life, McDermott showed open emotion in front of his adoring wife. He tried, and failed, to stop the tears pooling in his eyes. Molly rushed around to stand behind him, wrapping her arms around him, nestling her face into his hair.

'It's ok Harry, you old fool!'

McDermott blurted a laugh, before standing to face and embrace his wife. 'Ah Molly...why are you always right?'

'Took you a few years to realise it,' she replied with affection. 'Right, get yourself cleaned up and get in and see your buddies.'

~

Patterson milled about with the other eleven escorting officers. He thought it a bit of overkill on the Governor's behalf. Toal and Flagherty smiled, as they communicated in Gaelic from behind the bars of the holding cell, waiting for McGuigan to arrive. Patterson was primed. He no longer feared McGuigan. Destiny had instilled a confidence in him, almost a brashness. He was confident, McGuigan was aware of his relationship with Orla. But, so what? What if the death threat on him was from McGuigan? This domineering, so called 'hard man' who had beaten his trophy wife. Had isolated her. Was bereft of any feelings for her. No wonder she turned to a real man.

And McGuigan was not even hinted at in his destiny. He was too late anyway. The noise of the unrest from above, caught them all off guard as they hunched their shoulders in an automatic gesture of defence. The two in the holding cell laughed at their behaviour. Patterson, annoyed, gave them a steely look.

'Tiocfaidh ar la! Mo Chara,' spoke Toal in a slow sinister tone, contrived to drive fear into him. Patterson walked to the cell with its barred entrance. 'I'm not, nor ever will be, your friend, understand?' His bravado surprised, but was admired by most of the officers, apart from the few who wanted to avoid confrontation. They heard footsteps descend the staircase. McGuigan walked through the empty search box. His eyes widened slightly on noticing Patterson, who held his stare without flinching. McGuigan called upon all his techniques of meditation, his mind fighting to control every sinew in his body, resisting the urge to throttle his nemesis. His battle of self-control, confirmed to Patterson, that this was the one, above all, who wanted him dead. The cell door was opened and McGuigan entered. The others shook his hand followed by a light embrace. Toal was the first to speak to him in Gaelic.

'That black haired screw is a cocky wee bastard. I'd love to 'nut' him.'

McGuigan briefly glanced toward Patterson who was still staring at him. His thoughts raced. *'My wife, you bastard! You made a laughing stock of me. You will pay dearly for this...and soon!'* Though he still oozed control.

' Ignore him. His time will come.'

The conversation was interrupted by one of the two Principal Officers in the area.

'It's time to round them up and move them out.' He spoke directly to McGuigan, as he held three sets of cuffs in his hand. 'Padraig, we can do this the easy, or the hard way. If we don't cuff you for the long walk to freedom, I have to know that there will be no fucking about or acting the maggot in tunnel.'

McGuigan nodded. 'You have my word.'

The remaining PO tapped the darkened, re-enforced window of the control pod on the far wall at the start of the tunnel. A buzzer went off as the 1st part of the airlock was opened, followed by an override command that unlocked the exit grill down into the tunnel. The PO led the way, followed by the staff and the three inmates, who were dispersed between the escorting officers. It came as no surprise to McGuigan, that Patterson walked beside him. With every step along the seriously hot, cavernous tunnel that ran under the Crumlin Road to the Crown Courthouse, McGuigan fought with his inner self. *'I have the bastard beside me! Right here, right now! I should bounce his head off the radiators, crack his skull against the wall, jump on his head to squeeze the last remnants of life from the fucker!'* But he understood the discipline required of someone of his stature. If he did assault Patterson, he would not be released. He would be ostracised by the organization that had put so many resources, and time, into the operation he would lead. He kept his anger under control.

Patterson sauntered with confidence, an act to emphasise that this scumbag was merely just another prisoner. Terrorists were all the same in his eyes. He reminisced about Orla, something he hadn't done for a long time. He wanted to tease McGuigan, push him over the edge. He'd nothing to lose. He wanted to ask if she'd screamed out loud when she'd orgasmed, as she did with him. He wanted to tell how *she loved him and not you*. Would he even understand the meaning of the word? Did his so-called rank mean that he ordered her to love him? Destiny sparked up to remind him he was taking an enormous gamble, veering off the path that was written for him. He walked in silence. At the end of the tunnel, a small staircase led up to the officer's assembly point, where staff checked documentation, identity of the prisoners, what court they were appearing at, and at what time. Before McGuigan ascended the stairs, Patterson asked him a question.

'I think it's safe to say you'll not be making the return journey then.'

McGuigan stared at him with menacing eyes, before heading up the stairs, turning directly left, past the Officers area toward the plush, compared to the jail, holding cells, directly below Court 1. Patterson, in close pursuit, continued the taunt as if McGuigan was engaging. 'I guess you'll be glad to back to your own bed...' McGuigan had put one foot in the holding cell...'and your wife.'

McGuigan froze, turning on his heel and leaning within ten inches of Patterson's face.

'I'll see you around.'

Patterson, unblinking, retorted, 'Not if I see you first.'

He smiled, then winked before turning to leave. The door of the holding area was closed. McGuigan's knuckles were white with rage as he slammed himself down onto the bench. Nostrils flared to encourage more air in to calm him. Veins each side of his head above the ears were prominent, pulsating. Steely rods of hatred searing through his resolve. His comrades fell silent in a show of respect. Their commander resembled a powder keg about to blow.

McGuigan visualised how he could make Patterson suffer even more when he had him. He would pull out fingernails, extract teeth and burn off all his fingerprints whilst he was still compos mentis, then dismembering him and spreading the body parts all over the county. The officer who closed the door to the three, turned to Patterson. 'That was a bit rough. Do you know that's one of *the* big players?'

'Fuck him!' Patterson replied, before disappearing down the rabbit hole toward the tunnel.

Chapter 56

McDermott lifted the final, framed commendation off the wall, placing it in a cardboard box, before moving to the top of the filing cabinet that had served as a shelf for years. He retrieved the photograph of his daughter, Jacqui, and her family on a beach in Scotland. *'Who goes to the beach in Scotland?'* he thought to himself, a wry grin on his face. He stared intently at his two granddaughters in the picture. He was a tad jealous, but absolutely overwhelmed, that those two wee girls would have a normal life. Not being searched as they entered the town or any of its shops. No thirty-minute warnings to save their lives, before bombs went off. No hi-jacking, riots, petrol bombs, under car devices, booby traps or knee cappings. And no soldiers patrolling the streets. It sounded like a fantasy world, the world of normality. 'God, how will I cope with that?' he kidded himself. Although frustrated, he realised this process was cathartic. He'd reached the end of this particular road, and only because, unlike hundreds of others, he'd survived. Molly's insistence of focusing on the future with no foot in the past, was a good call. What was the point in constantly looking back? He couldn't change anything, or make things better. The atrocities had happened, and there was nothing he could do about it. His last chance of salvation in the Henderson case, had all but evaporated in front of his eyes. Trevor Wilson was a ghost, a very intelligent ghost at that. But that was the past. He was about to place the commandeered ashtray from the Belfast pub, he had on his desk into the box, but rejected it.

He was going to Scotland, new start, new way of life. Molly would have binned it anyway. Dropping it in the bin felt good. He'd promised to give up all tobacco when they emigrated, not wanting to taint or influence, his darling grandchildren along that path. Would he miss it? Would he miss here? Would his miss his previous life?

'Nah, I don't think so.'

McDermott felt more relieved than morose, knowing tomorrow was his last day. The day he signed his retirement papers, and his pension acceptance. He would be interviewed by his Inspector, and hand over the uniform, that had existed as a hermit during the last fifteen years in his locker. But he would keep the badge from his hat. Molly had discussed his personal weapon. Both were in agreement; he wouldn't need it on Planet sanity. His US made Ruger revolver, had served more as a comfort blanket, having never been fired in anger during his career. He wouldn't miss it. His only outstanding case would be handed over to his deputies, with a promise they would keep him up to speed when everything was resolved

 His notebooks would be given to the duty sergeant, to be logged and filed away for any future references. He smiled when he recalled Molly mentioning it was a Disney fairy tale ending. The large animated book slowly closing with the credits, and it was over, for good. The entrance of Douglas and Jackson, brought him back to the real world. He instantly realised by their demeanour and facial expressions they were no further forward.

'Thought you might have looked happier, being only twenty-four hours from seeing the back of me.'

They both shrugged and sat down at the big table, where McDermott joined them.

'Sorry Captain, but we're stuck in a dead end,' Douglas offered as Jackson nodded his head in agreement.

'Look fellas…' McDermott paused to compose himself, 'I can't thank you enough for the shifts you've put in. You performed the way I'd hoped…and then some. It's just a pity we were working against the clock.'

'We'll finish it Captain, you know that,' Jackson stated honestly.

'I know Jacko, and I thank you both for that. Lads, I have to say, it's been both a pleasure, and an honour, to have worked alongside you.' McDermott felt a small lump form in his throat, Douglas noticed.

'It's not over until the fat lady sings, and we've still twenty-four hours.' Douglas stated with reassurance.

'It's not the fat lady we need, it's a bloody miracle.'

~

The noise of the furore in A and C wings had dissipated, the show of strength and support completed, jail veterans quickly wanting to return to the normality of showering and routine. Arriving back in the Supergrass annexe, Patterson noticed Henderson's cell door was locked back in the open position. Jones was wrapped up well against the cold, as Henderson marched around the exercise yard.

Lightbody, had the names of the staff that would be at his, and acting SO Patterson's, disposal for the next week or so, until Henderson was either re-remanded, sentenced, or God forbid, released. It was a pool of twelve basic graders, to cover any eventuality. Lightbody had received a print out from the duty office that designated the shift patterns for their staff. Everything from day shift, association period, evening duty to night guard.

'Guess we'll have to get you a new nickname Paddy, now you've your foot on the ladder and won't be doing as many night guards.'

'Pity,' he replied, 'I quite liked the *Prince of Darkness*.'

Henderson opened one of the wooden doors in the walkway from the yard, the icy breeze grabbing hold of anyone within twenty feet, entered with him. His normally raging, red face and head, had a distinct blue hue. Jones, with only his eyes visible between his hat and the scarf he'd wrapped his face in, quickly followed.

'Jonesy, shut that bloody door will you!' barked Lightbody.

Henderson instantly recognised Patterson as he walked past the class office.

'Fucking Baltic out there!' he offered.

'It's a day the brass monkeys stay indoors.'

Henderson adopted a bizarre grin and nodded, as he turned and waddled his way back to his cell.

'Scumbag.' breathed Patterson.

'No bonus points for observation there, Paddy boy,' offered Lightbody.

Within half an hour, he had learned all he needed to know about being an SO. What was required, how to handle staff, collecting and signing for the key board assigned to the annexe, and all other responsibilities. Patterson had cleverly deceived his comrade into thinking that he was eager and listening. He knew he would never carry out any of the duties.

'Anyone want a scone from the mess?' he asked the other staff, who eagerly replied affirmative. Lightbody produced from his holdall, four catering size sachets of strawberry jam he'd 'borrowed', from the wee café he'd had breakfast in yesterday. As Patterson turned toward the mini airlock, Henderson called after him. 'Excuse me Mister!' Patterson turned as the troll walked toward him. Henderson spoke in a hushed voice, hoping the remaining staff wouldn't hear.

'Ahm...I just wanted to say thanks for...' he tilted his head slightly, 'well...you know...'

Patterson was emotionless. 'No! I don't know, enlighten me.'

Henderson, awkwardly shuffled from foot to foot, dropping his gaze to the floor in embarrassment before continuing.

'You know...for saving my life...' the last few words of his statement were barely audible. 'Thank you!'
He offered his hand to shake. Patterson ignored it and replied. 'I didn't save your life. I was just doing my job, that's all!'

Patterson turned toward the airlock. Henderson felt indignant that Patterson hadn't reacted in a more approachable manner. What had happened to the cocksure youngster he'd been introduced to on his first day of committal? But then what had he expected, a hug? Although his overriding thought was the one, he'd had on his first day of incarceration. Patterson reminded him of somebody, and he still couldn't put his finger on it.

~

McGuigan, instead of travelling in the boot of the car, lay in the well behind the driver and back passenger seats, covered by a tartan blanket. It gave him an opportunity to engage with his female driver. He mused about his day thus far. The anger he'd felt against the bastard screw, had been funnelled into his determination to execute his plan. He had never felt more focused. McGuigan smiled at how he, and his two co-accused refused to stand up when the clerk of the court announced the entrance of the judge. And how the judge had berated the Public Prosecution Service for over half an hour, for the waste of resources, lack of evidence and more importantly the withdrawal of witnesses, who would be dumped with heavy fines. The noise had been deafening from republican supporters in the court room when the case against the three was deemed it wouldn't be progressing, and that they were to be released. The flashing of cameras from the throng of reporters, already licking their lips at the birth of, yet another, disappointment by the PPS, was like a Halloween firework display.

Then being whisked off to the Greenan Lodge in a black taxi, and identifying the Special Crime Unit, unmarked car, that followed. McGuigan wondered how many of his entourage at the Lodge, would be sober, come early evening. His only downturn was when he instinctually, and without warning, thought about Orla. He would have loved to have been wrapped in her arms under the blanket that covered him. He would have made up for the lost years he had bestowed upon her. He would have proved his true love to her. But, deep down, McGuigan felt, no... *knew*, he would never see, feel, touch or smell her again. His driver, McGuigan reckoned, had been hand-picked; a welcome back present. Early thirties, long raven black hair, piercing blue eyes. She wore just enough make-up to look sultry, accented by huge steel hooped earrings. Her accosted Greenan Lodge uniform was tight, especially around her breasts, that McGuigan thought was deliberate, on her behalf. He knew by the way she had spoken to him, as they hurtled along the A1 past Hillsborough, that she wanted him as much as he needed her. She'd hinted that, if he didn't mind, she'd book a double room in a different hotel from where he would have his meeting, under her name, as she couldn't be bothered driving the whole way home and fancied a few drinks to relax. She had no idea of the night that lay ahead of her.

Chapter 57

FRIDAY Midnight-4pm

The ringing phone in the hallway, shattered the empty silence that had existed in the house for most of the night. Molly was first to react. She reached over to the bedside cabinet for her reading glasses, as McDermott stirred. Molly squinted at the bedside clock. It was just before 4am. The continuing ringing, brought her maternal instincts to the fore. She jumped out of bed and grabbed her dressing gown, putting it on as she raced down the stairs. Her mindset was all over the place.

'Who'd be ringing at this time of the morning?' Dread kicked in. 'I hope nothing's wrong. I hope it's nothing to do with my daughter or grandchildren!'

McDermott stirred.

'Molly, is that the phone?' he mumbled, probably still thinking he was dreaming.

'It's ok, I'll get it. Go back to sleep.'

Molly held her breath ready to face the inevitable, lifting the phone from its cradle.

'Hello?' she enquired sheepishly.

'Sorry for ringing at this ungodly hour Mrs. McDermott. It's DC Roy Jackson. Could I speak to DS McDermott please?'

Molly maintained her alertness. 'Is everything ok?'

'It's better than ok, Mrs. McDermott, in fact it's very good.'

Molly's shoulders dropped in relief.

'If you hold the line, I'll get him now.'

'Thank you.'

Within seconds, McDermott spoke.

'Jacko, what's happening?' he asked, unable to muster a theory about receiving a call this early.

'Do you know the miracle we were praying for? Well, it just happened!'

'Miracle? What miracle?' McDermott questioned, rubbing his eyes.

'A bruised and battered Trevor Wilson, is now under arrest whilst residing at the burns unit, Dundonald Hospital. He has dictated a confession!'

'Jesus Christ the night!' he shouted in amazement, the penny having well and fully dropped.

'Harry!! Language!!" Molly scolded from upstairs.

'Sorry love.' He apologised before returning back to Jackson. 'I'll be there within an hour. Make sure he doesn't try to do a runner.'

He heard his colleague laugh out loud. 'Not much chance of that Captain.'

McDermott hung up and leaned back against the wall in the hall. His grin turned to a broad beam, causing muscles in his cheeks to ache. He looked at the ceiling, imagining he could see through it, before whispering. 'Whatever or whoever you are...thank you!'

~

It had been arranged in the meeting of the previous night, that McGuigan and his three associates would cross the border at different locations, avoiding the partially manned main border crossing, outside Newry. None of the assembled squad, could afford to be held for questioning or bloody time-wasting harassment, by the bastard Brits. They would then board an Ulsterbus at the station in Newry, that would take them to the centre of Belfast, and close to the Church Street Black Taxi ranks. McGuigan had his female escort's phone number safely in his pocket. He would visit her again, only if Orla's whereabouts weren't located. He slipped on his jacket, and shouted into the bathroom. 'Five minutes! Downstairs.'
The escort was puzzled and deflated. He had been an exceptional lover the night before. Rough, the way she liked it.
She experienced elation, knowing *he really* wanted her. She was also aware of his importance within the organisation, and felt privileged. This morning, McGuigan was a different animal. He scowled when she wrapped her arms around him, in foreplay to a morning session in bed. He ignored her, seemingly wrapped up in his own importance. She had no idea of his plans for the day. He ordered her to get dressed at 6am, whilst he went for a walk.

He'd been gone nearly half an hour, and she still hadn't finished preparing her make-up. Now she would just have to make do. She inherently realised not to cross him. He'd seemed robotic and distant; from the moment she'd awakened. He'd given her orders, without discussion. She wondered if she would ever see him again after today.

~

Joseph Conlan stood in the hall of his three-bed roomed semi, baring his teeth. His face reddened, as he looked at his ladders, multiple paint tins and everything else he'd had in the back of his van. Except the sheets. The bastards had kept the sheets. He was in a Catch 22 situation and couldn't do anything about it. An early riser, he'd been having breakfast in his modest kitchen, when the banging had started at his front door. He heard his wife walking across the bedroom floor upstairs.

'Whoa! Take it easy, will you?' The banging continued as he walked the length of the hall.
'Do you want a fucking hammer?' he snapped as he opened the door. His verbal assault was cut short by the two IRA men at the door, who pushed him back into the hall.
'No! We want your fucking van! Now!' the taller of the two had ordered. He'd been instructed not to report it stolen, until they had revisited him.
'When will that be?' he stated vehemently.
The smaller one leaned into his face, and growled, 'When we return!'

~

In a bizarre act of reverence, Patterson carefully made his bed, smoothing any wrinkles he spied. On completion, he smiled and nodded, before leaving the room for the last time. He headed to the kitchen where the ironing board sat ready. He unwrapped the brand-new, blue shirt from its plastic home, laying it on the board, intent on smoothing out the wrapper's wrinkles, and creating razor sharp creases of his own making. He then ironed the new, dark blue, clip-on tie that was free from stains and murk. He wanted to make everything perfect. This part of his uniform wasn't for his five hours shift this morning, he'd grubbier stuff in his locker for that. This was for his gala performance this evening. He worked as an automaton, tunnelling his focus on the task that lay ahead. Payback. After a quick coffee, two cigarettes, and checking the list he'd made, Patterson engaged in his routines of checking outside.

Gun in hand, before entering the garage from the back door, and checking the underside of the car, for any lethal additions. He had already scanned the outside of the house to the front, and was confident enough to open the roll up garage door in safety.

After starting the car, he edged onto his driveway, and quickly got out to secure the garage door. Patterson decided to take a route to work via Moneyreagh and down the Castlereagh Road. He reckoned he would still avoid the rush hour easily. It was essential, that he avoid any harm, that could jeopardise his plans. But then again, Destiny was still on his side.

On leaving the driveway, Patterson turned left onto Muskett Road, the main artery in the development, and focused on the unoccupied semi to his right. He narrowed his eyes and pursed his lips. No 'For Sale' or 'To Let' signs. Or any hint of activity. Available houses in this development were snapped up within days. Still, it wouldn't be in his thoughts for much longer.

Chapter 58

McDermott arrived at Dundonald Hospital on the outskirts of East Belfast, shortly after 7am. It was obvious where to park, as the RUC, Grey Landrovers, had set up camp in the smaller of the two car parks, as close to the entrance as possible. Douglas had suggested they meet up in the canteen, so that he could get him up to speed, before visiting Wilson in the Burns Unit. Jackson and Douglas shared a Formica table with a senior E Division, Criminal Investigation Department, Sergeant, who had been called to the scene initially and had taken statements from Wilson. The CID Sergeant looked up when McDermott entered the canteen, before smiling, standing, and offering his hand.

'Harry McDermott. Are you wise? Getting involved on your last day? Thought you'd be at home, flicking through the zimmer frame catalogue.'

McDermott grinned, and they embraced briefly, before settling down at the table. Jackson fetched his boss tea. McDermott trawled through the hastily written statement, looking at Douglas with narrowed eyes.

'Take it you've read this already Doug? What are your thoughts?'

Douglas took a breath before replying. 'Part of me wants to believe all of it, and another part isn't so sure.'

'I know what you mean. There's a lot more detail in his confession to Montgomery's murder, and his description of the disguise he used, is spot on. I think we have him there. But Hamilton...'

McDermott turned to the Bangor CID Sergeant. 'So, how did you get him Tommy?'

'He's lucky to be alive at all to be honest, Harry. If it hadn't had been for the neighbours, who rolled him in bedclothes across the garden, he'd have burnt to a crisp. The smell of burnt flesh when we arrived was horrendous!'

McDermott and his entourage shuddered at the thought of it.

'It appears that he broke into their garage and retrieved a set of ladders, before clambering onto the roof, while lugging a five-gallon Bergen full of petrol, probably spilling some on himself. It seems he wanted to pour petrol down the chimneys, and then light it. But during his struggle of reaching the chimneys, we can only assume, that he'd spilled more petrol on himself. When he lit the match to ignite it, he must've had some shock when he went up in flames. Needless to say, in his struggle to put his personal fire out, he slipped and fell off the roof...still on fire. Unfortunately for him the Bergen, which was still half full, retraced his route to Terra Firma.'

McDermott, Jackson and Douglas flounced at the Sgt's description. Their conversation was interrupted by a nurse, who informed them that Wilson had regained consciousness. McDermott ignored the fresh tea, the group collectively heading to the Burns Unit. It looked like something from a movie. Armed, plain clothes officers, mingled in the corridor with hospital staff, in what had ostentatiously become, a 'secure' ward. One way in, one way out. As McDermott and his crew followed the CID Sgt to the room where Wilson suffered, a Staff Nurse appeared from the interior, in a bullish mood.

'Who's in charge here?' she lowly barked.

The CID Sgt looked toward McDermott. 'I am. Detective Sergeant Harry McDermott.'

She rounded on him, finger wagging to, display her disapproval. 'Let me tell you something Mr Detective Sgt! This patient has just recovered consciousness, and is still showing signs of severe trauma. He has second degree burns over most of his body, fractures in both legs, his collar bone, right arm and a few ribs. He could lose consciousness at any moment. You must not put him under any further stress.'

McDermott glared at her for a moment. He understood the dedication of hospital staff, but struggled being spoken to as a naughty child… by anyone.

'OK, let me tell you something. This murderer will be questioned, and we *will* conduct out interrogation with the upmost care.'
The staff nurse's face turned pale, blood disappearing from it, at the mention of the word 'murderer'. She stepped aside, permitting the entourage to enter. What they witnessed was abhorrent, and inhumane. The shell of Trevor Wilson, was propped up slightly on the bed. A nurse stood watching over his every move. His face was blackened, highlighting the bright red, almost pink, patches of skin that survived severe incineration. Two thirds of his face and head, was covered in gauze. Instead of regular casts on his broken legs and arms, there were light bandages covering the gauze, that had a cooling agent.

The parts of his fingers that protruded from the Gauze strapped right arm, were blistered and pink. His left arm was also covered in the cooling gauze. Numerous drips, were helping to keep him alive. His lips, barely open, were cracked and burnt. It took McDermott a few seconds to adjust to the image before him. Deep down, he felt sorrowful at the state of Wilson, but noticed that Wilson's eyes followed his every movement.

'Well, well, if it isn't the fiddler on the roof?' McDermott stated light-heartedly.

Wilson strained in pain to reply, his voice low and forced.
'Very droll, Sergeant'.
McDermott moved closer to hear, and avoid Wilson projecting his tone. 'It is Sergeant, isn't it? One of my position, surely wouldn't rank any higher?'

McDermott nodded in approval. 'I need to ask you a few questions?'

Wilson breathed in shallowly, his face creasing, inflicting more pain. 'Let me check my diary. Oh, you're lucky, question away.'

A part of McDermott admired the burnt man's tenacity. 'Why did you do it?'

Wilson closed his eyes, summoning up the strength to reply, the Nurse hovering cautiously around him.

'I could ask you the same thing, Sergeant.'

'Meaning?'

'I vie to eliminate, and you strive to protect those that cause so much pain and loss.'

'Difference is, it's my job to uphold the law.'

'Like you upheld the law in the 60's? When you fought hard to find the killers of another Loyalist scumbag, and confined my brother, to a dusty file on a shelf?'

McDermott felt uncomfortable. 'It wasn't like that, you're confused.'

McDermott had wandered into a verbal confrontation, he neither needed nor wanted. He inwardly struggled to defend his superiority, and total belief, in his opposition to the remarks. The nurse supplied Wilson with a glass of water that he gladly accepted, regardless of how painful it was to drink. He felt comfortable enough to continue, under the sad eye of the nurse, who thought he had already been overstretched.

'Don't insult my intelligence, Sergeant. Contrary to any doctor's reports, I am anything but confused. Yes, I suffered for many years after my brother's murder. But do you know the only medicine helped me to get through the darkest of times?' He paused for another painful sip of water. McDermott instinctively knew what was coming.

'Reprisal Sergeant... revenge… retri-fucking-bution!'

The annoyance in Wilson's tone was reflected in his abysmal frame, as he became angry. The nurse raced to calm him, providing water and sympathetic encouragement.

His eyes closed, fighting the agony racing throughout his entire body. His forced breaths were louder and the nurse looked at McDermott with a *do-you-not-think-he's-had-enough* glare. McDermott indicated to his troupe to return to the canteen.

~

There was a fresh determination and focus in Patterson's, mind as he strode along in front of the cottages on the way from the car park, on his penultimate journey into the jail. His sister, Shirley, the boys, Beattie, Pamela and Orla, were all compartmentalised and safely stored away, an unfathomable distance from his current mind set. But there was one other thought distraction, he needed to deal with before this evening. His Aunt Elsie. He would leave her with a print of her adopted daughter, her offspring and himself. He knew, she loved him as much as his mother had, and made so many sacrifices, to give him a normal upbringing. He smiled as he realised tonight, he would openly reciprocate his gratefulness, by telling her, he loved her too. A phrase he'd struggled with. That would be all mental baggage in eternal storage. The thoughts that couldn't be compartmentalised, were that of his father and the evil troll, Henderson. His father had morphed into the essence of his guiding light: Destiny. It was his father, who had contrived to make it possible for him to frame Henderson, and get him in the perfect killing arena. It was his father who had allowed him to save Henderson's life, and convince the Governor to promote him, and then take a lead role in Henderson's wellbeing.

It was his father who allowed him, evasion from capture after the slaying of Hamilton. Patterson looked up with a wink, and smiled, assuming it was also his father, who had given him Orla and Pamela.

'Nice one, Dad,' he whispered

His attention was now razor sharp. Little did he realise the intense focus, the belief in the coincidences, and the self-honour he now lived with daily, had nudged him closer to insanity.

Chapter 59

McGuigan hid as much of his features as possible with a woolen hat, not just as protection from the cold, but as a disguise against police and army patrols. Leaving the bus station in Gresham Street, he headed left, intent on skirting the city centre and the searches at the gates. He walked past the towering colossus, of the most bombed hotel in the world, The Europa, crossed over Grosvenor Road and on past the Royal Belfast Academical Institution. He was disgusted by the boy's only school, and the rich parents who sent them there, unaware of any child he could recall, from his working-class area, that had ever darkened its doors. This was not his world and even if he could afford it, he'd decline the invitation to mix with the city's elite, and their self-styled pretentious lives. People who'd never held a gun, who'd never fought for their homeland, who weren't determined to retain the six counties and drive the British out. That society, fought more for capital gain, and mansions where they could grow fat and die in peace. McGuigan continued past the 'Black Man' statue of the noted Evangelical Presbyterian minister, Dr Henry Cooke, before crossing the road, and walking along King Street. The other volunteers followed at a safe distance. The Limerick guy walked alone, whilst the couple from the rebel county of Cork, took in the surroundings together. On reaching Castle Street, they hailed a black taxi that took them to a series of lock up garages, off the upper part of the Whiterock Road. The taxi waited for them, as they inspected the interior of the dirty white van.

Everything was as expected. Hurley sticks, cloth bag for the head, industrial packing tape, thin steel chains and locks. Under the painter's sheets were their weapons. Two stolen police Ruger pistols, a 9mm Browning care of a part-time UDR soldier and an armalite rifle, from a cache of weapons provided by the Boston branch of NORAID, via a rocky inlet, off the Dingle peninsula. McGuigan ordered his comrades to check the weapons. There were no communications devices, as it was knowledge the RUC had been scanning radio frequencies, creating the downfall of previous operations. They were flying solo. There would be unmarked cars scouting in front of their every move, looking for any potential pitfalls and a tailing car, with enough firepower to help them out of any unforeseen misdemeanours. They were then driven to the Ballymurphy estate, and the safe house where they would receive food, have time to rest and go over the fine details of the abduction. The taxi driver refused to charge the fare, announcing, 'Good to see you back, Padraig,' to McGuigan, as they were alighting, before the driver re-joined the plethora of ant like taxis crawling in and out of the city.

Food was prepared by the sole female occupant of the safe house; a hand-picked, dedicated volunteer. During the meal, they re-discussed the plan to abduct Patterson. The obliging cook, had provided them with the information they required, whenever they reached their final destination. Hastily photocopied A5 flyers of 'Laverty and Sons Tar macadam Services' had been prepared. One of the rebels, acting as the sole passenger, would park in front of Patterson's driveway at an angle, to make witnessing the opening of the back and side doors, impossible to see from the house. Aware he would be watched; he would distribute leaflets around the other houses, while knocking on a few of the doors with vehicles in their driveways. His clean-shaven face, the black dye in his hair and the addition of clear glass spectacles, would be the description the RUC would use as a driving force, in their follow up investigations. He would be far removed from his normal appearance of, ginger hair and beard, without glasses. He'd cough out loud as a signal, letting those hiding in the back of the van, when he approached Patterson's front door, to carefully de-bus and prepare. It had been decided they would follow the main arterial route to Carryduff, the Saintfield Road. Mainly to avoid any of the frequent VCP's (vehicle check points) that could pop up on any of the less busy roads, during rush hour. Within a few hours, it would begin. As McGuigan relaxed, he thought of his target. He was ready, and would not sleep. A devilish grin etched on his face.

~

The holy trinity were in hushed, heated conversations in the Hospital canteen. They'd been there for two hours, waiting for Wilson to build up enough strength to resume questioning.

'I'm sorry lads, but his confession of the Hamilton killing seems too sparse. Do you know what I mean?'

'I'm … sort of…with you on this Captain.' replied a cautious Douglas.

'My only hang up, to use a Belfast expression, he might be stupid, but he's not daft,' interjected Jackson, 'I mean, why would he lie? Why would he want to confess to a murder he didn't commit? Remember his IQ score? It was off the scale.'

'Kudos? Ownership?' replied McDermott, feeling that he had lost some conviction in his own theory. He wanted this finished on his last day, and the easy way would be, to accept the statement in its entirety. What would he care tomorrow, when he would be nothing but a memory? He would love to be able to hand this guy on a plate to his dedicated deputies. They could receive well-earned promotions, or at least help them, and their reputations, of never giving up. Douglas, who'd never had the ambition of promotion, would be glad of it, and the higher pension it would provide in a few years' time. This could be the runway to higher things for the loveable oaf, Jackson, who deserved promotion, or at the very least, the transfer to the Serious Crimes Unit he had dreamt about.

'So, Harry, why won't you just accept the golden fleece and slide into retirement?' he questioned himself. *'Because I'm a cop, a good cop at that!'*

Jackson continued, 'it's only a thought without substance... but he described stabbing Hamilton in the neck, and watching him fall.'

Douglas assumed the role of the defence. 'He could have got a lot of information from the media. It was available to everyone. But, like Jacko says, this is a smart cookie. He could've convinced someone over the phone, to release information. He could've lied his way into the coroner's office.'

They were interrupted by the Bangor Sergeant, informing them, Wilson was ready to resume. McDermott knew the only way they would learn the truth, would be in the next half hour. The Staff Nurse was in attendance to Wilson, when they entered the room. She half- smiled apologetically at McDermott, for her previous outburst. He lightly touched her arm, 'Apologies if I appeared rude.' Her smile became genuine, shaking her head in acceptance. Wilson's breathing sounded as laboured and painful as before. McDermott was keen to get this over with.

'I understand your personal, yet unlawful motives for these crimes, but surely you knew that Henderson was already in Jail.'

Wilson breathed in through his nose carefully, before reacting. 'Yes Sgt, but you and I both know, it won't be for long.'

McDermott temporarily froze. Jackson and Douglas glanced at each other, gaping with shock. Wilson fought the torrent of pain flowing through him and continued.

'I so regret the misdemeanour I suffered last night. I wanted to make *him* suffer, before I *finally* sacrificed him. The first way to make him suffer, was to rape him of the material possession he craves the most. His God. Money! The unintelligent say that money is power. Destroy the money, and he is powerless. Defenceless.'

'Remind me how you killed both of them,' McDermott asked.

An excuse of a horrifically painful smile, slowly crept onto Wilson's face, the cracks on his lips widening minutely, inflicting more damage.

'Ah! A test! You're good Sgt, not brilliant, but good. The first animal was easy, a lamb to the slaughter,' Wilson considered a smile at his comparison, but realised the consequences. 'He stood paying homage to another of the animals, when I stabbed him in the neck. I prayed he would drown in his own blood, slowly. Did he drown?'

McDermott, and everyone within earshot, recoiled at Wilson's emotionless, callous account.

'The second, the faggot, took meticulous planning, and I hated it! I had to pretend to enter his world.' He closed his eyes.

The staff nurse, fearing the worst, attempted to attend to him, before his eye lids re-opened. His stare was frightening. She jolted, and backed off.

'I heard his head crash on the side of the ship, before the sea took him. If you excuse the pun Sgt, I executed my plan perfectly.'

McDermott moved to the corner of the room to speak to his deputies in private.

Wilson called out in his pitiful, loudest tone, as they assembled. 'Team talk Sgt? Corroboration? Good for the morale.'

They ignored him, conversing quietly.

'He's bloody convincing Captain,' breathed Douglas.

'This could be the jackpot we've been looking for… and you deserve,' added Jackson.

McDermott, reluctantly, half dared to dream. He took the written confession from his Bangor colleague, and stood close to Wilson, making sure he could see the confession in his hand.

'The confession you dictated this morning to my fellow Sergeant, needs your signature,' he motioned with his eyes, before returning his attention back to Wilson, 'I will read it out to you as you may have been confused after your trauma…'

Wilson interjected. 'I was not confused! There's no need to read it out! In this case, and this case only, I trust you implicitly. Now give me a pen.'

Douglas took a pen from his inside jacket pocket, and lifted the clip board that hung on the bottom end of the bed, to lean on. He held the pen out.

Wilson notioned toward his right hand, before seething, 'I could use some assistance here!'

Douglas then carefully, put the pen in the pink, seeping fingers.

He held the board close to facilitate the wretch, who winced as he held the pen. He squealed in pain, sweat rolling down his face, and slowly scribbled his signature at the bottom of the page.

McDermott's expression had changed, as he briefly inspected the signature. Miraculously, Wilson, breathing harder than he'd have liked to, responded. 'Are you annoyed Sgt, that you didn't catch me before I done you, and all of society, a favour?'

'You now rank down amongst those scumbags. Congratulations!'

Jackson entered the fray. 'Where did you get the breadknife, you stabbed Hamilton with?'

Wilson noted how solemn the three looked, standing shoulder to shoulder. He gloated inwardly, assuming the upper hand, observing how pitiful they were, and decided to cement his authority with sarcasm. 'In a fucking library! Where do you think Mr Intelligent?!' Although his pain had increased to the extent that he was close to passing out, Wilson mustered a gigantic effort to drink in the sight of the keystone cops. Jackson had a dead-pan expression as he looked at Douglas, who offered the slightest of nods. They both turned briefly to McDermott who had them in his peripheral vision, his direct vision aimed laser-like at Wilson. He took the confession in his hand, without deflecting his stare, and slowly crumpled the piece of paper, before letting it drop to the floor.

Wilson's expression changed dramatically. He ignored the pain of opening his eyes and widening his mouth. He'd been duped. 'No!' he shrieked in a tone considered impossible, as they turned to leave.

The heart monitor, attached to his arm screamed 'warning' and the staff nurse was joined by a colleague, to try and keep their patient alive. The Bangor Sgt was outraged, grabbing the crumpled confession from the floor and racing after the trio.

'Jesus Christ Harry! What the hell are you doing?!'

McDermott addressed him in a solemn tone. 'Interrogate him again Tommy, and charge him with Montgomery's murder. But he didn't kill Hamilton.'

'What?' The Sgt was dumbstruck.

Jackson intervened. 'Hamilton was stabbed with a pair of scissors, not a bread knife.'

The Sgt's jaw dropped in disbelief. Douglas took over. 'Not only that, but the forensic report stated emphatically, it was a left hander. That scumbag is right-handed!'

The Sgt struggled to talk, to form any cognisant reply, before blurting, 'Are you sure?'

McDermott brought the curtain down. 'Very sure Tommy,'

When they turned to leave, the last, and loudest of Wilson's verbal outbursts, echoed down the hall after them.

'Damn you all to hell!' his exertions being his final one, before slipping back into unconsciousness.

Chapter 60

It was a slow morning in the Supergrass annexe. Patterson was fed up drinking tea, wishing he'd brought coffee with him. Henderson had only once, left his opened cell for showering. He was now pouring through the Belfast Telegraph that had been left for him, by the previous night guard officer. The majority of staff were engrossed in a game of Jack-change-it. Patterson was sitting it out, other things pre-occupying his mind. Just before the dinner trolley arrived at mid-day, Henderson emerged, hopped up in as many clothes as he could muster, and requested the exercise yard. One of the day staff started to rise to facilitate him.

'It's ok,' Patterson intervened, grabbing his dark blue gabardine coat. 'Finish your game, I'll take him.' He took the yard keys from the shadow board, clipping them onto the spring hook at the end of his key chain, that was secured to another belt loop near the buckle. As he unlocked the entrance to the yard, Henderson stood close behind him. Instead of feeling rage, Patterson was remarkably calm, in the knowledge that only he *knew,* what was going to happen tonight. The grilles were locked back, and both wooden doors closed, to keep the cold out of the annexe. Henderson started pacing around the yard, keeping close to the walls, in a vain attempt to muster heat, as an icy wind swirled around. When his back was to Patterson, Patterson stared, thoughts racing through his mind. *'I'd love to let this rat know to enjoy his exercise! His last ever exercise.'*

Henderson stopped abruptly when his path brought him close to Patterson, motioning to open one of the wooden doors. 'Mister, I've left my cigarettes in my cell.'

'Here take one of these,' Patterson offered the open packet of Embassy Regal.

'Sure?'

'Yeah, work away.'

Henderson took the cigarette, and the offered light from Patterson's metallic petrol lighter, before grinning and thanking him. He waddled off like a Puffing Billy cartoon train. The exercise of offering a cigarette and light, displayed to Patterson how far he'd come. No sign of nerves, or apprehension, just steely determination. When Henderson had finished another lap, he stopped in front of him.

'Mister, hope you don't mind me asking, but there's something I've been meaning to ask you about.'

For a second, Patterson had a ridiculous notion that Henderson knew about his strategy for later.

'And?'

'It's about you.'

Patterson tensed, before going on the offensive. 'Whoa hang on! You're not some sort of shirt lifter, are you?'

'Fuck off! No! It's just… that you remind me of somebody. I felt that from the first time I met you when I was lifted. Could be someone from the TV, or a film. I just can't put my finger on it. We ever meet before?'

'Wouldn't think so! You're probably thinking of Mel Gibson, the actor?'

Henderson scrunched his features in bemusement.

'You've never heard of Mel Gibson? You need to get out more. Oops, I forgot, you can't.'

'That was fucking funny, wasn't it?' Henderson growled, striding back into the annexe and storming down to his cell. Patterson re-locked the grille to the yard and re-entered. The card players were on alert because of Henderson's reaction.

'Were you winding him up?' he was asked.

'I can see what you're doing here. You're mistaking me for someone who actually gives a shit about that scumbag.'

The others laughed, realising everything was in control. The steel door was opened to let the evening duty staff member enter. He wasn't happy.

'Davey, who ate the cream of your bun?' offered Patterson.

'Wankers in the duty office!'

Patterson dropped his eyebrows, tilting his head in puzzlement.

'We're heading off to Spain tonight. I'd already told them that! Only thing is, the flights at 10pm, because it was the best deal. They fucking knew that! And still… they detailed me evening duty. No chance of making that flight. Wankers!'

Patterson couldn't believe his ears. Destiny had embraced him once more. 'Don't worry about it mate, I've nothing else to do, I'll come in early for my night guard, and let you away. About 7? Would that be, ok?'

'Ah Paddy you're a star! Are you sure? You don't mind?'

'Not at all. I'd expect the same from you if I was stuck.'

The evening duty officer shook his hand. 'Brilliant! Thank you! I'll ring her on my break!'

Patterson removed his outdoor coat, and headed for the exit. 'Right troops, see you later.' He had to make two pit stops, en route home. He would call at the Art shop for the framed portrait, and then stop off at the library to collect a book on Criminology for tonight, maintaining the deception until the final act.

~

The Duty Sergeant wasn't surprised to see McDermott on his last day. He'd heard that he'd been up at the scrake of dawn, and managed to convict a murderer at the Ulster Hospital. The Duty Sergeant already had McDermott's notebooks and case details, that needed updated, ready to hand over.

'Thanks Robert,' he said when he lifted the package.

'No Problem, Captain, it's been a pleasure working with you.'

McDermott displayed a wry grin, before collecting his items and returning to the goldfish bowl, *his* goldfish bowl, for the last time. He sat alone, updating and initialing the new notes, along with a brief description of this morning's events. He grinned, closing his notebook for the last time, thinking back to Molly's Disney analogy. It was mid-afternoon and he was ravenous, the adrenalin rush of the morning's proceedings, had long since dissipated. He was disturbed by the wooden door to his office being opened and looked up to see his nemesis. The Superintendent stood proud, in front of McDermott's desk. He stayed seated.

'If it isn't Harry Houdini, making the great escape,' he announced in a pleasant tone. 'I'm sorry Harry, but I can't make your leaving bash tonight. I've a senior meeting at 6pm, and then I'm taking my wife to dinner, for her birthday.'

McDermott stood. 'No worries Super'.

'I also wanted to say, 'well done'. Your final actions on the force, vindicated your requests to re-open that historical inquiry. You got your man.'

McDermott shrugged, 'Well, one of them anyway. But my team will continue, with your blessing of course, to bring it to a conclusion. "By all means…' He hesitated for a while before continuing. 'Believe it or not Harry, I am going to miss you.'

McDermott was wary. 'Because you're like me, the last of a generation. A good old-fashioned cop, with integrity and drive, not frightened to get his hands dirty. We've both a foot in the old ways, and a toe in the new, technological ways. An advantage the new RUC generation won't have.'

McDermott understood exactly, and empathised. 'I think you're right, but on the other hand they'll probably solve more, in less time than we did, because of those technological advances.'

The Superintendent stifled a laugh, 'Yeah, probably, and hope to god this wee country settles down, and they never have the workload we had.' McDermott rose and walked around the table, offering his hand in a final handshake. The Superintendent ignored the hand and hugged him. 'You look after yourself, and cost the pensions people a fortune!'

The superintendent turned to leave but McDermott stopped him.

'Phil,' McDermott said in a raised voice to get his attention. 'There's one more thing I'd like to ask of you.'

The Superintendent turned; his eyebrows raised quizzically.

'Promise me you'll look after my two boys. They've been outstanding throughout this case.'

The Superintendent grinned, 'Balls already rolling Harry, they've been mentioned in dispatches. They'll be deservedly, well looked after. You have my word on that. Goodbye mate.' They shared a mutual nod, and one last smile, before the Superintendent strode out of the office.

.Alone, McDermott barely stemmed, an overriding rush of emotion sweeping over him. He fought hard to maintain it. *'What's wrong with you Harry?'* he thought. He reckoned it was merely nostalgia, mixed with change. The realisation of no longer being a part of the band of brothers, hit him hard. He sat down at the table outside his office, breathing deeply to regain control. He looked at the poorly painted, dark green walls, walls he would never see again. Although it had been a tough thirty-five years, he still had deep set feelings of security, and camaraderie in this place. He would miss the company, the banter, the successes, and the failures. He felt the same as he had, when Molly and he moved house 27 years ago. He thought he'd never get over not being in the house he'd carried Molly over the threshold in. But he did. And the house was now home to someone else. In fact, the occasion he was now enduring, made him think of that house, for the first time in years. But his was a cast iron retirement. No joining past members clubs. No playing golf, with long time acquaintances and friends. No reminiscing over a pint in the local. The logical side of his brain kicked in. No checking under your car, no fighting to get the seat that gave you a view of the entrance in every establishment you visited. No, always having to reverse into car parking spaces for easy exit. No 'putting up the sandbags' and reliving past operations, whenever he just wanted a pint. He took a deep breath and thought, *'it's over. I'm no longer a policeman.'* There was acceptance in his facial expression. He turned round as Jackson and Douglas entered, standing to address them. 'Well lads, there's one more thing I need you to do on my last day.'

'We could tell you to piss off, as you're no longer a peeler,' stated Jackson in a comical fashion. They all smiled.

'What is it Captain?' Douglas asked through a grin.

'You can take me out to lunch at the Skandia, as a normal civilian.'

Jackson immediately started rubbing his enormous girth. 'Mmm, Food! Be a pleasure, Mr Civilian.'

Chapter 61

Friday- post 4pm

The white van reversed up the driveway of the semi-detached house, the key dropped through the letterbox. No histrionics. A phantom delivery. McGuigan had heard it, and fought the adrenalin rush its arrival created. He breathed deeply, held it and slowly exhaled. He felt a calmness. But more than anything, he felt an overwhelming determination. He looked at his watch, a strange concept in itself, having been denied the timepiece whilst incarcerated. It was 4:15 pm, they would leave in 20 minutes.

~

Patterson aimlessly wandered throughout his home. Everything was in place, and as it should be. He visited each room that had once meant something to him. Two of the upstairs bedrooms were overlooked, as they had only ever been used for storage, and held no special memories. He opened *his* bedroom door and smiled. This had been his lair. Images of different female partners flooded his mind, each convinced they had found their eternal soul mate, each devastated when Patterson moved on. Sadness emerged, on realising he'd never had Orla here. *'In another world, in another time'* he sighed out loud. Pamela was delectable, but Orla was perfect. Neither mattered anymore. They were gone forever. He moved on to the tiled bathroom, checking the toilet bowl, ensuring it was spotless. He didn't want anyone to think he'd led the caricature life of a hermit.

Moving downstairs, he sat on the settee, recalling the time he had 'connected' with his father. He wanted to thank him for guiding him on his journey. For presenting the opportunities he had been blessed, with en route. He fell back into the settee and focused on the ceiling, smiling. 'Thanks Dad, I'll see you soon,' he said to the yellow, plastered ceiling. A single tear of fulfilment trickled down his cheek.

~

They left at 4:40PM, aware the rush hour on Friday, always kicked off earlier than the rest of the week. McGuigan, like the rest of his assault team, had extra layers of clothing, as the miserable heater in the front of the dirty white van was found wanting. It was already dark as one of the Cork duo drove down the Grosvenor Road, having crossed the west of the city from their base camp. McGuigan sat close to the back of the passenger couch, leaving enough room for viewing the path ahead. He instructed the driver to turn right, along College Avenue before turning left into Wellington Place and past the majestic City Hall. At the traffic lights, he merged onto Donegall Square West, then Alfred Street and on to Ormeau Avenue.

They stopped at traffic lights. Despite the yellow street lights, and the blanket of winter darkness making the cars appear colourless, McGuigan identified the scout car, two vehicles in front of them. It was a red, Datsun 120Y. Blind to their follow up vehicle, McGuigan already knew it to be a silver Ford Escort, driven by two armed female volunteers, dressed to look like typical office workers.

Both the scout, and trailing car's occupants, knew nothing about the operation or target, except their roles in it. The scout car would drive into the Muskett complex and follow the road up to Muskett Court and turn left. As soon as the white van appeared in their rear-view mirror, they would turn and wait back down Muskett Road until the van reappeared. The trailing car would be parked at a garage on the Comber Road, toward Lisburn and the motorway, and would fall in behind the white van. The amassed vehicles would drive to Banbridge, before entering the republican South Armagh area known as Bandit country. Here, they could comfortably cross the border into the republic. Spotters were already in place to ensure safe passage. Beyond the traffic lights, their journey began in earnest. They would shortly, be spewed out of Ormeau Avenue and onto the busy Ormeau Road. McGuigan was surprised with the amount of traffic that had already amassed. His frustration was advertised to his colleagues, as he mumbled incoherently, whilst staring at his closed hands, his fingers white. His breathing was shorter. His companions shared a glance of concern, witnessing this incoherent behaviour. They collectively thought he was starting to unravel.

~

Unbeknownst to Patterson, the lookout who tracked his every move, had orders to stand down at 5pm, after sweeping the empty house, leaving no trace of his presence. The operation had begun. He put the plastic chair and telephone, into the car idling outside, that had called to collect him.

The first thing the RUC would do on learning of the abduction, would be house to house calls, enquiring if anybody had seen anything out of the ordinary. Patterson was engrossed in packing his brown Gola sports holdall. He had struggled earlier. After a final inspection of his dwelling, he'd sat at the dining table with a pen and paper, intent on leaving a farewell note to his beloved sister. Every concoction of the first few lines he'd written, were scribbled out, dissatisfied with their frivolous content. He'd contemplated writing a will, which in law would have been useless, due to no witness signature. But what could he leave? Crippling debt on a house and car? He grinded his teeth, thinking of the rich bankers and financers, who would gloat at his demise. They'd sell the house, covering the cost of his mortgage, and then some. The car financers would lose money on their precious car, grieving for mugs like him, who poured money into a time-scaled must have, emptying their pockets just to display their deluded self-styled egos. Eventually, he decided on a short note, written in capital letters on a blank A4 Sheet.

'MY DARLING SISTER, I HAVE ALWAYS LOVED YOU AND THE BOYS. DON'T BE SAD, THE BOYS HAVE PROMISED ME THEY WILL ALWAYS LOVE AND LOOK AFTER YOU. YOUR BROTHER, WEE MAN. ☺'

Patterson folded the sheet, writing Shirley's address on the front of the envelope before applying a 1st class stamp. It would be his last action to post it, before entering the jail. All thoughts of his sister and her sons, were left behind in ink on the page.

He meticulously packed his bag. He set a blue towel at the bottom of the holdall, where he would hide his personal protection weapon. Ejecting the magazine from the Walther's grip, he set seven 9mm rounds on the table. He lifted the first round, studying it hypnotically. This was his escape, the last in the magazine to be fired. His stairway to heaven. He'd unsuccessfully created an alternative plan, acknowledging it was futile. He could never complete his task and walk away untouched. Even destiny, his father, couldn't rustle up a viable solution. Patterson understood, that to be successful, he must terminate his own existence. He could never contemplate being caught, and receiving a lengthy jail sentence. The thought terrified him. It was exasperated by the fact he would be a 'former screw', and a target for any other prisoner for the rest of his lengthy, prison term life. That couldn't, and wouldn't, happen. This special bullet would ensure that. Loading the rest of the shells into the spring-loaded magazine, he clicked it into place, within the pistol grip, ensuring the safety catch was deployed. Cocking the weapon caused the first round to be lifted into the breach by the returning top slide. He tucked into his belt, then placed two full rolls of industrial packing tape into the bag, one at each end before setting the heavy *Book of Criminology,* on top of the towel. He would play his deceptive role to the full. After adding a jar of coffee, Patterson set prepared ham sandwiches, wrapped in cling film on top of the book, and zipped the bag closed. He glanced at the kitchen clock. It was 5:20pm. He reckoned the rush hour would soon begin to peter out, estimating his journey to Aunt Elsie's, would be around 25 minutes. That would give him at least 45 final minutes to spend time in her company, and steal enough of her Temazepam tablets that were necessary, to complete his quest. He didn't really consider it stealing, happy in the fact that they would be automatically replaced by her health visitor. Patterson glanced at his reflection in the slim, full-length mirror in the living room, admiring what he saw. His shirt, clip-on tie, and trousers were immaculate. He was ready. Adorning his civilian coat to hide his uniform, he lifted the bag from the kitchen table. Ensuring the front door was locked and all lights were off, he headed out the back door, undertaking his regimental security check routine. After manoeuvring the BMW onto the drive from the garage, he left it idling as he locked the garage door, before pushing his house keys through the letter box of the front door. This section of his life, and routine, was finished. *'Let the games begin,'* he thought.

Chapter 62

The crawl through the rush hour traffic had seemed eternal. They had snail-paced their journey up the Ormeau Road, to the roundabout at the Ravenhill Road Junction.

McGuigan was concerned, momentarily thinking out loud, 'I could've walked this quicker!' without addressing anyone. His reassurance was, that they had a two-hour window.

Moving onto the Saintfield Road after the Supermac shopping complex, miraculously managing 40mph, and passing the Inns, Purdysburn Hospital and the Texaco garage. They neared the left-hand bend in the road where the Ivanhoe Inn was located. Passing it meant they were less than a mile from the roundabout, and the final countdown of the operation.

It was 5:10pm. The van came to a halt, the driver complaining. 'Jesus, would you look at that fucking traffic!?!' McGuigan had a sneak view. Both lanes were choc a block up to, and over the brow. A multitude of double, red brake lights bobbed, rather than moved, as they resumed erosion pace. Whenever they reached the brow at 5:15, they witnessed the reason for the hold up.

Minor collisions between two vehicles in their respective outside lanes of the Saintfield Road, city and country bound, 50 yards from the roundabout.

McGuigan slid into the shadows in the back of the van, noticing the RUC officers directing traffic in both directions.

'Stay in the inside lane. When you get closer, allow a couple of vehicles indicating from the outside lane in, in front of you. The fuckers will think you're a do-gooder. Nod and smile at them as you pass,' he ordered the driver. The driver detected an eager nervousness in his tone.

~

It took Patterson 5 minutes, to join the Ballynahinch Road and drive left toward the city. 'Must be something big happening in Ballynahinch,' he joked.

The music system in the car was almost deafening. He thought it relevant, as it filled his mind, dispelling any doubts that dare appear. He trundled amidst the throng, toward the traffic lights. It was almost 5:20pm, and he still hadn't reached 10mph, 500 yards from the roundabout. After Annavale Avenue, the lights had turned red at the final traffic lights prior to the roundabout. A female pensioner doddled her way across. Patterson was oblivious, singing along to Starship's *'Nothing's gonna stop us now,'* replacing the word 'us' with 'me'. The sound proofing of the BMW meant, that no other drivers had to endure the deafening noise.

~

The driver, although impressed with McGuigan's instructions for tackling the police, was worried, catching a cursory glance in the rear-view mirror. McGuigan's eyes were the size of dinner plates, his pupils dilated. Saliva dribbled, unattended, from both corners of his mouth. McGuigan had experienced an adrenaline rush like no other.

He was a lion closing in on its prey. Nothing else mattered. *Nothing*. They had circumnavigated the roundabout. The van slowed as it approached the lights on the inside lane, two cars back. McGuigan spied the pensioner shuffling across.

'Get out of the fucking way!' he growled demonically, his grotesque eyes following her every step. As she neared the far side, the lights turned to amber. McGuigan was fixated, as the removal of the pensioner, allowed him the see the BMW. The number plate identical to Patterson's. He spied the profile of his prey as the car slowly moved off toward the roundabout and the city. His universe shrank to minutiae.

'Stop the van!' he squealed hysterically.

The driver struggled to understand the relevance for a second, before feeling the barrel of the armalite pushed against his neck.

'Now!'

Brakes were dramatically applied, causing following cars to rear end the van, creating a domino effect back along the line. The hum drum world of the commute, was thrown into pandemonium. McGuigan and the driver braced themselves against the cars behind, unlike their colleagues who slid around the back of the van in a state of confusion. Before any of the three could complain, McGuigan slid back the side door and escaped. Angry drivers, ready to complain, cowered and dived as McGuigan leapt on to the crumpled bonnet of the Mercedes behind them, brandishing the Armalite.

Patterson had reached the roundabout. A quick glance to his right showed a line of cars backed up, blocking off the Downpatrick Road slipway. He was grinning as he sang, and car danced with somebody, who happened to be Whitney Houston, whilst joining the roundabout.

~

McGuigan felt invulnerable. His mind closed to his actions. He witnessed the car slowly crawl onto the roundabout. He didn't give a thought to the carefully constructed Operation. Nor any repercussions from the Organisation. Nor the police. This was nothing to do with anyone or any*thing*. This was his personal war. His animal behaviour had been bottled for too long. He was a warrior, and would prevail, irrespective of cost. The creature had ridiculed and embarrassed him. The audacity of stealing his wife was beyond reproach. It had to die

Leaping off the bonnet he held the hand guard of the rifle at his hip, firing a misguided round into the night sky. He sprinted toward the roundabout, all traffic now at a standstill, some mounted-on kerbs, while the majority appearing driverless, as people slid to the floor for cover. As he ran, he felt nothing. No wind or cold. He was aware that he was shouting. 'Stop you Bastard! Stop!' yet there was no noise, his universe engulfing him.
He never heard the van, speeding off to the Comber Road. The Saintfield Road that Patterson had just entered, seemed to glow in front of him. He had no sensation of his feet on the ground as he ran.

.

He came to a stop at the entrance to the roundabout, the car a mere 30 yards on the road in front of him. Time slowed, including the target, as his tunnel vision focused on the back windscreen of the car. An infernal smile slid across his face, as he raised the rifle, staring along the sights. The index finger on his right hand curled around the trigger. His thumb flicked the switch to 'automatic'. He controlled his breathing as he started to squeeze the pressure on the trigger.

Eight explosive rounds, blazed flashes into the night sky.

Women screamed and cried. The sound of exiting footsteps, mixed with the screeching of rubber tyres was prevalent, as onlookers fled for their lives. McGuigan flew backwards as the four Policemen, double-tapped their service Rugers, to ensure safety of innocents. All were confused that this lunatic had ignored their multiple screams to drop his weapon. He'd concocted his own fate.

Patterson continued on down the road out of sight, completely unaware that destiny was firmly on his side.

Chapter 63

McDermott struggled through the Ulster fry Molly had prepared. It would have fed four people. Two eggs, a fried soda farl, cut into two thick wedges, three bits of potato bread, four big rashers of bacon and two sausages, all covered in brown HP sauce. He glanced from the meal to his right. Molly was looking at him with a challenging glimmer in her eye.

'You have to eat all of that Harry McDermott! You need to line your stomach before you go out drinking tonight!'

'I'm just not overly hungry Molly, I had a sandwich in work with my colleagues. Bit like a re-enactment of the last supper.'

He didn't mention the curry and two slices of Pavlova he'd wolfed down in the Skandia restaurant, although he hated lying to her. In this case, it was for the good of his health. She smiled and walked over putting her arms around his shoulders before kissing him on the cheek.

'Just eat what you want love, it's ok.' McDermott smiled, glad to be off the hook.

'Do you think we'll get an Ulster fry in Scotland?'

Molly stepped back with her hands on her hips, mocking in a soft tone. 'And there's me thinking you were a detective, Harry McDermott? What do you think?'

'I'm not sure. After all, I'm just an ex-detective. Everything I learned and was stored in my head, was sucked out by a police machine this afternoon. It was awful.'

Molly laughed out loud. 'Away on with you!'

McDermott left the table to rest in his favourite chair in front of the fire. 'If I happen to fall asleep, would you wake me by 7pm? There's a taxi picking me up at 7.30.'

'What do you mean 'if'?' Of course, I will.'

McDermott was fatigued by the food he had consumed in the last three hours. He needed rest. As his eyes began to close, his body went straight into relaxation mode.

Molly shouted to him from the kitchen. 'Just to let you know, they have square sausages in Scotland.'

'Square sausages?' He thought, with a smile on his face, *'What have I let myself in for?'* Unaware of the pressures that had been lifted off him by his acceptance of finality in retirement, he drifted into a food induced slumber.

~

Elsie Patterson couldn't take her eyes off the portrait. It was beautiful. There was something about black and white photography, that gave rise to a beauty that couldn't be felt in colour. It was striking. The smiles on the faces of the children, a stunning reflection of their innocence. Shirley was beautiful, and open, caring and warm even without colour. So natural, so happy.

John was like a tower of strength, holding the portrait together, with that wonderfully, cheeky grin.

By God, his father could never have denied him. Although, there was something in his eyes that she kept returning to. It was if his eyes were striving to appear happy-go-lucky, but she didn't sense a naturalistic glare. *'Probably just my age,'* Elsie thought. Patterson had been in the bathroom on the first-floor landing. He accrued three Temazepam tablets from his aunt's stash. Elsie was delighted to see her adopted son, who had made her tea and stayed for a chat. He was such a good boy, going into work early to help a fellow officer. She had been pleasantly surprised when he'd rang ahead of his visit because he had 'a wee present' he'd brought from Blackpool. Although she had wrestled with the thought about that nice McDermott chap who called, and whether she should mention it. She knew that McDermott had retired, and hoped that the awful secret she shared with Shirley, would now be buried forever. John didn't need to know. Elsie turned, a genuine smile of pride on her face, as he ambled back into the parlour.

'I'll wash these dishes and then head on Auntie E.'

'Leave them son, I'll do them. I didn't mention how smart you look in your uniform by the way.'

Patterson sucked in his stomach and expanded his chest. He pointed a finger toward the blue epaulettes on the shoulder of his pale blue shirt. 'Setting an example for whenever I get a few silver pips sewn on my white shirt, when I officially become a Senior Officer.'

'As if you weren't already smart enough,' she gestured, whilst rising from her chair. He carefully assisted her, before putting on his civilian jacket. She walked him into the hall before saying, 'Thank you so much for the lovely picture son. I can't stop looking at it.'

'Pity I'm in it, or it would have been even lovelier.'

She tutted in denial, before smiling and opening her arms to embrace him. He hugged her tightly, but in a gentle way, before kissing her cheek and whispering into her ear, 'I love you auntie.' She automatically stepped back to look at his smiling face, so like his father, 'And I love, and am proud of you son.' When they untangled, she watched him leave out the front door. Patterson glanced quickly, up and down Cherryville Street, before hurrying across to Sherwood Street where his car was parked. Elsie stood looking through the glass vestibule door, as the red brake lights illuminated. When the car took off down the street toward his workplace, her pride and joy dissolved, when the car finally disappeared. Elsie quivered, a deep sadness racing through her entirety. She closed the outer front door and returned to the heat of the parlour, fearful as to how she was feeling, but more importantly, why? Was she ill? Was this it? Elsie gathered herself, felt her pulse and controlled her breathing, that was as good as it could have been. Maybe John's openness of emotion had put her in a mild state of shock? She looked at the floor and concentrated. Every thought process, and every analysis, lead her on a path of dread. Her mindset continually offering her only one solution. There was something wrong.

Something she instinctively knew, was dreadfully wrong. But she had no one to share this self-induced terror with. No one to talk to. She looked again at the portrait in aid of explanation, and realised the truth. Her features froze like a mask.

'It's John. There's something wrong with John,' she murmured quietly.

The eyes that had earlier perplexed her, now haunted her. Elsie turned the portrait around, to rid those challenging eyes, and wandered aimlessly around her house. She was so overwhelmed, she considered contacting the jail to make sure he was ok. But she didn't want to appear as an interfering old busy body, and embarrass him. She moved to the kitchen and boiled the milk for her nightly cocoa, before taking an extra sleeping tablet, in the hope that deep sleep could eradicate her fears. She would ring him tomorrow.

~

The iron gates had already crept open at Patterson's arrival. The officer operating the hand-held, opening device blinked rapidly, drawing his neck back in surprise, as Patterson drove in. The car window was down.

'You're a bit early,' he stated. 'Suppose you're nipping into the club for a few scoops to help you sleep?'

'No, I'm letting wee Davey McConkey away early. He's a plane to catch at ten o'clock.'

The officer shook his head in disgust. 'Shower of wankers in that duty office. Davy told me. Good on you Paddy.'

Patterson smiled, and drove to the nearest parking space beside the gate, that led to the cottages and the front of the jail. It meant a quick getaway in the morning. This was routine for night guard staff. He didn't want to raise any suspicions. On exiting the car, he placed the Walther inside the towel at the bottom of his bag. He then smoothed the bonnet and the body work of his vehicle with his fingertips, in an act of saying farewell. As he strode down the parallel route with the unseen Crumlin Road, Patterson had one thing on his mind. It wasn't the intricacies of how to successfully smuggle a gun into the jail. It wasn't the thoughts of how, throughout his life, he stood by his convictions and always helped the underdog. It was the line from the Eagles song, *Hotel California, 'you can check out anytime you like, but you can never leave'*. Patterson smiled, reckoning it was apt. On reaching the wicker gate in the enormous Iron Gate, the buzzer sounded for it to open. He was surprised to see the evening duty SO at the helm.

'You been demoted Trevor?'

'Not at all! Never mind me, have you pished the bed?'

A grin appeared on Patterson's face. 'I'm letting wee Davey away to catch a flight. Who's on here with you?'

'That dipso, Clarke.'

'Glutton for punishment,' Patterson replied.

'I know Paddy, he would bore the arse of you. I let him away early.'

They walked to the Tally Lodge, where Patterson dropped in his pass, noticing the rows of passes already lined up, for the horde that would soon descend, at the end of the remand association period. The Senior Officer led the way to the opening in the right-hand side of the giant airlock, and walked through the metal detector. Patterson set his bag on the table beside the detector and walked through without an alarm sounding. The SO unzipped the Gola bag. Patterson was unperturbed. He lifted out the book on criminology.

'Fuck me Paddy! A wee bit of light reading or what!'

'I'm studying. I've always wanted a degree,' he lied.

'What's with the duct tape?' he replied lifting out the roll from opposite ends of the bag, close to the pistol. Patterson completely disguised the terror flowing through him. What if he found the Walther? What course of action would he, in fact, *could* he take? It would ruin his plan. *'Help me father,'* echoed through his mind.

'Didn't even know it was in there,' Patterson laughed, 'I was in a rush, and grabbed the first bag I could see.'

The speaker from the tally lodge crackled into life. 'SO, there's a phone call for you.'

'I'm busy.'

'It's your wife. Still busy?'

Dropping the tape into the bag, the SO zipped it up and noticed the oil slick of staff descending the stairs toward their location, through the panels in the iron door, that led to the forecourt.

'Paddy, do me a favour and be crowd controller for a couple of minutes, while I take this call. You head on in afterwards, I'll ring down to the annexe to tell Davey to head on, as soon as I get this bloody woman off the phone.'

As he left, he heard the SO shouting sarcastically to the tally lodge, 'Funny fuckers, aren't you?' The reassuring grin rested itself once again on Patterson's face, as he looked skyward and winked. Insanity was beginning to take control.

Chapter 64

Douglas sat in the back of the taxi with McDermott. Jackson's huge frame wedged into the front seat beside the driver. The taxi firm had been vetted ages ago, and had a standing account with the RUC. McDermott stared out the window at the mansions lined side by side, whilst they travelled along the Malone Road, the affluent area of the city. He wondered how much money these people must have. He was fairly sure they hadn't been subject to the terror and devastation that he, and the normal people, had been immersed in throughout the troubles. No, the pain, suffering and loss, was almost entirely reserved for the working class. Ordinary people trying to exist in anything, but an ordinary world. It saddened him.

The taxi reached the lights at the junction, with Balmoral Avenue, turning left onto Newforge Lane, then left again to a path, more than a lane, with a private property sign that led to a manned barrier. There was a brick-built Sanger with an officer inside. The external officer, wielding a Sterling submachine gun, stood ominously at the barrier. The entourage knew that two other armed officers were constantly on patrol with dogs around the entire campus of the RUC Athletic Association. The driver was known to the barrier sentry, and in a break with tradition, the Sanger officer left his post and approached the taxi, before it moved off.

'Captain, all the best, you lucky old bastard!' he shouted in through the window.

McDermott smiled, before replying and shaking the hand that was offered. 'You're not too far behind me Smicker.'

'Bingo! But hey, you look after yourself and enjoy your retirement mate.'

'You too. It's been a pleasure.'

They were dropped off at the front door of the main building. As they approached, Douglas took McDermott on a brief journey down memory lane. 'Do you remember when this was nothing but Nissan huts and a concrete excuse for changing rooms?'

'How could I forget Sin City? The dances, or discos, as the young ones preferred to call them. The drink flowing like an over swollen Nile.' He recollected with a sigh. 'Those good old bad old days' Douglas put his arm around the shoulders of his soon to be departing friend.

'No point in sucking up to him now Doug, he can't help your career anymore,' Jackson intervened. McDermott would keep his knowledge of their futures a secret. The two-storey block construction, was a world away from the Nissan huts he'd been used to. It was welcome progress. A place where comrades, and future officers, could relax in safety, away from the eternal threats they lived with daily.

He stopped at the glass entrance doors and looked left. On the outside wall was the crest of the RUC Athletic Association. It had been established in 1928 and the word Athletic, had been used in its broadest sense, encompassing many other sports. McDermott's focus was on the plaque underneath the crest. A role of honour for lost members.

McDermott carefully read through the lists, dormant memories erupting, as he recognised friends who were no longer alive. He would honour them with a toast tonight.

'There but for the grace of God, go I,' he whispered mournfully.

This was only his second visit to the relatively new building. McDermott was impressed. The first thing that caught his attention was the photograph collections on the white painted, block walls, that seemed endless throughout the complex. Every conceivable achievement in all the sports, had been historically recorded by both black and white, and more recently, coloured images. He wondered if his own photograph, one of the thirteen monochrome faces, would be there, when 'C' Division had been inter- divisional football champions back in 1970. To their right, the new restaurant 'McCleave's Lock', named after the *actual* lock in the River Lagan, located down below the buildings elevated plot, although no longer visible due to tree growth. To his left, an office, then a corridor that turned right to run parallel with the corridor he was in. He knew the physiotherapy room, changing rooms and gymnasium were housed there. Just past the corridor was a souvenir shop. McDermott stopped and looked through the window of the, now closed, shop, admiring the craftsmanship amidst the surfeit of tankards, glass ware, miniature statues, badges and other memorabilia.

'This is what it all boils down to Harry,' he contemplated, *'thirty-five years with an ornament to remind you.'*

McDermott noticed a sign with a print of the Titanic, that had 'Captain's Table' scrawled under it, and a crudely drawn directional arrow pointing upstairs, toward the bar room on the second floor.

'Jacko, you're a laugh a minute,' he sarcastically stated to his giant colleague who smiled and fiddled with his tie in a tribute to Stan Laurel. McDermott grinned like a Cheshire cat, feeling immensely proud at having had the opportunity to work alongside such a character.

~

In the toilet area within the locker room, Patterson worked swiftly and methodically. The 3 Temazepam tablets were in a brown envelope. He used his truncheon to crush them into a fine powder. When complete, he left the truncheon inside the locker, closing it for the final time. He then climbed the stairs to the hall that began the inner sanctum of the Victorian jail. The new, young recruit covering the Glass Door during evening duty, had a vacant expression, staring at the tiles below his feet, before rising to insert a key into the manual lock. He turned, looking at his reflection in the two-way glass that the electronic button pusher hid behind. Before the grille into the circle was released a crackling, voice discharged from a speaker on the wall. 'You're in early tonight, Paddy.'
' It's a long story,' Patterson replied, without turning around. He walked toward D Wing, calling out to the circle officer, hiding in the empty Chief Officer's Bunk, who continued to read his book as he rose and moved toward him. Patterson wasn't too annoyed, knowing that Davey was by, now long gone.

He then walked the length of D wing and downstairs to the entrance of the annexe. The spy hole in the metal stayed closed as the electronic lock buzzed, allowing him to enter. Lightbody met him at the inner metal mesh, that was unlocked. A blue prison issue, tea mug sitting on the desk in the makeshift office, looked out of place.

'Where's lover boy Billy?'

'He's on the shitter Paddy. He could shite for Ulster.'

They shared a grin. Although Henderson was a remand prisoner, he enjoyed the benefits of being treated as a sentenced inmate, due to his location under D wing. He would be locked in his cell 45 minutes after the remand wings were secured for the night.

'Hot waters already been called Paddy, so if the troll gets the finger out, I'll be able to get away early.'

Henderson trundled toward the office. Patterson thought he looked uglier than ever, if that were possible. He nodded at Patterson before entering the office, lifting the mug that Lightbody was about to fill with tea from the plastic container.

'It's ok mister. I couldn't drink anymore of that stuff. It's leaping!' protested Henderson.

Patterson produced the jar of coffee from his bag.

'Want a drop of this?'

Henderson's eyes lit up with delight, Patterson flicked the switch on the previously boiled kettle.

'Fuck me, that would be great.'

Henderson hesitated for a second, before speaking again with an apologetic tone. 'I'm nipping down to my cell for a minute.'

As Henderson left, Lightbody went into the yard for a final check before locking and mastering the grilles. Patterson leapt into action. He poured the powdered drugs into Henderson's mug and covered it with a dose of coffee and a splash of milk from the mini fridge under the desk. Most of the powdered drugs dissolved without trace, but a few speckles floating on the surface, could advertise their presence. Without fear or thought, Patterson dipped his index finger in the scalding coffee, stirring it until there was no trace of the Temazepam. He felt no pain. Seconds later, Henderson reappeared, clutching a packet of cigarettes. Instead of offering his hand to shake, in fear of refusal, he spoke.

'These aren't just for the coffee; I owe you one, for acting like an arsehole this morning in the yard. No Hard feelings?' he stated humbly.

"Wise up. None taken.'

He lifted the coffee before continuing. 'You know something? You're alright for a screw. Well, that's me for the night. Only four days to go.'

Patterson revealed a wry half-smile as Henderson walked back to his cell, where the SO awaited his arrival. Patterson had a delicious thought. *'Four Days to go? We'll see about that later.'*

Chapter 65

McDermott climbed the stairs, continuing to glance at the sporting prowess of photographs on the walls. He was fairly sure his old photograph wouldn't be there. And he was right. He walked with the others along the corridor, turning right, opposite the council room and toilets, into the upstairs bar. The bar was to his right where the place opened up, suffused with bays and tables. He was surprised how empty it was. He'd expected at least, two or three old comrades to show up and wish him well. He sighed, dropping his shoulders. Jackson noticed McDermott's disappointment and moved to his left wrapping his bear like, right arm around his shoulders, whilst manoeuvring him toward the bar. 'At least we're here for you Captain,' he whispered. The barman deliberately engaged in inane chat with McDermott, and with Jackson cutting off his left line of sight, the throng that had been hiding in the back bar, slipped out and into place, directly behind McDermott. A handful of the gathering held, at waist height, a banner that read, *'Thought you would never leave Captain.'* Jackson had one eye on Douglas who gave him the nod. McDermott lifted his 1st pint of Guinness and took a hefty swallow. 'At least the Guinness is good,' he announced with a hint of melancholy.

Jackson's grip intensified. 'There's one thing you need to know Captain.'

McDermott's head tilted, and his eyes narrowed with confusion. Jackson spun him around to face the attendees, who erupted into cavalcades of welcomes, whistles, cheers and a round of applause. McDermott was so stunned, he released his grip on the pint, that met a timely death, the glass smashing on the solid floor, dark liquid spreading in all directions. A comic from the crowd shouted, 'Will I be like that when I'm your age Harry?' It was complimented by loud, outrageous belly laughs. McDermott was dumbfounded, his focus bouncing from face to face, some close colleagues, and some vaguely familiar. On another level, he fought to suppress the emotion rising. After all, the last thirty-five years, had been worth it. McDermott felt immense pride and respect, as much as being overwhelmed. Before he could collapse in on himself, he was whisked by his giant minder toward the doors of the back bar, where a few tables had been placed together, covered with a white table cloth. There were assorted packages on each table. Jackson manoeuvred him to stand behind the table and address the crowd. 'Speech!' the crowd demanded, as Douglas placed a fresh pint in front of him. He raised his brow, thinking back to the fate of his previous pint. 'Not sure the white tablecloth is a good idea?' Laughter rippled around the room. McDermott composed himself as much as possible, before beginning.

'Thanks to each, and every one of you, for taking the trouble, and time, to be here tonight. I really appreciate it and know how much you're looking forward to the free drink I'm meant to supply.'

A light-hearted snicker came from the crowd.

'Before we do anything my friends, brothers and comrades, there's something I would like us *all* to do.' McDermott's tone cast a hush around the room. 'I noticed on my way in, the plaque dedicated to our 'lost members'. This is something we should never forget.' Muted voices announced a chorus of 'hear hears.' 'I would like to remember all of our forces losses, and suggest we have a minute silence to reflect, and respect the people who made the ultimate sacrifice, in making this force, *our* force, one of the greatest on the planet.' Only the noise of the fruit machine could be heard as everyone in the bar, including those not part of his leaving party, stood in absolute silence. Sorrowful faces dominated the emotions on display. After one minute, McDermott broke the silence, 'Raise your glasses people. I propose a toast to our lost members!' The combined toast, rippled through the room, everyone united in praise. McDermott noticed that Douglas had erected an easel behind him, that held a white board covered by another tablecloth.

'I have no idea what all this is about, but will no doubt, find out soon,' he stated, eyeing the covered parcels on the table and the easel. 'Without further ado, and this breaks my heart, in the golfing tradition of getting a hole in one, where you have to buy everyone a drink. Well according to Herbie,' Herbie Long's face beamed in confirmation. 'I know this because Herbie *did* have a hole in one, only in his case, he was talking about his socks.'

Laughter rang out again. 'Seriously people, it would be my pleasure to offer you all a drink at my expense, as a thank you for all those years.' A loud cheer erupted, as the race for the bar got under way, making it difficult for McDermott to be heard. 'Remember, I'm a pensioner now, so don't rip the arse out of it!'

~

It was as quiet as a crematorium in the annexe. Patterson, the epitome of control. He no longer let his mind wander to anything, that would divert him from the task ahead. He had performed the charade of checking on Henderson every 30 minutes to placate the beady, intrusive eyes of the night guard control room officers. This was it. This was the killing ground. He had been guided by his father, and would complete his mission. It would be the final, and greatest, highlight of his troubled existence, and he embraced it. It was 9:30pm. Patterson had decided that 10pm would be the beginning of the final act, in the life of the scumbag Henderson. 10 was the perfect choice. He'd had a girlfriend in his late teens, who was fanatical about Mathematics, and explained how important the number 10 really was. She'd explained that, not only was 10 the first number that needed a separate part, it also symbolized the completion of a cycle, as well as being the number of heaven, the world and the universal creation. It seemed appropriate.

His only other consideration, had been the camera mounted above the grille near the ceiling. It provided a panoramic, live view of the annexe

He would use the floor brush in the office, to tilt it toward the floor, and frustrate the attention of the Control room officers, letting him complete his destiny, in relative privacy. That would be just before, he raised a false alarm. The less the outside world knew of his operation, would create conspiracy theories, to confuse those racing to the rescue. Who was in danger? What was happening? He relished the confusion he was about to create. This was his show. Boiling the kettle, he made himself a cup of strong coffee before lighting, what was to be, his last ever cigarette. He inhaled deeply and slowly exhaled, watching the blue grey smoke spiralling, briefly maintaining its density, until it separated and faded, becoming an invisible part of the atmosphere. It reflected the brief life existence of the human race. He lit another cigarette when that one ended.

'Another one won't kill me?' he stated aloud, almost laughing at his quip. He checked his watch. Twenty minutes to show time.

Chapter 66

McDermott took a sharp intake of breath when handed the bar bill. He would never reveal the amount to Molly, she'd kill him, although the evening had been terrific. He'd mingled with as many of the crowd as possible, including the late comers. Recruits from the depot from thirty-five years ago. A few lads stationed in Fermanagh and Tyrone, who'd insisted on attending, to mark his farewell. Colleagues from his Willowfield days. The list seemed endless. So many promises of keeping in touch, or visiting him from time to time in Scotland. Although he was aware the promises, in time, would fade like melting snow. He did, however, feel humbled. But in a strange way, feel also like a relic, whose name may occasionally be mentioned in conversation. He acknowledged the lifetime membership to this club, and would always be welcomed by serving and future officers. He was also, aware of the unlikelihood of ever setting foot in it again, after his Scottish migration. His light had gone out. McDermott smiled, when he unveiled the white board and opened his farewell presents. On the board, were mainly black and white photographs, stirring personal memories. As a recruit in the depot, on duty at the remembrance parades, and patrolling pitch side at Windsor Park football ground. There was even the photograph of the 'C' division champions. He'd asked Douglas, if he'd had to take that one out of the frame that had been on the wall, within the complex, and been told to 'wise up.' It had been found it in a store room in Tennent Street.

The presents were both welcome, and somewhat absurd. One, a hat that would help him 'blend in' to his new surroundings, was a tartan cap with a partial red, untidy wig, sewn into the back of it. Another, he was informed, was 'to show the Scottish what real whisky was' and came in the form of a crate of Bushmills. McDermott didn't have the heart to tell them he hated the stuff. His most treasured gift, was that of a miniature, pewter statuette, a detailed portrayal of an RUC Officer in full uniform. It was mounted on a black onyx plinth, that had a full colour RUC metallic badge with his name, police number and years of service, delicately engraved below. He would cherish it forever. After the presentation ceremony, around 9:15, he was beginning to tire of making small talk, and wanted to sit and savour a few pints. His wish was granted when, unexpectedly, his good friend, PO Pete Clydesdale walked into the room, wearing a civvie coat, the only thing covering his uniform.

'Thought you were night guard Pete?'

Clydesdale laughed. 'I am. Let me tell you Harry, monkeys could run that place at night. Everything and everybody, are safely locked away. And did you honestly think I wouldn't be at your retirement do?'

McDermott stood and embraced him, 'It's really good to see you mate. Can I get you a drink?'

'Does a bear shit in the woods? Although I'm only having a couple, got to drive back to the Hotel for the lost and lonely.'

They walked to the bar, McDermott politely avoiding being captured in conversation by anyone in the, almost inebriated, band of brothers, before returning to their seats for an old fashion chinwag.

'How are the kids?'

'Great Harry. You know Denise is in Australia now? She working for Qantas.'

'Wow! That's brilliant. That's some airline. You both must miss her though?'

'Of course. We were out a few years ago. Some place. Hoping to get out again in July. She gets one of us out free.'

'Oh...before it slips my mind, I need to ask you about that young fellow, Patterson. Is he keeping, ok?'

'He's not doing too badly, or as well as can be expected after...what happened.'

McDermott felt remorse for the young officer, and how he'd had to cope, after his friend was murdered. 'Has he changed much?'

Clydesdale sighed before replying. 'He has a bit, Harry. You just *know* he's not himself. He doesn't play in the card schools any more. He's like, quieter, more reserved ...if you know what I mean? In saying that it hasn't affected his performance. He saved that whore Henderson from being stabbed.'

A hint of recognition flew across McDermott's face. 'I'd heard about that, but not about Patterson's involvement.'

'Tell you where he's sadly missed though, the snooker team. Some player, ' Clydesdale grinned, 'though he plays arse about face.'

McDermott scrunched up his face. 'He does what?'

Clydesdale laughed. 'He's a klute Harry... the only left hander in the entire league!'

McDermott only just disguised a gasp, before the flow of conversation was interrupted by the vibrating of Clydesdale's pager. Checking it, his expression turned serious. It read, 'Need you back. ASAP.'

Clydesdale rose, simultaneously downing the remainder of his pint. 'Sorry Harry, got to get back.'

'Something wrong?'

'Looks like it. I'll ring you over the weekend and we'll grab a bite to eat, before you head off and start wearing skirts in Scotland.'

'No problem, Pete. Do me a favour. Ring the bar here when you get back and let me know everything's ok.'

'Will do mate.'

As Clydesdale hurried out the door, McDermott had a feeling of foreboding. Had he got it wrong all along? He knew unequivocally, that Henderson, nor Montgomery, nor Wilson had murdered Hamilton. Maybe, just maybe, Patterson already knew.

'Oh my god,' he thought, in an eye of a storm dilemma. He wrestled with the idea that Elsie was lying, before dismissing it... reluctantly.

He had promised that poor woman he would never reveal Patterson's true identity, to anyone. He was in a quandary. What he retained of his Detective brain, fighting against a sincere oath. He decided to keep his word, his policing career finishing in a few hours' time. McDermott convinced himself Patterson, the lifesaving, bomb evading, Prison Officer, had been dealt enough bum cards in his life.

~

Two staff in the control room, were settling down for the night. The room was similar to the flight deck of the Star ship Enterprise, located one floor above the duty office, up a stairwell. Banks of video screens, displayed coarse, monochrome images of different areas, within and on the outer skin, of the prison. There was a walkway, patrolled by a dog handler, between the outer protection wall and the sprawling campus that formed the inner workings of the jail. Each exterior wall section was numbered in oversized, white painted numbers, making location quick and easy. At the wall that ran parallel to The Mater hospital, was an inbuilt secure Sanger, manned 24 hours a day by a Grenadier Guardsman, the current incumbent regiment. The Sanger's were sporadically positioned around the entire perimeter of the external walls in what was calculated as, the most vulnerable areas, not only in escape attempts, but for illegal entry.

The cameras of those areas, were the main focus for staff on night guard, as well as the camera overseeing the tunnel area. The camera watching over the Supergrass annexe was all but ignored. The sole inmate was secured within a cell, and the Night guard officer was in attendance. The staff had already undertaken a cursory check, witnessing Patterson making his deliberations of checking through a metallic flap, at the state of his charge. All was good, or like the majority of night guards, boring. It was difficult to keep sole attention, on such an amount of black and white images. One of the staff needed the toilet, with his accomplice's approval. They'd already agreed to two-hour stints, giving the other a chance to sleep using two upholstered, soft chairs as a makeshift bed. Although welcome, the sleep was never deep, nor satisfying. Left alone, the remaining officer had a quick read of the sports pages in the Belfast Telegraph. Neither had witnessed the image on the Supergrass annexe camera, transforming from a panoramic vista, to an extreme close up of the red tiled floor.

Chapter 67

The time of contemplation had elapsed. No more thinking, only doing. Patterson was aware his first act could create suspicion. He lifted the floor brush and stood under the camera above the grill. He could see the camera lens was attached to a ball within a circular housing, enabling the exact angle to be secured. The only remote factor was the image being displayed. Using the base of the brush carefully, and slowly, he nudged the lens attention toward the floor. He was supremely confident of his success. Returning to the office, Patterson dialled the internal line to the Key Room, where the Night Guard PO and two SO's were located.

'Yo?'

'Colin, there's a problem down here,' Patterson feigned urgency.

'Ok, Kid, calm down. What sort of problem?' In the background, the remaining SO was already sending a message to PO Clydesdale's pager.

'I've been checking on your man Henderson from about 8 o'clock, and there's something that doesn't look right. It's strange. He hasn't moved.'

'Like sleeping?'

'That's what I thought, but he looks more unconscious. I've been banging on his door for the last five minutes. I'm surprised you didn't hear me up there! The fucker hasn't moved an inch!'

'Are you sure Paddy?'

'Positive Colin, there's something wrong!'

'Ok, we're on our way down.'

He turned toward his partner. 'Fuck this for a game of marbles! There's me hoping for a quiet night. Throw me over the master, and a cell key, for the annexe. Contact control and let them know what's happening, if they don't already know. Have you contacted...?'

His question was cut short. 'Already done. on his way.'

'Good man.'

The SO lifted a radio from the block of those on a charging consul.

'Ring wee Gerry in the hospital, and get him over here. You go down and unlock the Bravo 2 grille. Oh, and for god's sake, let the Delta call sign know what's happening. We don't want somebody losing an arm, if the dogs off the lead. One catastrophe a night is enough.' He turned his attention to the radio. 'Hello control this is Sierra One joining the net. Awaiting arrival of Hotel One before going to the annexe. Over.'

'Roger Sierra One. And do us a favour when you're down there. Have a look at that stupid camera. Looks like it's slipped...again...It's pointing at the floor.'

'Will do. Out.'

Within five minutes, the Hospital Officer arrived at the key room and was briefed. Patterson had been asked for an update. The situation remained the same.

Shortly, the pair arrived at the door to the annexe, that was electronically unlocked by Patterson. PO Clydesdale had arrived in the key room and was being brought up to speed. The SO, had a quick glance at the obsolete camera above his head as he entered, making a mental note to fix it on his departure. The pair witnessed the catatonic condition of Henderson, whilst they banged on the cell door. Patterson went to the office to retrieve the door stop mechanism and, unseen, the gun from his bag, that he slipped into his belt at the base of his back under his jumper. Each cell, throughout the jail, had an iron door that filled one half of a metallic frame. On the blank side of the frame was a hollow indent, allowing the cell door to be opened to its fullest, the handle of the door resting in the hollow, and flush with the wall, before being locked into position. It was normally used on orderlies' cells, saving the staff from having to open and close their doors multitudinously, or whenever staff were carrying out cell searches. The door stop that Patterson collected was a heavy metallic, long box shape, that sat neatly into the bottom of the frame, adjacent to the door. It had a welded attachment of heavy metal near its end, protruding out at 25 degrees away from the frame. The door could now, only be opened a few inches, the pressure of the open door, jamming the doorstop in the frame. A safety mechanism. Patterson set it in place, as the hospital officer shouted toward Henderson. No response.

'Colin, we have to go in, this guys in trouble!'

'I'm not happy about this Gerry.'

'But there's three of us,' Patterson added.

'Right! Do what you have to do!' The SO replied, bending down to remove the doorstop, the Hospital Officer grabbing the handle to open the door fully. Patterson took a step backward, removing the pistol from his belt.

'It's ok gentlemen, I'll take it from here.' he said, with cold blooded calm.

They turned to face him.

'Paddy, what the fuck do you think you're doing?' The SO's tone was mixed with confusion, anger, but moreso, fear. The hospital officer was braver.

'Wise up Paddy,' he said motioning to walk forward.

The face of his colleague had changed. It was demonic, and brimmed with intent. He pulled the hammer of the weapon back, making it ready to fire. The Hospital Officer froze, wary any sudden movement may make this ...thing... that Patterson had become, agitated. Both he and the SO, had wide-eyed expressions of bewilderment, lightly veneered on their faces, not completely covering their terror. Both minds ferociously calculated survival.

'Listen to me very carefully, and you will both come to no harm.'

The SO felt Patterson had grown in size. He seemed in total control, yet his eyes were terrifying. A blank stare from a lost soul. He realised he was now, only a pawn in this macabre game. And pawns were expendable.

'I have no intention of hurting either of you. But if there's any heroics, make no mistake, I will respond.'

The SO suppressed a gasp of shock, when Patterson continued, thinking he could read his mind.

'Colin. Don't panic. This isn't an escape attempt. No-one's going anywhere.'

The Hospital Officer was practically hypnotised by Patterson's every word.

'Do exactly as I say, and stay close together. Any sudden moves could be misinterpreted as a threat. That can't happen!' There was a finality, and determination, to Patterson's characterless voice.

'Both of you step back against the wall. Gerry, take the batteries out of both radios. Throw them down the landing.'

The HO had a brief inclination of throwing the batteries at Patterson, in an effort to overpower him, but erred on the side of caution, realising Patterson's aim had a bead on his head. Bizarrely, the HO felt pity for the younger officer.

Radios disabled, they moved to the office, where the SO, under orders, disabled the phone connection to the key room by unplugging its cable. Patterson turned to leave the office, but raised his pistol and aimed between the SO's eyes. 'Leave the master key on the table, Colin.' He obeyed without hesitation, frightened to put any doubt into the mind of this abomination that was once Patterson. Patterson ordered them to walk down the landing.

~

PO Clydesdale tried the radio again. 'Hello, Sierra One this is Papa One, over.' He dropped the radio on the floor and grabbed another from the charging bank. 'Fucking thing hasn't charged!'
The replacement radio was the same. The landline rang.

'Thank Christ, they've decided to call in. Malcolm, go down and find out what's happening.' ordered PO Clydesdale. He lifted the phone and spoke with a hint of relief. 'Thought you were never going to get in touch!'

'Sorry PO. This is the control room. We have a serious problem here. We have no comms with the annexe. Radio or landline. And the stupid camera has moved, showing us only the floor.'

'Shit!' Clydesdale felt a chill wash over him.

'We'll wait to hear from Sierra Two, before contacting the Northern Ireland Office.'

'Good thinking.'

The supposed, defunct radio crackled into life, and the voice on the other end was hurried and repetitive. 'Papa One, this is Sierra Two. Papa One this is Sierra Two.'

'Papa One send, over.'

'Pete, this is fucking serious. No-one's answering the door, or radio down here. I haven't a clue what's going on. I can't get in to find out!'

'Calm down Malcolm.'

'Control to Papa One. Sierra Two's communication is the key. Contacting the NIO now. Do we deploy the Army?'

'Immediately. Two armed squaddies, with a ranker to keep them under control.'

PO Clydesdale rang C Wing, ordering the Golf 1 officer out to the front gate, on the Crumlin Road, to await arrival of the Governor and the NIO Official. He then contacted B Wing for an officer to unlock the Golf 2 area, as he lifted the key boards of both areas and passed them to the respective staff when they'd checked into the key room. There was nothing left to do but wait. Pulling his diary from his back pocket, he flicked through the phone numbers he had collected. Within seconds, he was connected to the RUC Athletic Association.

'Hello, Harry McDermott here.'

'It's Pete. We have a massive problem here Harry.'

McDermott listened intently, as Clydesdale went through the chain of events meticulously. The mention of Patterson's inclusion, questioned his earlier decision to exclude him from any investigation, or reveal to his deputies, the connection to Smallwood. In a far-off tone, McDermott could hear the pleading of Elsie Patterson. For now, he would keep the status quo, until they reached the jail. Sadly, he realised he would have to reverse his decision of ignorance, and uncover Patterson's life story. It was a bizarre anomaly he had plunged into.

'Think Henderson has pulled a fast one?'

'It's the only thing I can think of Harry. Are you still a peeler?'

McDermott looked at his watch. 'Well, for the next hour and a half.'

'We're going to need police on the scene at some stage. I know you have a vested interest in this scumbag. If you grab your two mates, and hotfoot it down here, the job's yours.'

'Easiest interview I've ever had. We're on our way.'

McDermott handed the phone back to the barman, requesting he order them a taxi from the trusted pool immediately. He trawled the room for his deputies, ignoring the false farewells.

As they bounded downstairs like trained dogs behind him, McDermott announced they were on their way to jail.

'Tonight, wasn't that bad captain, was it?'

McDermott grinned ruefully. 'Shut up Jacko. I'll fill you both in while the taxi is on its way.'

Chapter 68

On reaching the end of the landing, Patterson ordered the SO to unlock the last two cells.

'Leave the key in the lock, Colin.'

The SO stared at him, before nodding his compliance. Patterson motioned with his pistol that the SO enter the empty cell. He felt deflated, utterly powerless and fearful, convinced a bullet would crash through the rear of his skull when he entered the cell. He called upon his last ounce of bravery and reason, and turned around.

'Look Paddy, think about what you're doing. There's no escape.' He hesitated and attempted to dig into the compassion he knew existed in the former Patterson. 'Be careful kid. We all think a lot of you.' he offered, hoping to put a chink in Patterson's unfathomable armour.

'Thank you, Colin, I appreciate your sentiment. No more talking from here on in. Ok?' Patterson sounded like a robot giving commands. The SO acceded, nodding ruefully.

'You can trust me kid, I'll be quiet,' he promised, his voice breaking.

Before Patterson moved to close the door, he ordered the HO to hug the wall and move toward the next cell. Before closing it, the SO swore he noticed a childlike emotion, ripple over Patterson's expression.

'Colin, it's been a pleasure to have known, and served with you.'

The Hospital Officer was now confident, death would be a stranger to him tonight. He rushed into the other opened cell, as previously requested, and stood in the middle. The Patterson he knew reminded him of his oldest son. Fear had been replaced, by remorse and pity for this traumatised boy. He looked directly into those far away eyes of the thing that now controlled the mindset of his colleague.

'Why Paddy? Why son?'

'It's a long story Gerry, and to be honest, I haven't time right now. I'm sorry if I scared you both, it wasn't intentional. You and Colin are now safe, I swear it. Gerry, please tell the lads I done you no harm.'

The HO nodded, struggling to hold back tears of grief, feeling the pain his young friend was immersed in. When the door closed, he sat on the edge of the bed and wept and prayed, for one so young. Patterson worked fast, having guaranteed his safety from fellow officers. He went inside the open grille toward the heavy metal outer door. It was one of the few doors that had a 'through lock', that could be opened from either side. The main difference being that this door also had to be electronically opened from the inside. There was an over-ride button in the control room, but only for the electronics, which the physical locks weren't. Patterson locked the outer door from his side, leaving the key in the lock, before inserting the master key in the smaller lock and leaving it in place.

Lifting the heavy metal door stop, he hammered at both keys, until they were bent out of shape, impossible to remove, or allowing anyone to enter. He returned to the office, grabbing the duct tape. The show was well under way.

~

Tony McQuillan stood in the small, freezing, concrete 'hut', located beside the outer gate, the pedestrian entrance from the Crumlin Road. He ignored the cold, adrenalin pumping through his veins. There was something serious happening, and even being on the peripheral, excited his mood. The antiquated Tannoy on the wall came to life. 'Tony, they're coming up the road now.' It was his first of two sets of visitors, the second set, arriving by taxi and entering through the pedestrian gate. Three policemen, led by Detective Sergeant, Harry McDermott. He fled from the shelter, hastily unlocking the outer main gate, as the lights from the Mercedes spilled in underneath.

~

Henderson struggled to open his eyes. He felt drowsy, bordering on surreal. The walls and ceiling expanded, unfocused, before dissipating. His head was spinning, his face wet.

'This must be a dream,' he convinced himself.

Whenever he tried to lift his arms in an effort to regain control, there was no movement. He was constricted. The overriding fear of his self-diagnosed predicament, was obvious.

'Oh God, I've had a stroke!'

Henderson attempted to shout for help, but his mouth remained closed. Fear raced through him. He could feel his fingers, move them slightly, but this gave him false hope. On attempting to sit up, his muscles re-acted as normal, but he remained pinned down. He focused on the ceiling above. It was the same ceiling he had stared at for the last few weeks. Abnormally, in the near distance, he heard soft humming of the theme song from *'Love story'*. Henderson took comfort that he had finally awakened, and rid himself of the horrific nightmare he'd been trapped in. He attempted shouting for help again, to no avail, his mouth still not responding. The humming continued and confusion reigned. Patterson, unseen, sat in a plastic chair close to the bed, noticed that Henderson had regained consciousness. He softly sang the words he had previously hummed, rising to his feet.

'Where do I begin...la, la, la, la, la, la, la,'

Still out of Henderson's eye line he started to talk.

'Where, exactly do I begin?'

Patterson was content the duct tape he'd used, would keep the animal at bay. He had taped his shoulders tightly looping the tape around the frame of the bed. His arms were secured, taped to his sides, lapping over his considerable girth for extra security.

His hands, hips, knees and ankles were applied in the fashion of the shoulders. Totally immobile.

Patterson was undergoing a schaden freude experience, wallowing in the peril Henderson was experiencing. He felt invincible.

'Ah Sleepy head, you're awake at last.'

Henderson thought the voice sounded friendly, almost soothing, praying this was still a dream.

'Am I still dreaming? Bet that's what you're thinking, isn't it?' The tone turned sinister. 'Or is it a nightmare?' Henderson's un-obscured view of the ceiling disappeared to be replaced by a close-up of Patterson's fiendish expression, inches from his face. 'Boo!'

Henderson closed his eyes in defence, the only defence available. His heart went into overdrive. He felt the warmth of urine on his legs. In a voice, dissimilar to any he'd heard so far, Henderson listened once more to Patterson.

'Ohh, Little red riding hood, the big bad wolf is frightened, he's done pee pee's,' Patterson looked down at Henderson, enabling a view of himself. His expression had changed, bordering on normality. 'Right let's get this thing sorted. I can categorically assure you, you're very much awake. Apologies for pouring water over your face, I thought you'd never wake up. Boy, we've so many things to talk about, and so little time. The number of questions going through your mind must be enormous...and still you don't speak?'

He roared a demonic laugh. Henderson started to cry. He knew this was his end.

'I forgot. You can't! There's that prison humour of mine again. Now, don't go storming off in a huff like you did this morning.' He leant close to Henderson's head; a maniacal grin etched on his face. 'But then, you can't do that either. Can you?'

He paced up and down out of sight to Henderson. Leaning in, Patterson resumed a normal tone. He held the cigarettes Henderson presented him earlier. 'I was really touched by your peace offering.'

He displayed them close to Henderson's face, before lifting them away and pacing.

'Nice touch, but those things are bad for you, and you should really give them up. I've an idea,' he said, inches away from Henderson's face, speaking in a normal tone. 'Let's give them up tonight, together. What do you say?'

The face disappeared; the pacing reinstated. Henderson could hear him mumbling, arguing with whatever other personas filled his mind, and expected to see him crawl on the ceiling like a demon in a film. The pacing stopped, the steps toward the bed growing louder. 'I've been a bad boy. I told you lies.' The tone had the innocence of a child. 'So, to make it up, I'll tell you the truth.' Patterson stood, powerful and almighty over Henderson, clutching the cigarettes. He fought minuscule twinges in his face, his head jerking side to side. His face shot up to look straight at the ceiling, a calmness set in, before the face that now looked at Henderson, was hideous. Scary eyes glaring, piercing his soul. Patterson studied the cigarettes in his grasp.

'These?' Patterson crumbled them, the loose tobacco falling on Henderson's face. He shut his eyes. 'I would rather have seen you sticking each one of these, up your own arse!'

Henderson had seen the devil. Patterson disappeared from view for a few seconds before a different guise returned, and brushed the tobacco from Henderson's face.

'Please excuse my manners. I really should explain what is happening here.'

Irrespective of the demeanour and normal tone, Henderson had lost hope, not knowing which Patterson was which, and reckoning, correctly, that the dark side dominated. The banging from outside, bled a smidgeon of rescue.

'So, I'll start at the very beginning,' Patterson started talking to himself. 'That's a song, isn't it? Or do I start from the end and work backward? Yes, I'll work backward.' He came back into view. 'You don't mind, do you?'

Chapter 69

The night guard Trades Officer, who'd been enjoying a quiet night in the cosy boiler room below the circle, was working through his bag of tools, in an attempt to breach the lock and gain entrance to the annexe.

'Both the master and servant locks are jammed. It'll take forever to unscrew the housing and even at that, there'll be some force required to unhinge the thing from the wall SO.'

'Shite!' the remaining SO exclaimed in frustration, before returning to the metal door and banging it.

'Colin! Gerry! Paddy! Can you hear me?' All he received in return was inaudible muffled sounds of the incarcerates shouting from behind cell doors. He tried the radio again. 'Hello Control, Sierra 2. Any contact yet? Any coverage?'

'Control, nothing. We'll keep you informed. Boss has arrived. Over.'

The trades Officer, caught his attention, hurriedly speaking, 'Let them know I'm going over to the stores to get the Angle grinder. That's the ticket!'

The SO nodded in agreement.

~

Patterson, lost in his own world, was oblivious to the banging and shouting that cascaded in behind him. He had pulled a chair closer, allowing his quarry visuals. There was a determination in his tone.

'You're probably wondering how, and why, you're in this position right now? I know I'd be.' Henderson shuddered, noting that whenever Patterson was addressing him, even in this disarranged state, a part of his mind, was reminding him of time restrictions.

'You could call it planning, and a bit of luck. Good and bad luck of course, although, more good, than bad,' he self-affirmed. 'But thank fuck for bad luck, or you wouldn't have any at all.' He chuckled at his own anecdote. 'So … why did you fall soundly asleep so quickly? It's all down to a tiny pill called, Temazepam. But then, you must know that anyway, you're probably already stealing, and selling them.' He leant close again, teeth showing, eyes blazing, 'To kids!! To ruin lives! You helped me along the way, by leaving your coffee in the office when you went for your… peace offering! It's much better this way, with the tape and all. I don't think I could've listened to you whining, and begging, for mercy. Not your scene. I had considered simply poisoning you, but reckoned you might be interested in what I have to say.' Henderson's eyes, as wide as saucepans, squealed terror. His chest contracted faster than normal, within its tight bounds. The application of tape, couldn't prevent his lips from trembling. Patterson noticed and adopted a calming tone. He brushed the cool metal of the pistol on Henderson's cheeks. 'There, there, stay with me. How did I get the Temazepam?' Patterson's eyes began to fill with tears, showing genuine remorse. 'I did a bad thing. I borrowed them without asking, and it really cuts me up inside.' Patterson's voice was just about audible, during his confession.

In an instant, the disturbed side of his character took control. 'Do you know what else? It brought me down to your level!' Henderson shut his eyes while Patterson began what seemed like a confessional. 'I feel terrible because of the person I've become. A person that *you* helped shape.'

Henderson's gaze was clouded.

'You don't know who I am, but maybe that's a question you should ask yourself. Who, or what, are you?' Patterson was enjoying watching the mental torture he was inflicting on his victim. 'I don't even think you know the answer. You could be described as an animal, devoid of guilt or emotion. But that would be a slur on animals. You spent your life removing any obstacles in your way, without thought or compassion. Yes, I've done my homework on you… Mr Fucking Bulldog.'

Henderson's expanded nostrils blew out a series of short breaths, in an attempt to gain control.

'You specialised in killing Catholics, innocent or not. But if you hated Catholics so much, why did you fucking marry one?'
The tirade continued, growing in intensity, Patterson fought against slipping into eternal insanity, a bitterness etched into his features.
'Is it because you could feel justified in beating her. Did it make you feel important? Powerful?! Let me tell you exactly what you are. You're a paradox! An Oxymoron!'
He leant in closer. 'You're a contradiction in fucking terms!'

Patterson delivered a forceful back handed slap to Henderson's face, who by now, had almost no vision., his eyes clouded by the tears he sobbed.

~

One of the three-night guard officers in A wing, took over in the key room, the PO racing to the vehicle airlock. He was aware there was something happening in the annexe, but wasn't exactly sure what. On arrival, he met the 1st Lieutenant, and two armed sergeants. When the Mercedes was in the airlock, Governor Bleasdale and his civil service nemesis, Tomlinson, de-bussed. The three soldiers stood behind the PO. Tomlinson began to rant, flexing some ministerial muscle. 'How the hell did this happen? And more to the point, who's responsible?

Bleasdale narrowed his eyes in disgust, before angrily intervening. 'This is no time to look for heads. We have a very serious situation here!' He turned to Clydesdale. 'Pete, is this a hostage situation?' '

Clydesdale offered his synopsis. 'To be truthful Sir, we have no idea. What we do know, is that around 10 o'clock, young Patterson contacted us on the landline, worried about the state of health of the inmate, Henderson. Control informed us, that they witnessed Patterson banging on Henderson's door for at least 5 minutes, before that. He was in a panic when he contacted the key room. However, we know that shortly after the SO and MO entered the annexe...' He hesitated, '...we've lost all communications.'

'What about the camera?'

'It's been moved to point at the floor sir, there's nothing.'

'Jesus Christ, I've three staff down there,' he mused to himself. He had reached beyond the point of standing around talking, and addressed the Lieutenant and his armed sergeants.

'Lieutenant, you and the lads follow me. Weapons at the ready.'

The command went way beyond everything Tomlinson stood for. 'This is preposterous! You could jeopardise the safety of the entire jail! This is a police matter!'

Clydesdale responded first, ignoring Tomlinson, and spoke directly to Bleasdale. 'Police are on their way sir.'

Bleasdale's features warped in anger, suggesting he was about to explode, as he marched toward Tomlinson. 'Shut your fucking bureaucratic, cake hole! I have made a decision. We have three staff and, or, an inmate, all of whom may be in serious trouble. We are going down to assist right now. You stay here and under no circumstances do you delay the police when they arrive. Understand?!' Unfamiliar with facing such a directed tirade, Tomlinson turned deathly white, meekly nodding in agreement.

Chapter 70

Patterson was as close to normality, as the calm section of his mind would allow. Still speaking rapidly, he continued with Henderson's torture.

'Ok, we've ascertained what you are. But me? Am I (A) a Provo, (B) Loyalist or (C) none of the above? I'll make it crystal clear very soon. Seeing that you've no objections, I'll give you a bit of my background. I was fortunate, and unfortunate, as a child. I never really knew my parents because, they died when I was very young. However, I was lucky to be brought up by my wonderful adopted parents. Up until about 6 months ago, I believed my parents were killed in a road accident. Then, I discovered the truth. Sorry, I know truth, isn't a term you're familiar with. I was actually worried I could lose my job, if people connected me to my natural parents.' Patterson leaned in close to Henderson before growling, 'Do you know how that feels?!' It took a few seconds for Patterson to return to a passive state. 'I'll give you one thing though, you've a hell of a memory. You said I reminded you of someone. Apparently, I'm not unlike my father, and believe me, you're in a better position to make that comparison than I could ever be. You knew him better than I ever did. Well, am I like him! Well!?' The agitated tone had reached its crescendo, Patterson slipping into a false civility. 'Oh, I do apologise, I haven't told you, his name. It's Jackie Smallwood.' Henderson's eyeballs threatened to explode, as he vainly struggled to escape his bonds, his breathing shorter and faster.

~

The Governor, Army guard commander, armed sergeants and PO Clydesdale, joined the SO at the annexes' closed door. Within seconds, the Trades Officer arrived with the angle grinder. The Governor addressed the PO. 'Pete, get onto control and inform the Delta call signs to continue patrolling the perimeter wall, in case this is a distraction. Deploy all night guard staff, to cover all wing entrance grilles.' He then spun round and spoke to the Guard commander. 'Liaise with your network to get armed guards, patrolling with the dog handlers.' The Trades Officer cranked the angle grinder into life. Deafening noise reverberated around D wing. Immediately, complaints started to spill out from behind closed doors. 'Any fucking chance?' 'Keep the fucking noise down, there's people trying sleep here!?' Those not complaining, decided to make the most of this opportunity to create havoc, by banging their plastic mugs against their metal doors.

Clydesdale addressed the SO. 'Get the wing night guard staff to shut those monkeys up, or I'll have an awful lot of charges to deal with in the morning.'

~

'So, you see, everyone has skeletons in their cupboards. You thought you could dump all yours by making them disappear.' Patterson shook his head. 'No way Jose! Let me enlighten you about your bad luck.'

Henderson, drained and frightened, reckoned his heart was about to explode.

'All of this ...' Patterson motioned with his hands, 'came about by chance. When I had discovered the truth about my father, as a mark of respect I decided to visit his final resting place. And who should I meet there? None other than that dopey big lad, Hamilton, who made the mistake of being, a *wee* bit aggressive, to little old me. He told me everything, the stuff that the police knew nothing about, albeit the pistol between his eyes probably played a part in his confession. He hated you, and after confessing, he even offered to help me, get to you. I mean, can you believe that?' Patterson stopped abruptly in mid flow. He registered noises from outside the metal door, of a gaggle of people and a loud buzzing sound of, well... something. 'Too many cooks would have spoiled the broth don't you think? I knew from that very moment; I'd begun my journey beyond the point of no return. So, I created a plan. I broke into your house to leave the murder weapon. You're wife's a nice arse, by the way. I then rang the confidential line to frame you, before posting a letter to the Loyalist council. I'd just undertaken my plan, and then don't you know...' He slapped his thigh, '...somebody goes and beats me to it. I've no idea who killed that other faggot, but I'm sure they had good reason. Unlucky for you, this accelerated my plans, because I didn't want anyone to rob me of this moment. Your loyalists aren't too loyal to you, are they? How much respect do you think they offer you?' Patterson advanced closer to Henderson, who lay still as a corpse. 'Absolutely zero. And who could blame them? I wouldn't be surprised if there's a queue already forming around the City Hall, to kick you when you're down. How does that dose of your own medicine taste? I bet it's fucking awful.'

~

McDermott, Jackson and Douglas were briefed loosely by Tomlinson on arrival. On learning of Patterson's presence, McDermott momentarily presented a pained expression, noticed by Douglas. They could hear the high-pitched shrieking of the angle grinder echoing out from the empty wing, that served as an amplifier. Their passage stalled, as Control waited for confirmation that the Delta call signs were aware of them crossing the forecourt.

'Everything ok Captain?'

McDermott had a profusion of thoughts racing through his mind. Had Henderson set a trap? How had they arrived at this situation? Was it collusion with a staff member, that had been intimidated on the outside? His final thought, the one he wanted to, but couldn't ignore. Was Patterson aware of his past? Had he discovered the mystery killer? Cursing inwardly, the realization that he was obligated to disclose, potentially vital information, he apologised to Elsie Patterson. He wouldn't have time to discuss it now.

'I'm ok Doug, thanks.'

They raced across the forecourt, up the steps and along the chequered hall to the Glass Door, where their journey briefly halted, as the sole member of staff in the key room had to operate the electronic release for the grille.

~

The heavy metal door, crashed onto the tiled floor inside the annexe, its noise reverberating throughout the ghostly, now silent jail. The Army Guard Commander indicated with his hand, for the remainder of the gathering to move away from the now open portal, to a safe area, further along the outer wall. He issued silent signals of communication with his armed sergeants. They gave a thumbs up. The first tiptoed inside the grille, Browning Pistol housed in both hands, pointing at the floor. He hugged its side wall, shuffling crab-like along its length, before motioning for his partner to follow suit. Both heard muffled talking and eyeballed the only open cell door. The staff locked in respective cells, aware an operation of some sort was underway, decided to maintain silence for its duration, not wanting to upset any equilibrium.

~

Sections of Patterson's mind worked individually. One part registered the silence and the soft noise of squeaky boots, getting closer, suggesting the need for urgency. Henderson knew his time was up. Patterson's demeanour, now locked on serious determination. Yet, when he spoke, it was without fear, worry or emotion. He held the pistol in his left hand, the barrel forced against the middle of Henderson's forehead.

'There's an old Chinese proverb about riding the Tiger. It says *'you can ride the Tiger as long as you like, no matter how angry he becomes. But be careful when you get off, the Tiger will still be angry.'* Patterson leaned in close for the final time, pushing the barrel harder against Henderson's skull. 'You have just got off the tiger, arsehole.' Patterson stood upright, and clasped his right hand over his left on the pistol grip, keeping the aim no further than a foot away from its original target. The soldiers slid silently across the landing, hugging the wall that contained the only open door. After what seemed like forever, McDermott and his aides had been given access to D Wing. They picked up the pace and ran.

The first soldier, motioned that he was about to engage, and required cover. They counted down with their fingers, 3, 2, 1.
He left the safety of the wall, beginning to raise the browning pistol in both hands, whilst swiveling to face directly into the open cell. His training allowed him to dismiss the surroundings therein and the body taped to the bed, focusing solely on the target that held a pistol.

'Drop the pistol now or I will shoot!' he roared with inbred army authority.
Without displacing his aim, Patterson turned his head, to drink in the sight of his potential executioner. His facial expressions displayed countless emotions of doubt, deliberation and reminisce. His conscious, wrestled with his subconscious. His mind was a firework display of thoughts. Until he adopted a vacant expression.

The roulette wheel of decision making inside his mind, had stopped spinning, and the ball that determined his destiny, had found its home. He looked at the soldier, dolefully, and then responded. 'No!'

~

McDermott, Jackson and Douglas were roughly two thirds along the landing, fifteen feet from the small stairway down to the annexe, when they heard the two separate single gunshots. The trio skidded to a halt; they were too late.

EPILOGUE

3 months later.

Late January, early February, was rightly described as the most depressing time of the year. All thoughts and memories of Christmas, were long forgotten, replaced by bills and debt that the time of great cheer had created. The weather added to the misery. It was bitterly cold, an eastern wind plummeting the temperature. Belfast was lit by yellow sodium lights under a star-studded black sky. From a distance it appeared as a normal city. Close inspection begged to differ. Inside the Royal Victoria Hospital, was a sanctuary of warmth. A nurse had run the gauntlet of reaching the secure Intensive Care Unit, past four men, two police and two prison officers, who were housed in a makeshift corridor at the end of a dedicated wing, behind a bomb proof iron door. It had a spy hole, and was supplemented by exterior cameras that surveyed the entire outer area. At the end of their inner corridor, a space where a door should have been, led to the Intensive Care Unit. She was glad all four of the 'guards' were glued to the black and white portable Television in the corner, watching a Live European cup match involving Liverpool. Thankfully they didn't pay much attention to her, as she felt she looked dreadful.

She hated her frumpy shape. Her frizzy, auburn hair was a mess. Blotchy skin, sporadic pimples, oversize glasses and prominent teeth, completed her self-deprecating mood.

As soon as she stepped into the ICU to check on its sole inhabitant, she instantaneously, became the consummate professional. This was her world. She, like all nurses from the dawn of time, seemed to glide across the highly polished floor.

She lifted notes from the board at the end of the bed, before beginning her routine check list.

~

The police and prison staff, huddled around the Television. They had checked in at 6pm for their twelve-hour shift, accompanied by officers from two police Land Rovers, such was the potential threat in the west of the city. Both sets worked four nights on, three off completing their mandatory forty-eight-hour week. They all received subsistence, shift allowance and travelling expenses, boosting their pay. Apart from the handovers, it was as easy a shift as could be. The likelihood of hassle from a comatose patient was zero, giving that he hadn't moved, or responded, for three months. The police pair was made up of two officers, worlds apart in age and experience. The two prison officers were middle aged, veterans of hospital guards. The television set was barely audible, in a modicum of respect for the nurse, and the patient.

~

The nurse studied the emaciated body on the bed, feeling a hint of remorse, witnessing that, only the machines were alert. She carefully lifted, and peeled back, the tape that held the eyelids closed, before administering eye drops and resealing them again. Open eyes in a patient of this nature would dry up, the involuntary blinking no longer in operation. She moved methodically, amidst the cornucopia of whirring, and clicking, artificial intelligence, checking in turn, the life sustaining equipment connected to, and inserted into, the patient. An arterial line monitor, advertised blood pressure and concentrations of oxygen and carbon dioxide within the blood, was showing as normal. A Central Venous line, registered the blood pressure as it returned to the heart. Brain Stem Evoked Response equipment, monitored painless sound waves relayed to the brain stem, via headphones, were being received, by the remaining vestiges of life within the body. Beside the various monitors was the ECG Machine, the most recognisable to non-medical staff, thanks to the continued over usage in cinema, as a dramatic indication that a person had 'flat-lined'. The Intracranial Pressure Transducer, silently completed its tasks, with continuing readouts of brain pressure, thanks the subarachnoid bolt attached to the patient's skull. She inspected the tubes, inserted in the chest between the lungs and the ribs, used to remove any excess fluid or air, and to prevent the collapse of the lungs. The catheter at the end of the bed that collected waste fluids, was less than a quarter full, as was the catheter that held the flow of urine from the bladder. Before finally checking the various intravenous medications, she logged the rate of artificial respiration being rhythmically supplied by the respirator, as it accordioned the humidified air into the non-breathing body, via an Endotracheal tube in the patient's mouth. It made a noise akin to a mother 'shushing' her children quietly to sleep, sixteen times a minute. Finally, she paid close attention the dosage of various medication being administered via intravenous drips. She paid special attention to the drips that merged, and electronically produced, an infusion of 0.3% of Potassium Chloride and 5% Glucose; Potassium levels within the body, being essential.

~

The football on the TV had reached the end of the first half of extra time, balancing the result on a knife edge. Although animated conversation and analysis was abundant, one of the seasoned prison officers stood, went to the door, and expertly surveyed the exterior, using the spy hole and cameras, before opening it, to allow the nurse to leave. They exchanged smiles of appreciation. Although only one true Liverpool supporter amongst their ranks, the remainder were fully supportive, adopting the mantra of, supporting your local sheriff. They were fed up with the diving, remonstrating and arrogance of the overpaid Italians. There was bated breath as the match went into the dreaded, penalty shootout, but disappointment mixed with abhorrence of the Italians overtly celebrating, putting a damper on the mood. It didn't last long. The elder three of the quartet, settled down into one of the comfortable chairs provided, alongside newspapers, books and crossword puzzle magazines.

The youngest police officer, flicking through the few channels available on TV, was frustrated, already counting the hours and minutes that he would be in this cocoon of a place. He hadn't joined the RUC to babysit comatose patients. He wanted to be out on patrol, in the thick of it, doing a proper police job. Another 20 years of service would change his attitude. He grabbed a two-day old copy of the Belfast Telegraph, praying that reading would send him off to sleep.

~

Tonya Whyte, paid cash at the bursar's desk on the same floor as the main entrance onto the Belfast Car Ferries, for her single overnight cabin. She was dog tired, and didn't fancy mingling with the eternal drinkers in the bar, or attempting to find comfort in the main passenger deck with its rigid seats. She had a nine-hour overnight crossing to Liverpool. Inside the cabin, she noticed new bed linen, clean if not wafer thin. Extra blankets were under the bed beside her life jacket. She quickly read, and remembered, the green assembly point's notification on the back of the cabin door. Due to her fatigue, she could've slept on the floor, but there was something she had to do. Ensuring the lock was firmly on the door, she tipped her belongings from her rucksack onto the bed and stripped off, before stepping into a miniscule shower, that barely mouthed water over her body, but was warm enough. She washed her hair, face and body rigorously, and slipped into a fresh set of clothing that included a heavy Harris Tweed, polo neck.

Once dressed, she shoved all her other items of clothing and toiletries back into the rucksack before retrieving a plastic bag from its front pocket. She was desperate to lie on the bed, but was resigned to stuffing a few items in the bag, and grabbing her coat on completion. She stepped out into the long corridor of doors and badly designed carpet, then locked the cabin door.

~

The older occupants slipped seamlessly into relaxation mode. The younger officer was bored shitless. He attempted to instigate a conversation.

'Do you lads do a lot of these shifts.'

'Course we do. It's money from America, and gets you away from the jail,' the first prison officer replied. The remaining incumbents were engrossed in a book and crossword puzzle, simultaneously.

'Bores the arse of me,' huffed the young RUC officer. He had already, exhausted his repertoire, and became inquisitive.

'Did you know that prison officer...you know the one ...?' asked the young RUC officer, before indicating and nodding toward the space that was the gateway.

'Yeah.' replied the inactive, stony-faced prison officer.

'Fuck, he must have been some sort of looper.'

The conversation turned cold with the slamming closed of a hardback book. The second prisoner officer stood up and glared at the young policeman, the elder policeman diverting his eyes from the crossword, ascertaining the situation.

'What did you just call him?' Every word was menacing.

The young constable felt contrite, and attempted make amends. 'I was just asking if youse knew him, that's all.'

'Were you fuck! You were slabbering about someone you don't know. Do me, and yourself, a favour son, never, again refer to our friend in that manner.'

The prison officer's fists clenched as he leaned closer, his blood boiling. The senior police officer leapt up between the two.

'Right lads, knock it on the head. We've a long night to put in here.'

The second PO took stock, relaxed and backed away. The young RUC officer felt depleted. His elder mouthed the word 'sorry' to him, out of sight of the PO's.

'Look mate, I'm really sorry about…'

The first PO displayed a knowing smile of acceptance, striving to get back to his book. The other, a grunted acceptance. In an attempt to save face, the young constable, diverted to an alternative conversation topic.

'Pity we weren't on last night. Mate of mine was saying the wee blonde nurse on then, is a cracker. Unlike the Hattie Jacques we have.'

Even the irritated second PO found it hard to stifle a smile. The seasoned constable glanced toward the cameras as he rose. 'Well, well, lover boy, looks like your boat has just come in.'

The grey, fuzzy TV picture of the blond-haired nurse, done nothing to distract them from her face and body shape, as she deliberately swung her hips on approach, enjoying these sessions of adoration. The young constable grinned then blushed, at the next comment from the senior police officer. 'Want me tell her what your mate called her?'

'Shit no' he whispered.

She entered with a smile plastered over the width of her face, noticing the staff, were glancing and drinking in her cleavage, in a uniform that was 'just-too-small.'.

'Good evening gentlemen, and how are we all doing tonight?'

The grinning foursome were transfixed, before their youngest stood up, stretching to his full height, and sucking in his midriff, in an effort to make his chest look bigger.

'All the better for seeing you,' he bleated in an inane effort to impress her. She winked at him.

'That may well be true, but I have to check on my other admirer first,' as she began to walk toward the ICU unit. The senior policeman, still grinning, stated, 'you must have got your wires crossed love, the other nurse was here about an hour ago.'

She stopped in her tracks, turning to face him; her flirtatious face expression absent.

'What other nurse?'

As she relayed the last syllable, the first of many of the machines, began to squeal out from the other room, indicating danger. She gasped, swivelled and raced into the ICU unit, followed by the guard force. Every machine, except the ventilator, was now, out of harmony, squealing for attention. She raced around the comatose body, checking everything, panic displaying her manner. She stopped, and gasped when she reached the IV unit. There was, what appeared to be water, on the floor, but was actually glucose. The infuser of the formerly double tubes, was clinging to it. She looked at the Potassium Chloride bag that had previously dripped life enhancing, diluted amounts, and was now completely empty. All three green lines on the ICU monitor, ran parallel, not a hint of the patient's stability or existence in sight. She turned, ashen faced and announced to the others, 'Mister Henderson's dead!'

~

Tonya, was the sole passenger on the upper outside of the ship. She ignored the biting cold, gazing wondrously at the stars, that shone brighter than the twinkling lights of Helen's Bay. The sea and sky had become one. She opened the plastic bag and lifted out a pair of thick lensed reading glasses, that she threw overboard. With the upper deck being at the rear, and the ship picking up a head of steam toward open water, she found it impossible to watch them hit the sea.

She gazed back at the stars for a minute, hypnotised, unaware that her eyes had begun to water. Next, she tossed an upper set of comical false teeth purchased in a fancy-dress shop that also, impossibly disappeared. In quick succession, she lobbed a dark, red wig from the same shop. In her mind, that was the last vestige of Tonya Whyte, her existence brief. The tears felt warm on her face as she resumed her true identity. She looked skyward, focusing on three stars that were close together, and although she struggled with her quote, she had the same determination as her brother, as she whispered through the tears,

'Mummy and Daddy, you can rest peacefully now,' Shirley blurted out through tears at the mention of her beloved brother, 'How's the wee man? Tell him, me and the kids miss him an awful lot. But let him know it's all over now. We love all of you. Night, night.'

THE END

ACKNOWLEDGEMENTS

First and foremost, I want to acknowledge my wife, Karen, who has had to endure listening to me droning on, relentlessly, about plots, ideas, characters, scenarios and everything else to boot. The other side of that fence, is that she is way more talented than I, especially whenever it comes to cooking and organising. She feeds me like a king. I am blessed.

My editor, Chelsea Terry, is meticulous and leaves no stone unturned. I get annoyed sometimes whenever I receive her feedback, mainly because I have a mountain of work thereafter. But... hey, she's always correct and helps me get my books to where they should be. ☐

My next dear neighbour, over the back fence, Daryl Young, is a high-class photographer and helped me bring the idea I had for the front cover to life. Outstanding mate.

Thanks also to a long-time friend, Pat McGailie, a retired Policeman, who described everything I required, in detail, about the Police World.

My constant sparring partner in the novel and screenwriting universe, Spencer Wright, helps me no end. I run nearly every idea I have, past him, and get honest feedback every time. He is a clever, and very funny, bunny. And I'm glad he's there.

Gavin Bates, owner of the White Horse, and his head barman, Robin, who looked after me when I was writing most of this book, upstairs in the pub. I received food and never-ending coffee. Cheers guys.

Also, a big thank to, now retired, Dr Watterson who provided me with all the medical information I could handle, and needed for the book.

I can't ignore my 'first readers', who all provided me with essential feedback.

And finally, I can't thank enough, the woman who was the rock throughout my life. My Nanny Shaw, who sadly passed away from dementia in 2012. I love and miss her every day.

Printed in Great Britain
by Amazon